The Legend Thief

SIMON & SCHUSTER BOOKS FOR YOUNG READERS
NEW YORK • LONDON • TORONTO • SYDNEY • NEW DELHI

The Legend Thief

✦ E. J. Patten ✦

ILLUSTRATED BY John Rocco

Also by E. J. Patten
The Hunter Chronicles: Return to Exile

SIMON & SCHUSTER BOOKS FOR YOUNG READERS
An imprint of Simon & Schuster Children's Publishing Division
1230 Avenue of the Americas, New York, New York 10020
Text copyright © 2013 by Eric Patten
Illustrations copyright © 2013 by John Rocco
For information about special discounts for bulk purchases, please contact Simon & Schuster
Special Sales at 1-866-506-1949 or business@simonandschuster.com.
The Simon & Schuster Speakers Bureau can bring authors to your live event. For more information
or to book an event, contact the Simon & Schuster Speakers Bureau at 1-866-248-3049 or
visit our website at www.simonspeakers.com.
Also available in a Simon & Schuster Books for Young Readers hardcover edition
Book design by Laurent Linn
The text for this book is set in Minister Std Light.
The illustrations for this book are rendered digitally.
Manufactured in the United States of America • 0314 MTN
First Simon & Schuster Books for Young Readers paperback edition April 2014
2 4 6 8 10 9 7 5 3 1
The Library of Congress has cataloged the hardcover edition as follows:
Patten, E. J., 1974–
The legend thief / E. J. Patten ; [illustrator: John Rocco]
p. cm.—(The Hunter chronicles; 2)
Summary: Twelve-year-old Skye must continue to fight monsters
and discovers that the other Hunters want him dead.
ISBN 978-1-4424-2035-9 (hc)
[1. Hunters—Fiction. 2. Monsters—Fiction. 3. Supernatural—Fiction.] I. Rocco, John, ill. II.
Title.
PZ7.P2759Le 2012
[Fic]—dc23
2012012578
ISBN 978-1-4424-2036-6 (pbk)
ISBN 978-1-4424-2037-3 (eBook)

To Jordan, Lucas, and Connor, the thieves of my heart

WITHDRAWN

· CONTENTS ·

The Legend Thief

The Binding of Bedlam

December 25, 1592

Alexander Drake tightened his grip on his burlap sack and marched through the fiery crags dressed like a pirate. He was seventeen, slightly skinny, mostly handsome, and smattered with grit, both figuratively and literally.

He also wore a monocle.

The pirates who plundered the Atlantic and manned the ship *Le Pamplemousse Terrible* didn't commonly wear monocles, particularly thick white ones covered with strange latches and rings; but then, Alexander Drake was no common pirate.

A dark shadow passed through the ash cloud overhead. Alexander stopped and slowly reached for a long shimmering blade hanging from a strap on his shoulder. He let his hand rest on the handle. Waiting. Waiting. Sounds bounced strangely through the haze, nearby and far away—muffled screaming and creatures shrieking. Dying.

The shadow passed and Alexander marched on, trying to silence his misgivings. He followed a worn path through a sleepy volcanic crater, passing bubbling streams and hardy tropical trees struggling to survive. Ahead, the path led up the side of a smaller volcano within the main crater, one of three such peaks within the broader volcanic valley.

He reached a ledge near the top and popped out above the ash cloud so that he could see the other two peaks and the surrounding ridge of the main volcano which, from above, resembled a human skull.

Alexander found Solomon Rose waiting for him on the ledge.

"I was beginning to think I'd have to go on without you," said Solomon grimly. Solomon was dressed like a nobleman in fine black breeches and hose and a black doublet adorned with golden clasps that looked like roses.

Other than the clothing, Solomon was identical to Alexander in every way—nose, eyes, ears, height, weight, everything—even down to the faint white mark, like a small eye, that sat on his palm: the Hunter's Mark, which Alexander had inherited at birth and Solomon had miraculously and dangerously inherited much more recently. They could've been twins. In a very real way, they were, but not by birth.

Alexander scowled. "You look like a fop, Solomon. Worse, you make *me* look like a fop."

"A fop?" Solomon asked, sounding confused.

"A fop. A coxcomb. A jackanapes. A lordly mountebank," Alexander rattled off.

Solomon raised an eyebrow.

"A well-dressed *fool*," Alexander clarified.

"Ah, I see," Solomon replied. "You mean because I look

like you. Or rather, I look as I would if I didn't have to drink your nasty concoctions every day of my life."

"Don't be so dramatic—it's not every day. And it was part of the deal, Solomon, when I made you what you are," said Alexander tartly.

"You mean when you made us what *we* are," Solomon corrected. "We're the same, you and I."

"We are most assuredly *not* the same," Alexander retorted, his eyes sweeping the crater below and catching fleeting glimpses of a massive winged shadow flying through the haze. With a fearful gulp, he lowered his voice. "When I merged our blood under my birth moon and did that which was forbidden, then—at that moment only—we became the same, save in will and general disposition—an important distinction, I might add. And while I admit that we are still bound together in strange and unusual ways, we are *not* the same. Not now. Not in any way that matters."

"I'm well aware of our differences," said Solomon. "That's why I'm in Austria risking my life to hunt the Arkhon and you're in Exile, hiding and playing with plants. And just because it doesn't matter to you doesn't mean it doesn't matter at all. My point was that we are *both* Changelings, not just me. When you Changed us, you made us both something else. You are a Changeling."

"Yes, yes, I know." Alexander sighed, feeling annoyed with the whole conversation and wishing Solomon would speak more softly. "I'm not trying to suggest that I'm better than you; we both know that's not true. But this isn't something either of us should discuss, especially out loud. If the other hunters found out what we are, they would kill us. You know the risks as well as I."

"If you don't want to discuss it, then just say what you mean; if you mean 'we,' say 'we,' and if you mean 'well-dressed fool,' then say it," Solomon retorted. "You can't hide behind words forever, Alexander."

"I said precisely what I meant and nothing more," Alexander snapped. He turned away from the smoky crater below and its circling shadows and marched along the ledge toward a large cave. "I assume everything is in place?" he asked, changing the subject. He could feel Solomon watching him intently.

"My hunters drank your Slippery Wick Brew and are inside," Solomon replied after a moment, finally lowering his voice as he fell into step beside Alexander. "Bedlam doesn't suspect a thing."

"You'd better hope not or your hunt of the Arkhon may reach a premature conclusion, and that would end badly for the both of us." Alexander glanced over and saw that Solomon had taken the Slippery Wick Brew once again, just as he had for the last several years, to maintain his disguise. The Brew allowed Solomon to move his fat around so that his jaw was now chiseled. The baby fat that had been there moments before had hardened and moved to his arms to make him look even stronger. His nose was now long and sloped at the tip, his ears slightly larger, while the fat of his midsection had moved to the balls of his feet to add a bit of height. Thankfully, he now looked nothing like Alexander, aside from the white Hunter's Mark on his palm.

They passed into the black cave, marching ever deeper into the volcano's boiling heart. Strange creeping mosses glowed green on the tunnel walls, and far ahead, Alexander could see faint red light rising from rivers of molten rock.

Alexander offered Solomon some moldy brown leaves. "Shove it up your nose."

"Shove it up *your* nose," Solomon replied tersely. "You insult me, sir."

Alexander rolled his eyes. "No, really—insert this substance into your nasal cavity. And there's no need to get formal, your lordship."

"What is it?" Solomon asked, refusing to touch the nasty leaves.

"Barrow weed," Alexander replied. "It will keep Bedlam from edgewalking into your mind, or at least make it harder."

"I've grown beyond such trappings," Solomon boasted, refusing to take the barrow weed. "Bedlam holds no power over me."

Alexander scoffed. Bedlam held power over everyone. As one of Legend's five remaining children, Bedlam was perhaps the most powerful monster alive.

Solomon was a good monster hunter—perhaps the greatest since the original thirteen Hunters of Legend—but Bedlam was a force of nature.

Solomon wouldn't stand a chance.

Rather than argue the point, Alexander shoved barrow weed up his own nose and kept quiet.

Ahead, the tunnel opened into a gigantic glittering cavern, the top of which was so full of rubies, emeralds, and diamonds that it looked like stars sparkling in the night sky. Molten rock flowed in rivers through the cave, and heat washed over Alexander, growing hotter and hotter as he crossed bridges of hardened lava leading to the center.

They passed dozens of creatures—twenty-foot-tall Harrow Knights with rusted smoldering skin, and their human-size siblings, the Harrow Wights, who rode massive burrowing Gossymer spiders. But Alexander and Solomon had come this way many times before as welcomed guests, and nothing tried to stop them. *If only they knew*, Alexander thought.

Bedlam's giant obsidian throne sat in the center of the enormous cavern. The monster Bedlam sat on the throne and stared at them with burning eyes. He had a jumbled face of charred gray flesh and rusted green copper, hardened like plate armor. On Bedlam's forehead, Alexander saw a black scar that looked like an eye and belched out writhing puffs and strands of darkness that distorted the light around it.

The Eye of Legend.

"My friends, my pupils . . . I sense that you have come to lie to me," Bedlam rumbled disapprovingly, his voice as gravelly as the earth. "Since you were young, I've trained you to walk the storms of the Edge—the invisible space all around us where light and darkness war. I've taught you how to cross those unseen lands and enter the minds of others, to see what they see, to dwell in their memories, and haunt or bless their dreams. I've taught you as one of my own Edgewalkers, my own children. But you are no longer those boys I once knew. I see the fire stirring in your minds—I know what you seek."

"We have come to ask for your aid in stopping the Arkhon, your brother, who has unjustly declared war on the hunters," said Alexander nervously. "We keep no secrets from you."

"You mix your words well, Alexander, with speckles of truth. You know that I am tired of war—I want no part of it. So let's be honest, shall we? It's not my presence you desire in this war; it's my Eye." Bedlam tapped the black Eye of Legend on his forehead. "It cannot be taken by force without dire consequences, which you know, and so you have come to ask me to hand it over to you willingly."

Alexander and Solomon glanced at each other.

"Well," Alexander began, "we were hoping that since you're tired of war, and since none of the hunters has an Eye of Legend quite as powerful, that you might see fit to—"

Bedlam started laughing. "Ah, Alexander. When did you start taking me for a fool? My Eye is only the first in your hunt. What you truly desire is to claim *all* the Eyes, to reforge the cold and terrible darkness my father used in his attempt to reshape the world—you want to possess the force that gave him power over nearly all other forces and nature itself."

Bedlam's burning eyes bored into Alexander and Solomon, challenging them to deny it.

"Centuries have passed since the First Hunter trapped my father's power and gave half to me and my four siblings, and half to her chosen thirteen Hunters, binding that power in our very flesh, in the Eye marks that each of us guard. The Eye of Legend is a curse upon all who carry its burden, not a blessing. To use Legend's power, you must control his will, and the more of his power you obtain—the more Eyes you reforge— the more lost you will become until *he* is all that is left."

"The Hunter's Mark will allow us to control it," Alexander insisted, holding up his hand to show Bedlam the pale white eye on his palm. "Its warming light can cut through the dark, just as it did centuries ago. We can reforge the Eyes and use Legend's power for good!"

"The First Hunter held my father's power in her hands and she gave it up. Are you greater than she?" Bedlam asked.

Alexander looked away, unable to meet Bedlam's piercing, copper-flecked eyes.

"Enough of this!" Solomon spat, drawing his long shimmering blade. "Will you give us the Eye and help us stop the Arkhon from destroying the hunters—your supposed allies—or not?"

Bedlam stood from his throne, dragging a massive great sword from the shadows. He stood over ten feet tall, and the sword was just as long. "My allies? Is this how allies treat one another? I give you one last chance—for what you were. Leave me now, in peace, while you still can. Turn from your path. Cease your lying. Seek not the wasting darkness."

Each command struck Alexander like a punch to the head. More than anything, he wanted to do exactly what Bedlam said, to leave this path of madness and return to his plants and his botany in London, or Exile, or even—heaven forbid—*Paris*, but he breathed in the barrow weed and his mind cleared of Bedlam's unnatural influence.

Looking over, he saw Solomon, impassive—a single bead of sweat sliding down his forehead.

"I know your secrets, Bedlam," said Solomon quietly. "My mind is my own. Legend's power will be ours. And with it, we will change the world forever."

"That is precisely what I fear." Bedlam swung his great sword into the ground. The earth split. A gaping crack opened where the sword hit, racing all the way to Solomon. Fire and molten rock spewed out, setting Solomon's clothes aflame as he dove out of the way.

Solomon rolled as he landed, dousing the flames. When he regained his feet, his fine doublet and hose were scorched and covered in ash. On Solomon's face, Alexander saw something he never would have expected: fear.

Giant spiderlike Gossymers spilled out of the ground and lava pools, charging. Humongous Knights burst into flame, their flesh sloughing off as boiling metal seeped through their pores, rising from hidden pockets and heated by their rage. Great gobs of burning copper pooled in the Knights' palms, ready to throw, and the smaller Wights charged with them, cold and restless.

The Knights drew back their arms and threw, casting fiery gobs of metal at Alexander and Solomon, who bobbed and weaved to stay out of the copper's burning path.

Solomon whistled, and the pockmarked but human-looking Wights suddenly turned on the giant Knights and spiderlike Gossymers, attacking with silvery knives and swords that produced strange effects, turning Knights to stone and Gossymers to ash.

For the first time, Bedlam looked surprised.

Solomon shot forward, moving inhumanly fast. He cut through two Gossymers without slowing. His shimmering blade, aglow with bright colors—so unlike the dull weapons of the other hunters—struck Bedlam's rusted skin with a clang and bounced off. Solomon stared at his blade, disbelieving.

Without bothering to raise his great sword, Bedlam grabbed Solomon's blade and yanked him close until their faces were almost touching. Wispy darkness, like smoke, crept out of the night-black Eye on Bedlam's forehead.

Solomon raised his Hunter's Mark and a stream of cloudy white light vomited out, striking the smoky darkness. The two forces crashed together like raging storm clouds, swelled, and then exploded with a deafening thunder clap. Solomon flew tumbling back without his blade and Bedlam staggered—Solomon's blade in hand, which was no longer shimmering.

Alexander shadow slipped, jumping from shadow to shadow unseen. Darkness swirled around him, cold and terrifying. He appeared behind Bedlam. With a mighty heave, he swung his burlap sack. A glittering powder mixed with bright-white leaves that looked like the tail feathers of a dove exploded out, filling the air. Alexander held his breath, eyes watering as the powder churned around him in a blizzard of frantic movement and zaps of electricity.

Bedlam turned to face him, dazed. As Alexander watched, the fire in Bedlam seemed to die. His face softened. Green rust oozed out of his pores as the strange powder weakened his defenses.

Alexander drew his shimmering blade and drove it into Bedlam's heart. The blade sank deep. Golden ichor spilled out.

Alexander let go of the hilt and sprang backward and out of the surging cloud of sparking energy and glittering powder, leaving his sword in Bedlam's chest.

Caught in the midst of the cloud, Bedlam stared down at the blade and then at Alexander. Their eyes met, and Alexander could feel Bedlam rifling through his thoughts. Alexander looked away, cursing himself for allowing that to happen.

"You have trapped me," Bedlam rumbled. "But I see in your mind that you will not kill me. Even *you* would not risk the consequences of taking the Eye by force."

Bedlam's wound looked bad, but Alexander's shimmering blade wouldn't kill Bedlam—not at the moment—and Bedlam now knew it; he wasn't going to give up the Eye willingly.

The glittering powder rushed toward Alexander's shimmering blade and began to harden into a waxy, frozen cocoon around Bedlam, spreading outward from the blade itself.

"You carry the Hunter's Mark and the key to her power," Bedlam whispered, his breathing labored as the strange semitranslucent cocoon formed around him. "But you are not her heir—you are a thief and a liar. A traitor! The hunters have fallen! When I awake, I will sweep you all from the face of the earth until not a soul remains. I will hunt the hunters as I once did long ago, and then you will remember *fear*. By my blood . . . and by my fire . . . I will do it."

The cocoon closed around the Eye of Legend last of all. Darkness, like thick black tar, exploded out of the Eye one final time, knocking Alexander to the ground. Then the waxy substance crystallized and Bedlam's chrysalislike prison toppled backward with a thump.

The cavern fell silent.

Alexander got to his feet. Through the strange material, he could see Bedlam sleeping and wisps of darkness slipping from the Eye. Alexander climbed on top of Bedlam's waxy coffin. Slowly, he withdrew his blade. Golden blood dripped down its length. The blade shimmered brightly, and then the blood was absorbed into the blade itself and turned into tiny golden lights that joined the other colors floating within.

Alexander stared at the weapon in his hands, wondering if he'd done the right thing. Bedlam's words had shaken him. Even if they could control Legend's will with the Hunter's Mark, was his power really worth all the lies and betrayal?

"Is that the only key?" Solomon asked, startling Alexander. Alexander looked around, noting that the Knights and Gossymers had died or been driven away to join their kin beneath the earth.

Over a dozen hunters gathered around the Chrysalis, their faces stretching and snapping back into place like rubber bands as the Slippery Wick Brew wore off and they resumed their normal appearances, no longer posing as Wights.

"Alexander, is your blade the only key?" Solomon asked again.

Alexander nodded. "Yes. Unless I die or give it up willingly, no one will be able to use it to free Bedlam."

"Good," said Solomon. He surveyed Alexander, looking thoughtful. Then he offered his hand. Alexander hesitated and then took it and climbed down.

They stared at the strange Chrysalis prison together.

"Looks like we'll have to try our luck with the Arkhon," said Alexander.

Solomon nodded, his expression grim. "I suppose we will."

"Or we could give up our hunt for the Eyes," Alexander suggested.

Solomon looked at him coldly, but didn't say anything.

"It was just an idea," Alexander muttered. He spotted Solomon's shimmering blade within the Chrysalis. "Sorry about your blade."

Solomon shrugged. "The First Hunter made thirteen of them—I'll find another."

Solomon turned and walked away with the other hunters, his own private, handpicked army, loyal only to him.

Alexander glanced down at his shimmering blade. "And who will you kill to get that, I wonder. . . ." For a moment he considered attacking Solomon and ending things before they got any worse. He, with his shimmering blade; Solomon, weaponless— Alexander thought he might stand a small chance of winning. A *very* small chance. But Solomon was closer than a brother, despite their petty arguments. They were bound together in ways neither could explain. He couldn't just kill Solomon, even if he could, even if killing Solomon with his own hands would return blood to blood and un-Change him, thus making him a full-blooded hunter once again and freeing him from Solomon forever.

He wouldn't just kill Solomon.

Not today.

With a deep sigh, Alexander shoved one of the last remaining shimmering blades into his sheath, stole a final regretful look at Bedlam, and followed Solomon Rose to his death.

CHAPTER 1

Down in the Dumps

Over Four Hundred Years Later

Y ou think it's wired?" Sky asked, surveying the bowling alley's broken back door from his hiding place next to the Dumpster.

A high falsetto voice sang from the bowling alley like a cat strangling another cat that was, in turn, being strangled by a man with very small hands and a personal vendetta against cats.

"I hope not," said Andrew, dumping an armload of garbage out of the Dumpster. Sky sifted through it until he found an old soda fountain hose to replace the one on his Pounder that he'd lost to an overaggressive Barrow Hag earlier that day. He hated taking the time for it, especially while they were so close to finding the Marrowick monster they'd tracked since nightfall, but their gear was in sorry shape: Pounder hand-cannons on the fritz, low on ICE freezing solution, dead car batteries on the Shocker gloves and the Cross-Shocker crossbow that they used to electrify the ICE solution and thereby freeze the monsters; it was a wonder they'd managed to freeze anything at all recently.

They were too busy; that was the problem—too much going on. But if they didn't take time to do some quick repairs now, they'd end up fighting the Marrowick with their bare hands, and that wouldn't end well for anyone except the Marrowick. And maybe T-Bone, with his huge frame.

Besides, no one was in any immediate danger since the bowling alley was supposedly closed for the night. But if that were true, then who was killing those poor defenseless cats?

"If the door was wired," Andrew continued, "the Marrowick's already tripped it by breaking the door, which means the police will be here soon."

"All the more reason to hurry," T-Bone chided, attaching a few small wires to the modified car battery that powered his electrified Shocker gloves. "I'm beginning to think you like it in there, Andrew."

Sky applied some crazy-strong adhesive to the soda fountain hose before duct-taping it on his Pounder hand-cannon. Then, acting in as nonchalant a manner as he possibly could, he scooted closer to Crystal and Hands, trying to stay out of the argument he knew was coming.

"Next time, *you* do the Dumpster diving," Andrew retorted as he climbed out of the Dumpster and began sifting through the trash for spare parts. "Maybe you could search with your hands *and* your mouth. That would speed things up and put your mouth to good use for once."

T-Bone chucked a soda pop can at Andrew, hitting him on the head. Andrew jumped to his feet and charged T-Bone, who, at fifteen, was two years older and more than twice his size. But before he could get there, Crystal leaped between them.

"Would you two cool it!" she exclaimed. "You're ruining Sky's birthday!"

Sky chuckled at the absurdity of the statement—as if his birthday wasn't already a disaster. A fistfight with Crenshaw. Mystery fish for lunch. Detention with Malvidia. A sub for gym class. And now they'd tracked the Marrowick for nearly an hour, and they still didn't know why it had wandered into Exile, let alone the bowling alley. He was surprised anyone *remembered* his birthday. Even his parents hadn't said a word when he'd left for school that morning.

Still, as bad as it was, it beat his last birthday, when Uncle Phineas had disappeared, only to die two days later. Nothing could top that. For a time, Sky and the others had believed Phineas was still alive, that he hadn't died in the Jack, and that he'd left them clues in his will. But after a year . . . well, Sky still hoped, but if Phineas was alive, then where was he?

"You two should be ashamed," Hands rebuked, wagging his finger at T-Bone and Andrew. "Things were going splendidly until you started fighting. Now you've spoiled our picnic."

Sky laughed.

Crystal glared at them until their smiles faded. Then she turned her glare back on Andrew and T-Bone. Andrew huffed, walked over to his equipment, and put it on while T-Bone tugged on his Core shoulder pads.

"Let's just finish this so Hands and I can catch the end of football practice," T-Bone grumbled. "We've still got a long night ahead, and tomorrow's the homecoming game against Quindlemore."

"Coach Blackburn is making you practice the night before the homecoming game?" Sky asked, surprised.

"Are you kidding?" Hands replied. "Coach Blackburn is making us practice the *day* of homecoming—right after school. He'd pull the entire team out of school and make us practice morning, noon, and night if he thought he could get away with it. The man is insane."

Sky finished duct-taping and suited up: Core shoulder pads to control his gear, Pounder hand-cannon for freezing monsters, jetpacklike Jumpers, fog-spewing Foggers, three-second force-field–like Shimmer. Lastly, he pulled on a black cloak to hide it all. Their gear was made out of garbage; it *needed* to be hidden.

"Look, I know everyone's tired," Crystal stated, to groans and nods, "but we can't start turning on each other. We've got enough enemies as it is—monsters, Malvidia and her Exile hunters, Solomon Rose, and who knows what else; we've got to stick together. A *band of one*, remember? That's what Phineas wanted."

Everyone nodded. Last year Phineas's weird poem, *Enof Od Naba Ban Do Fone* ("A Band of One" when read from the middle out), had helped them find the three keys to the Arkhon's prison: two funky monocles and a pocket watch. The three keys had connected together on a giant pendulum in Pimiscule Manor, allowing them to relock the prison before the Arkhon (or, really, the Hunter of Legend *Solomon Rose*, as they'd discovered) could escape and destroy the world. They'd lost Phineas's monocle shortly after—how and where, they had no idea—but Sky still had the other monocle and the watch, and he kept them close at all times. They used to joke that Phineas had stolen his monocle back because he was blind without it, or that maybe he was giving them another clue that he was still alive. They didn't joke about that anymore. Now Sky just hoped Phineas's lost monocle hadn't fallen into the wrong hands.

He glanced at his fellow monster hunters: Crystal, Andrew, Hands, and T-Bone. Phineas had wanted them to hunt together, to be unified, to be a band of one, but they were all broken in one way or another. Crystal's mom was still lost, Andrew's parents were still dead, Hands's parents were still jerks, and T-Bone's family was still big (and one kid bigger again since they'd found his little brother last year).

And then there was Sky, the most broken of all.

He glanced at the two separate and distinct marks on his palm: the warm white Hunter's Mark and the cold black Eye of Legend surrounding it (or "trix" as he used to call the Eye before learning its real name). Two marks, two opposing forces—light and dark, hot and cold, unify and destroy—same boy. Was he conflicted? Yes. Was he confused? Yes. Did he hate asking himself rhetorical questions? Yes. Yes, he did.

He could talk to monsters, thanks to the Hunter's Mark. Other than that, and a few random experiences with the Eye last year, he was clueless as to their purpose and use.

If the two puzzling marks were the extent of his childhood trauma, Sky felt he'd be okay. Weird, but okay. The real problem was *how* he got both marks. He started with just one—which one, he didn't know. The other he'd acquired as a baby when a person he called "Shadow Man" turned him and another boy, Errand, into Changelings. *Monsters.* They'd become physically identical in every way at the moment of Change, and deeply connected thereafter.

And then, within hours of Sky discovering that Errand was real, Solomon Rose had thrown Errand over an enormous wall.

Like Phineas, Errand was simply gone, and Sky felt like part of himself was missing. Was he a monster? Was he a hunter? Had he stolen Errand's life?

Only the Shadow Man knew.

For the last year Sky, Crystal, Andrew, Hands, and T-Bone had run themselves ragged hunting down monsters like the Marrowick that had escaped from Solomon's prison. Now they were all tired and broken, even if they usually managed to put a good face on it.

A band of one. That's what Phineas wanted them to be. But how could you possibly take five broken things and make something that wasn't also broken?

"Are you sure they're closing early tonight?" Sky asked.

"Positive," said Hands, whose mother owned the bowling alley. "Madge should've left over an hour ago. Marrowicks aren't violent, are they?"

"They're walking wax plants," T-Bone replied. "How violent can they be?"

"Gee, I don't know," Andrew responded sarcastically, "I seem to remember a certain Jack and Dovetail plant kicking our trash last summer."

"And Solomon Rose smacked us around with his Echo branches," Hands added. "I still have slivers in places I'd rather not mention."

T-Bone grunted in grudging agreement. Sky understood; it was hard to admit you'd been beaten up by a plant.

They jammed the spare garbage into their duffels and T-Bone dropped everything into a nearby sewer grate while everyone else waited by the Dumpster.

"So what's a Marrowick doing in a bowling alley in Exile? Why leave the safety of the north cemetery now after a year of hiding?" Crystal asked, staring thoughtfully at the bowling alley's broken door.

Sky raised his hood as he stepped from hiding. The others fell in line behind him. Since he was the only one who could talk to monsters, the others had selected him to lead the charge—*every* charge, even though talking almost never worked and monsters invariably mauled him as a result.

T-Bone and Hands thought it was hilarious.

"No idea why it's here," Sky replied. "Let's find out."

Shockers crackled. Steam hissed. Metal creaked against metal.

Cats died.

Cringing against the agonizing disco beats, Sky reached for the door handle . . . at which point the door promptly exploded off its remaining hinges and hammered him into the ground.

CHAPTER 2
Cut to the Wick

Sky scrambled out from under the door as a three-foot-tall monster lurched through. The monster—a Marrowick—walked on small stumpy feet and the tips of waxy wings that sprouted from its back and folded over its shoulders. Its melted face quirked to the right and sloped down into sunken cheeks and a lopsided chin. It stared at Sky with empty eye sockets, and as Sky watched, shiny white eyes bubbled to the surface, forming out of the wax.

The Marrowick let out a pathetic-sounding hiss as Sky climbed to his feet and slowly backed away.

"That doesn't look so bad," T-Bone muttered.

"Where's its mom, do you think?" Hands asked, looking around nervously.

"I don't think they have moms," Andrew replied. "They're plants."

"Everything's got a mom," Hands stated.

Andrew and Crystal glared at him.

"Present company excluded, of course," Hands corrected.

"We want to help you—" Sky started, but before he could finish, the Marrowick charged.

Surprised, Sky raised his Pounder and pulled the trigger.

A glob of goopy ICE solution shot out and smashed into the Marrowick. The ICE ripped through the creature, splitting it in half. Sky stared at the two halves in horror, wondering what had gone so terribly wrong. He'd meant to freeze it, not hurt it!

And then, before his eyes, the halves re-formed, changing into two smaller versions of the original Marrowick.

Sky backed away.

A fluttering sound filled the alley, coming from the open door.

"That sounds menacing," Andrew commented, raising his Cross-Shocker.

Scores of pint-size Marrowicks burst out of the bowling alley, shrieking, waxy fingers grasping.

"Oh, come on!" Sky yelled in frustration, hardly believing his bad luck. He fired and fired.

Marrowicks swooped at him. Sky hit his protective Shimmer and a blue nimbus of light shot up around him. The first horde of foot-tall Marrowicks crashed into the light and bounced off.

From the corner of his eye, he saw flashes of electricity and globs of ICE flying.

The Shimmer fell and another horde hit, lifting Sky into the air.

Crystal hit a Marrowick with ICE, and Andrew shot his Cross-Shocker, sending two electrified prongs into the waxy creature, freezing it before it could split. The Marrowick crashed to the ground, the ICE shattered, and two Marrowicks emerged from the rubble.

Hands swung his electrified Collapser staff around like a bat, while T-Bone swatted with his electrified Shocker gloves, knocking Marrowicks from the air.

More flashes, more ICE. Marrowicks split and split again with each hit, swarming them as they grew smaller and smaller.

Warm wax flowed across Sky's skin, leaving a tingling feeling where it touched as dozens of tiny Marrowicks dragged him through the air. He hit his Shimmer again and the Marrowicks blew away from him, spinning. He crashed to the asphalt.

Marrowicks swooped down, gobbling up their fallen comrades, becoming bigger and bigger as they did. With a *whoosh*, scores of small Marrowicks rushed together, smashing into one another.

Sky struggled to his feet. Before he could get all the way up, the Marrowicks re-formed into a single twelve-foot-tall monster right behind him.

Sky turned. "B-big," he stuttered dumbly, staring up at it.

For the third time in as many minutes, Sky hit his protective Shimmer as the Marrowick backhanded him, sending him flying through the open door and into the bowling alley snack bar, where he smashed into a bucket of nacho cheese.

Outside, he saw Andrew flailing in the air, firing his Cross-Shocker at the few Marrowicks that hadn't merged yet as they carried him toward the main body and its greedy hands. Electrified prongs from the Cross-Shocker sailed everywhere, lighting up the alley bright as day.

Beyond Andrew, Sky saw T-Bone punching Marrowicks from the air until they swarmed around him like mosquitoes. Hands and Crystal worked around T-Bone, Hands dancing about like a madman, while Crystal fired from behind the Dumpster, kicking at Marrowicks trying to drag her from hiding.

But the ICE wasn't holding.

Through the bowling alley windows near the front, Sky saw red and blue flashing lights and shadows creeping close, guns out, flashlights swinging. He had seconds to act.

Planting his feet against the snack bar, he hit his jetpack-like Jumpers. The force shot him through the splatter of nacho cheese and built-up deep-fryer grease caking the floor. He slapped a button on his Core shoulder pads as he slid, and nasty thick Fog streamed behind him, filling the bowling alley, and then he was through the shattered doorway and back outside. He crashed into the largest Marrowick, knocking it down as the smaller ones released Andrew.

Andrew landed on top of the Marrowick just behind the wings and rode the Marrowick like a bronco as it struggled to rise.

The force of the Jumpers slammed Sky into the curb at the far side of the alley. He lurched to his feet, flinging clumps of grease and cheese everywhere. The Marrowick noticed the police flashlights coming through the bowling alley and around the building. With a screech, it burst into hundreds of miniature Marrowicks and swarmed away like angry bees, knocking everyone to the ground. Sky's Fog petered out.

He helped Crystal to her feet, but before they could chase after the Marrowick, dozens of monstrous black-and-white birds shot out of the nearby woods, cawing madly. They were smart (but not that smart), loved homemade phosphorescent crackers, and their skeletons glowed green under a black light. But, most important, they'd saved Sky from Solomon Rose last year.

Piebalds.

"Calm down! I can't understand you all at once!" Sky hissed, anxiously watching the police close in.

The Piebalds kept chattering.

"What? Now? I can't do that now!"

"CAW! CAW! CAW!"

Something was terribly wrong, but he couldn't understand what amidst all the chatter. He glanced at the bowling alley, the forest, the road, taking it all in; he could make it if he rushed.

"All right, but it'd better be quick." Frustrated, Sky closed his eyes, opened his senses, and let his mind fill in the blanks— a trap-building technique Phineas had taught him years ago.

He imagined himself standing in front of a window. Through the window, he imagined the Piebalds flapping and cawing, the moon rising, the trees growing, until the image in his mind vaguely resembled his actual surroundings. He spotted the nearest Piebald and imagined a rope leading from the window to the Piebald—from his body to the Piebald's body, as it were.

Sky opened his imaginary window and stepped to the Edge, doing something Phineas had never taught him—something he'd figured out after edgewalking with Errand last year.

A strange wind picked up, arising from everywhere and nowhere, buffeting Sky. He struggled to hold his imagined world together, fixing more and more details until the winds calmed down. Normally, he'd spend several minutes working on details and shaping the Edge—the strange space his mind had to cross to reach the Piebald—until it was stable and safe, but he only had seconds, not minutes.

Taking a deep, calming breath, he stepped onto the rope

and lurched forward, leaving his body behind. Almost immediately the winds rose up again, stronger than before. Sky made the mistake of glancing down. The road below shifted and the asphalt began to boil. Frantic, he pushed on, focusing on the rope and the Piebald.

The wind uprooted the trees and sent them flying through the air. Sky's imagined world fell apart around him. A raging storm of darkness and crackling energy seeped through the road. Sky focused, recalling detail after detail. But as the road re-formed—driving the storm back—the tightrope began to shake and the Piebald's feathers shifted color. Sky focused all his attention on the rope and the Piebald, letting the rest of his world fall apart.

The storm roared in from all directions, throwing the fractured remnants of his world to the four winds. Boiling light and freezing darkness tore at his mind. He stumbled and, for a moment, feared he'd fall as he had the first time he'd edge-walked, when Errand had pushed him into Rauschtlot's mind and he'd tumbled through that storm and felt his consciousness torn apart until he'd nearly forgotten who he was.

The tightrope slipped away and Sky jumped the last few feet, reaching for the Piebald. As he touched it, the world shifted around him and he was suddenly in the Piebald's head, seeing the memory it wanted to show him, the whole complicated process over in less than five seconds.

And what he saw terrified him.

CHAPTER 3
Unexpected Guests

Frantic, and hoping the monster hunters noticed his collapsed body, Sky forgot about all else and leaped from Piebald to Piebald, heedless of the distance and the rushing storms ripping at him—the tightrope barely formed before he jumped to the next. Sky moved faster and faster, ignoring more and more details until Piebald stick figures flew over childlike landscapes that ripped apart the second he entered them. He leaped before the next Piebald's image even formed in his mind. Wings sprouted from his back and the storm exploded around him. He sailed through the hidden forces of the world, the chaos of the Edge.

Gale-force winds pounded him, tearing at his mind, ripping him apart.

He smashed into the last Piebald and the storm finally disappeared. In seconds, he'd leaped across a distance that would've taken a Piebald precious minutes to fly.

Pimiscule Manor spread out below him with its domed

tower, wandering corridors, and sprawling wings, and he saw in real time what he'd only glimpsed in the Piebald's memory: dozens of dark figures creeping through the woods, gardens, and fields surrounding the manor, closing in on his home and his unsuspecting family within.

He heard a rumbling on the cobblestone drive, and then Hannah, his sister, pulled up in front of the manor in her beater car—a gift for her sixteenth birthday. She climbed out and casually strolled into their brightly lit home carrying her pom-poms, perfect as ever. A sign on the door read HAPPY THIRTEEN SKY!

The Piebald whose mind Sky was in dropped lower and Sky saw that the figures wore dark cloaks and hoods and had bows and arrows slung over their shoulders. Some carried silver knives, boomerangs, and bolas, and other, stranger weapons and gear. They were all clearly hunters . . . but from where? Who were they?

Sky found it hard to focus. He'd never edgewalked like this before. He tried to flap his wings, realized he wasn't the Piebald—just a passenger in one—and asked it to swoop in for a closer look.

He spotted more hunters creeping through the grove of dead trees east of the manor—how many, Sky couldn't tell, but a lot. A *whole lot*. And more farther down the hill to the east, near his school, Arkhon Academy. Ages varied—old, young, male, female. Some looked no older than Sky, and he didn't recognize any of them.

There were still a few hunters in Exile—mostly retired—whose identities Malvidia, the head of the Exile hunters, kept secret. Sky didn't number himself or his friends among the Exile hunters, nor did Malvidia, for that matter, so he didn't know much about them. The Exile hunters' ranks had swelled last year when Solomon's prison had opened and several hunt-ers, previously thought dead, had emerged after being locked in time for eleven years. But even so, Sky felt certain that the Exile hunters had nowhere near these numbers, not by half. Not by half of a half.

These hunters weren't from Exile. Sky didn't know much about it, but he knew there were different hunter orders and societies in different parts of the world. He also knew that every hunter order outside of Exile answered to the same group: the Hunters of Legend. They were the oldest order of hunters, the most powerful, founded by a mysterious woman known only as the First Hunter. There were never more than thirteen at a time, and they'd gotten their name centuries ago when they'd hunted Legend, the most evil monster in the history of the world. Sky had only read bits and pieces here and there about their origin, but he'd read plenty of stories about their indi-vidual members. And he knew something else, too: Phineas had once been a Hunter of Legend, and so had Solomon Rose.

But if these hunters answered to the Hunters of Legend, then what were they doing here, in Exile? And, more impor-tant, *why were they at his house?*

Sky saw a redhaired boy at the front of the group hold up his hand, and all the hunters came to a stop a short distance from the manor. They took up watchful positions and then seemed to meld into the shadows, disappearing from his sight. The Piebald, and Sky within, swooped toward the redhaired boy who'd held up his hand, and who appeared to be their leader.

As Sky drew closer, he spotted a large group of hunters dragging someone toward the leader. When he realized who it was, he groaned. It was Sheriff Beau, his friend, in need of help, and Sky was stuck in a bird!

Beau's hands were tied behind his back and his face was battered. His clothes were torn and he had cuts everywhere. The dozen or so hunters guarding him looked even worse. They pushed him forward until he collapsed at the feet of the red-haired boy, who looked fourteen or fifteen and was roughly the same height as Sky, but with a stockier, more muscular build.

The boy looked surprised when he saw Beau, but then his expression changed and a smirk appeared on his face as if he were laughing at some private joke.

"Hello, mates," said the boy with a thick British accent. "What's all this, then?"

"We found zis guy sneaking up behind us, Chase," said one of the hunters with a faint Austrian accent. "Claims to be ze sheriff, but he fights like an Academy of Legend–trained hunter. He took out ten of us before we realized he was zere."

Beau spit out a mouthful of blood. "Where's Morton, kid? It's time he and I had a little chat."

"Busy, I'm afraid," Chase replied.

"You realize you're violating a treaty by coming here, right?" said Beau. "You stay out of Exile, we stay out of Europe—that was the deal. That's been the deal for four hundred years."

"Your treaty with the Hunters of Legend died with Bartholomew Lem," Chase replied. "He was one of the thirteen, and he died on your watch."

Beau scoffed. "So, because your envoy got eaten by a Wargarou, you're going to break a four-hundred-year-old treaty? Are you sure you're not here because *Phineas* finally died, so you thought you could step in and take control of Exile? Because I promise you, Phineas wasn't the only thing in Exile you should fear."

Chase shrugged. "You'll have to talk to Morton about all

that, mate. Really, I'm just here for the boy." Chase gestured vaguely at the manor.

"Boy? You mean Sky?" Beau's eyes narrowed dangerously. "You touch a hair on Sky's head and I will personally kill every single one of you."

The Piebald squawked in agreement.

Sky was too stunned to react, both by Beau's defense of him and by the truth of it: These foreign hunters were here for him; but why?

Chase glanced up at the Piebald, looked away, did a double take. He narrowed his eyes.

Sky felt a sharp stab. A painful cold raced through him, and the Piebald's beak started to chatter. Before Sky or the Piebald could react, Chase looked away and the pain was gone.

"Things change," Chase muttered, looking back at Beau. "The others have made up their mind about Sky and there's nothing we can do about it, even if we wanted to—and I do, mate. Honest. It's a shame what they're planning with the hunt and all. But there's no need for us to be enemies; we didn't come here for that—quite the opposite, in fact. We're here to help you." Chase shooed away the other hunters and offered Beau his hand. "I'm Chase Shroud—Hunter of Legend."

Beau grinned. Then, faster than Sky could blink, Beau grabbed Chase's hand, yanked him forward, drew a long knife from Chase's belt, spun Chase around, and put the knife to his throat.

"I'm Beau—Sheriff of Exile, kid. Now call off your hunters and take me to Morton Thresher or I'll shove this knife down your throat."

Chase held up his hands, ordering the others to back away. Then he disappeared in a wisp of black smoke, shadow slipping just like a Wargarou. He reappeared behind Beau.

Beau spun with the knife, but Chase was a touch faster. He blocked and snatched the knife from Beau's hand. Then he spun Beau around and pushed him back to the ground with his foot.

Chase tossed the knife next to him. "Keep it—you'll need it."

Beau rolled over to face Chase, chuckling. "I wouldn't have believed it—a kid your age chosen as one of the thirteen? But they taught you, all right. You must be the youngest Hunter of Legend since Alexander Drake."

"Solomon Rose, actually," said Chase. "He beat Alexander to the honor by a full year."

"Honor?" Beau harrumphed. "Whatever, kid."

For the first time, Chase scowled. "Not all of us can be *sheriffs*, mate. The world's population of jam doughnuts would never survive."

"Hey now, just a minute—" Beau started to protest, sounding highly offended.

"Bedlam is coming to Exile, Mr. Sheriff, *sir*," Chase cut in. "I recommend you start listening."

The forest seemed to grow quiet, and Sky along with it. After a year of studying the books in Phineas's library, he knew the stories. Bedlam, the oldest living son of the ancient terror Legend, who nearly destroyed the world with his dark powers. Bedlam, brother to the Arkhon—the *real* Arkhon. Husband of the nightmarish Darkhorn. Father of the giant Harrow Knights, the human-size Harrow Wights, and the spiderlike Gossymers, as well as the Edgewalkers that Solomon Rose had hunted to extinction. Bedlam, master of the Edge, who could steal into your mind and terrorize your dreams, or drag you into his and lock you away in undying madness.

Bedlam, the monster whom Solomon Rose and Alexander Drake imprisoned in Skull Valley.

Bedlam. If possible, even more frightening than the Arkhon.

"We believe Bedlam is already here, edgewalking," Chase continued. "His army will arrive no later than tomorrow night with his body, which—lucky for all you Exile hunters—remains trapped in the Chrysalis thanks to Solomon Rose and Alexander Drake, both *Hunters of Legend*, I might add."

"Bedlam escaped. . . . How is that even possible?" Beau asked, sounding stunned as he slowly climbed to his feet without picking up the knife.

Chase shrugged. "No idea, mate. But you know the story. After Solomon and Alexander locked him away, Bedlam promised to hunt down every last hunter. Maybe he's coming here for his brother, or maybe he thinks something here can free his body. Whatever the case, it looks like he's figured out a way to edgewalk from his Chrysalis and, lucky you, he's starting his hunt in Exile."

Beau spit blood on Chase's foot. "Lucky us."

Chase glanced at the blood, looking even more amused. "I'm on your side, mate. It's all bollocks. I don't want to see Sky hurt any more than you do. . . ." Chase glanced up at the Piebald, and Sky felt certain that Chase knew he was watching. "But I'm a minority, and Bedlam's arrival has forced Morton's hand. By taking control of Sky, Bedlam could get everything he wants. Sky's marks would make him more powerful than if he reclaimed his own body, and with the keys to the Arkhon's prison, Bedlam could free his brother. We can't let that happen. Morton believes, and the other hunters agree, that if Bedlam hasn't already taken control of Sky, he soon will. Sky is untrained, weak-minded, and weak-willed—there's simply no way he could resist. And so, at Morton's request, the Hunters of Legend have declared a hunt. Tonight, one way or another, Sky *will* die."

Sky startled. They were here to kill him? *That's* what they wanted? Why couldn't anyone ever hunt him down for brunch?

Chase looked back at the Piebald. "If I were Sky, I would run and I wouldn't stop. If we don't find him, Bedlam will before the night is over. Death, madness, or escape; those are Sky's only options. Sky should run from Exile and he should start right now, before we find his friends wandering Exile's sewers with his body."

Sky startled. Chase definitely knew he was there. What's more, he knew where to find him. But was he warning him away or leading him into a trap? And if he was warning him, why?

"Take him to Morton," Chase instructed his hunters, gesturing at Beau. "I'm going to pay a visit to Sky's family to see if he's been acting strange lately. Looks like it's his birthday today—I do hope they saved me some cake."

The Piebald let out a squawk, or maybe Sky let out a squawk. . . . He was so confused. Either way, they took to the air.

"Remember what I promised, Chase," Beau called out as Chase strolled toward the manor. "Any harm comes to Sky and I'll hunt you down after I deal with Morton! I swear it!"

Sky caught a glimpse of the hunters surrounding Beau. Beau kicked the knife into his hand and attacked in a flurry, quickly disappearing beneath a mountain of bodies.

Sky sped south, jumping from Piebald to Piebald like a madman, but by the time he returned to his body, it was already too late.

CHAPTER 4
A Deadly Collapse

Sky opened his eyes and stared down at T-Bone's butt. "What in the . . ."

"He's awake!" Andrew yelled.

They raced through the sewers. Sky kept smacking his head into T-Bone's back, slung as he was over T-Bone's shoulder. Behind them, Sky saw flashlights swinging this way and that.

"About time," T-Bone huffed, sounding winded.

"Can you run?" Crystal asked.

"Yes," Sky croaked between slams. "No. Who is that?"

"Police," said Crystal. "Next time give us some warning. Okay? We barely got you out of there."

Sky nodded, but since he nodded with each bouncing step T-Bone took, Crystal probably couldn't tell the difference.

"We need to get out of here!" Sky exclaimed.

"You think?" said Hands.

"Tunnel's ahead," said Crystal. "Andrew, drop a can."

Andrew flipped on a Fog canister and threw it behind

them. Flashlight beams disappeared behind a thick cloud of Fog. They reached the tunnels—dozens of branching passages—and T-Bone banked right toward their secret lair.

"We can't go this way!" Sky exclaimed.

"What?" asked Crystal. "Why?"

"Set me down!" said Sky.

T-Bone dropped him to the ground. Sky stumbled. The world spun around him.

Hands grabbed Sky by one arm and T-Bone took the other and they started running again, dragging Sky between them. Crystal led them through the tunnels with her black light. Finally Sky got his feet under him and ran on his own.

The tunnel forked ahead.

"Don't go to the lair! Go home—you should be safe there. I'll find you guys when this is over." *Assuming I'm not dead*, Sky thought. He headed for the passage on the right.

"Ohhh no you don't!" Crystal exclaimed, snatching his arm. "You're not going anywhere until you tell us what happened."

Voices sounded back down the tunnel—hunters or police, he couldn't be sure. But either way, he was running out of time. He didn't want to put Crystal and the others in danger, and if they stayed with him, that's exactly where they'd be. Hunting monsters was one thing; endangering his friends to try to save himself was another matter entirely. The question was, could he lie well enough to keep them safe?

"I'm going to visit Rauschtlot."

Crystal stared at him skeptically.

"The police are coming," Sky pointed out.

"Some time in jail might give us all a rest," Crystal replied. "Now *talk*."

Sky sighed. "The Hunters of Legend are here to kill me.

They've got Beau and they'll soon have my family and if you don't go, they'll take you or kill you as well. Now will you go?"

"No." Crystal took the passage to the right. "I assume you have a plan?"

They started running again. While they ran, Sky explained what he'd seen.

"Wait, you're telling us there's an army of hunters camped outside your house and you're running *toward* them?" Hands asked.

"Yep," said Sky, watching the tunnels ahead.

"Now that's my kind of crazy!" Hands replied, grinning.

They reached a large natural cavern beneath the east cemetery—the home where Rauschtlot the Gnomon had raised her daughter, Nackles, and protected dozens of children from the Wargarou last year, including T-Bone's brother, Dickens.

Tree roots, rocks, and dirt sprouted from the top of the cave. Small streams raced past shattered coffins, which had sunk through from above, and wove between rock formations before disappearing down passages Sky had never explored that led farther into the earth.

If what Chase said was true, then Bedlam was going to try to edgewalk into Sky and take control tonight. Then he would use Sky's prison keys and whatever weird powers were in Sky's marks to free the creature everyone thought was the Arkhon—but was really Solomon Rose—and destroy Exile. Sky couldn't let that happen. He *wouldn't* let that happen.

He veered off, leading Crystal and the others along a narrow passage toward the tomb of Andrew's mother, Emaline Livingstone, and the exit into the east cemetery. There was still no sign of Rauschtlot or Nackles, which was odd. Normally

Nackles would've tackled him to the ground by now with her shovel-like four-fingered hands and smothered him in kisses from one of her dozens of razor-sharp rock-shattering mouths—most of which were on her head and hidden by a knit cap.

"What exactly do you hope to accomplish by rushing up there?" Crystal asked.

"I'm going to lead them into the Sleeping Lands."

Everyone was quiet. The Sleeping Lands included the north cemetery and much more besides—swamps and crags, broken woods, flooded rivers, floating corpses, ancient monsters, and death . . . more death than Sky could name.

T-Bone whistled. "Risky . . . you're as likely to die there—maybe more. I know you've laid a lot of traps up there over the last year to keep the monsters away, but your traps are nonlethal; what happens when the hunters escape?"

Sky was quiet. He'd thought about it; if there was any other way to force the Hunters of Legend from Exile, he'd take it. But there wasn't.

"He's not going for the traps, T," said Andrew.

T-Bone looked confused. "What . . . the monsters? You can't mean . . ."

Hands started laughing. "The Bolgers! Sky, you devil! Remind me to never get on your bad side!"

Sky gave Hands a tight grin.

Last Christmas, T-Bone's family had decided they wanted a fresh-cut Christmas tree. So, T-Bone had cut one down while on a hunt in the north cemetery and dragged it home—an unfortunate decision that had led to an even more unfortunate incident. The incident had involved Wormwood, T-Bone's gigantic mutt with shaggy hair and a neurotic personality. The incident had also involved two dozen jumbo-size Yule log gift sets (made up of both the log-shaped dessert and the actual hardwood log) and a flood of Bolgers, ugly green-skinned creatures that tended to shrink to the size of a pine needle and hibernate when hungry, but grow to the size of a pine tree when fed Yule logs (either kind, but they preferred the dessert).

Worst Christmas ever. Fortunately, when deprived of Yule logs and other foods, the Bolgers shrank back down to pine needles and resumed hibernating on their favorite tree, so it could've been a lot worse.

"I need you guys to do something for me," said Sky. "Find Malvidia and tell her I'll deliver a present in the next few hours, if I survive. Tell her they've taken Beau to Morton Thresher, Bedlam's army is coming, and Bedlam is *not* controlling me. Tell her she owes me for last year—it's time to pay up."

"Sky, you're nuts if you think we're leaving you for even a minute," said Crystal. "Besides, how do we know Malvidia's not helping them?"

Sky held up his hand for silence as footsteps sounded in the tunnel ahead.

"The light—turn it off!" Sky hissed. Crystal flipped off her black light as three hunters in dark cloaks emerged into a crossroads where several tunnels met less than fifty feet away. Sky clutched the Pounder hand-cannon and pressed himself against the wall beside Crystal.

"What's going on?" Crystal whispered. Sky could see perfectly well in the dark; he often forgot that the others couldn't. Fortunately, Sky always carried the remaining two keys to Solomon's prison with him: the monocle and the watch. And the monocle, as they'd discovered last year, allowed the wearer to see in the dark. He pulled the monocle from his pocket and pressed it into Crystal's hand.

The hunters moved slowly into the crossroads, searching each passage with strange, glowing green eyes. Sky held his breath, refusing to move, hoping they'd choose a different passage.

His Hunter's Mark suddenly warmed, something that only happened when he talked to monsters, or when his Eye of Legend freaked out. He sensed a slight tremble in the wall through his Hunter's Mark.

He groaned inwardly at the timing. His Hunter's Mark translated the vibrations, allowing him to communicate in Earthspeak, a Gnomon language composed of complex rhythms sent through the earth like miniature earthquakes. Sky ignored the incoming greeting and, in Earthspeak, yelled . . .

RUN!

Farther up one of the passages, beyond the hunters, Nackles the Gnomon—Rauschtlot's daughter—dropped silently through the ceiling and shook the dirt from her back. She took in the hunters, who hadn't yet noticed her, and her semitranslucent skin suddenly went from gray to blue.

Blue as she stills, Black as she flies, Red as she kills, Sky thought. She was waiting and watching. There was still a chance the hunters might just move on down a different passage.

The hunters raised their bows, aiming at Sky.

"Shimmer!" Crystal screamed, apparently realizing at the same moment as Sky that the hunters could see them.

The hunters fired.

Sky hit his force-field–like Shimmer and a blue nimbus of light shot up around him.

Green flames flickered to life around the thick, bone-white arrows as they sped through the air. The flames disturbed him, and despite his Shimmer, Sky dove.

All three arrows streaked past him. Hands deflected the first shot into the ceiling with his electrified Collapser staff and pure, dumb luck. The second just missed Andrew and hit the wall. The third arrow streaked toward Crystal. It struck her Shimmer's blue nimbus, slowed, and then stopped a few inches from her heart. The arrow hung harmlessly in the air for a moment, and then it fell, flaring brighter and brighter as it approached the ground.

Crystal threw herself backward, away from the arrow, just as it exploded.

The force—far greater than it had any right to be—launched Sky, who was in front of the others, up the passage, tumbling toward the hunters. He caught a quick glimpse of Crystal, Andrew, Hands, and T-Bone spinning away in the opposite direction back down the passage, and then two more massive explosions buffeted him and the tunnel collapsed, separating him from Crystal and the others.

Sky rolled to his back. Every bone in his body ached. He stared down the ruined tunnel, desperately hoping his friends were okay.

A hunter grabbed Sky by the hair and dragged him to his feet. From his coat, the hunter pulled a long silver knife. He pressed it against Sky's throat and inspected him, his glowing green eyes staring out of his dark face. "You are not as Morton led me to believe." His accent was strange, short and clipped, as if he was biting his words.

"'Agos, kill ze boy and let us leave zis 'orrible place," yelled a French woman, even though she stood but a few steps away. Sky wondered if the collapse had affected her hearing.

"Patience, Solange. I do not believe Bedlam has yet taken

control of the boy. . . ." Hagos furrowed his brow, but before he could do anything more, Nackles the Gnomon—her skin deep red—rose up behind Hagos, grabbed his head, and smashed it into the wall. Solange turned, but Nackles already had her. With her immense strength—a strength Sky knew all too well—Nackles threw Solange down one of the side passages.

The last hunter raised her bow.

Nackles dove into the earth as if it was water and rocketed out of the ceiling, burying the hunter in rubble as she loosed her arrow at Sky.

Sky hit his Shimmer. The fiery arrow exploded as it hit, flinging him backward. He slammed into the far wall and crashed to the ground as the crossroads started to cave in.

Dirt and rock fell everywhere. Sky stumbled to his feet, dodging debris, trying to get back down the tunnel to find a way to his friends. A rock smashed into his shoulder, driving him to the ground, his Core shoulder pads taking the hit. Through the shower of earth, he saw Nackles toss Hagos and the nameless hunter down the passage with Solange and to safety, her skin gray once again.

As boulders tumbled around her, Nackles smacked the rocks out of the air as though they were gnats hardly worth considering. Her knit cap fell off and mouths all over her body chewed through the falling earth, passed it right through, and spit it out of other mouths.

She was in her natural habitat, perfectly comfortable amidst the avalanche. Sky, though, was far from comfortable. He backed away—there was no way through, and the cave-in was just getting started. He pressed his Hunter's Mark to the ground and shouted in Earthspeak: *Nackles, my friends might be trapped! Please find them, get them out!*

Nackles spun around and seemed surprised to see him still there. She began punching the wall, responding in Earthspeak, her words coming through amidst random noise.

I will help—YOU RUN!

Sky ran. As the collapse began to spread out from the crossroads, chunks of earth fell from the ceiling, battering him. He reeled to and fro, stumbling and dodging as he raced through the tunnels for the exit at Emaline's tomb. He threw his shoulders against the stone tile and crawled up and out into the dark stone room.

The floor collapsed around him, and he leaped from tile to tile. Emaline's stone coffin cracked and fell apart. Sky rolled out of the way, remembering thankfully that the coffin was empty, as they'd never found Emaline's body.

As the broken sarcophagus sank into the ground, Sky latched onto it and launched himself across an impossible gap. He hit the other side hard and scrambled for the door, shooting through and out as the tomb toppled in on itself.

He raced north as the earth continued to sink around him. He ran and ran until the ground stopped trembling and the rumbling stopped rumbling. When he turned around, he saw something that made him cry out: The entire east cemetery had collapsed into the earth. All that remained were a few scattered tombstones, some broken statues, and a hole as deep as an open grave.

CHAPTER 5

Sky Hunters

Sky wiped tears from his eyes and started running north even though every part of him wanted nothing more than to race back and find his friends and make sure they'd survived. But that was exactly what he couldn't do, not without endangering them all over again, not without first taking care of the hunters. He had to trust that Nackles would get them out. He couldn't give in to his fears. Not now.

Sky pulled two cans of Fog from his backpack as he slipped into the woods, racing toward his traps and the Sleeping Lands. Too many had died for him already. The entire east cemetery was littered with the bodies of hunters who'd died protecting him when he was just a baby, and now even those bodies were gone. Phineas, Errand, Andrew's mother and father, even Crystal's mother, Cassandra, who'd disappeared near Skull Valley years ago while looking for answers about Sky—all gone now. And for what? For some stupid marks on his hand?

Sky just couldn't lose anyone else. Crystal. Andrew. T-Bone.

Hands. They'd spent months tired and upset with one another, and it all seemed so stupid now. They were his best friends, the first real friends he'd had that weren't related to him or imaginary, or imaginarily related to him. They'd be okay. Nackles would get them out. She would. He had to believe that.

He replaced the used cans on his Fogger and reached out for the Piebalds. He found one sitting on a branch nearby, watching him. The bird seemed bigger than the others he had seen, and older somehow—more scarred, some of its black feathers gray with age.

The strange Piebald swooped after him.

"What's your name?" Sky asked.

"CAW."

"Fred?" said Sky, confused. "What kind of a Piebald name is that?"

"CAW!"

"All right, all right," said Sky, holding up his hands, "I get it! You're not from around here. I'm sure Fred's a fine Piebald name where you come from." Sky tossed the Piebald a cracker from his pocket, but the bird turned up its beak and the cracker dropped to the ground. Sky had never met a Piebald that didn't like crackers before, especially the uniquely disgusting phosphorescent kind Andrew and Hands made from superexplosive distilled urine.

Before he could wonder too much, a murder of Piebalds arrived and snatched up the cracker amidst a flurry of wings and snapping beaks.

"I need eyes," said Sky, throwing more crackers.

The murder squawked at him and then took off. Sky slung his backpack over his shoulders, where it rested snugly between his ICE containers. He adjusted his cloak and continued jogging roughly northwest. He'd planned to get the hunters' attention so he could lure them away from the manor; he was pretty sure he had it now, and more than he wanted.

Fred flew next to him, ignoring the other Piebalds. Sky didn't have the time or focus to edgewalk into the Piebalds to see through their eyes, which meant he'd have to rely on their judgment and verbal warnings, a terrifying prospect in its own right.

"CAW!" a Piebald screeched.

Sky dove to the side and an arrow struck a tree beside him, just missing his head.

Sky stared at the quivering black arrow, heart pounding. The arrow began to smoke, and black lines—like veins—spread through the tree, and then it crumbled to ash.

A shout went up behind him. Sky gulped, switched on his Fogger, and hit his jetpacklike Jumpers. He shot through the air, leaving a massive cloud of Fog in his wake. A giant tree branch rose in front of him and he bounced off of it and onto the next, and the next, canvassing the area as arrows whizzed past. He heard traps snapping below and hunters screaming and yelling. With a final leap to a lower branch, he plunged back to the ground and rolled amidst the blue light of his Shimmer. Then he veered from the path and started running in earnest.

He definitely had their attention.

More arrows whizzed past. He crashed through the undergrowth, jumped a log, and rolled to the side. The trap sprung and the hunter behind him dropped into a pit.

Sky scrambled to his feet and kept running. He hopscotched through a clearing as his Fog petered out. Hunters dove at him with knives and swords. Logs swung down from trees, knocking hunters to the sides. Saplings sprang from the ground, tangling the hunters in knots, and still more hunters vaulted into the air as slabs of spring-loaded bark exploded and vines dragged them away.

Stinging Lizzies, double bogies, and dozens of other traps Phineas had taught him sprang up, snatching the hunters. But for every one caught, two more appeared.

Sky sprinted down a hill and crashed through a small creek. On the other side, the ground leveled and grew mushy.

A hunter dropped out of a tree in front of him, eyes glowing green.

"Whoa!" Sky faked right. The hunter took a step and a vine closed around first one ankle and then the other, yanking the hunter crotch first into a tree—Montezuma's revenge, one of Uncle Phineas's favorite traps. Sky raced past, heart pounding. He heard more traps going off behind him and to the sides.

Piebalds called out warnings from above, steering him away from the larger groups. For a moment he thought he saw Chase Shroud rushing through the trees to his right, but then the hunter veered off and sped away, leaving Sky perplexed and, if possible, even more frightened.

Sky hit his Core, and the Pounder slid into his hand. He raced along an old animal trail, lengthening his lead. A year of running from monsters had made him fast. Very fast. Hopefully fast enough.

Another green-eyed hunter leaped at him. Sky shot her with the Pounder, driving her back into a trap. He took out two more, racing on.

Ancient trees stretched out above him, blocking the moonlight. He navigated his way across the swampy ground and into the craggy, tombstone-covered moors that marked the beginning of the north cemetery, the border of the Sleeping Lands. Old and flooded hunter tombs leading to underground family crypts lay scattered ahead, rising from the bog.

"CAW!" the Piebalds warned, but Sky was too slow and a hunter tackled him from the shadows, pinning him in the mud. As he struggled to get free, he caught a glimpse of a slightly older boy with blond hair, high cheekbones, and puffy lips.

"Crenshaw?" Sky sputtered in amazement. Last year Crenshaw and his cronies—Ren (T-Bone's brother), Cordelia, Marcus, and Alexis—had made a pact with the child-eating Wargarou and become giant, wolflike Shadow Wargs. They'd tried to kill Sky. Since then, most of the cronies had left him alone, but Crenshaw still blamed Sky for the death of his mother—a hunter who'd died when the Arkhon had attacked twelve years earlier. Crenshaw picked fights with Sky whenever he thought he could get away with it; in other words, *all the time*.

Fortunately, Crenshaw wasn't a Shadow Warg anymore, thanks to Ursula. Unfortunately, he was still bigger and stronger than Sky.

Crenshaw smiled at him. "You're done for, Sky. Morton sought me out personally to track you down tonight, and I'm not the only one."

"Malvidia's not going to be happy when she finds out you sided against her," said Sky, probing to see if Crenshaw knew anything of Malvidia's allegiance; his entire plan hinged on her.

"Sided against her? You have no idea what you're talking about," Crenshaw spat. "I finally get to kill you, and the Hunters of Legend will call me a hero for doing it!"

A long silvery knife flashed into Crenshaw's hand. Sky raised the Pounder and Crenshaw sliced through the recently repaired hoses before he could shoot. Compressed gasses rushed out, spraying into Crenshaw's face.

Crenshaw raised his hands to block the spray. Fred swooped down, clawing and thrashing at Crenshaw with his wings.

Sky rolled and threw his feet out, launching Crenshaw into the nearby swamp water. Vines exploded upward, trapping Crenshaw in a watery net.

Sky jumped to his feet and started running again, troubled on so many levels. If Malvidia and the Exile hunters were really helping Morton, what chance did he have?

He passed the first tomb, a large, gaudy entrance to Crenshaw's forgotten family crypt, the perfect place for Crenshaw to lurk. The epitaph on the Argrave tomb simply read: ARGRAVE IS YOUR GRAVE.

He moved past, running deeper into the Sleeping Lands or, more accurately, Nasty Dead-Hunter Soup, the one-time burial lands of the hunters before the swamps had come and the land itself had chewed up the dead and spit them out.

Hunters were closing in. Sky could hear them all around him now, slogging through the swamp.

Sky leaped across a bog, trying not to imagine what kinds of fetid flesh floated beneath the surface. At some point, maybe ten years ago, maybe a hundred for all he knew, the Vulpine River a few miles west had overflowed its bounds, creating the swamps and washing away grave sites. Whether because of the icy waters, or because of some long-forgotten preservation ritual performed upon the dead, many of the bodies were miraculously well pickled. With the topsoil washed away, these coffinless dead, these ancient hunters stared out of the water with sightless eyes and graying flesh.

Though Sky had now visited the Sleeping Lands many times, he couldn't help but fear that with each leap, he would feel a gnarled hand on his ankle, waiting to drag him down to join the dead in their eternal frozen slumber.

As if maniacal hunters bent on killing him weren't bad enough.

Shivering, Sky raced after the Piebalds.

His traps—meant to keep the worst of the monsters away from Exile—were nearly spent, and Sky felt weary to the bone. Adrenaline and a year of one of the worst exercise routines imaginable were the only things keeping him on his feet.

Ahead, sitting on a small island in the middle of a swampy wasteland, he saw a gigantic gnarled tree bristling with green needles, and he knew he was nearly there.

Sky ditched his cloak and gear as he ran—everything but his waterproof, fire-retardant backpack—and then dove into the stagnant water and swam deep beneath the surface, past corpse after corpse in this, the most disturbing part of the Sleeping Lands. Arrows zipped by, trailing bubbles.

Sky dove deeper, skirting tombstones, mausoleums, broken statues, and the bodies of hunters long dead who drifted with the waves and watched him with milky, indifferent eyes.

An arrow landed in the chest of the corpse next to him, a man with only half a face, the other half whittled to the moldy-green bone. The corpse rolled with the impact and drifted backward in the water, its arms rising up as if to grab Sky. A sightless white eye stared out of the man's broken face. On the corpse's forehead, Sky thought he saw another Eye, black and scarred, spilling inky darkness into the water: the Eye of Legend.

Freezing pain, answering darkness, and tarlike blood erupted from the matching Eye on Sky's palm.

The corpse smiled at him.

Sky screamed and bubbles exploded from his mouth—Bedlam had found him, just as the hunters predicted.

Water froze around Sky, above him, frozen by the cold and terrible darkness spilling from the Eyes, and he could feel Bedlam pressing at his mind. Sky swam frantically to stay ahead of the ice and grew disoriented in a blackness so deep that even his eyes couldn't penetrate it. Laughing corpses lurched into his path. He swatted them away and left them in his wake. His lungs burned; his skin froze. Finally his feet touched bottom and he sprang upward, crashing through the ice. With scrambling hands, he dragged himself onto the small island and collapsed in the mud, shaking uncontrollably.

Dead faces stared up at him, laughing and locked within the dark ring of frozen swamp that spread out from the island and reached halfway to the far shore. He saw the half-faced man far away near the ice's edge, just beneath the surface yet seemingly close enough to touch—the half face a rictus of frozen laughter, and Sky could hear the corpse, in his head, laughing still. And laughing. And laughing still.

Living, grim-faced hunters clambered out of the swamp waters and burst out of the ice, creeping ever closer as Sky fought to push Bedlam from his mind.

The cold moved through Sky—his body, his blood—reaching for his heart, clasping at his mind. He pushed at it, wrestling it like a living thing, fighting to keep the darkness away.

The world around him went pale and gray. He flopped onto his back and jerked spastically, unable to stop. The moon above began to tremble and crumble to pieces, crashing in the swamp all around and shaking the earth. Burning trees bowed to him, water boiled with the pale dead, and haunted creatures for miles around let up a long and terrible wail.

Sky's screams joined the wailing, and he'd never felt more frightened in all his life. But as dark blood from the Eye spilled across the white Hunter's Mark, soft, weak light slipped out, so faint he almost missed it. He focused on that light—that speck of brightness and warmth—and clung to it through terror and madness until the moon settled, the fires died, his screaming turned to quiet sobs, and the waking nightmare ended and returned everything as it was. No fires. No shaking earth and crumbling moon. No bowing trees.

No Bedlam.

But the creatures of the night still wailed and the dead still stared out of frozen waters with sightless eyes, and Sky's Eye of Legend still bled black. For the moment, at least, he'd fought off Bedlam. He was still in control.

Piebalds squawked around him, urging him to run as hunters crept slowly across the cracking ice. His thrashing and fight for control against Bedlam, which had seemed like hours, had taken but minutes. Still, the ice and Sky's early lead were the only things keeping him alive, but not for much longer.

Fred landed a few feet away and watched him quietly, almost as if he knew what Sky had just gone through.

Sky took a deep, steadying breath and then began scooping up great handfuls of mud and smearing them all over himself as fast as he could—through his hair, on his arms, his face—until every exposed inch of him was covered. Then he stumbled toward the humongous tree covered with little green hibernating and very hungry needles.

The giant trunk spread out before him, four arm lengths around at its base, and the top stretched upward, reaching for the moon. Sky wedged his hands and feet into the deep grooves of the bark and with a weary breath began climbing. His arms shook with the effort, and he wished he hadn't thrown away his Jumpers with his other gear, but he pushed on, climbing higher and higher.

"CAW?" the Piebalds offered.

"No!" Sky barked, adding more gently between breaths, "No . . . I can get to the top on my own, but thank you." They wanted to fly him up, but he wasn't about to put the Piebalds in any more danger just to save himself. They'd done enough, *more* than enough. Nobody else was going to die for him. "I'll meet you at the top."

Cawing and yammering petulantly, the Piebalds swooped away—all except for Fred, who flew at his side the entire way, cawing encouragements whenever Sky began to slow. By the time Sky reached the top and moved out of bow range, his whole body trembled and he thought he might fall from pure exhaustion. The Piebalds landed on the narrow branch and flapped about to hold him upright while he struggled to pull himself together.

Looking down, he saw the first few hunters gathering around the base of the tree, watching him. Dozens more waded through the waters, across the ice, and up the muddy beach, followed by even more emerging from the bogs and swampy woods, until finally hundreds of hunters surrounded the base of the Bolger tree.

Sky stared down at them all, wondering if Bedlam's waking nightmare had started up again.

"This night really stinks, you know that?" Sky muttered in

exhaustion. The Piebalds squawked in agreement and Fred nodded wisely.

A few of the more senior hunters seemed to be arguing about what to do, but Sky wasn't planning to let them decide; this was *his* trap, after all.

As the last hunter stepped onto the island, Sky pulled a small petrified Yule log from his backpack—something he'd carried with him ever since the Bolger incident last Christmas. He weighed it in his hands, took aim, and dropped it with an immense sense of satisfaction.

The Yule log tumbled end over end, bouncing from branch to branch. It fell down and down, leaving small cracked bits behind until it finally shattered at a hunter's feet, as only a hardened sugary dessert named after a log could. The hunter looked up at him, and then back at the smashed dessert, obviously confused.

A few of the bolder hunters began climbing, apparently incensed by the flagrant pastry attack.

Sky put his Hunter's Mark on the tree and in perfect Bolger whispered, "Dinner's on," into the wood, causing the entire tree to tremble.

The pine needles shivered and then shifted ever so slightly. The Piebalds launched into the air and darted away as fast as their wings could carry them.

A low chattering started up, growing into a yawning buzz that sounded like a twenty-story hive of groggy bees. Tiny green wings sprouted from the pine needles, which weren't really pine needles but starving Bolgers angry at being woken from hibernation.

And then, in a terrible swirling cloud, thousands upon thousands of Bolgers dropped from their branches and swarmed the hunters. The Bolgers fought over every scrap of Yule log and stung every bit of exposed hunter flesh they could find.

Sky hunched down, making himself as small as possible. He was covered in mud, but with Bolgers, you could never be too careful. A swarm of passing Bolgers paused a few feet away, looking—Sky knew—for exposed flesh. He held his breath, waiting. Finally they swooped off, and he sighed in relief.

The pine-needle–like swarms spun around like a green tornado, flinging hunters into the air. A few of the luckier Bolgers gobbled up their Yule-log winnings and grew larger and larger with each bite, until they looked like inflated balloons. Green, impish faces popped out of their bodies, followed by pointy ears, stocky arms, a long needle nose, and bulbous grasshopper legs. These newer, fatter Bolgers sprang into the hunters and began knocking them down and stinging them with their noses.

The hunters hacked and stabbed with their swords and knives, sending green pus everywhere, but the fat Bolgers pressed on even while they shrank. In return, the Bolgers poked and prodded the hunters in the behinds while smaller Bolgers licked up the pools of green pus, grew bigger, and leaped into the fray.

It was gross even by Sky's standards, and he used weapons made out of garbage.

The hunters fell back, sliding across the ice and splashing into the water, their faces green and swollen to twice their normal sizes from the Bolger stings. They looked almost like Bolgers themselves.

Sky concentrated on the Bolgers until he felt his Hunter's Mark warm. Then he spoke softly in their language, his voice joining the buzz until the Bolgers backed away from the hunters and sped west in search of a Yule log that wasn't there.

"You have thirty minutes to find the cure for Bolger venom before your body slips into hibernation mode for the rest of winter!" Sky yelled. "And when you wake up—if you wake up—I promise you won't like what you find!"

The green-faced hunters stared up at him, silent and angry and very, very trapped.

"If you leave now," Sky continued, "you can reach Malvidia at Arkhon Academy before it's too late. I happen to know she has the cure on hand. Thirty minutes—make it count!"

The hunters fled. Crenshaw, who'd apparently escaped his trap, scowled up at Sky with a puffy green face, and then he too turned and ran.

Sky watched them scramble away until every last one of them was gone. He'd just handed the Hunters of Legend over to Malvidia to do with as she pleased. He'd given her the ultimate bargaining chip—their very lives—and he'd shown he wasn't Bedlam by sparing them. Malvidia was horrible, but she always kept her word, and she'd promised to repay Sky for saving her life, hopefully by saving his. If she was on his side, he'd soon be rid of these hunters and the death sentence hanging over him; they might even gain some allies against Bedlam. Of course, if Malvidia wasn't on his side, these hunters would soon return, angrier than ever. And two of the thirteen Hunters of Legend—Morton Thresher and Chase Shroud, wherever they were—would lead the hunt this time.

Whatever the case, Sky had done all he could. It was time to turn his attention elsewhere.

He called the Piebalds back. The Bolgers would return soon. They hated leaving their tree, especially with winter coming on, and it wouldn't take them long to realize there were no

Yule logs around. A Bolger's intelligence increased with size, and Sky had yet to discover a limit to how big they could get. But right now even the largest Bolger here was still too small to reason with, which was why he needed to get moving.

It was time to find out what'd happened to his friends.

It was time to return to Exile.

CHAPTER 6
Indecent Descent

But first he had to get down.

"Can you guys give me a hand, er . . . beak?" Sky asked, hanging from his perch on the Bolger tree. He glanced down at the island and the surrounding ring of ice with its grisly contents. He shivered. He didn't think he could bring himself to cross that again—he honestly didn't. "And not to the island, either," he added, trying to keep the fear from his voice, "to my gear. It'll . . . it'll save us some time."

Fred narrowed his eyes—as much as a giant bird monster *could* narrow its eyes. The Piebalds were smart, but they had simple needs and short attention spans. And yet, there was something about Fred. He was different, more attentive, more complex, more connected—in a word: wiser. And that word was about as un-Piebaldish a word as Sky could imagine.

"What? I'm not afraid," Sky stated unconvincingly under Fred's wilting stare. He was a better liar than he used to be, at least with creatures he didn't know, but he wasn't *that* good.

Fred plucked at his feathers and remained silent.

The other Piebalds flapped around Sky and snatched up his clothes. Fred watched, refusing to help.

With a terrifying lurch, Sky fell from the Bolger tree, dragging the madly flapping Piebalds with him. As they plunged earthward, the thought occurred to Sky that he might be getting too big for this.

Before they dropped too far, Fred flew to the rescue, yanking at big chunks of Sky's hair.

"Ow ow ow owwww!" Sky cried.

Fred began to loosen his grip and Sky started to drop again.

"No, no! Don't let go!"

Fred's grip tightened and they leveled out, even rising a little.

Sky gritted his teeth. "There's got to be a better way to fly."

"CAW!" the Piebalds croaked.

"Yeah?" Sky replied. "Well, the Darkhorn is terribly cool in the stories—I'm not sure I'd use the words 'terrifying yet stone-cold awesome,' but you're entitled to your opinions."

"CAW! CAW! CAW!"

"What do you mean you've seen her around?"

"CAW! CAW!"

"She does? I knew the Darkhorn and Bedlam had a thing going, even if she is some kind of weird giant flying horse—to each his own, I guess—but that's a little exotic by any standard. And you say she doesn't cook you beforehand or use any spices?"

"CAW! CAW! CAW!"

"Gross. I'd never eat a Piebald that way."

"CAW! CAW! CAW! CAW! CAW!"

"It was a joke!" Sky yelped, smarting at a particularly vicious jerk from Fred. "I'd never eat a Piebald at all—you guys are like family to me, and I have a strict policy against eating family, especially without proper cooking and spices."

"CAW! CAW!" squawked the Piebalds, sounding slightly mollified. Fred gave Sky's hair one more yank, apparently not as impressed with the apology.

Sky's grin turned into a cringe, and not just because of the hair pull. He was putting on a good show of bravado, but he'd seldom felt more troubled. Bedlam's attack meant that he was nearby, maybe even controlling one of the hunters or watching from the shadows.

The Darkhorn's arrival made matters even worse. She was not only Bedlam's bride, she was his harbinger, his front-runner—the one he sent first into battles in stories like *The Edge of Oblivion* and *Legend Most Legendary*. She was a terror in her own right—a giant flying nightmare with a twisted horn of darkness (or many, by some accounts) jutting from her fore-head. A fleshy glowing bulb that dangled from the horn could mesmerize victims and put them to sleep. Where Bedlam was the father of the Edgewalkers, the Darkhorn was their mother and the dreamer of Nightmares—literally her "horses of the night," born from her broken horns.

Last year, Beau had told Sky that the Arkhon had once posed as the Darkhorn and attacked a hunter stronghold. In that conversation, Beau had mentioned that the Darkhorn could be captured with a dog-hair net. Why? Sky had no idea, but hunters believed it would work. Unfortunately, Sky was now fresh out of dogs, and dog hairs, and nearly out of his own hairs at the rate Fred was pulling.

If the Darkhorn was in Exile, then Bedlam's army wasn't

far behind—less than a day away, according to what Chase Shroud had told Beau, but how could an entire army get from Skull Valley to Exile without someone noticing?

Sky took in his surroundings as the Piebalds left the island and its ice ring behind. They sailed over the unfrozen part of the swamp waters and started to descend toward the far shore, where he'd ditched his gear. The Bolger tree was one of the tallest in the Sleeping Lands, and from this height, Sky could see quite a lot, though Fred had to turn his head for him. To the west, he saw the Bolger swarms returning, looking angrier than ever. Southeast, the hunters sprinted through the swamps toward Arkhon Academy. He saw other things—dark things—moving in the trees. The creatures of the night had stopped their mournful wailing, but Sky still shivered at the memory. The sooner he left this place, the better.

And then to the east, he saw something flying low through the trees—not the Darkhorn, as he'd feared, or Bedlam's army swooping in, but something he'd almost forgotten about in his mad dash: the Marrowick from the bowling alley.

They'd never figured out why the Marrowick had gone to the bowling alley in the first place, and now it was moving swiftly and sticking to the shadows as if hunting something just out of Sky's sight. Sky frowned. The timing of the Marrowick's strange behavior, occurring so close to the arrival of the hunters and Bedlam, was too odd to be a coincidence. Was the Marrowick somehow involved in all this? As much as Sky hated it, he knew that Exile would have to wait.

"We need to hurry," Sky muttered, "before he gets away."

Fred cawed and let go of Sky's hair, flying off to the east.

"No, wait! Fred!" Sky plummeted.

The other Piebalds squawked and tugged to no avail, and

then let go entirely to save themselves, leaving Sky to plunge into the icy waters.

He came up gasping for air, then paddled for shore. As he dragged himself onto dry land and collapsed to his hands and knees, he spotted his Core a few feet away.

"CAW!" called out the Piebalds, landing nearby, but not *too* nearby.

"Thanks a lot," said Sky, picking up his Core and putting it on.

"CAW!"

"Yes, the mud is all gone, but if I'd wanted a bath, I would've given myself one—and not in a swamp full of dead bodies!" Sky slammed a Cheez Whiz canister full of Fog into place.

"CAW."

"I know it's not your fault," said Sky. "Fred and I are going to have a long talk when he shows his face again."

He pulled a Baggie full of crackers from his backpack and tossed several to the Piebalds. "Here, P-crackers—your favorite—made fresh at the lair four months ago."

"CAW!" the Piebalds complained, dancing around the crackers.

"I meant *P* as in phosphorus! Of course they're not actually soaked in pee! That's preposterous!" The Piebalds leaped onto the crackers, snatching them up. Under his breath, Sky added, "As far as you know."

He tracked down his other gear, reassembling it as he went. Last of all, he found his cloak sitting next to the broken Pounder. He surveyed the sliced tubing—cut by Crenshaw's knife—and decided, sadly, that he couldn't fix it.

Sky pulled out his pocket watch, the only key to Solomon's prison he still possessed. One monocle he'd lost last year. He'd given the other to Crystal before the east cemetery imploded. He thought about her and the others and remembered something Phineas had told him years ago after finding him, crying and stuck in his own trap with a pair of woven branch pants wrapped around his head. After showing Sky how he could've broken free if he'd just thought it through, he'd said, "We are hunters, Sky—tears are our lot. But we mustn't allow our sorrows to trap us. At night, we hunt evil in all its forms and we survive. There's plenty of time for tears in the morning, and often you'll find, when the light shines, the tears will come for entirely different reasons."

Sky checked the time. Less than an hour had passed since he'd left Crystal, Andrew, Hands, and T-Bone behind, buried in the earth and in Nackles's hands. One lousy hour, and the night was still young. Part of him was afraid to return, afraid of what he might find.

He sighed heavily. "Come on, let's find Fred and the Marrowick before something else decides to kill me."

He set off through the swamp after the Piebalds, running northeast.

It took him some time and a few roundabout paths to find any trace of Fred and the Marrowick. And when he finally found that trace, it was confusing.

He knelt down and examined a glob of soft Marrowick wax on the tip of a small gray feather. He rubbed the glob between his fingers, which caused them to tingle strangely. He stood and stepped carefully around the pools of wax and feathers that littered the ground.

The Piebalds watched him quietly, perched on the surrounding trees.

Ahead, the hill sloped upward into dry, uncharted terrain. He'd never gone this far into the Sleeping Lands before, both because it was a horrible place and because it was incredibly dangerous, even if you could talk to monsters. He wasn't even sure he was *in* the Sleeping Lands anymore since he hadn't seen a grave or a floating corpse for nearly fifteen minutes—a record for the night, by his estimates. When had his life gotten so odd that the absence of a dead body was more noticeable than its presence?

He shook the thought away and turned his attention back to the feathers.

"CAW?" the Piebalds inquired.

"No, not the Darkhorn," said Sky, inspecting a broken branch covered in wax. "Though I suppose the Darkhorn could've attacked both of them. . . . Does the Darkhorn eat Marrowicks?"

"CAW! CAW!"

"I didn't think so," Sky replied, dropping the branch. "I suspect the Marrowick would give the Darkhorn horrible indigestion."

Sky stared thoughtfully at the battleground, noting that the trail of feathers and wax seemed to veer off to the east. He reached out with his senses, but there was no sign of Fred anywhere. "Where are you, Fred?"

The Piebalds squawked and cawed, gossiping amongst themselves about Fred and horror stories they'd heard about unprovoked Darkhorn attacks on innocent Piebalds. By the sounds of it, Piebalds were the Darkhorn's favorite food.

As Sky continued surveying the grove, his eyes settled on an old oak tree and something sticking out of the trunk. When he reached it, he found a thick, gray hunter's arrow wedged deep into the bark. The shaft was coated in fine white powder that numbed his fingers in an all-too-familiar way—not the tingling of the Marrowick wax, but a numbing weariness that made him want to give up, lie down, and sleep.

Dovetail.

Last year the gargantuan Dovetail maze had poked him so many times, he couldn't help but recognize it. A little Dovetail put you to sleep so the plant could eat you at its leisure. A lot of Dovetail made you hallucinate. A little more and you never woke up.

The arrow, though, was the wrong color for Dovetail—gray, not jet-black. And it was strangely gnarled and twisted, like a corkscrew—not at all like the sleek green-flame and glossy-black arrows the hunters had shot at him.

And yet it was definitely a hunter's arrow; it was too crazy not to be.

Near the tip, Sky spotted a piece of torn cloak like those the hunters wore and a streak of fresh blood smeared lengthwise across the bark, pointing north. He backtracked, re-creating the scene in his mind: two hunters, one the shooter, the other the prey. The prey is shot—grazed by the looks of it—and flees north. And Fred and the Marrowick—how did they fit in? When Sky saw the Marrowick earlier, it'd looked like it was stalking something—one of the two hunters, possibly. Fred must've caught up to the Marrowick, and then . . . what?

Sky analyzed the angle of the arrow and found the likely spot where the shooter had stood. The ground was covered in feathers and wax, which meant that Fred and the Marrowick had either attacked the shooter together, or that one had attacked the shooter and the other had defended the shooter from the attack. Either way, the prey had fled north while Fred and the Marrowick followed the shooter east.

Sky scratched his head. *What in the world was going on here?*

Sky reached out for Fred again. Nothing. He reached out further through the Edge, striving to touch Fred's mind and get a sense of his whereabouts. As he focused on Fred, the grove suddenly grew very, very quiet. Sky gave up his search and glanced at the Piebalds, wondering why they'd ceased their incessant gossiping. What he saw chilled him. Not a single feather moved, not an eye twitched. The Piebalds sat, tense and perfectly still, their beaks raised to the night.

Sky looked up and saw a shadow streak across the moon, high above the thin and scattered forest—its gigantic wings blotting out the light. A blink, and then it was gone.

Sky held his breath, afraid to move.

Straight in front of him, he saw one of the Piebalds shuffle from one foot to the other.

No . . . no, don't, Sky wanted to scream.

The Piebald looked at him. Sky shook his head—*No,* he mouthed.

The Piebald twitched nervously and began to spread its wings.

No, no, no! Sky shook his head violently, willing the Piebald to stay in place.

With a downward thrust, the Piebald launched into the air.

"NO!" Sky screamed. But before he could even finish, a giant winged shadow—moving faster than he could track—darted out of nowhere and snatched up the Piebald in its gaping mouth. Sky caught a glimpse of a twisted horn and a mesmerizing blue light dangling from it, and then the creature was gone.

The grove erupted into chaos. Piebalds threw themselves

from their perches, cawing and yammering madly in their frantic race to save themselves.

The Darkhorn reappeared, swooping through the Piebalds, knocking aside trees and boulders that got in her way to get at her favorite food.

Sky sprang sideways, dodging a falling tree. The Darkhorn hurtled over him, scooping up another Piebald. Sky reached for his Pounder, but the Pounder didn't work. He cursed Crenshaw, reached for his Fogger, and detached a canister as the Darkhorn came in for another pass.

He flicked it on and chucked it into the air, trying to hide not only himself, but the Piebalds as well. Before Fog could cover any of them, the Darkhorn apparently mistook the canister for a Piebald and swallowed it whole as she rocketed past.

She screeched angrily, a high-pitched neighing that shook Sky to his bones.

He scrambled for cover and reached for his last can of Fog, but before he could grab it, the Darkhorn dropped to the ground in front of him. She was massive and sleek and stood almost twenty feet tall. Thick Fog billowed from her mouth, swirling around her in strange geometries as she folded her wings to her sides. The glowing blue ball of light dangled from her mangled black horn, swinging back and forth.

Her angry screeching suddenly changed into the most disturbingly beautiful sound he'd ever heard, like a thousand broken harps accompanying a thousand fallen angels. The sound pulled at him, dragging him close, step by longing step. And standing above him now was the most glorious woman, robed in light, her arms beckoning, beckoning. Strands of bright white hair swirled around her head and she smiled warmly, waving him closer.

Sky took another step. Another. He knew something was wrong, but he couldn't stop himself.

Something cawed off to his right and the woman suddenly reached out and snatched a Piebald from the air, shoving it in her mouth. In that instant Sky saw the Darkhorn in place of the beautiful woman, and he threw himself to the side as the Darkhorn's slavering maw plunged toward him, just missing.

Sky rolled to his feet, slammed his Jumpers and Foggers at the same time, and shot into the air. Putrid Fog rolled around him as the Darkhorn's teeth snapped shut behind him. He landed on a high tree branch and scampered along its length as she let out a hideous shriek.

The Darkhorn rocketed out of the Fog and felled the tree next to him.

At the end of the limb, Sky lunged forward and dropped to a new branch, hugging it as he landed. He pulled himself up and dashed toward the trunk. The Darkhorn rammed the tree, and Sky hit his Jumpers—a quick burst—and sailed into the next tree. He veered sharply toward a new branch and a new tree. Another burst.

The Darkhorn shot past, snapping branches.

Sky bounced free-form, without his Jumpers, from limb to limb and tree to tree, frantically trying to stay ahead. Branches and bark showered him.

He spun, changing direction again and again. One more burst and the Jumpers fizzled—out of juice.

Sky plummeted. He slapped his Shimmer and crashed into a branch, snapping it in two. He ricocheted down the tree, bouncing around, and then he smashed into the ground.

His Shimmer flickered out at the same time as his Fog and he rolled to his back, groaning.

Dense Fog coated the forest. The Darkhorn screeched, but she sounded far away, and getting farther. Sky's twists and turns within the Fog had thrown her from his trail. He was safe for now.

Rocks poked him in the back and a branch had worked its way into an awkward position, but he didn't care. Piebalds had died tonight because of his stupidity. He should've known better than to reach out for Fred like that with the Darkhorn and Bedlam nearby. That reaching was part of edgewalking, part of Bedlam and the Darkhorn's domain, and they were infinitely better at it than him. If he'd thought it through, he would've realized: If he could reach out, *they* could reach back. Why did everything and everyone around him keep dying? The Piebalds, hundreds of hunters when he was young, including several of his friends' parents, and Phineas, Errand, Crystal, Andrew, Hands, T-Bone . . . Sky stopped himself. Not them. Not the monster hunters. Not his friends. Nackles would get them out. He had to believe that, even if it was hard.

Something crunched nearby, and Sky stopped berating himself. He sat up hesitantly and looked around, but the Fog remained as impenetrable as ever.

More crunching, and then quiet.

Fearing that the Darkhorn had circled back, Sky climbed to his feet and stepped around the tree. On the other side, he found a scruffy man with a scraggly beard wearing a dingy blue jump-suit. The man sat casually on a tree stump, holding a torn picture in one hand and eating from a bag of Doritos with the other.

Sky glanced around nervously, wondering if the Darkhorn was messing with him—if she'd pulled him into a nightmare without him knowing. And then he realized that he recognized the man.

"Mister . . ." Sky didn't know the man's last name. "Mister Janitor, are you okay?"

Crunch, crunch, crunch. Orange cheese and bits of tortilla chip lived in the mangy beard like squirrels nestling down for winter.

Sky stepped closer. The poor man had mental problems, he knew. Last year the janitor had helped him out of a bind with Crenshaw, and then he'd made the strangest comment about urinal cakes.

"Forest saltines taste like urinal cakes," the janitor now muttered.

A comment very much like that, in fact.

Without taking his eyes from the picture, the janitor held out the bag of Doritos, not to Sky, but to the empty space slightly to the left of Sky.

Sky glanced over, afraid he might find someone there. No one was, but that made him more frightened, not less.

"Are you lost?" Sky asked hesitantly; he was beginning to think he might prefer the Darkhorn. "Do you need help finding your way back to Exile?"

The janitor ate another Dorito. A checkered picnic blanket was spread out in front of him.

Slowly, Sky stepped up behind him and looked down at the picture, which had been ripped from top to bottom so that half was missing. The picture showed a woman who looked somehow familiar. She wore jeans and a grungy T-shirt and her charcoal hair was long and pulled back in a ponytail. In the background, he saw one of the spires of Arkhon Academy. An arm clothed in a white dress shirt was wrapped around the woman's shoulder.

The more Sky stared at the woman, the more familiar she seemed.

"I know her . . . ," Sky muttered, the memory nagging at him.

The Dorito paused halfway to the janitor's mouth.

"We won't let anything hurt you," the janitor promised without turning, his voice gentle, as if he were talking to a small child.

Sky shied away, taking several steps back. "Excuse me?"

"Not monsters, not hunters, not the Arkhon himself, no matter how badly he wants you," the janitor continued. "You'll grow up with my son and the others."

"Your son?" Sky backed away, utterly creeped out. "Who's your son?"

The janitor turned to look at him. "We'll teach you how a hunter *should* act. All of us, we'll start aga—"

The janitor suddenly stopped and stared at nothing.

A chill shot down Sky's spine. He'd heard these words before . . . last year while edgewalking through the memory of when he was a baby. They were the words spoken in the library the night the hunters captured Solomon Rose, whom they believed then, and believed still, to be the Arkhon.

A man had held Sky in his arms and spoken those very words to him, promising something he could never deliver, promising Sky safety. The man had cut down a ring of monsters around the pendulum before fighting the Shadow Man, the one who could slip through shadows, the one who'd turned Sky and Errand into Changelings that very night.

Sky's great protector had fallen while defending him. White light, like a physical thing, had whipped out of the Hunter's Mark during the Changing and plunged through the monocle, into his protector's eye.

Sky stared at the janitor and imagined him clean-shaven, with cropped hair, a long black trench coat covering slacks and a dress shirt, and a thick white monocle on his eye. His great protector, the one who'd given up so much for him, had been right in front of him the whole time, and Sky had never spared him a second look.

"You're Nikola," Sky said, bewildered, the puzzle pieces snapping into place. "You're the hunter who built the Arkhon's prison with Phineas. You protected me."

Nikola glanced back at Sky, looking past him rather than at him.

"They'll never find it that way," Nikola muttered, dumping out his Doritos and putting the bag over his head. "The coffin is empty."

"What?" Sky glanced over his shoulder, but once again there was nothing there save Fog and forest.

Nikola dropped the picture and picked up his picnic blanket. "Why do the good ones always die? You'd better hurry if you want to save her."

"Save who?" Sky asked.

Muttering to himself about nacho cheese, urinal cakes, and glowing saltines, Nikola spun and walked away, disappearing into the Fog. Sky picked up the picture and raced after him.

"Wait! Who is this? Who's your son?" Sky yelled.

But Nikola—the Genius, the Protector, the Mad Janitor of Exile—was gone.

CHAPTER 7

Grove of the Fallen

The wind dragged the Fog through the forest, thinning it and spreading it out for miles around. From the growth of moss on the trees, Sky knew he was heading north. He'd contemplated circling back to follow the trail of wax and feathers and, presumably, the shooter, Fred, and the Marrowick, but he'd given up the idea, fearing that the Darkhorn might have the same thought.

Besides, an injured hunter hid somewhere to the north, judging by the trail of blood. This hunter and the other—the shooter—hadn't tried to kill him or they'd both be at Arkhon Academy right now getting treated for Bolger venom. They'd defied Morton's orders. That meant one or both might be potential allies against Morton, should Sky's plan fail, and against Bedlam. Or, they might just kill him while trying to kill each other. Either way, they were up here for some reason, and he meant to find out why and how Fred and the Marrowick were tied up in all this.

Still troubled by Nikola but not sure what to do about it, Sky closed himself off completely to the Piebalds to prevent the Darkhorn and Bedlam from tracking him so easily. He left the swamps behind, moving deeper into the unknown. Without the Piebalds guiding him, he felt exposed and traveled more slowly than he liked, fearing what he'd encounter. Here, the forest thinned and the ancient trees grew taller and broader and somehow more disturbing—the angles wrong, bent and twisted.

Following the trail of blood, he circled around a massive hole that seemed to go down forever. He passed a row of barrows—dark burial hills—and black trees that sent shivers through him. As he continued on, the land, if possible, became even more wretched than the swamps. The numerous crags became pitted and charred and jutted from the earth like a long-forgotten palace or the remains of a swallowed city. Dozens of black streams raced between the rocks, some continuing southwest to join the rivers and swamps, others disappearing into the cracks and gaping holes, great waterfalls of darkness falling into nothing.

Ancient trees grew tall and few, their black branches long and spread out, wrapped together like fingers high above him.

He had never had the time, nor the inclination, to explore this dark and dangerous wasteland. He didn't want to explore it now, but instinct and a certain morbid curiosity were driving him on. Who were these two hunters and why were they here in the Sleeping Lands? And why now? Once again, he thought the timing wasn't a coincidence. Bedlam's army was on its way to destroy Exile, the foreign hunters were here to stop Bedlam, and these two hunters were somehow involved.

Everything seemed to revolve around Bedlam, and Sky suspected that Bedlam's arrival was somehow driving these two hunters as well.

Of course, the real question was: Why had Bedlam come to Exile in the first place?

Sky had read about Solomon and Alexander's heroic capture of the terrible monster Bedlam at the beginning of *The Edge of Oblivion*. He remembered reading about how Bedlam was plotting to destroy the hunters, and how Solomon and Alexander pleaded with him to change his ways. Bedlam had refused and sworn that he would reclaim his father's throne and wipe the hunters from the face of the earth before making all people bow to him. Then, he'd attacked Solomon and Alexander on the spot. They defended themselves with their shimmering blades, while begging Bedlam to give up his mad quest. Finally, with no other options, Solomon and Alexander had wrapped Bedlam in threads of light and trapped him in an unbreakable shell—the Chrysalis. They promised him that one day, when his heart was pure and filled with love, he would emerge like a butterfly.

It was the beginning of the Edgewalker Wars. The rest of the book detailed the brutal wars and how Solomon tracked down and killed every last Edgewalker.

Of course, Alexander and a few other chroniclers had written the book, and as Sky had learned last year and numerous times since, hunters lied. It was quite possible that nothing in the story was true, in which case Sky had little to go on to figure out why Bedlam had come to Exile. Clearly Bedlam hated the hunters and had every intention of destroying Exile; one didn't bring an army to make friends. At the same time, there were relatively few hunters in Exile. If Bedlam had just wanted to kill hunters, he could have gone anywhere, such as the Academy of Legend Chase had mentioned. Whatever and wherever the Academy of Legend was, it sounded like a good place to start. They had to have more hunters there, based on how many they'd sent to Exile.

But Bedlam had chosen to attack Exile first, and that meant he wanted something here, something more than just to kill hunters. If Bedlam somehow knew about Solomon taking the Arkhon's body—a secret known by almost no one—then he could, feasibly, have come for revenge. Bedlam would have to hate Solomon more than just about anyone, besides maybe Alexander, who had died centuries ago due to an unfortunate sword through the neck from an unknown assassin. But if Sky were trapped, the first thing he would do was free himself, especially if he had failed to take control of the one person—namely him—who could have given him an advantage.

But to free himself, Bedlam would have to escape an unbreakable Chrysalis, and to do that, he'd have to have a pure heart filled with love.

Sky laughed.

Even as a small boy, he had thought the idea was not only cheesy, but completely ridiculous: If Bedlam's mind and body were trapped, how could his heart ever change? But there had to be some way for Bedlam to free himself. It was the only reason for coming to Exile that made sense.

Sky could only hope that the hunter he was tracking knew more about it than he did.

As he came around an immense, sharp-edged crag, he found an inscription beside a narrow gap:

Grove of the Fallen,
Chosen of the First.
No slowly seeping poison
taints their morbid thirst.

Disturb their slumber
—disregard this sign—
and join them six feet under,
with maggots in thy mind.

Feeling anxious, Sky walked through the narrow gap and down a steep path. Gray-and-black rock towered over him on both sides, growing taller the farther down he went until he was hundreds of feet below the highest point.

His Pounder hand-cannon was busted, his Jumpers empty, and he'd used up his last can of Fog. The protective Shimmer would recharge on its own eventually, but, at best, he had one or two zaps left. If this place lived up to its engraving, he was destined for brain maggots.

On the other side of the gap, he found himself standing in front of a strange grove. Sheer gray-and-black cliffs, spattered with waterfalls, surrounded the grove entirely, with a few gaps leading out. Lush white trees covered in sparkling leaves and twinkling blue fruit lit up the grove—its very beauty making Sky leery, and reminding him of why he hated botany: Things that looked that good were never that good.

The trail of blood he'd first noticed near the swamps had long since disappeared, but the injured hunter was in a hurry and sloppy, leaving Sky plenty of tracks to follow. He crept into the grove, staying as far away from the trees as he could. Fireflies of all colors darted here and there, and eerie green moss rustled on tree trunks and slunk across earth and obsidian like slugs. He passed odd, bright, bell-shaped flowers and silvery grass that hummed in the wind like an eerie choir. Golden reeds strummed together like cellos, and the trees swayed and whispered until the grove was filled with haunting music.

Sky felt his tension and anxiety slip away, little by little. The air felt cleaner here, the night brighter, his heart more hopeful. Glancing down, he was surprised to find his Hunter's Mark warm and glowing, the light in the Mark mingling with the light in the grove. The light seemed to move through him, washing away aches and pains he didn't even know he had, and others he was all too aware of. He wanted to be wary—to watch for the traps that must be lying in wait—but for the first time in nearly a year, he felt something he'd almost forgotten. . . .

In the ghostly melodies of this unnatural grove, he felt *peaceful*.

He pressed his fingernails into his Eye of Legend, the pain helping him focus. Now wasn't the time to get all peaceful; this place was dangerous. If he didn't pay attention, the only peace he would find would be the eternal kind.

In the center of the grove, Sky came upon a clearing and an enormous stone statue, easily a hundred feet tall, of a woman rising from the earth. Ivy shrouded the lower half of her body as it twirled out of the ground like a sickly gray beanstalk.

Her left arm and part of her face had sloughed off and Sky could see the remains strewn across the smaller monuments, statues, and graves that surrounded her, many of which had been crushed to rubble. Her right hand was stretched out in front of her, hovering over the statue of a kneeling man. On her palm, Sky saw the Hunter's Mark.

He crept forward, feeling more and more confused. He'd seen a lot of things in the last year—man-eating pumpkin patches, aggressive pine trees, hardened desserts, even a half man, half manatee (a Humanatee), not to mention a crazy janitor with a Doritos bag on his head—but he'd never dreamed of a place like this. Everything else was so horrible, so nightmarishly awful, but this . . . *this* . . . was wonderful—mindblowingly creepy, yet magical at the same time.

Phineas had once told him that there was no such thing as magic, just some *very* misunderstood natural forces. But as Sky looked up at the statue, and heard the symphony of the grove, and felt the light and warmth flowing through him, he couldn't help believing that maybe Phineas had gotten it wrong; maybe there was no such thing as natural forces—just some very misunderstood *magic*.

Sky passed by the woman's giant stone sword, still clasped in her broken left hand, sitting atop a row of crushed monuments. The blade shimmered strangely as moonlight reflected off particles of precious metals locked within. He remembered reading about such blades—the real blades, not this stone replica. Shimmering blades, they were called, the swords of the Hunters of Legend, like those Solomon and Alexander had used to fight Bedlam in *The Edge of Oblivion*. Phineas had even carried one, a blade that now sat, Sky supposed, in the belly of the Jack.

Sky recognized many of the names etched into the monuments and graves, Hunters of Legend whose stories he'd studied for as long as he could remember. Nathaniel the Noteworthy, who'd shared delicious toast with Samuel the Simpleton while searching for the Tourmaline of Foresight. And Gladys Goodright, the first (and last) hunter to fall in love with a Humanatee. He passed the gaudy tomb of Esteban, a hunter so vain he believed other hunters should recognize him from a single name. The fact that it was true had annoyed Phineas to no end, Sky remembered with a smile. And Studious Kelp, who'd cornered the poultry market in London to stop a Satyrn invasion—an invasion that Studious invented in order to corner the poultry market in London.

He passed other hunters, too, *real* hunters of the heroic kind. Portense Happenstance, who brought light to the Morospawn giants under the sea and found the cure to Creeper venom. And Frederick von Gooseburg, who gave his life to protect an insignificant village from a cadre of fellow hunters who wanted to destroy it for its wealth of Gilead root.

Sky shook his head in amazement; there were far more bad hunters than good, and even the good ones he'd worshipped as a boy, such as Solomon Rose, hadn't turned out so great. Morton Thresher was another raging disappointment, if Chase was to be believed. Sky found it hard to fathom that one of his idols wanted him dead. With the Hunters of Legend set on killing him simply because of what he might become, Sky found it hard to imagine any of them as heroes. Were any of the stories true? Were there any heroes left?

As Sky rounded the sword, the statue of the kneeling man came into view. Sky guffawed. A stone cloak rested on the man's shoulders, hood down, with a giant rose carved into the back, making it obvious who it was supposed to represent.

Solomon Rose.

The statue lorded over the other monuments, second in size only to the statue of the woman. Solomon had a chiseled jaw and ski-jump nose and looked young, barely out of his teens. He knelt piously under the woman's outstretched hand—directly under the Hunter's Mark—signifying, no doubt, that he was much cooler than everyone else. Solomon leaned on a shimmering stone sword like the woman's, a knight pledging himself to his liege lord. But who was the woman?

Sky stepped forward and read the words etched into the stone:

> Solomon Rose
> Hunter of Legend,
> Star of the First Hunter,
> Keeper of the Light

Sky pondered vandalizing the statue, but at that moment, he heard the sounds of digging. He crept closer. A short distance away, he spotted a humble grave with a large rock at the head. Heaps of dirt were piled around the hole, with more dirt flying out all the time. Someone had rigged together an ingenious pulley system made of branches and vines that looped around a nearby tree.

A woman's head popped out of the hole and Sky ducked back, holding his breath. Her face was covered with dirt, but hidden beneath that dirt, Sky saw short brown hair, a grim face, and sunken eyes. After a moment the pulley creaked, the vines dropped into the hole, and she disappeared again.

Sky darted closer and dove behind the mound of dirt. Peeking over the mound, he saw the hunter attach vines to the coffin within. Blood stained her arm, and she'd wrapped a cloth around it to stop the bleeding; this was definitely his injured hunter.

He glanced at the rock to see who was worth digging up and was surprised to see the name Alexander Drake.

Sky glanced around nervously, remembering the warning from the inscription outside the grove:

> Disturb their slumber
> —disregard this sign—
> and join them six feet under,
> with maggots in thy mind.

He realized that the grove had grown still—no eerie music, no wind, just the whispers of firefly wings as they flew around the monuments.

Sky ducked back down as the hunter stood and tested the ties. Then she leaped from the hole with supernatural grace.

She grabbed a vine and pulled. Slowly the coffin rose into the air and then dropped to the ground with a thump.

Sky peeked over the mound again. He still had no idea who this hunter was or why she'd dug up Alexander Drake. Sky had one of Alexander's journals, which had helped him survive the Jack last year, and he owned the series *A Botanist's Guide to Botany: Botany Through the Ages*, also by Drake, which was every bit as tedious as it sounded and was really only good for hiding monocles.

And, of course, Alexander had trapped Bedlam alongside Solomon; *that*, Sky suspected, was the most important detail. Once again, it all led back to Bedlam.

The hunter flipped open the coffin lid and Sky peered in: The coffin was empty except for a gray sludge that filled the bottom. The hunter dipped a scarred finger into the sludge and then licked the sludge off her finger. She threw back her head and laughed.

She kicked over the coffin, spilling the sludge. Before Sky could decide whether to show himself or slip away to a safer hiding place, he noticed writing on the inside of the coffin lid: "With Hunter's Mark the buried dead shall shimmering blade hold in my stead."

Sky stared at the words, as if staring would force them to make sense.

"You might as well come out," said the hunter. "I know you're there."

Sky's heart froze in his chest.

"Come on, don't be shy—I won't bite," she promised.

Sky stood from the mound, dusted himself off, and stepped from hiding.

The hunter looked him over. "Ahh. I see. This is . . . unexpected."

"Who were you expecting?" Sky asked, looking for a way out if things went bad. As he looked, he noticed the strange fireflies starting to swarm.

"An old friend," she replied. "Why'd you come here?"

"Got lost on my way to school," said Sky.

"Funny," said the woman, without laughing. "Grab the other side of this coffin, would you?"

Sky looked around. "Who, me?"

"No. The smart-aleck kid *behind* you," she said, picking up one side of the coffin.

Sky hesitated.

"Well, go on, pick it up," said the hunter. "Unless you want that swarm of Porp-a-lorps to bury us."

"Porpa-whats?"

The hunter sighed in frustration. "Just pick it up."

Sky grabbed the coffin and struggled to lift it. It was just a thin pine box, not a true coffin. Still, it was heavy.

She raised her eyebrows. "And here I thought you were a hunter."

Sky dropped the coffin, walked over to the pulley, surveyed it, and then tipped it and rearranged the pieces into a sled in under a minute.

The woman grinned. "Nice sled."

"You have no idea who I am, do you?" Sky asked, pulling the coffin onto the sled.

The hunter snatched the coffin from the sled and put it on her shoulder, holding it with one arm. "No. Should I? Are you like Esteban, where everyone should know your name because it's Esteban?"

Sky shook his head. "Who *are* you?"

"The only thing keeping you alive at the moment," the woman replied. "Now bring the sled and stay close to me—I might get tired. And while you're at it, tell me what you're *really* doing here."

The Porpa-whatevers swarmed around them, but for some reason none of them came close.

"I'm looking for my bird," said Sky, dragging his sled. "You might've seen him—gray feathers, goes by the name Fred, saved your life earlier. Maybe."

The hunter glanced at him from the corner of her eye. "The Marrowick yours, too?"

"I claim no affiliations," Sky replied. "How about you?"

She smiled. "I claim all sorts of affiliations; doesn't mean they claim me."

"So you're not working with Morton to kill me?" Sky asked.

"Morton? You mean *Morton Thresher*?"

Sky nodded.

"Good golly, kid, you don't aim low at all, do you?" she said, sounding impressed. "What'd you do, backtalk during one of his lectures?"

Sky felt flummoxed. "You really don't know what's going on?"

"Been out of the game for a while."

They reached the edge of the clearing and the hunter set the coffin on its end and leaned against it, catching her breath.

"A few things you should know before we make a run for it," said the hunter. "First, shove this up your nose." She offered him some moldy brown leaves.

"Barrow weed?" said Sky, recognizing the nasty leaves he'd used on Phineas last year.

"To keep Bedlam and the Darkhorn out of your head," she said. "Porp-a-lorps don't like it much either."

Sky shoved the barrow weed up his nose and the weird firefly things seemed to back off. It tickled.

"I really could've used this earlier. What are the side effects?" Sky asked. Phineas once told him things like this had a cost, like the black rutabaga that could make you jump like a Barrow Hag but gave you severe constipation and an inordinate amount of nose hair for a week.

"Ugly brown leaves hanging out of your nose isn't bad enough?" the hunter asked.

Sky shrugged.

"Not every monster secret has a side effect," said the hunter. "Of course, you might smell the color brown for a few hours after."

"Brown?" said Sky, perplexed.

"The next thing you need to know," the hunter continued, "is that until a short time ago, I was Bedlam—or rather, he was me. He trapped my mind temporarily, I'm embarrassed to say. 'Just sprinkle the dust on Bedlam's Chrysalis to find your answer,' she told me. 'Only Alexander's blade can free Bedlam; you'll be fine,' she claimed. Yeah. Right. Free his body maybe, but that dust worked perfectly well at freeing him to edgewalk right into my head."

"Wait, *you* freed Bedlam?" Sky asked, dumbfounded.

"Not on purpose. I was tricked," the hunter replied.

"By who?"

"Vulpine, Bedlam's sister," said the hunter. "The whole family is tricky. I thought she was okay—never steered me wrong before. Salt of the earth kind of woman . . . er . . . plant. Whatever she is."

"So let me get this straight," said Sky. "A plant woman—one of Legend's daughters—told you to sprinkle dust on her trapped brother's Chrysalis—a Chrysalis that only a dead hunter's shimmering blade could open—and you actually did it?"

"Well, when you put it that way, it sounds kind of stupid," said the hunter. "Look, if anything happens to me, you need to get this coffin to Phineas T. Pimiscule. Got that?"

Sky stared at her, and a huge lump caught in his throat.

"Phineas lived in the manor south of here," the hunter continued, "but he went into hiding nine years ago, so he might be hard to find—"

"Twelve years ago," Sky corrected, choking on the words.

"Excuse me?"

"Phineas went into hiding twelve years ago," Sky said

again, fighting to keep tears from his eyes. "He died last year in the Jack."

"Last year? That's impossible . . . I couldn't have been . . . I mean, it took some time for Bedlam to raise his army, and I was locked in the Edge for a while, but . . ." The woman shook her head. "You must be mistaken."

She threw the coffin over her shoulder and stormed off before Sky could reply.

He ran to catch up to her, dragging his sled.

The strange grove came to life around him, churning out its haunting tune. Only, this time the music was frenetic, disturbed, all sense of peace gone.

The hunter stopped at the edge of the grove and set down the coffin. She held up her hand for silence as Sky came up behind her.

Before he could comply, he caught a flash of movement from the corner of his eye. The woman staggered, a thick gray arrow sticking out of her chest.

She looked at Sky, eyes unfocused. Then she fell to the ground.

Sky dove behind the coffin. He scanned the surrounding cliffs but saw nothing.

He stared at the hunter for a moment, her chest slowly rising and falling. She lived, but for how long?

He cast his eyes around and spotted the Porp-a-lorps hovering a few feet away. He watched their shifting lights, heard the discordant sounds of the grove . . .

He focused on his Hunter's Mark and felt it warm. He spoke to the grove and his voice filled with music. The grove responded, and the Porp-a-lorps zoomed off to find and bury the shooter.

Sky caught a glimpse of a cloaked figure racing away. Then he stopped speaking and the music faded.

With a heave, Sky dragged the hunter into the coffin, fearing that he knew exactly who she was and that she might die. Then he looped the vines around his chest and started to pull, desperately hoping the coffin would float.

He'd hoped to sneak home and lay low until he found out what had happened to his friends and if Malvidia had worked out a deal to save his life. But there was no time for stealth now. Whether the Hunters of Legend planned to kill him or not, he was going home, even if it cost him his life.

CHAPTER 8
A Surprise Party

Sky dragged the coffin out of the water and stopped to catch his breath. Sky and his dying cargo had floated through the Sleeping Lands on their morbid ship, moving swiftly with the currents and rowing through the swamps using branches he picked up along the way. He pulled out his pocket watch, checked the time (half past late), and started moving again.

The grove had rejuvenated him and filled him with new-found strength, but the high had long since faded. Exhausted, he pushed on, refusing to let this woman die. The birthday sign still hung on the manor door when he crashed through, dragging the coffin behind him.

He was so tired, he hardly noticed all the people in birthday hats staring at him. Someone tooted a party horn, making a sad sound.

Sky collapsed to the ground, sucking air.

"Sky!" Mom cried, rushing over. "Where have you been?"

"Ewww! Is that a coffin?" Hannah chirped, sounding

disgusted. Next to her stood Derek Webber, the captain of the swim team, her latest "friend," since she'd broken the football captain's heart a few months ago. Derek was tall, with long, muscly arms, a perfect smile, and dark, tanned skin. He stared at Sky with an expression of perplexed horror. In his mouth he held a recently tooted party horn.

In the corner Sky saw Andrew and Crystal, very dirty, but alive. His heart skipped a beat and he nearly started to cry. He had reassured himself over and over that they had survived—that Nackles had gotten them out—but until now, he hadn't believed it. He had hoped, but hope had abandoned him so many times. He had chased after the Marrowick and then the hunter as much out of curiosity and instinct as out of fear of what he might find when he returned home. But he should have remembered what Phineas had taught him: "Sometimes the hardest things to believe are the only things worth believing at all."

He wiped his eyes and smiled at them. They looked every bit as relieved as he did. Sky glanced around, wondering where T-Bone and Hands were hiding. And why were his parents still throwing a surprise party? Hadn't Andrew and Crystal told them what had happened?

Then, in the shadows behind Andrew and Crystal, Sky saw Chase Shroud. Chase raised a plate of cake, toasting Sky in greeting, before taking a humongous bite and, by the looks of it, enjoying it thoroughly.

Before Sky could figure out what was going on, the hunter in the pine box groaned.

"There's a woman in this box!" Dad exclaimed. "Helen! She's injured! Get your supplies!"

As Mom raced for the kitchen, the others gathered around.

Sky stood, still wheezing. He watched Crystal, worried at how she might react. "I think it's—"

"My mom . . . ," Crystal muttered in shocked disbelief. Her mouth hung open and her eyes were wide. Reaching down hesitantly, as if fearing she might slip away, Crystal took her mother's hand and started to cry.

Sky's heart broke as he watched the flood of agony wash over Crystal's face. She was always the strong one, the glue that held them together; he had never seen her look so anguished before. For three years Crystal had believed her mother was lost, and now Cass was lying in a coffin with an arrow in her heart, dying in front of her. Sky couldn't imagine how Crystal must feel. He could get close, maybe, because of what he had suffered with Phineas and Errand, but he had learned over the last year that pains were like snowflakes: Each one was unique. Sky wanted to reach out to Crystal, to help her as she had helped him so many times before, but he didn't know what to do, and fear of doing the wrong thing—of making her grief worse—paralyzed him.

Before Sky could figure it out, Andrew put his arm around Crystal—the gesture awkward, but sincere. Crystal seemed to relax the tiniest bit and her tears fell more freely, in great drops.

Mom rushed back in carrying a small bag, her fingers deftly sorting through it. She reached the coffin and her face froze. "Cass . . ." She glanced at Cassandra, then at Crystal. She put her hand on Crystal's shoulder, giving it a squeeze. "She'll be okay." With her normal efficiency, Mom shook herself out of her stupor and set to work. "Herman, Chase—carry the coffin into the kitchen."

"Of course, Mrs. Weathers," said Chase sweetly, taking one last humongous bite of cake. Chase handed his plate to

Sky. "Stay close," Chase whispered, "we need to talk."

"Hannah, my bag." Mom shoved her bag into Hannah's hands. "Crystal, just . . . hold on."

"Shouldn't we call an ambulance? Or the police?" asked Derek.

Everyone stared at Derek. He was the only one in the room who knew nothing about monsters and hunters.

"It'll be okay, Derek," Dad said reassuringly. "Helen's well trained, and Sheriff Beau should be along shortly. Can you grab that corner of the coffin?"

Derek hesitated and then, reluctantly, helped with the coffin.

Andrew detached himself from Crystal. He whispered something in her ear and she nodded. Then he crossed to join Sky, holding him back as the others left the room.

Sky stood watching as they carried the coffin out of the foyer, too tired to follow even if Andrew hadn't stopped him. He could hear Mom barking orders down the hall, and then her voice trailed off and disappeared as they headed for the distant kitchen in the east wing. If anyone could save Cass, Mom could.

Sky and Andrew shuffled their feet. Sky wasn't quite sure what to say and, apparently, neither was Andrew. The problem was, he had so much to say and didn't know how to say any of it. So instead, he gave Andrew a quick pat on the arm, and Andrew grinned.

"I thought you were dead," said Sky.

"Nope," Andrew replied eloquently.

Sky grinned. "Where are T-Bone and Hands?"

"T-Bone went to find Malvidia," said Andrew. "Hands is tracking down Tick, Lazy Eye, and Squid. Everyone was supposed to meet here to start our search for you. We saw the hunters come back all green and puffy, so we knew you were still alive."

"Tick's coming?" Sky asked, surprised despite all that had happened. Tick was, of course, the football team captain, who Hannah had dumped a few months ago. He—along with Hannah, Lazy Eye, and Squid—had also been instrumental in locking Solomon's prison last year.

"Yeah. According to T-Bone, he's still heartbroken over Hannah, but he hasn't given up," said Andrew. "Plus, after we made them honorary monster hunters last year . . . well, we didn't really know where else to turn if Malvidia refused to help."

"Tick's persistent, I'll give him that," said Sky. He paused. "What happened down there?"

"You saw the explosions," said Andrew. "They knocked us back and out of the worst of it. Nackles led us to the surface after the cemetery collapsed. By then, you were gone. So we split up. Crystal, Nackles, and I waited until the hunters returned, to make sure you were still alive. Then Nackles took off—"

"Where?"

"The Sleeping Lands somewhere—she didn't say," said Andrew. "Either that or she did say and I couldn't understand her. My Gnomon isn't really all that great. But they've been there for a few days, by the sounds of it—her and Rauschtlot. They're working on something. She wanted to come here, to help search for you, but with so many hunters around, we thought it wouldn't be safe. She was only back in the cave to collect some kind of baking fungus from the walls when she heard us."

"Baking fungus?" Sky scoffed. "I wonder what they're up to?"

Andrew shrugged. "Beats me. Crystal and I came back here to wait. That's when we found Chase. He's the Hunter of Legend you mentioned—the one who fought Beau and led the hunters to the manor, right?"

"The same," Sky replied, wondering how Beau was faring. Whatever else happened, Sky felt certain that Malvidia would work out a deal to save Beau. Even though Beau wasn't technically a hunter anymore, Malvidia relied on him far too much to let these hunters have him.

"Well, Chase is pretending to be a friend from school—a *hunter* friend," said Andrew. "We've played along because we weren't sure what he'd do if we didn't."

"So that's why you didn't say anything to my parents . . . ," said Sky.

Andrew nodded. "We need to get you into hiding. T-Bone should've been back by now—not a promising sign. You handed these hunters over to Malvidia, but if she was on their side to begin with—"

"She'll keep her promise," Sky insisted, hoping it was true. "She's a heartless killer and a horrible person, but once she gives her word, she keeps it."

"Then maybe something else went wrong," said Andrew, sounding skeptical. "But whatever the case, if the hunters honestly believe Bedlam's controlling you, they're going to hunt you no matter what Malvidia does. We need to get you out of here."

"I'm not running anymore," said Sky, shaking his head. "Crystal needs me, and maybe T-Bone and Beau, too. Besides, I'm tired and it won't do any good. They know I'm here." Sky gestured at the hall where Chase had disappeared. "They're not going to just let me leave, and if I tried now, a lot of people could get hurt."

"And you think we're all just going to stand around and watch while they kill you?" Andrew asked. "People are going to get hurt one way or another."

"Not if I can help it," said Sky. "Look, my plan either worked or it didn't. If it did, great. If not, I'll improvise. I told them where to find the antidote for Bolger venom—I let them live even after they tried to kill me. That has to count for something. Plus, I know things now, things they'll want to know about Bedlam and what he's after. I have leverage."

Andrew frowned. "All right, Sky. If this is what you want, we're with you. But if things go badly, don't think we're just going to stand by and watch."

Sky nodded to show that he had heard Andrew, not that he agreed with him.

Through the window, he saw Hands approaching with Tick, Lazy Eye, and Squid. They were all dressed in full hunter gear: Pounders, Shockers, Jumpers . . . everything. "Looks like reinforcements have arrived."

As they watched, Lazy Eye accidentally set off his crossbowlike Cross-Shocker. Electrified prongs and trailing wires rocketed out and hit Squid, who fell to the ground writhing while Tick and Hands laughed.

Andrew scoffed at the sight. "We're dead, aren't we?"

After briefing them on the situation and making sure Squid hadn't suffered any permanent damage, Sky led the new arrivals to the kitchen where they found Crystal and the others. They'd removed Cass from Alexander's coffin and placed her on the table, lying on her side. Crystal stood by her mother, holding her. From where he stood, Sky could see the arrowhead sticking out of Cass's back.

Mom shuffled in and out of the pantry, bringing out her strange medicinal supplies.

Andrew crossed to the table, putting himself protectively between Chase, who was helping hold Cass in place, and Crystal. Hands positioned himself on Chase's other side, staying out of the way, but close enough to intervene if Chase got any ideas. Crystal looked up. Her eyes were red and puffy. Sky gave her a weak smile. Brushing a strand of hair out of her face, she dropped her gaze.

There was no more space around the table, so Sky, Tick, Lazy Eye, and Squid moved to the bar to join Hannah and Derek.

Derek looked them over. He gave Tick a curt nod—captain to captain, rival to rival—before pitching his voice low, but not low enough that Sky couldn't hear him. "Why are they dressed like that? I didn't know . . . I mean . . . they're not . . . they're not *goths*, are they?"

Hannah shushed him.

Dad held the arrow steady and Chase grabbed it with some cutters. "One, two, three . . ."

SNAP!

Chase cut off the fletching.

"This is nuts," said Derek. "She should be in a hospital."

Hannah grabbed Derek's hand, holding it tight. Sky saw Tick cringe.

Dad examined the cut. "It's more bone than branch—looks like you were right, Helen. It's either Dovetail or Gilead . . . possibly Harksplitter. . . . It's so hard to tell what it is without the bark. We can hope it's Harksplitter, though I don't know why anyone would use it on Cass. Sky, did you get a look at who did this?"

"No," said Sky, glancing at Chase suspiciously. He remembered seeing Chase in the swamps, but Chase hadn't gone to the Bolger tree. He wondered what time Andrew and Crystal had arrived. Could Chase have had enough time to shoot Cass in the Grove of the Fallen and get back before Andrew and Crystal showed up? It wasn't likely, but it was worth looking into. Chase had told Sky to run; he had known Sky was watching through the Piebald's eyes and he had warned him about the hunt. Chase had an end game, and Sky had no idea what it was.

He glanced at Derek, wondering how much he was taking in. Too much, probably.

"Worry about the shooter later," said Mom. "Use the Bardolph Blend for now, Herman."

Dad began throwing bits of plants, powders, and unidentifiable substances into the blender as it ran at high speed. Mom spooned a thick yellow paste out of the blender and smeared it around the remains of the tail end of the shaft. The paste, the spoon, and the shaft suddenly burst into flames.

Derek yelped.

Mom threw the spoon in the sink and Dad smothered it in baking soda until the flames went out.

The fire on the arrow faded to a dull yellow.

"I think it's ready, Helen," said Dad.

Mom grabbed the tip of the arrow poking out of Cassandra's back. "You kids might want to look away for this part."

"You can't be serious!" Derek declared, jumping from his seat. "You're going to kill her! It's a miracle you haven't already! This woman needs a hospital!"

"A hospital couldn't help her right now, mate," said Chase calmly.

"Well, I say otherwise," Derek retorted, puffing out his chest. "I'm not going to let you kill her. I'm calling an ambulance!"

"Give it a rest, Derek," said Squid. "Don't get your Speedo in a wad."

"Yeah," added Lazy Eye, "wadded Speedos are very uncomfortable."

Derek glared at Squid and Lazy Eye.

"Helen, the arrow," said Dad, drawing Mom's attention back to Cassandra.

Mom pulled on the arrow and Sky looked away. Even so, he could hear a hiss and crackle, and the room suddenly smelled like burnt hair. When he looked back, Mom held the arrow in her hands; the fire had gone out.

"This is the worst birthday party I've ever been to," said Derek.

"Here, drink this," said Hannah, handing Derek a steaming mug.

"What is it?" asked Derek suspiciously.

"It's a love potion, Derek," said Hannah sarcastically. "Geez, what do you think it is? It's an herbal tea. Drink it."

"Right. Sorry," said Derek. He took a sip. "I'm just a little jumpy. It's not every day you see a dead wo—"

Hannah snatched the cup from Derek as he collapsed to the floor.

"You knocked out your boyfriend," said Squid, sounding astonished and slightly impressed.

Dad glanced up, nodding in approval.

"He's not my boyfriend," said Hannah waspishly, adding, sadly, "not anymore."

"What'd you give him?" Sky asked, sniffing the mug.

"Dovetail and Gossymer thread," said Hannah.

"Gossymer thread? Like, from the huge burrowing spider thingies that burst into flame?" asked Sky.

"I don't know!" Hannah exclaimed, clearly flustered. "I got it from the pantry! Mom told me that mixing the right amounts can help people forget things, only . . . I think I overdid the Dovetail. And the Gossymer thread. And maybe the water was a touch warm."

Tick, Squid, and Lazy Eye hovered over Derek, gawping. Derek's head rested at an odd angle and his arms and legs splayed out as if he were swimming the backstroke. A small stream of drool, or possibly tea, dribbled from his mouth.

"He looks so peaceful," said Lazy Eye softly. "Like a little angel."

Squid smacked Lazy Eye on the back of the head.

"Would you three stop staring and help him up?" Hannah reproved.

"What do you want us to do with him?" asked Squid.

"Put him in a chair or something!" Hannah exclaimed. "Linemen—ugh!"

Lazy Eye grabbed Derek's legs while Squid lifted under the shoulders. Tick, seemingly lost in thought, grabbed an arm, which hung limply in his hands and—through some strange physics—kept slapping Derek in the face. They dumped Derek in a chair. Tick walked back to Sky and Hannah, leaving Derek to slide out of the chair.

"Tick!" Hannah shouted.

Tick glanced back at Derek, and looked surprised to find him on the floor.

Squid grabbed Derek under the arms again and hoisted

him back onto the chair. "Got it covered, bro—make your move."

Squid winked and Tick gave him a thumbs-up, crossing back to stand by Hannah. Hannah rolled her eyes.

"Hand me that apron, Lazy Eye," said Squid, his face squashed against the back of the chair.

"This one with the flowers?" asked Lazy Eye.

"Yes, that one with the flowers! Do you see another apron?" said Squid.

Lazy Eye looked around. "Well, there's that one over there on the door."

"Just hand me the apron!" Squid exclaimed.

Lazy Eye hesitated.

"The one with the flowers, you idiot!" said Squid.

Lazy Eye tossed the apron to Squid. "I like the one with the flowers," said Lazy Eye. "They remind me of lemon drops."

"We need to get you a stronger helmet, bro," said Squid. He finished tying the apron to Derek, looping it under one arm, around the rungs of the chair, and across Derek's neck.

"There, see?" said Squid, looking over Derek, who sat slumped in the chair, tongue lolling out, right arm raised in a salute. "Linemen aren't so dumb."

Mom, Dad, and Chase worked on Cassandra, occasionally calling on Hands or Andrew for help. Sky watched quietly, feeling like he should do something, but not quite sure what. He could barely stand as it was.

"Hey. You okay?" Tick asked.

Sky thought Tick was talking to him, but then he saw him leaning against the counter making goo-goo eyes at Hannah.

Sky longed to move out of earshot, but there was nowhere else to go.

Hannah rolled her eyes. "I'm fine, Tick. It's not like this kind of thing doesn't happen *all the time*." She glared at Sky.

"Not involved. I'm not involved," Sky muttered, sliding farther away and looking everywhere but at Hannah and Tick.

"Oh. That's good," said Tick, his eyes never leaving Hannah. "I just wanted to make sure you were okay. You know . . . in case you weren't. Okay, that is."

Hannah watched him for a moment, opened her mouth to speak, and then closed it again. "I need to check on Derek."

"Yeah. Sure. I understand," said Tick.

Hannah looked at Tick a minute more and then crossed to Derek, yelling at Squid and Lazy Eye to get out of the way.

Tick glanced at Sky. "I should probably help her, shouldn't I? She probably needs my help. Swimmers, you know." Without waiting for an answer, Tick set off after Hannah.

Sky sighed, wishing he had his Rubik's Cube, or any puzzle really, just something to keep his hands occupied. He circled the counter, opening drawers. He found some thread spools, twine, some paper clips. He started playing with them, throwing in some knives and forks. He tossed in some spatulas, paper towels, and rubber bands.

As his hands worked, his eyes drifted to the coffin. Someone had left a message on the inside of the lid: "With Hunter's Mark the buried dead shall shimmering blade hold in my stead." Clearly Cass had dug up the grave looking for Alexander's shimmering blade, hoping, Sky supposed, to find it before Bedlam did. But someone had beaten her to it and, based on the clumps of grass Sky had seen mixed in with the dirt piles, he suspected that the robbery had happened a long time ago. The grave robber, whoever it was, had taken the blade and Alexander's body as well. But who would take it, and why? And was the riddle really saying what he thought it was saying: namely, that to get the blade, someone with a Hunter's Mark had to bury himself in the coffin? He hoped not.

According to Phineas, Sky was the only creature alive who had a Hunter's Mark. It was the reason Solomon Rose had come to Exile in the first place—to steal Sky's Hunter's Mark by becoming a Changeling with him. It was the only way to get it if you weren't born with it, and Solomon had lost his Hunter's Mark when he'd taken the Arkhon's body. In the process, Solomon had gained the Eye of Legend, but he wanted both marks—the Eye of Legend and the Hunter's Mark. He had even complained to Sky that someone had cheated him out of both marks centuries ago. Maybe there were lots of Eyes of Legend—Bedlam had one, after all—but according to Phineas, there was only ever supposed to be one creature at a time with the Hunter's Mark, and Sky was the first to have it in over four hundred years. Or maybe Errand was the first. Either way, Errand was gone, and Sky was once again the only person with the Hunter's Mark, which meant—if his interpretation of the riddle was correct—that he was the only one who could recover Alexander's shimmering blade.

Of course, he wasn't about to bury himself to find out if he was right.

Sky lost track of time, his hands moving, his mind wandering, looking for answers but only finding more questions.

"Sky?"

Sky looked up and found Mom watching him, a strange look on her face. "What are you building?"

Glancing down, Sky saw that he'd inadvertently built a very complex trap. The bottom of the trap looked almost like a stage, with paper towels overlaying a framework of twine and spatulas stacked end-to-end. A hole surrounded by mounds of wadded paper towel was cut in the middle, and a small coffin made of stacked knives bound with twine sat next to the hole. Forks and spoons rose like trees across the stage, and he'd threaded twine through the utensils, attaching it to various thread spools to serve as weights and counterweights. A small person made of bent paper clips and paper towel stood on the edge of the utensil forest, a loop of twine under his feet.

Sky flicked a fork, causing it to topple. Vines tugged, weights shifted, trees fell. The loop closed around the paper-clip person's legs, jerking him into the air, where he hung upside down. An arm made of knives set in a T swung him over the stage, dropping him into the coffin. The coffin lid closed and the coffin flipped into the hole.

Sky blew on the mounds of paper towel and they drifted in, filling the hole.

"How . . . unique," said Mom, apparently at a loss for words.

Sky glanced around and saw that the procedure was over—Dad was cleaning up. Cass lay on her back, unconscious, the wounds bandaged. Crystal stood over her, holding her mother's hand. Andrew and Hands hovered nearby. Hannah, Tick, Lazy Eye, and Squid had disappeared somewhere, while Derek slumped in his chair, arm still raised in a salute.

There was no sign of T-Bone, which was worrisome. If the hunters had captured him, as they had Beau, then things were going to get very complicated very quickly. Sky had played nice so far, even if the hunters hadn't. He'd given them a chance. He'd left it up to Malvidia to make a deal that kept everyone alive—a risk since she was still an unknown, but a risk worth taking. Plus, Sky might still have some leverage. He knew that

Alexander's shimmering blade could somehow be used to free Bedlam, and it was quite possible the hunters didn't have that information. It wasn't in any of the stories Sky had read, the ones like *The Edge of Oblivion* that claimed Bedlam wouldn't break free until his heart was pure and filled with love—so ridiculous. Not to mention that if the hunters did know how important the blade was, they never would have buried it with Alexander in the first place.

Phineas had taught Sky how to build traps and solve puzzles, but the greatest lesson he'd taught him was that true hunters didn't hunt creatures; they hunted *peace*, the most elusive prey of all. Sky had given the hunters a chance, but if he had to raise every monster in Exile and make a deal with Bedlam and the Darkhorn to save T-Bone and Beau, he'd do it. Nobody messed with his friends. Nobody.

Chase stepped up behind Mom, and Sky tensed. "Hey, Sky."

"Hey, Chase, old buddy," said Sky, trying to sound friendly even though they'd never spoken before. "So good to see you."

"Got a minute, mate?" Chase asked.

Andrew and Hands stepped closer, but Sky shooed them away. "Sure, *mate*. Let's talk."

Mom looked back and forth between them, furrowing her brow. "All right, Sky. But afterward, you and I are going to have a long chat about your activities over the last year and your . . . *distance*."

Sky looked away. A year, and he still hadn't told his parents what he was or about Errand. How could he possibly tell them that he might not be their son? What if they didn't love him anymore?

"Your father and I have given you a lot of latitude when it comes to these things, but this . . ." She glanced back at Cass.

"We trust you, Sky, but we're not blind; it's time you trusted us."

Sky nodded without making eye contact, without letting her see the lie. He'd rather face the Darkhorn again than have that conversation.

Mom harrumphed and went back to help Dad with the cleanup.

"Shall we take a walk?" Chase asked.

"After you," said Sky.

Chase smirked and walked out of the kitchen.

CHAPTER 9
Thresher

"Why are you still here, Sky?" Chase asked.

They strolled down the hall toward the main body of the manor and the entry—or, as Sky liked to think of it, the *exit*. For Chase.

"I live here. Why are *you* here?" Sky knew he should feel nervous—by his own admission, Chase was a Hunter of Legend, after all, here to kill him—but Sky was just too tired.

"I thought I made that clear when you were spying on me earlier," Chase replied. "I'm trying to save your life."

"*Save* my life?" Sky sputtered, not bothering to deny his spying. "I must've heard a different conversation. And how did you even know I was there?"

"The behavior of the bird," Chase replied.

"What?" Sky asked, perplexed.

"Birds don't stay in one place that long and neither do most monstrous birds like Piebalds, especially in the presence of loud noises and fighting," said Chase. "I'd heard about your trick with the Arkhon last year—the Quadruple Quandary, I believe you called it?"

Sky nodded, realizing what Chase was getting at: Sky had used the Piebalds as part of his trap, a fact every hunter now knew.

"I was aware of your special relationship with the Piebalds," Chase continued, obviously enjoying himself. "And while neither I nor any other known hunter has any idea how to edgewalk, I've read of the possibilities. Putting two and two together—the unmoving Piebald and your relationship with the Piebalds—I realized you must know how to edgewalk, though I have no idea where you would've learned such a thing."

"That's quite a leap," Sky pointed out, watching Chase with renewed interest. Sky knew Chase could fight—he had watched him take down Beau—but discovering that he was also clever was disturbing, to say the least.

"I'm good at leaping," Chase replied smugly. "Unfortunately, so is Morton. He already knows far more than you realize."

"What's that supposed to mean?" Sky asked, coming to a stop as they reached the foyer.

"It means be cautious, Sky," said Chase. "I'm aware of what happened tonight. You've outmaneuvered Morton and everyone knows it; he won't like that one bit. He'll agree to Malvidia's demands, as you guessed, but not for the reasons you suppose. You've outwitted him; he'll want to humiliate you in front of the other hunters before he kills you now."

"Even if he thinks Bedlam's going to take control of me and destroy the hunters?" Sky asked.

"You spared his hunters, which means you're probably not

Bedlam, and you have barrow weed sticking out of your nose," said Chase. "That alone will keep him away, not to mention any girls you might fancy."

Sky blushed, but mostly with anger. "Then why not just give me the barrow weed to begin with? Why try to kill me if barrow weed is all it takes to keep Bedlam out of my head?"

"This hunt was only partly about Bedlam," said Chase. "It was mostly about *you*. Morton and the others fear what you might become."

"And what's that?"

"A terror or a hero," Chase replied. "Do you have any idea what the Hunter's Mark is, Sky?"

"It lets me talk to monsters," Sky replied hesitantly, not wanting to admit how little he knew. "And it holds some sort of unifying force in it."

"It's a birthright that hasn't been seen in nearly four hundred years," said Chase. "It marks you as a descendant of the First Hunter—her chosen heir, destined to rule the hunters during dark times. The hunters are terrified."

Sky shook his head, refusing to believe it. "That's not possible."

Chase smiled. "You can deny it if you like, mate, but it won't make it go away. There are still a few hunters walking around—members of the original thirteen, like Morton—who saw the First Hunter give the Mark to her son and heard her speak the words. They remember. But the Hunters of Legend have ruled the other hunters for a long time; they won't give up power easily, and the Eye of Legend on your palm complicates an already complex situation."

"I don't want their power," Sky replied. "And you say 'they' as if you aren't one of them."

"I'm a newer member," Chase replied, "not so entrenched as some of the others. But if I'd lived for fifteen hundred years or more, I might have a problem taking orders from a twelve-year-old."

"I'm thirteen," Sky retorted.

"Right. Sorry, mate. I'm sure that extra year will make all the difference," Chase quipped.

"How's it even possible for hunters to live that long?" Sky asked. The question had bothered him for some time, ever since he learned that Phineas had lived for centuries. Sky didn't know how many centuries, precisely, but he knew that it was too many for Phineas to be his real uncle. Still, Sky couldn't imagine Phineas as anything else.

"That's a hunter secret, I'm afraid," Chase replied.

"But you just said I'm the First Hunter's heir, destined to rule the hunters during dark times," Sky pointed out. "Seems like you should tell me."

"Nice try," said Chase, "but a Mark doesn't make you a hunter and hunters don't obey a Mark, destiny or not. Alexander had a Hunter's Mark at the same time as Solomon—a miracle in its own right given the singular nature and rarity of the Mark's appearance, yet one the hunters rejoiced over because, sadly, Alexander was not a popular man. Solomon is the one hunters remember, he's the one hunters followed and called the First Hunter's heir. From what I understand, Alexander just wanted to be left alone."

"That's not a reason not to tell me," Sky pointed out.

"Secrets are the currency of the hunters," Chase replied. "No one just gives them away. But if you survive all this and come to the Academy of Legend to train as a hunter, you'll learn this secret and more besides."

"If no one gives away secrets, then why are you telling me all this?" Sky asked.

"Because, mate, despite how it may look, I want to help you," said Chase, sounding sincere.

"Like you did in the Sleeping Lands?" Sky watched Chase closely, looking for a reaction. He was nearly positive he had seen Chase in the swamps earlier, right before he had reached the Bolger tree.

"Been here all night, mate," Chase replied, smiling. "And I believe Morton Thresher's at your door."

Glancing over his shoulder, Sky spotted a distinguished-looking older gentleman peeking through the window. He wore a snappy gray suit, a cravat, and a round bowler hat that would've looked out of style fifty years ago.

Morton Thresher, Hunter of Legend, tapped on the door with his cane.

Chase grabbed Sky by the collar. "Please disregard anything I might say or do in the coming hours. Honestly, I don't mean a word of it."

Chase dragged Sky to the door and threw it open.

"Here's the little bugger, as promised," said Chase, tossing Sky at Morton's feet. Sky scowled up at Chase, but Chase just gave him a wink.

Morton strode in, followed by Malvidia, a bruised and battered Beau, T-Bone, and two hunters Sky recognized from Rauschtlot's cave. In the woods and gardens surrounding the house, Sky saw hundreds of hunters silently watching. Given that none of them was green and hibernating, he had to assume negotiations had gone well—for Malvidia, at least. The fact that the house was surrounded by hunters might mean they hadn't gone well for him. Whatever the case,

Morton clearly wasn't taking any chances with him this time.

"Well done, Chase," said Morton. "I see now that I should've listened to you in the beginning and simply allowed the boy to come to us."

Sky started to open his mouth to say something profoundly witty, but Malvidia shook her head, her eyes flashing a warning. Chase grabbed Sky by the cloak and dragged him to his feet.

Morton circled the foyer, examining the paintings, the stairs, the chandelier, and the coffin tracks.

"Quite a home you have here," said Morton, his voice deep and commanding as he turned to face Sky. Morton's eyes bored into him, seeing all, and Sky felt small and insignificant before him.

"Er . . . thanks," said Sky, at a loss for words. Morton petrified him. Morton was the kind of hunter Sky had always imagined: ancient, dangerous, and powerful. What made it even worse was that Sky had read books about Morton all his life: *The Barrow Hags of Hagerby*, *Dark Night Black Day*, *Demon Wraiths of Windsor*, *The Errant Alchemy of Ebanezar Alton Thorne*, and a dozen more.

But most intimidating of all, Sky suddenly remembered as he thought of those books, Morton Thresher had personally trained Solomon Rose, and that made him troubling, to say the least.

"Your parents must throw a fantastic party," said Morton, gesturing with his cane at the mud tracks the coffin had left behind. "I'm sorry I missed the surprise."

"It was something," said Sky.

"I'm sure it was," said Morton. "Excuse me, I'm being rude—Morton Thresher." He offered his hand.

"Uh . . . Sky Weathers," said Sky, reaching out to take it.

Morton's eyes darted down, staring at the Hunter's Mark and the Eye of Legend on Sky's dirt-caked palm. As they touched, a cold, painful jolt shot through Sky.

"You've got a strong handshake, Sky," said Morton. "A little sweaty—are you nervous?"

Sky pulled away and wiped his hand on his dirty pants, wondering what'd just happened. "Running for your life is a wet business, I guess."

"Ah. That must be it, then," said Morton, seemingly unfazed by Sky's casual reference to the hunt. "I wouldn't have expected nerves from a boy who just bested my entire coterie of hunters—some of the Academy of Legend's best, mind you."

Sky smiled awkwardly, not sure how to take that.

"I assume you all know each other?" said Morton, sweeping his hand around the room to take everyone in. Sky's eyes settled on Beau and T-Bone and two of the hunters from Rauschtlot's cave standing behind them pressing knives into their backs. Beau grinned reassuringly, but his muscles bulged as if he was getting ready to pounce. T-Bone, if possible, looked even less restrained.

"Ah, yes," said Morton, glancing at the hunters. "Two of my associates from the Hunters of Legend: Hagos Adera and Solange Avaray. I understand you met briefly?"

Hagos scowled at Morton. "Get on with it, Morton. Make your peace. Clearly the boy is not Bedlam—he has barrow weed in his nostrils."

Solange nodded in agreement, her lips pouty. "Yes, make your peas! Make your broccoli—I do not care! Finish zis so I can sleep!"

"Yes, quite," said Morton, chewing on the words with apparent distaste. "As you are aware, Sky, we've run into a bit of a snag: We wish to kill you and you, by all accounts, do not wish to be killed."

Sky laughed uncomfortably.

"My old friend Malvidia has suggested another possibility that might work, if you're agreeable?" Morton said.

Sky knew Morton was only humoring him; he was surrounded and out of options—Morton could easily kill him. It was time to see if Malvidia had kept her promise.

"What do you have in mind?" Sky asked.

"Oh, nothing too terrible, I expect," Morton replied. "First of all, you must keep the barrow weed with you at all times until this situation with Bedlam is resolved."

"Easy enough," said Sky hesitantly, remembering Chase's warning. Morton still wanted to kill him, but Morton would humiliate him first. Sky thought that having brown stuff sticking out of his nose was a good first step.

"Good," said Morton. "Next, we believe Bedlam is searching for a certain blade that may lie in Exile."

It was all Sky could do not to choke. Knowledge of the blade was his one leverage point, but it appeared that Morton, somehow, already knew about it.

"The blade belonged to Alexander Drake," Morton continued. "I trust you are familiar with him?"

Sky nodded hesitantly.

"Excellent!" Morton declared. "It has recently come to my attention that this specific blade may hold the secret to freeing Bedlam from his Chrysalis. I have dispatched hunters to the Grove of the Fallen to determine if the blade was buried with Alexander's body, as was rumored after his death, though I expect they will not find it. The few remaining blades are priceless—one does not simply bury them, no matter how sentimental the reasons."

"What does this have to do with me?" Sky asked.

"Possibly nothing," said Morton, examining him. "But should you learn anything about said blade—or happen to remember something a *supposedly* dead relative might have told you regarding its whereabouts—you must bring it to my personal attention. Agreed?"

"Agreed," Sky replied, having no intention of telling Morton anything unless he had to. Even if Morton knew about the blade, he likely didn't know about the inscription on the lid of the coffin, especially since Morton didn't seem to realize that Alexander's coffin was sitting in Sky's kitchen. Sky still had secrets he could trade, if he needed to. Secrets were, after all, the currency of the hunters, according to Chase.

Of course, as soon as Morton's hunters returned with news that the coffin was missing, the secret would get Sky in serious trouble. The mud and coffin tracks on the foyer tiles weren't exactly subtle, and Morton would doubtless make the connection.

What intrigued Sky most was that Morton not only seemed to believe that Phineas was still alive (the "supposedly" dead relative), but also that Phineas might have told him something about Alexander's blade. Phineas had seldom talked about Alexander or the shimmering blades, and never at the same time. And yet Morton clearly thought there was a connection between Phineas and Alexander's blade. Sky racked his brain but couldn't come up with anything Phineas might have said, or why Morton would suspect a connection in the first place.

"Next," Morton continued, "we believe that should Bedlam free himself or manage to take control of you despite our precautions"—Morton looked pointedly at the barrow weed sticking out of Sky's nose—"he will attempt to free his brother, the Arkhon."

Sky nodded; he had guessed as much. Bedlam would have quite an unpleasant surprise when he found Solomon Rose tromping around in the Arkhon's body, assuming Bedlam got that far. Sky had no idea where the real Arkhon was, or even if he was still alive.

Sky looked up from his thoughts and found Morton's eyes drilling into him again. An uncomfortable silence passed, and Sky began to fidget. Morton couldn't possibly know about Solomon, could he?

Morton finally broke eye contact, and Sky felt as though a weight had lifted from his shoulders.

"No one, of course," said Morton, "wants the Arkhon roaming free any more than we want Bedlam roaming free. This brings us to the crux of our problem . . ."

"You want the keys," said Sky, his stomach dropping.

"Smart boy," said Morton. "You *will* give us the keys. Finally, there's a question of loyalties. Your previous mentor was . . . how shall I put this delicately? Of questionable character."

Sky bristled. "There was nothing questionable about Phineas's character."

Morton smiled indulgently. "Of course. Nevertheless, after extensive discussions on the matter, we've determined that your education is incomplete. If you choose to accept our conditions, and live, you must declare your loyalty to the Hunters of Legend, train with us, and take a new master."

A chill went through Sky. "And who's that?"

Morton's smile grew even bigger. "Myself, of course."

Sky gulped. This was the humiliating part. Morton wasn't a gracious loser; Sky had embarrassed him. Now Sky would pay. A training accident, a dangerous hunt gone bad, maybe just a knife in the dark, but if he put himself in Morton's hands, Sky had the feeling he'd wind up just as dead as saying no.

"It's a great honor," Morton assured him. "It's your choice, Sky: Use the barrow weed, give us information on the blade, hand over the keys, and accept me as your new master. Or . . . die. Make your choice."

CHAPTER 10
Vengeance

Sky shook his head. "That's the worst choice I've ever heard."

"Morton, I've got a choice for you: Accept my challenge—fight like a hunter," Beau spat. "Stop picking on children."

"But, my dear Beau, you are *not* a hunter," Morton replied. "Phineas booted you out himself. And why was that again? Ah, yes. For marrying a creature who was not only a daughter of the Arkhon, whom you were sworn to hunt, but a Whisper *spy* as well."

Sky perked up. He knew Beau had left the hunters years ago—at least in name—but he never knew why, not really. Beau had told him that the hunters had booted him out when they'd discovered that Ursula was a Whisper, a monster who could shift into just about anything over the three days of the full moon. But he'd left out a big chunk of story.

"I don't have the keys," Sky muttered, derailing Morton and Beau's conversation.

For the first time Morton looked confused. "What?"

"I don't have them," said Sky. "I've only got the watch."

Morton glanced at Malvidia.

"Sky, this isn't the time for games," said Malvidia urgently. "Give Morton the keys."

Sky glared at Malvidia. He didn't notice a knife in *her* back. He'd handed her the hunters, and she'd negotiated one of the worst deals in history. She'd sold him out; she'd sold all of them out.

"He's telling the truth," T-Bone jumped in. "We lost one of the keys last year."

"You *lost* one of the keys," Morton scoffed. "You've got to be joking. Where's the other?"

"Here."

Sky turned around and saw Crystal standing in the hall, holding up the remaining monocle.

Behind her, the hall was full of people: Andrew, Hands, Mom, Dad, and Hannah—even Tick, Lazy Eye, and Squid, dragging a still unconscious Derek between them. Slowly they entered the foyer, spreading out.

"The happy family and friends," said Morton, watching as Tick, Lazy Eye, and Squid dropped Derek to the floor none to carefully and reached for their weapons. "Helen, Herman—nice to see you again. It's been a long time since the Academy."

Chase started backing away with Sky. This was exactly what Sky didn't want to happen.

"It has," said Mom, her voice strained, a butcher knife suddenly in her hand. "What brings you to Exile, Morton?"

"A grim business, I'm afraid," Morton replied, ignoring the weapons.

"Take the keys and leave him alone," said Crystal, throwing

the monocle at Morton's head. He deftly snatched it out of the air with hardly a glance.

"Two keys is more than enough to stop Bedlam from opening the prison," Andrew added, holding his Cross-Shocker casually at his side. "You don't need the other key to keep it shut."

"Andrew has a point for once," Malvidia chimed in. "Surely Sky accepts the other terms you've offered?"

She glanced at Sky, her expression cold.

He looked around at all his friends, his family. They'd fight to keep him alive. They'd *die* to keep him alive. This wasn't just his life on the line anymore.

"Sky, you don't have to do anything," Dad insisted, inching forward, putting himself between Sky and Morton. "We won't let anyone hurt you."

A chill shot through Sky at those familiar words, and he thought of Nikola, his great protector, his tragic and broken champion, and he realized: Nobody could protect him. Not from this. But right now, he could protect *them*.

Sky nodded at Malvidia—a curt, quick jerk. He had doomed himself, but he had saved everyone else. Besides, he was probably doomed anyway.

"The boy is slow, but he's not stupid," said Malvidia. "What do you say, Morton—do we have a deal?"

Morton examined the monocle, ignoring Malvidia and Dad and everyone else. "Marvelous things, these monocles," he said, adjusting several of the monocle's knobs. "I was there the day the First Hunter forged them, you know. So long ago, now . . . The War of Legend wasn't going our way. High casualties in the Sahara; the Balkans overrun; Legend pushing through the Alps with an army of Erabin and Vindikites. We tried to cut him off at Grimsel Pass, but the Cloying took us. The First Hunter forged the monocles and named them Hope and Vengeance; the watch, Patience. They were symbols more than anything— not powerful like the shimmering blades she would later create. Still, they had their uses, as far as they went."

Nobody spoke as Morton put on the monocle.

Sky felt a sudden bump from behind and fell to the floor. He glared back at Chase, who had pushed him.

"Fortunately," Morton continued, "one of those uses will help us spot a liar." Morton started looking around the room, staring at each of the hunters as if he could see through them. "No . . . no . . . no . . ." The monocle settled on Sky. "Ah, there he is. Sky, would you be so kind as to hand over the monocle in your pocket?"

"What?" Sky asked, confused.

"Two keys is not enough, you see," said Morton. "It's all three or death for thee."

Slowly Sky reached into the pocket Morton was looking at and pulled out the missing monocle. He stared at it in wonder. "I . . . I don't know how—"

"It's all right," Morton cut in, snatching the watch and monocle from him. "The deal is done." Morton pulled the monocle from his eye. "We're going to have so much fun together, Sky—I just know it."

Morton nodded at Hagos and Solange, and they released Beau and T-Bone.

"You've fallen a long way, Hagos," said Beau, straightening his coat. He looked at Solange. "Solange, you haven't fallen far enough."

Solange stuck her tongue out at him like a little girl.

Morton strode toward the door. "See you tomorrow, Sky, bright and early. We've got a blade to find, and you've got much to learn and little time before Bedlam's army arrives!"

Morton paused halfway out the door. "Oh, and Sky—lie to me again and your punishment will be most creative. Don't let the bowler hat fool you; I am not a nice man."

With that, Morton left, followed by Malvidia and the other hunters. Chase left last of all. He gave Sky a cheeky wink and closed the door behind him.

"The *nerve*," Mom complained after they left. "And that Chase, pretending to be your friend."

"We'll fight this, Sky," Beau promised. "Morton's out of control. No one will expect you to go through with this ridiculous apprenticeship, no matter how many hunters witnessed the contract—"

"Beau," Sky cut in. "I have to go through with it. You said it yourself: Morton's out of control. Who knows what he'd do if I tried to back out? He might burn Exile to the ground before Bedlam's army ever gets here! Besides, he won't hurt me—not really. If anything happened to me, he'd lose face again. He won't let that happen," Sky lied. Poorly. Morton would make him pay, Sky had no doubt. Fortunately, most of them seemed to buy it, but not the monster hunters. Crystal frowned at him.

"Look," Sky continued, "let's focus on stopping Bedlam and we'll worry about Morton *after*."

Mom and Dad exchanged *the look*.

"And you promise you'll tell us if Morton steps out of line?" Dad asked.

Sky nodded. Another lie.

"All right," said Mom. "We'll play along for now. You should shower and go to sleep. And so should your friends. And get that poor boy off the ground!"

Tick, Lazy Eye, and Squid scrambled to pick up Derek, accidentally ramming his head into a table.

"Careful!" Hannah cried. "You're going to damage his best parts!"

"His brains?" asked Lazy Eye.

"His eyebrows!"

Dad scowled. "I don't want you looking at boys' eyebrows, Hannah."

Mom sighed. "Hannah, please just take everyone home. It's been a long day."

"I'll walk them to the car," said Sky.

"Okay," said Mom, "but be careful. We'll sort this all out tomorrow."

"Would it be okay if I stayed here, Mrs. Weathers," said Crystal, "with *her*?"

Mom pursed her lips. "Won't your father be worried? We really should call him—"

"He's out of town," said Crystal.

"And he didn't leave a number? The name of the hotel where he was staying?" asked Mom.

"Could have," said Crystal, shrugging.

Hannah, Tick, Lazy Eye, and Squid shuffled out the door with Derek, banging him into the wall.

"Careful!" Mom cried. She turned back to Crystal. "Maybe Beau could check the house—"

"No, no!" said Crystal, perking up. "I mean, the house is a mess; I'd hate to waste Sheriff Beau's time. I can check in the morning. I think I remember where it is. And I'd hate to worry Dad when he's overseas and couldn't catch a flight this late anyway."

"I suppose . . . ," said Mom hesitantly. "But are you sure

you wouldn't prefer to stay in one of the spare rooms?"

"I'd like to be by her," said Crystal, "in case she wakes up."

"All right," Mom conceded. "I'll get you a blanket . . . but try to get some sleep."

"I will," Crystal assured her.

Mom, Dad, and Beau left, leaving Sky alone with Crystal and the others.

"Do you want us to look for the phone number?" Sky offered, exhausted, but desperate to help in some way.

"Don't worry about it," said Crystal, waving her hand dismissively.

"We'll stay, too, if you want," Andrew offered. T-Bone and Hands nodded.

"Go home! I'm fine," said Crystal. "Seriously. I'll see you guys tomorrow."

"All right," said T-Bone, "but call us if anything changes and don't do anything . . . anything . . ."

"Stupid?" Crystal supplied.

"I was going to say don't do anything Sky would do," said T-Bone.

"Hey," said Sky, "I'm right here, you know."

"But mostly," said Hands, "don't do anything without us."

"Don't worry, I'll wait until we can be stupid together," said Crystal.

"That's all I ask," said Hands.

They left Crystal behind and walked out the door toward Hannah's car.

"I'm curious," said T-Bone, looking ponderous, "has anyone ever *met* Crystal's dad?"

"I did," said Andrew as they stepped onto the cobblestone

path. "A few years ago. He's a journalist of some sort, always on assignment."

T-Bone grunted.

"I'm still completely lost," said Hands. "What exactly happened tonight?"

"You guys aren't going to like this," said Sky.

He filled them in as quickly as he could while Tick, Lazy Eye, and Squid attempted to shove Derek into Hannah's rather small car.

"That's just freaky," said Andrew. "Why would Crystal's mom dig up a dead body?"

"Maybe she's a *vampire*," said Hands, "Nosferatu. The unholy scourge. The walking dead with pointy teeth."

"You do realize that vampires were just weak shifters who ate dead people, right?" said Sky.

"A boy can dream, can't he?" said Hands.

"So what are you going to do, Sky?" asked T-Bone. "You aren't seriously thinking of going through with this apprentice thing, are you?"

"I have to," said Sky. "Morton's too old—I think his brain's rotted. You heard him in there; he'd destroy Exile if I blinked at him weird. Besides, now that Bedlam's lost control of Crystal's mom, he's likely wandering around in someone else's body. Bedlam's probably the one who shot Cass, and Morton wasn't on the hunt tonight."

"You think Morton is Bedlam?" Andrew asked.

Sky shrugged. "Morton, Chase—who knows? Bedlam's looking for Alexander's blade, so he's likely to pick someone in the know, and neither of them was at the Bolger tree."

"It's not Chase," said Andrew. "He was here when Crystal and I arrived."

"And he was here the whole time?" Sky asked.

Andrew nodded. "The whole time we were here. It took us a while to dig out, so maybe he could've slipped away before we got here. But there's no way he could've shot Cass and made it back in time."

"Get in the car!" Hannah yelled.

"Looks like it's time for us to go," said Hands, looking at Hannah's beat-up car nervously. "She's a good driver, right?"

"That car was new when she got it," Sky lied, but it was a lie close to the truth; the car was beat-up when she'd gotten it, but it was far more beat-up now.

Hands guffawed.

"Before you go, shove this up your nose," said Sky, handing them some barrow weed he'd taken from Mom's pantry.

They looked at him as if he were crazy.

"It's barrow weed," Sky assured them. "It'll keep Bedlam and the Darkhorn out of your head."

Hannah laid on the horn. "Now!"

T-Bone, Hands, and Andrew glanced nervously at the car, and then back at the barrow weed. They shoved it up their noses.

Hands sniffed. "Why can I smell the color brown?"

"Side effect," said Sky.

"It's mintier than I would've expected," said Hands.

Sky smiled.

Hannah laid on the horn again, and this time she didn't let up.

"See you guys tomorrow," said Sky as they scuttled away, saying good-bye. "I hope."

CHAPTER 11
Darkhorn Dreams

Sky ran through thick vines. Gourds as big as houses smashed around him. A shriek shook the earth. Spinning, Sky found a fiery face staring into his soul, burning green eyes malevolent and menacing. The Jack's awful mouth seemed to smile, and the green fires inside its skull flared even brighter. The giant jack-o'-lantern head rose up, and the Jack pulled a broken man forward and held him up for Sky to see.

"Phineas . . . ," Sky muttered, his voice cracking with emotion.

Phineas looked up, his face bleeding and terrible . . . and then the Jack yanked Phineas back and away, and Phineas disappeared beneath a mountain of vines and gourds and flaming green fire.

Sky screamed as he stumbled and plunged into a swamp filled with laughing corpses. He swam frantically, the water freezing around him. A giant man latched onto him and pulled him close, his face half pockmarked flesh, half coppery metal.

A black Eye of Legend on his forehead stared back at Sky, darkness spilling out.

"Hello again," Bedlam cackled.

Sky screamed.

He raised his hand and light shot out of his Hunter's Mark, driving the monster back. Sky fell through the swamp as if it were air, water splashing around him. His nostrils filled with smoke, and then he stood on a mountain ledge overlooking a charred wasteland. The mountain he was on sat in the middle of a much larger volcanic crater. Rivers of molten rock flowed through a strange blackened forest below, and he saw two more mountains, also within the crater, off in the distance. Fires burned bright in the wasteland, their crackling filling the night with haze and haunting sounds.

Sky reeled back from the edge. Behind him, a giant cave led deep into the mountain's fiery heart. A shadowy figure stood in the mouth of the cave, gesturing for him to come closer.

Sky approached, knowing it was stupid but unable to stop himself.

The man's hood covered his face so that Sky could only see the lower half. Sky's heart beat against his ribs, threatening to break through. The Shadow Man . . . it had to be the Shadow Man . . . the one who'd ruined his life, who'd turned him into a Changeling with Errand. Finally Sky would know who he was. . . .

Sky reached out to pull back the man's hood. . . .

And found nothing. The empty cloak dropped to the ground.

Sky felt a hand on his shoulder and jumped ten feet in the air.

Errand started laughing.

"Errand?" said Sky, shocked beyond words. "Errand! You jerk! If you weren't already dead, I'd kill you!"

"That was classic!" Errand chortled. "Seriously. You should've seen your face."

Sky threw a stick at him.

"Hey!" Errand cried. "Lighten up—aren't you happy to see me?"

"I would be if you were real and not just another part of this nightmare," Sky replied.

"Sky, it's me. I'm really here," Errand insisted. "I pulled you out of your dream and brought you to this place. We're edgewalking."

"Yeah, right," said Sky. "That's exactly what I would say if I wanted to convince myself that you were still alive."

Errand sighed. "Look, this is dangerous, and I don't have much time. How about if I tell you something you couldn't possibly know? Would that convince you that this isn't a dream, that I'm not some figment of your imagination?"

"Maybe," Sky replied hesitantly. "That would depend on what it was. After all, if I didn't know it, how could I be sure I wasn't lying to myself? If I really wanted to believe you were still alive, wouldn't I just make something up that sounded real, even if it wasn't?"

Errand kneaded the bridge of his nose as if a headache was coming on. "That is messed up in so many ways."

Sky shrugged. "I'm a complicated guy; what can I say?"

"Look, Sky, Morton doesn't care about saving Exile. He and Phineas are mortal enemies and have been for centuries. Maybe he thought you were Bedlam, and maybe he's afraid of what you might become with the marks, but I suspect his hatred of Phineas was part of it as well. Morton would love to see Exile burn to the ground."

"If he doesn't care about Exile, then why is he here?" Sky asked. "Why bring all the hunters if he doesn't want to stop Bedlam?"

"I didn't say that he didn't want to stop Bedlam," said Errand. "Morton does want to stop Bedlam—that's why he's after the blade—but he only cares about stopping Bedlam from destroying his *own* hunters. Morton believes that if he can find the blade first, we'll lose our only possible bargaining chip. Bedlam and his army will destroy Exile, and then Morton and his hunters can march in and either finish off what's left of Bedlam's army, or—if needed—use the blade, and the promise of freedom, to strike a deal with Bedlam. But getting the blade, stopping Bedlam, and destroying Exile—those are all secondary. That's not why he came."

"So why, then?" Sky asked. "If Morton was so afraid that Phineas might rise from the dead, then why come here at all?"

"Think about it," said Errand. "What connection could Morton possibly have to Exile that would force him to come out of hiding and face his bitterest enemy, the hunter he fears more than anyone or anything else?"

"What . . . you can't mean Solomon Rose," Sky scoffed. "I'm surprised that's the best you—and by 'you,' I mean 'I'— can come up with."

Errand smiled. "Solomon was more than just Morton's apprentice—he was his adopted son. Until recently, Morton believed that Solomon died fighting the Arkhon. It came as quite a shock when Morton discovered that Solomon really had taken the Arkhon's body. The funniest part is that Solomon spent centuries trying to tell Morton precisely that, but every time Solomon tried, hunters trapped him. The Arkhon was one of the greatest liars in history, so none of the hunters believed him when he claimed to be the great Solomon Rose!"

Errand laughed like it was the funniest thing in the world, but Sky didn't join in.

"What's wrong?" Errand asked. "You have to admit that's funny."

"It's just . . . ," Sky said slowly, "that's a horrible lie. Parts of it are just ludicrous, and the other parts absurd. It also implies that *you're* the one who told Morton that Solomon was the Arkhon, since no one else knows, but that doesn't make any sense, either, because why in the world would you ever do that? And, seriously, could that story be any more complicated? It's not the kind of lie I would make up because it's so outrageous that I'd never believe it. There's nothing in it that makes me want to believe you're still alive. If anything, the opposite is true, which makes me think you might just be telling the truth . . ."

Errand grinned broadly and held out his arms, welcoming a hug.

Sky picked up a rock and threw it at him.

"Ouch! Hey! What was that for?" Errand complained.

"It's been a year, Errand! A YEAR!" Sky bellowed, pushing Errand repeatedly. "And you told Morton about Solomon! Are you insane?"

"Sorry," Errand yelped as he fended off Sky's blows.

"Sorry? SORRY? That's all you can say?" Sky yelled, punching him. "You let me believe you were dead for a year, and Morton's hunters nearly killed me! What happened, Errand? Why didn't you come and find me?"

Errand pushed Sky back. "And then what, Sky? Would you have brought me home to meet your parents? To become part of your family? Maybe like a new pet?"

"Yes!" Sky shouted.

"Really?" Errand shouted back. "Because from what I hear, you still haven't told them about me—or about *you*."

"Wha . . . how do you know that?" Sky asked.

"Does it matter?" said Errand, looking Sky in the eyes.

Sky squirmed. He unclenched his fists and turned away, unable to meet Errand's gaze. "Look, you disappeared. What did you expect me to do? Say, 'Hey, Mom and Dad, let me tell you about this kid who might be your son, but now he's dead, and oh, by the way, *I'm also a Changeling*?'"

"Ah, I see," said Errand, "so you didn't tell them about me to protect *their feelings*."

"Yes!"

Errand raised an eyebrow.

"Fine. No," Sky admitted. "I didn't tell them about you because . . . because . . ."

"Because you didn't want them to wonder if you were really their son," said Errand, "or worse: resent you for taking his place."

Sky clenched his fists and looked away.

"I know how you feel," said Errand.

They looked across the burning valley for a time, each lost in his own thoughts.

"What is this place?" Sky asked, finally breaking the silence.

"A small volcanic island in the Caribbean," Errand replied. "We're on one of the three smaller mountains within the main crater, a crater you might know better as Skull Valley."

"Skull Valley! This is where Cass disappeared—where

Phineas found her journal! This is where she freed Bedlam!" Sky exclaimed. "We searched everywhere for this place, even California!"

"Bedlam keeps it well hidden," said Errand. "You won't find it or remember it unless he wants you to, or you know how to avoid him. This is where Solomon and Alexander trapped him, and where he spent years gathering his army once he awoke and took control of Crystal's mom. I visited here a short time ago. This is my memory of the place."

"How do you know all this, Errand?"

A fiery ball suddenly appeared over the distant mountains.

"Is that . . . is that the sun?" Sky asked.

Errand glanced over. "We should get moving."

He grabbed Sky's arm and the mountain fell apart around them. Sky yelped.

They plunged into nothing, dropped through a swirling electrical storm that Sky recognized as the Edge, and crash-landed in a forest.

Sky jumped to his feet. "Warn me next time!"

Errand grinned. "Where's the fun in that?"

In the distance Sky saw a massive glowing wall made of multicolored stained glass that was filled with bizarre mechanisms, dark liquids, and odd mists, like breath captured on a cold morning.

Sky marched toward the wall. "I don't understand. . . . Why is Solomon's prison here? Is this a memory, too?"

"An Edge Memory generated by Phineas and Nikola's machines," Errand replied, examining the strange colors roving through the wall. "And more than that: a one-of-a-kind singularity."

"Isn't 'one of a kind' the definition of a singularity?" Sky quipped. He stopped in front of the wall and raised his hand to touch it.

"Careful," Errand warned. "Not too close."

Sky paused. Beyond the wall he saw Pimiscule Manor and the broken grove where he and Errand had fought each other. And within the grove he saw one tree still standing, arms reaching upward, giant black wings unfurled . . . just as he remembered. "Solomon."

Before entering the prison, Solomon had shifted into an Echo—a gigantic treelike creature that could either grow deep roots and dream with other Echo, or break those roots and fly. Centuries ago, before Solomon took the Arkhon's body, he gouged out the eyes of every last Echo and left them blind, save for the sensory organs in their branches. Last year, during their fight with Solomon, Errand had gouged out Solomon's eyes with a candleholder.

Through the wall, Sky could see those terrible dripping eyes, as if Errand had just ripped them open a minute ago rather than a year.

Sky backed away from the wall. Solomon didn't move.

"You still don't get it," said Errand. "Solomon and I were never trapped in time; not really. We were trapped *here*. In the Edge. In a memory of Exile."

"Still not getting it," Sky admitted. "Isn't the Edge that stormy place between minds, the place we just dropped through?"

"The same," said Errand. "A trained edgewalker can create places in the Edge by weaving those forces together—the light and dark. They're called Edge Memories. But that's all they are: memories. Shadows of places. Most fade over time or are ripped apart by the storms. So long as your dreams and memories stay in your head, they're protected. But once you put them out here in the Edge, the storms will do their best to rip them apart. Still, a few Edge Memories survive—places like this, places I might show you someday. Amazing places. And horrible places . . ."

Errand went silent and stared at the prison where he had spent eleven years of his life.

"I'm sorry you were trapped here," Sky said, feeling horrible. "I'm sorry I didn't tell Mom and Dad about you. I'd planned to, but each day I didn't made it that much harder. But now you're back! Come with me and let's tell them together."

Errand smiled wryly. "I don't think that's a good idea."

"Why not?" asked Sky.

"A lot can happen in a year," said Errand, staring up into the sky. He sniffed the air, frowning. "I'm not the same person I was when you found me. I don't need your pity or your family."

"This isn't about pity," said Sky. "It's about hope."

"It's about *vengeance*," Errand countered. "*Our* vengeance, Sky. They weren't so different from us, you know."

"Who?"

"Solomon and Alexander," said Errand. "I'm close to something, Sky. Very close. Soon we'll have answers . . . and more besides. We'll have everything we need to get our revenge."

A light exploded high above and then disappeared. Thunder rolled through the valley.

"We tried to keep you out of all this—you should've left when you had the chance—but you've made a mess of it now," said Errand.

"Who's 'we'?"

Errand grinned. "You'll find out soon enough. Next time

pack the barrow weed in tighter. You snort when you sleep. Better yet, try not to sleep at all."

"That should be easy enough," said Sky.

"I'll lead them away," said Errand. "Try to survive the night."

"Wait . . . lead who away?" Sky looked up and saw another light streak across the sky. "What is that? And what about Morton? Why tell him about Solomon?"

"Stay away from Morton if you can," Errand replied. "Focus on the blade, Sky. We have to find it. Everything depends on it. It will take Morton time to figure out how to open the prison. But even if he does figure it out, he won't free Solomon until he either has the blade or is certain we won't find it before Bedlam's army arrives. He'll wait as long as he can."

Errand turned and started walking away.

"What if he tries to kill me?" Sky yelled after him as another light—a fireball—streaked through the night.

"Don't let him!" Errand shouted over his shoulder. Then he raced away, moving inhumanly fast. Sky watched him and then ran in the other direction. He saw lights streaking across the night sky in the direction Errand had disappeared. Whatever those lights were, Errand seemed to be leading them away.

Ahead, he saw Emaline Livingstone's tomb, still intact, as it had been a year ago, before the east cemetery had sunk into the ground. He looked up and saw a ball of fire, like a comet, crashing toward the earth. Within that fiery ball he saw the Darkhorn, her giant wings folded back and burning. A dozen silvery Nightmares trotted at her side. The Nightmares were smaller than the Darkhorn, with fiery manes, hooves made of stars, and bodies of moonlight.

Raging fear took hold and Sky shot forward, but not fast enough. The Darkhorn smashed into the earth behind him—a star fallen from heaven—and then it was fire and darkness, rippling earth, falling trees, the sounds of frenzied neighing and clomping hooves.

Something pecked Sky on the nose, and then he plunged through the ground into darkness and terror, the madman in his ear laughing in a perfect imitation of his own voice.

CHAPTER 12

Perspicacious Bodacity

Sky woke up laughing madly.

Something pecked his nose and he felt something slimy enter his nostrils.

"Ow! Stop that! Stop that! I'm awake! I'm awake!" Sky covered his face and sat up in bed, sending Fred the Piebald fluttering away. Black blood trickled from Sky's Eye of Legend, touched by a faint white light drifting up, mistlike, from his Hunter's Mark.

He found a wad of barrow weed on his bed. Another piece was partially shoved up his nose, by Fred, he guessed. Sky finished the job, packing it in tight.

Wind blew through Sky's room, gusting through a cracked and broken window, and glass shards covered the floor like flecks of snow.

"You broke my window?" Sky asked, the shock he'd felt upon waking starting to fade despite the lingering sense of terror. "Where have you been?"

Fred dropped a note on Sky's bed.

"What's this?"

"CAW!" Fred croaked, explaining nothing before flying out the broken window.

Sky threw his blankets back and swung his legs over the edge of the bed. "Stupid birds."

He surveyed the glass and let out a long sigh. It was everywhere.

He picked up the note Fred had dropped. It was smudged and covered with bird droppings, and the penmanship was bad enough that Sky wondered if Fred had written it himself. It was so bad, in fact, that Sky nearly mistook it for his *own* writing.

"BEING WATCHED. MEET IN MISS TERRY'S OFFICE AS SOON AS POSSIBLE. I HAVE SOMETHING FOR YOU."

Sky slapped his face to make sure he was really awake. Since when did Piebalds deliver notes? They weren't pigeons. Or owls. For that matter, since when did Piebalds write? Either way—delivery bird or author—it was odd.

"Fred, my friend, you are one weird bird."

He spotted his slippers sitting across the room next to his desk. "Perfect."

He ripped the sheets off his bed and wrapped them around his feet. He surveyed his handiwork, remembering how happy Mom had been when she'd found these fifteen-hundred-thread-count sheets for 30 percent off. "She's going to kill me."

He stepped down onto the glass. He could feel it popping through the material, leaving, he suspected, dozens of tiny holes, but the fabric held well enough to protect his feet.

Moments later Sky threw on some jeans, zipped up a faded

yellow hoodie as high as it would go to hide an even uglier Valentine's Day shirt—the only clean shirt he had—beneath, put on his shoes, and used the torn bedsheets to sweep the glass into a pile.

He grabbed Fred's note, shoved it in the pocket of his hoodie, and set out for the kitchen.

"Late again, squirt," said Hannah, walking up behind him. Her hair was still wet from showering after, Sky knew, her rigorous early-morning workout. "Nice hoodie," she added with a smirk.

"What's wrong with my hoodie?"

"Nothing," said Hannah. "That color was really cool in the eighties."

"You weren't even born in the eighties," Sky pointed out.

"I saw *E.T.*," Hannah replied tartly, as if there was nothing more to know about the decade of denim. "Oh, and thanks for the great party last night. It's no wonder you're so popular."

"Sorry. Next time I'll leave my friend's mom to die in the woods," Sky snapped.

"Derek was still knocked out when I got him home," Hannah continued, sounding heartbroken. "He didn't even give me a good-night kiss!" She snorted as if a boy not wanting to give her a good-night kiss were the most absurd possibility in the world. "Lazy Eye and Squid offered to move his lips, but it wouldn't have been the same. Derek never moves his lips. Besides, Tick wouldn't let them."

"Amazing," said Sky, shaking his head mockingly. "I mean, the *nerve* of that guy."

Hannah sniffed. "Yes, well," she muttered, "Derek's mom thought he was on drugs; she blamed me, if you can believe it."

"What did you tell her?" asked Sky.

"I lied and told her someone—probably *you*—spiked his

fruit punch with Nyquil," said Hannah. "She'll never let me see him again."

"Do you really want to?" Sky asked.

"Maybe," Hannah replied guardedly. "What's it to you? Is Dad paying you to spy on me now?"

"Why? Do you think he would?"

Hannah laughed. "Probably." She paused, and then gave him a very serious look, especially for Hannah. "Sky, are you okay?"

"You mean, like, in the head?" Sky joked.

"I was thinking more in the heart," Hannah replied.

"Sure," Sky replied, refusing to look at her. "Why wouldn't I be?"

"Gee, I don't know," Hannah said, voice dripping with sarcasm. "Maybe because your life is nuts? I know you feel like this whole monster hunting thing is Phineas's legacy and all, but I've watched what it's done to you over the last year. You're not the same . . . something's changed."

Sky met her eyes. "You couldn't be more right, Hannah."

Hannah puffed her lips in apparent frustration.

"Look, I'm fine," Sky lied, not wanting to talk about it, or drag her any further into his messed-up life. "I'm just tired. Last night was bad, but it's all settled now. Really. To be honest, I'm more worried about you. I hear Coach Blackburn is making the team practice today right before the homecoming game. Does that mean you're practicing after school as well?"

Hannah didn't look like she believed him, and his sad attempt to change the subject was completely obvious, but she didn't press.

"The man is nuts," said Hannah, "but we're not about to let football players out-nuts us. We'll practice until there's not a player left on the field."

Sky glanced out the window as they passed, noting that it was still dark despite all the colored light coming from the massive stained glass wall surrounding the manor.

He stopped. *Stained glass wall?*

"Sky, are you all right?" Hannah asked, sounding concerned even though she couldn't see outside the window from where she was standing.

Sky rushed to the window, and his stomach dropped. Outside, he saw monsters in the yard, frozen in place. In the distance—in the light of the glowing wall—he saw Solomon Rose standing motionless, his branchy Echo arms raised.

"Sky?"

"Wait for me in the kitchen—don't leave until I get back!"

Sky darted through the dark and winding halls of Pimiscule Manor.

He reached the humongous library in the center of the manor and burst through the doors. Six stories above, he saw the stained glass dome. The pendulum hung from the dome, swinging back and forth in its terrible arc—a pendulum that, he knew, hadn't been there since they'd reset the prison last year.

Sky raced between the empty bookshelves, the books donated to Arkhon Academy years ago. In the center of the room, in the shallow concave pit that made up the floor, he found Morton Thresher standing quite still, watching the pendulum's erratic, unnatural swings. In his hands he held Sky's pocket watch . . . or, rather, Sky's *former* pocket watch.

Sky stopped.

Morton wore the two monocles, but they weren't connected together, nor were they connected to the watch. In other words, they weren't a band of one. Morton had somehow figured out how to make the prison appear, but he hadn't yet deduced how to open it—a good thing since, according to Errand, opening it was precisely what he wanted to do.

Morton glanced up. "There you are." He adjusted a few dials on the watch, and then, very suddenly, the pendulum disappeared. Calmly, as if nothing had happened, Morton turned to face him. He removed the monocles and shoved them in his pocket.

"Hello, Sky," said Morton. "Lovely morning."

"I've had better," Sky replied. "For example, once I woke up and a Hunter of Legend *wasn't* standing in my library trying to kill everyone."

"That only happened once, did it?" asked Morton.

"Rough neighborhood," said Sky.

Morton's mouth curved. "I see your wit is as sharp as your uncle's. Years ago I saw him argue with a bird for over an hour on the best flavor of ice cream. Phineas favored butter pecan, as I recall."

"And the bird?" asked Sky.

"Mint jubilee," said Morton. "Of course, I had to take your uncle's word for it since I don't speak bird."

"Who won the argument?" asked Sky.

"The bird, I suspect," said Morton. "I didn't stay to find out."

"Are you sure they weren't just trying to get rid of you?" Sky asked in all sincerity.

The corner of Morton's mouth twitched. "I can tell you're going to be a tenacious apprentice—perspicacious, as well."

"And maybe capacious, audacious, and loquacious—I can use big words, too. Years of word puzzles from Uncle Phineas has made me bodacious," Sky replied. "That still doesn't change the fact that you shouldn't be in here."

"Tell me Sky, where is your uncle? What is he up to? I promise, you can tell me. Despite our disagreements, your uncle and I were friends once."

"Up to? He's not *up* to anything," said Sky, bristling. "He's dead."

"And you claim that he hasn't contacted you since his death?" asked Morton, his eyes intent.

"No," said Sky. "That's generally the way it works."

Morton frowned. "Most unfortunate; I'd expected him to reveal himself by now. This business with Bedlam reeks of his traps."

"Phineas is *dead*," said Sky. "D-E-A-D. Dead. I don't know how to spell it out more clearly."

An ingratiating grin tipped the corners of Morton's mouth. "My dear boy, I have known Phineas for over fifteen hundred years. He snookered the Barrow Hags and charmed the Silversaff out of enough secrets to outfit the army of Erachnus. He bested Reemspun the Elder in a contest of wits, captured the Wimbledon Cleaver, and claimed the Moonriders as our mounts after spending over forty years in the Mountains of Moldy Foreboding just to learn their language. Phineas T. Pimiscule is the only man in the history of the world to go toe-to-toe with Legend and survive. He is the nightmare of monsters, the bane of hunters, and the consort of the First Hunter before her passing. I know his games. I know his tricks. One does not live as long as he has without some measure of ingenuity. I assure you, Sky, despite what you may think, Phineas is very much alive."

Sky reeled at both the overload of unbelievable stories he had never heard about his uncle and the revelation that Morton honestly believed Phineas was still alive. Morton had insinuated it before, Sky knew, but to hear him say it outright . . .

Sky wanted to believe it, too, but how could he? A year had passed since he'd watched Phineas die in the Jack. He'd watched him be consumed in that haunting inferno and crushed beneath that unbearable weight, giving his life for them. If Phineas were still alive, then where was he? And why hadn't he shown himself when Morton's hunters were trying to kill Sky last night?

"I'm curious," said Morton, cutting off Sky's thoughts. "Do you commonly dig up the dead—figuratively speaking, of course?"

"Do you commonly attack children, Morton, especially when you claim to be friends with their uncles?" Sky countered, fearing that Morton already knew about the Grove of the Fallen and Alexander Drake's coffin, his words clearly a thinly veiled reference.

"When necessary," Morton replied. "My former friendship with your uncle is the only reason you're still alive. I'm sure a smart boy like you has wondered why I didn't join in the hunt personally. If I had, I promise you, we wouldn't be having this conversation."

"I've had a few thoughts," Sky replied. "Hearing you talk about my uncle has given me a few more. You couldn't possibly be afraid of Phineas, could you?"

"He who has no fear of his enemies has no enemies," Morton retorted.

"Because he has friends?"

"Because he is dead," Morton stated. "But surely there are other reasons you've considered for my absence; perhaps you think I'm Bedlam?"

Sky furrowed his brow: He had thought that, mostly because he thought of everyone as a possible host for Bedlam. Morton hadn't participated in the hunt, which meant that if he was Bedlam, he could have attacked Sky in the swamp, and he could have shot Cass. Plus, Morton was in charge—it made sense for Bedlam to choose Morton. But if Morton was really Bedlam, why would he raise the question?

"Don't look so surprised," said Morton. "I thought the same thing about you when I learned you outwitted my hunters . . . until I saw the barrow weed. It's not a perfect barrier—completely ineffective once he's in your head—but it's enough to forestall entrapment, especially for one of such *prodigious wit* as yourself."

Morton sauntered around the library, inspecting the empty bookshelves, the concave pit, and the stained glass dome high above. "Now, Apprentice, it's time for you to keep the last part of our bargain: Where is Alexander Drake's body and his shimmering blade?"

"I don't know," Sky snapped. "Why don't you tell me why you made the prison appear?"

Morton's face tightened like a painter's canvas pulled too far across a frame. "DO NOT TRY ME!" he barked, turning on Sky. "My hunters told me what they found at Alexander's grave! I have visited the Grove of the Fallen myself! I have seen the coffin and Cassandra and your little friend, her daughter, peacefully sleeping on your kitchen table! So I ask you again: *Where is the blade?*"

Sky started backing away toward the bookshelves and the exit, trying to act casual, but frightened by the mad gleam in Morton's eyes. Morton might want to humiliate him first, Sky supposed, but that look said Morton would happily kill him right now.

"You know I'm not Bedlam," said Sky, trying to keep his voice from quivering, "but how do I know you're not?"

Morton smiled grimly and slowly walked toward Sky. "Do you feel cold, Sky? A slight chill, perhaps?"

Sky felt a sudden stabbing sensation in the Eye of Legend on his palm, and cold radiated through his hand. "How . . . how did you . . . ?" Black veins spread out from the Eye and his hand started to turn blue. "What are you doing to me?"

"Me? No, Sky—you are doing this to yourself," Morton replied. "Oh dear, it appears to be spreading up your arm. . . ."

Sky looked and saw black veins rising into his wrist and up his forearm. "Stop it." He cringed against the freezing pain and fell to his knees. He rubbed at his arm frantically, trying to drive the darkness back.

It spread up his arm . . . to his neck. Just behind the veins—wherever they touched—his skin turned midnight blue and froze into a solid, unbreakable mass. His chilled muscles grew taught and ropy, like a Gnomon's, his bones solid and heavy.

And then, as the veins reached his head, he saw visions flash before his eyes. He saw the arrow entering Cass, the Wargarou gutting Beau last year, and the Jack rising up behind Phineas. "Stop it!"

"Only *you* can stop it, Sky. You hold a piece of Legend—part of his terrible power—in that Eye. You could so easily destroy me. Let it free. . . . Use it. . . ." Morton leaned close and whispered in Sky's ear. "*Make* me stop it."

Sky saw Emaline's tomb sinking into the earth with all the hunters who'd died to protect him, and Piebalds snatched out of the air by the Darkhorn, never to fly again. He saw Errand, a baby, trapped in Pimiscule Manor for eleven years and Solomon Rose throwing Errand over the stained glass wall after claiming to love him—and that desperate need in Errand's eyes.

Sky lashed out with his frozen fist. Strength he didn't possess flowed into the punch as it shot at Morton's face.

Morton caught Sky's knuckles in a hand every bit as frozen and strong. Sky experienced a moment of surprise, and then the black veins in both their arms rushed back toward their palms. Darkness exploded out of Sky's Eye of Legend, matching the darkness exploding from an Eye of Legend on Morton's palm.

Sky felt a jolt as the two forces met—an anger coming from the darkness, a terrible will—and then a shove that sent him flying backward through the air. He crashed to the floor, the darkness spent, the cold gone. He started to rise but found Morton's shoe on his head, holding him down.

A long shimmering blade plunged past Sky's nose, missing by an inch, before sinking effortlessly into the floor. Morton leaned close again. "You wonder why we really hunted you?" he whispered. "*That* is why."

Morton removed his foot and spun away, leaving the shimmering blade quivering in place. "You are untrained! Undisciplined! *Flawed!* The First Hunter gave the Eye to the Hunters of Legend to protect—it does not belong to you! You are not worthy of the Hunter's Mark you bear! You are not the First Hunter's heir, no matter what trick Phineas played to give you her Mark! Solomon Rose on his worst day wouldn't have allowed himself to lose control like that!"

Sky laughed. If Morton believed that, he didn't know Solomon Rose.

Morton spun on him. "Is there something you'd like to tell me? Some *joke* you'd like to share, perhaps?"

Sky didn't say anything. According to Errand, Morton already knew the Arkhon was Solomon, which is why he planned to free him, but Sky wasn't about to reveal that he knew Morton's secret.

Morton curled his lip. "You were never meant to have the Eye of Legend, Sky. You cannot guard it, not from Bedlam, not even from *yourself*. There is a will in the Eye—Legend's will. Learning to control it takes lifetimes. Use it too much and too often, and he will control you."

Morton turned away and stared into the shadows quietly.

As Sky sat up, he noticed the Eye of Legend fading from Morton's palm, the skin somehow folding in around it until it disappeared completely.

The shimmering blade quivered in front of Sky. The blade itself was translucent and waxy, with thousands of flecks of what appeared to be gems encased within. The flecks twinkled like stars and shifted colors, drifting around to create the shimmering effect. The crosspiece of the sword was long and black, the grip as well, with a simple silver knob on the end.

Sky glanced at Morton, who still had his back to him. Fearfully, Sky reached out to touch the blade, wondering if it was Alexander's and why Morton would ask for it if he already had it, but the moment Sky's fingers connected, the shimmering died.

In an instant the waxy substance turned to rusted iron, the strange, twinkling gems disappeared, and all that was left was a long, corroded sword with a black hilt and silver pommel.

Sky climbed to his feet and yanked at the sword, struggling to pull it from the floor before Morton saw what he'd done.

"The blade only responds to its owner," said Morton, shoving Sky to the side and drawing the blade from the floor with ease. As soon as he touched it, the blade stirred to life, shimmering brightly. "This one is mine."

Sky backed away warily.

Morton pressed the silver pommel and the crosspiece collapsed, folding down until the blade disappeared and Morton was left with his cane. "Unfortunately, the one I need to find belonged to Alexander Drake."

"I don't know where it is," Sky insisted. "The coffin was empty."

Morton stared at him intently. After a moment he pursed his lips and nodded in a satisfied sort of way. "I believe you."

Morton spun on his heels and headed for the door. "Your education starts in one hour at the grounds north of Arkhon Academy. We have much to do before Bedlam's army arrives, including finding that blade! I've invited your friends—don't be late!"

CHAPTER 13
The Finger of Erachnus

Sky, T-Bone, and Hands walked onto Arkhon Academy's old hunter training grounds. Andrew had shown up early and opted to stay with Crystal and Cass at the manor rather than answer Morton's summons, a you're-not-the-boss-of-me move if Sky ever saw one. T-Bone and Hands had nearly stayed as well, but ultimately decided to go with Sky for moral support and to pound anyone who got too close to him.

The grounds were hidden in the woods and hills north of Arkhon Academy near the Sleeping Lands. Despite its close proximity, they'd never traveled here before, though they had spied on the hunters from a distance once or twice.

Broken bleachers sat around open spaces for sparring, and precut material for traps were scattered around foreign trees, bodies of quicksand and strange liquids, and all kinds of pits. A few areas had been cordoned off and were covered with signs warning of danger and traps—obstacle courses, Sky supposed.

But by and large the most obvious feature was a gigantic

smooth black stone that curled from the earth like a finger and stretched four stories high in the middle of the main field.

Malvidia had shut down Arkhon Academy's hunter school after the death and loss of the majority of Exile's hunters during Solomon's attack twelve years ago. But last year, when dozens of hunters had emerged from the prison, Malvidia had reopened pieces of the hunter school, including the grounds, during a grand ceremony.

Sky and his friends had not been invited.

As they approached the main bleachers where the hunters had gathered, an eerie silence descended. The hunters—grim men and women of all ages, from young teens to decrepit adults—stopped what they were doing and watched them pass. The hunters were covered in bruises, cuts, and scrapes from Sky's traps, and nearly all had pale, sickly green skin from the Bolger venom.

Sky took them all in, refusing to look away from these people who had tried to kill him.

He spotted a few familiar faces. Crenshaw was there, of course, his skin a deeper green than the others', as he'd waited longer to get the cure. T-Bone's massive younger brother and bitter rival, Ren, stood next to Crenshaw, pointedly ignoring T-Bone. Sky and Ren weren't really friends, but they weren't enemies, either, and Sky was glad to see that Ren's skin wasn't green, which likely meant that he hadn't joined in the hunt.

Sky recognized several Exile hunters they had saved from Solomon's prison last year. These hunters gave him warm smiles and almost friendly nods. Like Ren, none had green skin or cuts, nor did most of Exile's hunters. Maybe they had refused to kill him, or maybe they simply hadn't known about the hunt. Either way, Sky could clearly see that they were a minority, vastly outnumbered by Morton's hunters.

Sky spotted Malvidia's apprentices, Lazar and Lucretia, normal-colored and watching him closely, and the rest of Crenshaw's former Shadow Warg pack—Alexis (green-skinned) and Cordelia and Marcus (normal-skinned). Marcus avoided eye contact, while Cordelia gave him a big smile and crossed to join them in their lonely walk.

Cordelia had changed over the last year, introducing smidgens of color to her normally black outfits, and smiling on occasion. Her long, straight hair was fiery red—accentuating her milky skin—and pulled back in a ponytail. Like many of the hunters, she wore a long coat filled with hidden pockets for storing weapons, botanical supplies, and other sundries. A belt hung across her chest, with a number of finger-length throwing knives sticking out and an actual sword and sheath hanging from the end by her hip.

"Exciting, isn't it?" said Cordelia, pushing T-Bone aside and falling into step beside Sky.

T-Bone and Hands raised their eyebrows questioningly, but he ignored them.

"Exciting?" Sky replied. "I've got a target on my chest."

He glanced back and saw Crenshaw—who had a one-way crush on Cordelia—scowling.

"A target could only improve that sweatshirt you're wearing," Cordelia quipped.

"It's a hoo—" Sky glanced over and found her smiling. It was the kind of smile he'd seen girls give to other boys, but he'd never expected to see one directed at him.

"—hoodie," he finished lamely. The smile caught him off guard and all he could manage was a weak lip curl in return.

Hands cleared his throat and Sky tore his eyes away from

Cordelia. They'd reached the towering curved black stone. Morton stood at the base of the stone, staring up at it with Chase Shroud, Hagos Adera, and Solange Avaray—the four of them locked in whispered conversation.

Apparently taking Sky's arrival as a signal, the hunters closed in and formed a circle around Sky, Hands, T-Bone, and Cordelia, with the huge stone at the center.

Sky glanced around, knowing he was trapped but doing his best not to act like it. If Morton wanted to toy with him and humiliate him, he was welcome to it. Sky's only concern was for Exile.

A low murmur arose from the hundreds of gathered hunters as they engaged in whispered conversations. He noted that most of the Exile hunters were huddled in a small group directly behind him. Where Morton's hunters were talking, Malvidia's hunters were silent. Their hands hovered near their weapons and their expressions were strangely determined.

Finally Morton ended his whispered conversation with Chase, Hagos, and Solange and turned to face them.

Chase winked at Sky, but Sky ignored him. Whatever game Chase was playing, Sky didn't want to be a part of it.

A hush fell on the hunters as Morton inspected them. His eyes took in Sky, T-Bone, Hands, and Cordelia, and then swept past. He walked around the circle, staring down his hunters.

"You. Are. Stupid," Morton stated. He paused and came to a stop near Sky, but his eyes remained locked on his hunters. Sky thought Morton was done and that the speech might just be the worst he had ever heard, but Morton started up again.

"Last night," Morton barked, "this group of untrained

children bested you." Morton gestured vaguely at Sky, T-Bone, and Hands. "And this boy"—Morton pointed at Sky—"*humiliated* you."

"Hunters are only as good as the hand that guides them, I always say." The Exile hunters parted and a man Sky had never seen before strode through. He was unusually thin, with a narrow face, big ears, and a sharp nose. He wore a battered trench coat and slacks, with a bullwhip looped through his belt, and he was covered in dirt from head to toe.

Behind the man, Sky saw Malvidia, Beau, and—most surprising of all—Dad. T-Bone's mother, a huge Polynesian woman, was also there, along with Hands's grandfather, Osmer, whom Sky had met at the nursing home a few times.

Before the circle closed, Sky saw Nikola, his mad childhood protector, walking alone and unseen in the dawn shadows of the distant trees to the west, heading into the Sleeping Lands. He carried a checkered blanket, like the one he'd had the night before, and a small picnic basket on his arm. Sky's heart lurched painfully at the sad sight, and then the circle closed and Nikola disappeared from view.

Sky glanced at Dad, who gave him a warm smile before turning his attention back to Morton.

Rather than feeling comforted, Sky's general unease skyrocketed into full-blown panic. Morton wanted to humiliate him, to make him suffer, and Sky was willing to endure it for the sake of Exile, for his family and friends, but he knew Dad would never allow it; he'd never just stand by and watch Sky suffer, even if it meant saving himself and all of Exile.

The dirt-covered man strolled toward the black stone, looking up at it, his back to Morton. "That's a mighty large finger," the man muttered appreciatively, his accent British and as thick as Morton's. "After all this time, I'd nearly forgotten how enormous Erachnus was."

Sky looked around for a giant finger, and then realized that the man was talking about the black stone. Sky stared up at it. *Erachnus?*

"Winston Snavely," Morton sneered. "What on earth are you doing here?"

Winston spun around to face Morton. "I heard there was a surprise party and thought I'd drop in for cake—lemon, I hope."

"The party is over, I'm afraid," Morton replied, sounding annoyed.

Winston shook his head sadly. "More's the pity. Though from what I understand, Sky threw the party, and the surprise was yours. Or perhaps the surprise is still on its way?"

"If you're implying that I mean to harm the boy after giving my word and taking him as my apprentice, then the surprise is yours," Morton stated. "Or perhaps you've come to inform me that Bedlam is loose and his army marching here as we speak? I assure you, I'm well aware. The other Hunters of Legend have given me full leave to handle the Exile situation."

"So I've been given to understand," Winston said evenly. "Though decisions made in darkened rooms with a minority of fellows are hardly binding."

"Binding enough," Morton snapped. "Though you're welcome to challenge the decision if you can find a majority . . . unless, of course, you're proposing to resolve this another way?" Morton raised his eyebrows questioningly and Sky saw his hand tighten around the pommel of his cane.

Winston grinned and held up his hands in a gesture of peace, steering clear of his bullwhip. "Perhaps another time . . . I'm simply here for the party."

"Ah, yes! There's the Winston I remember!" Morton laughed derisively. "Cowardly as ever."

Winston frowned deeply. There was a flash of anger and Sky thought Winston might attack. But the anger disappeared so quickly, Sky wondered if he'd seen it at all.

"Quite," Winston mumbled, adding more loudly. "Let's get this party started, shall we?"

"A fine idea, Winston," Morton agreed, "the first I've heard all day. Since Malvidia has evidently persuaded you to represent Exile's interests among the thirteen, why don't we start with a friendly wager: Exile's finest young hunter"—he gestured at Sky—"versus our finest young hunter"—he waved at Chase, who grinned, obviously relishing the idea.

Winston looked skeptical. "I suppose . . ."

Chase's smile broadened and he sauntered closer, drawing a shiny silver sword from a hidden sheath. Sky blanched, then tensed as he saw Dad and Beau reaching into their coats.

Fortunately, Sky had anticipated just this sort of thing. He strode forward and put himself within Morton's reach, ensuring that Dad and Beau couldn't do anything to save him if fighting started, and thus removing the reason for the fight. Frustration cracked Dad's ever-smiling face and Beau gave Sky a crooked grin. Sky had just trapped them, and they both clearly knew it.

Winston examined Sky, Dad, and Beau, apparently noticing the silent exchange. He gave Sky an approving nod before addressing Morton and Chase.

"Perhaps we should start with something a little less pointy," Winston proposed, gesturing at Chase's shiny sword. "Might I suggest wooden swords?"

"Oh, come now, Winston," Morton chided, "we use real swords at the Academy."

"And we kill real creatures with them, and sometimes not the ones we intend," Winston retorted. "Malvidia and her hunters have already entertained this whimsical farce long enough by practicing when they—and *we*—should be hunting Bedlam and preparing for his army. Let's not add to the discourtesy by detracting from their numbers."

Morton sighed dramatically. "Very well, then," he growled, "if you wish to coddle the boy, wooden swords it is."

Chase put his silver blade away with an indifferent shrug, and a hunter stepped forward and handed Sky and Chase wooden practice swords.

"Anything else we can get for you, Your Highness?" Morton sneered condescendingly. "A warm glass of milk, perhaps?"

Several of the hunters snickered.

"If you have one, I wouldn't say no," Sky retorted. Morton's smile tightened, and Sky kicked himself for not holding his tongue. Trying to appear braver than he felt, Sky walked over to Chase and held the sword out in front of him. He'd never held a sword in his life, not even a wooden one.

Chase bowed to him and Sky gave a halfhearted twirl of the hand. "Can we just get on with this?"

Chase grinned, dropped into a stance, and motioned for Sky to attack.

With an exasperated sigh, Sky swung at Chase. Chase flicked his sword away, barely moving. Sky feigned right and then lunged. Chase sidestepped, thrust Sky past with his elbow, and then swatted him on the rump as he fell.

The hunters laughed and Chase took a bow, soaking up their adoration.

Sky climbed to his feet and dusted himself off. Then he likewise took a bow. T-Bone and Hands whooped it up, cheering, and Chase laughed, but the other hunters went silent, suddenly realizing he was mocking them. As the laughter died, Sky berated himself yet again: He needed allies, not enemies, but he kept making things worse.

Sky attacked and Chase parried. Then, wanting to put on a good show for his audience, Sky attacked wildly. Swing. Thrust. Hack. Dive. Hack. Roll. Hack, hack, hack. He knew it was a stupid way to fight, but he wasn't trying to win.

Chase parried everything and then stepped to the side and swatted Sky across the arm. Sky rolled past Chase's next swing, coming up behind him.

Sky swung. Chase stepped to the side.

Then Chase let loose with a series of blows that left Sky reeling. Chase gave him one final smack and Sky fell hard.

"Well, that was entertaining," Chase observed, staring down at Sky.

Morton's hunters cheered.

"Come now, Chase," Morton chortled, "it appears our 'farce,' as Winston put it, is over. There's no need to *humiliate* the boy. We'll have plenty of time for that later."

Morton's hunters laughed and cheered some more.

Chase offered Sky his hand and Sky took it.

"No hard feelings?" said Chase, sounding sincere.

Sky leaned forward so that Chase could hear him over the cheering. "I know you put the monocle in my pocket—where did you get it?"

"I'm sure I have no idea what you're talking about," Chase replied. He turned and walked away to join Morton and his hunters in their celebration and mockery.

Sky threw down his sword. He was tempted to take another bow—he'd just put on a wicked show, after all—but this time he stopped himself before he messed up his advantage.

Winston appeared, along with a worried-looking Dad, several smiling friends, and a small gathering of grim-faced hunters from Exile. Winston looked him over. "We'll have to work on your swordplay, I suppose."

And they did. For the next two hours Winston, Dad, Beau, and a few of the other Exile hunters drilled him over and over again. Even Hands and T-Bone joined in. They seemed so sincere in their efforts that Sky didn't have the heart to tell them he'd thrown the fight. He might have lost anyway—probably would have—but he hadn't even tried to win. He'd fought for a different reason entirely.

In a matter of seconds he'd moved from public enemy number one to a weak boy hardly worth noticing. For the moment, at least, he'd earned a breather from the hunters. Now he could turn his attention to more important things, like finding Alexander's blade and stopping Bedlam.

He'd come here to lose, and that's precisely what he'd done, and by losing he'd won.

CHAPTER 24

A Spy Among Us

The office door hung from a single hinge, like a loose tooth waiting for a strong belch. Warily, Sky crept into the room, watching the shadows. Bits of wood from the doorframe littered the floor immediately around the door and, farther in, Sky saw toppled bookshelves, broken furniture, and holes in the walls—artwork hanging askew or tossed upon the floor. Black, white, and gray Piebald feathers were scattered everywhere and bits of Marrowick wax clung to shattered glass fragments of the window.

"Miss Terry," Sky whispered, using Ursula's "school" name. "Are you here?"

He pulled out the note he'd gotten from Fred and double-checked it to make sure he wasn't missing anything.

BEING WATCHED. MEET IN MISS TERRY'S OFFICE AS SOON AS POSSIBLE. I HAVE SOMETHING FOR YOU.

That was it. Nothing else.

Sky stepped gingerly around the scattered books and papers. He lifted the corner of a bookshelf, peering underneath to make sure she wasn't buried. Had Ursula been in here when this had happened?

He hadn't seen her for . . . how long had it been? Certainly not since the last full moon. He'd had subs in gym class since then, though he'd never heard why and he'd been too busy to check.

He dropped the bookshelf and walked across it to get to the desk. He'd spent many hours in this office over the last year, enough hours that Ursula had actually stuck an old recliner in the corner for him. He could see it there now, lying on its side, the stuffing ripped out. Ursula was the only adult who knew he was a Changeling, and while Crystal and the others were very understanding about it all, they still didn't *understand* what it was like. But Ursula, on the other hand, was a monster like him; she understood perfectly.

Sky slipped around the desk. The drawers had been pried open, the folders and papers thrown out. He found a personal calendar on the floor and saw that she'd marked out the entire month with the word "Vacation." Sky sighed in relief. She had been gone for over a week—she couldn't have been here when this had happened. But he had to wonder: Where did a Whisper, who could change into anything over the three days of the full moon simply by biting it, go for vacation?

More important, who sent the note?

Sky looked around the room but didn't see anything obvious, nothing he could've imagined the sender of the note— whoever that was—wanting him to have.

He stood back, examining the desk. It was large and thick,

old, made of some ornamented dark wood. He knew that old desks such as this sometimes held secret compartments; Phineas had even made him build a few to see if Sky could create a compartment Phineas couldn't find.

Of course, whoever had torn apart Ursula's office probably knew about secret compartments as well. But had they had time to look?

Sky circled the desk, looking for movable parts. As he ran his hands along the surface, he noticed discoloration in a few spots, areas lighter than the rest where the lacquer had worn off from rubbing. He found six knobs, only three of which were discolored and moved when he pushed them. Next, he found two hidden latches. He clicked these and the sides of the desk popped open. Empty. Already cleaned out.

He pushed the three worn knobs and another compartment opened on the back—also cleaned out. He tried pressing the other knobs, but they either wouldn't move now that the desk was open, or pressing them had no effect.

Sky felt frustrated. He stared at the desk, imagining it as a giant trap . . . no, not a trap, an *anti*-trap: a device meant to repel rather than snare. Sky started walking through the situation in his mind. How would thieves react when they saw this desk?

First, they would start with the drawers—the obvious. If they were persistent, they would find the latches and open the sides. Most would stop there, believing they'd found the secret, but anything stored there would be a misdirection, something that looked important, but wasn't. The truly clever would keep searching. They'd find the knobs and the second compartment, which only opened after the first. They'd press the other knobs and search some more, just as Sky had, and then, finding nothing, they'd conclude they'd found everything of value and leave. But if the builder was truly clever, he'd understand the psychology of the thief, know that the thief would find those "secret" compartments, and hide the real treasure elsewhere.

A careful thief would open one drawer at a time. A thief in a hurry would open everything at once. But only someone who wasn't a thief at all wouldn't open anything.

Sky closed all the drawers and compartments.

He pressed the discolored knobs again. They locked into place and the sides popped open.

"That's not right . . . ," said Sky, closing the sides again. He stared at the knobs. Something wasn't . . . and then it occurred to him. More misdirection. Those weren't discolored by rubbing— they were discolored on purpose!

He pressed the three colored knobs that wouldn't depress before, and the knobs locked into place. Catches released and the entire desktop lifted up a smidge.

Sky pushed on a side and the desktop pivoted a few inches, revealing a narrow compartment underneath.

Inside, he found a letter and a few pictures. Sky flipped through the pictures: photos of the hunters who'd escaped the prison last year, a policeman, a bagger at the grocery store, a bowling alley manager, his parent's accountant, his parents! Some, he knew, were hunters. Others were just random people. He flipped through a few more, stopping on a picture of Mr. Dibble, his music teacher.

"Weird . . . ," said Sky. He flipped the picture over. On the back, he read: "Alistair Dibble: Tuba Lover."

"Really weird." Sky returned the picture to the stack, which he shoved in his backpack. He could find out why Ursula had these the next time he saw her. For now he needed to figure out what the note sender planned to give him and, somehow, he didn't think weird pictures of random people in Exile was it.

He pulled out a stack of letters bundled together with red yarn. He opened one, realized it was a love letter from Beau, and quickly shut it. He found several pictures tucked between the letters: Beau eating alone at a café next to a river; Beau dressed in odd clothing and riding a camel; Beau sitting alone on a mountain ridge watching the stars. And in each picture Beau didn't seem to notice the camera.

Feeling like an intruder, Sky returned the letter and pictures to the stack and retied the yarn. He slipped the bundle into his backpack, intending to return all of these things to Ursula when he found her.

Sky pulled the last letter from the compartment.

U,

Still hunting C. P and E are Slippery and in place. Give love and picture to N. Look for the Marrowick delivery on the setter in the pit between the bedposts—sponsor is unclear . . . beware. C wants it, too; watch out for Harrow Nights.

-M

Sky stared at the hastily scrawled note. This looked more promising. And, with Fred's recent run-ins with the Marrowick, it seemed like just the thing someone—whoever sent him the note—might want him to have. He stored it in his backpack to examine later.

He started to push the desktop back into place when a thought occurred to him: Could there be one more secret compartment, the place where Ursula stored her greatest treasures?

Sky examined the desk once again, searching. As he ran his hand along the side of the compartment he'd just emptied, he felt a small catch. He pulled it, and a tiny door flipped open. He reached into the opening and found another small stack of pictures . . . every one of which was of him. And they weren't just recent; they seemed to span his entire life! Sky at five at a park in Phoenix. Sky at nine eating corn on the cob. Sky at two waving at the camera.

Dozens of pictures, all of him.

Before Sky could process this latest discovery, he heard footsteps. He shoved the pictures into his backpack and slung it over his shoulder. Then he darted for the door.

"All right, thanks for the help, Miss Terry," Sky called as he left, waving behind him. He slid the door closed, holding it in place as Mr. Dibble walked up.

"Sky? What are you doing here?" asked Mr. Dibble.

"Mr. Dibble! I was just coming to find you!" said Sky, diverting Mr. Dibble back the way he came.

"You were?" said Mr. Dibble, sounding suspicious.

"Of course!" said Sky, speaking loudly to cover the sound of the door falling to the floor behind him.

Mr. Dibble glanced back, but Sky continued on, dragging

Mr. Dibble with him. "I've been . . . er . . . thinking that I'd like to get better at the tuba. Do you have time to teach me how to do the, er . . . that one thing I do poorly?"

Sky wanted to get Mr. Dibble out of there. If Mr. Dibble entered Ursula's office, he'd accuse Sky of demolishing it, and Sky didn't have time to waste. Better a quick few minutes practicing tuba with Mr. Dibble than an afternoon spent talking to teachers and police.

Probably.

"Which one thing?" said Mr. Dibble. "You do it all poorly."

"You know," Sky persisted, "the part with the buttons and all."

"The valves?" Mr. Dibble offered.

"Yeah—those!" said Sky. "So do you have time?"

"Don't you have class right now?" asked Mr. Dibble.

"Canceled," said Sky.

"That doesn't happen," said Mr. Dibble. "Ever."

Sky smiled nervously.

"You missed my class this morning," Mr. Dibble pointed out. "And homecoming is tonight. You are planning to play, aren't you?"

"Uh . . ."

"Your fellow bandmates are counting on you," Mr. Dibble continued. "You're not thinking of letting them down, are you?"

"Er . . ."

"Sky, clearly you're hoping to use me as an excuse to miss your next class," said Mr. Dibble. "I'm more than willing to help you. Nothing is more important than the tuba, after all. But first, you must help me. Can I count on you tonight?"

"Ah . . . sure," Sky lied. He wanted to support his bandmates and Mr. Dibble—even if he did hate the tuba—but he suspected he would be busy with Bedlam's army tonight. "Now can we go?"

"Well, I did have an appointment with Miss Terry. Perhaps if I told her . . . ," said Mr. Dibble, starting to turn back.

"Already canceled," said Sky, steering Mr. Dibble down the hall.

"Really?" asked Mr. Dibble.

"No," said Sky. "But she'll understand. Fifteen minutes, Mr. Dibble. That's all I'm asking for. Fifteen minutes, and my tuba will sing your praises."

"I'd like to hear your tuba sing *anything*," said Mr. Dibble.

"Great!" Sky exclaimed. "To the tuba room!"

Mr. Dibble sighed heavily and rubbed his temples.

Ursula's door gave one final crash as the last hinge broke free. Sky gave a nervous laugh, and then they were around the corner, heading for the music room.

CHAPTER 15
Angry Ostriches & Cockroach Eyebrows

That is quite possibly the worst tuba playing I have ever heard," said Mr. Dibble.

Discordant noise wafted through the band room like acidic vapor, slowly eating away at Sky's ears; the fact that he was causing it didn't make it any less acidic. Mr. Dibble stood at Sky's shoulder, watching him strangle his tuba. But no matter how much Sky tightened his fingers, he couldn't seem to kill it. Ignoring Mr. Dibble's criticism, Sky continued pumping his fingers and blowing into the mouthpiece, his eyes fixed on the clock.

Once he'd committed, he couldn't think of a good excuse to back out.

"It sounds like an angry ostrich searching for its babies," Mr. Dibble continued. "What are we going to do with you, Sky?"

The bell rang and Sky sighed in relief as he began putting away his tuba.

"Sorry, Mr. Dibble," said Sky. "I'll practice more. I've just been sort of busy lately."

"You're *always* busy," said Mr. Dibble. "How am I supposed to give you first seat at the homecoming game if you keep playing like that?"

"I don't know," said Sky. "Maybe because I'm the only tuba player in Exile? To be honest, I don't really care."

"Don't settle for mediocrity," Mr. Dibble retorted.

"I don't settle for it," said Sky. "It settles for me."

Mr. Dibble snorted and then gave Sky a disappointed shake of the head.

Sky put his tuba away with the other instruments. He had to get out of there. Fast. He'd wasted enough time. He needed to find Alexander's blade, not to mention that he had a riddle from a bird to solve.

"The janitor will transport the instruments to the field later," said Mr. Dibble. "Assuming, of course, the fool can remember where it is. Hopefully, we won't get a repeat of last year when he lost Eugene's trumpet and the school had to pay to replace it."

Sky stopped what he was doing. He felt a sudden surge of anger. "His name's Nikola," he growled, "and he's not a fool."

"Whose name is what?" Mr. Dibble asked, seemingly distracted as he sorted through a stack of sheet music.

"The janitor," Sky snapped. "His name is Nikola—don't make fun of him."

Mr. Dibble stopped what he was doing and examined Sky, a curious expression on his face. Then his lip curled in the slightest hint of a smirk. "My apologies. I didn't realize the two of you were on a first-name basis."

Sky snatched his backpack. "We are." He headed for the door. "I'll be back this afternoon."

"Why? We're not meeting here—we're meeting on the field this evening before the game," said Mr. Dibble, looking confused.

Sky paused at the door. "Nikola will need help moving the instruments." And then he walked out, leaving behind a baffled Mr. Dibble. Sky knew it was stupid. Amidst all the horrible things happening around him, helping Nikola move a bunch of instruments was not the brightest idea. But once upon a time, when Sky was a baby and couldn't protect himself, Nikola had guarded him, and lost everything as a result. Now it was time for Sky to return the favor, even if the best he could do was tell off a snarky teacher and move a few instruments. And if Bedlam's army showed up, or Morton finally decided the time was right to kill Sky, then so be it. Nikola had put his life on the line for Sky; how could Sky do any less?

Up ahead, Sky spotted Hannah talking to Derek by his locker.

"Have you seen T-Bone or Hands around?" Sky asked when he reached them. It was only after he asked that he noticed Hannah was frowning.

"Do I look like a member of the T-Bone and Hands fan club?" Hannah retorted.

"They have a fan club?" Sky asked. "Always the last to know."

Derek stared at Sky, brows creased.

"Hey, Derek," said Sky.

"Sorry, do I know you?" said Derek.

Sky started to laugh, and then he realized that Derek was serious.

"Oh, er . . . that's not good," Sky opined.

"No. It's not," said Hannah tartly.

"What are you two talking about?" Derek asked, looking flustered. "Do I have something in my eyebrows?"

Derek began weeding his thick blond eyebrows like a monkey looking for bugs.

"There's nothing in your eyebrows Derek," said Hannah. "They're as gorgeous as ever." She sighed.

"That's—that's good to know," Derek stumbled, sounding confused. "Sometimes, with the chlorine buildup in the pool, and the cockroach problem . . . little buggers can swim fast . . . like . . . like an arrow . . ." Derek shook his head, lost in thought. "Well, I'd best be running along," he said cheerfully, as if he hadn't just rambled on about having cockroaches in his eyebrows.

Derek shut his locker, gave Hannah a winning smile, ignored Sky completely, and walked off down the hall.

"Why does he have to have such gorgeous eyebrows?" Hannah muttered, watching Derek leave, not looking at his eyebrows at all, as far as Sky could tell.

"*Cockroach* eyebrows, in case you weren't listening. And they are quite large," said Sky. "Almost *too* large . . . Are you certain he's human?"

"He doesn't even remember we were dating," Hannah muttered. She spun around and began walking in the opposite direction. Sky followed.

"He had the nerve to ask me out all over again. Can you believe that?" Hannah said, sounding affronted.

"Shocking," said Sky with feigned sympathy. "Of course, you did wipe his memory."

"I know," said Hannah wistfully. "He's forgotten last night

and everything he ever knew about anyone at our house. He's forgotten our first kiss. And our second one. And the one under the bleachers—"

"I get the idea," Sky cut in. "The fish-lipped cockroach boy has forgotten you."

"This is all *your fault*, you know," said Hannah accusingly. "If you hadn't dragged that corpse in . . ."

"She's not a corpse," said Sky, "she's just life challenged. And I don't see how this is my fault. I couldn't just leave her there."

"You shouldn't have been there in the first place! What kind of person wanders a graveyard dragging corpses around on their birthday? Tell me!" Hannah exclaimed.

A few passing students glanced their way.

"Maybe we should talk about this at home," said Sky.

"My life used to be so *normal*," said Hannah, hanging her head. "Cheerleading practice. Boys chasing me. Now I've got creatures of the night chasing me, and none of them is the least bit attractive."

"Normal. Right. Well, maybe not all of us have that luxury," said Sky darkly.

"What's that supposed to mean?" asked Hannah, apparently catching his tone.

"Nothing," said Sky, regretting he'd said anything. Now wasn't the time for a heart-to-heart about his abnormality. "Just forget it. So have you seen T-Bone and Hands or not?"

"In the commons, talking to their *bros*, no doubt," said Hannah. "But the bell's about to ring—they'll be on their way to class by now."

"Since when do football players go to class?" Sky asked.

"Good point," Hannah replied. "Of course, since when do you?"

"Touché. Maybe I should try out for the football team."

Hannah laughed. "Now *that* would be a disaster. It would be like Tick trying out for cheerleading, which, unlike football, is actually hard. Just try doubling down from a chin-chin at full extension. I'm sorry—*quarterback*? Honestly, how hard can it be? No offense."

"No offense? It's *all* offense when you're quarterback," Sky quipped.

Hannah gave a well-deserved groan. "Sorry, Sky—didn't mean to put you two rungs below a cheerleader in the pecking order. But that pun more than makes up for my insult. Is he still following us?"

"What? Who?" said Sky, looking around, suddenly nervous.

"Tick," said Hannah.

Sky looked over his shoulder and spotted Tick skulking some distance behind them.

"T-BONE AND HANDS WENT TO THE LIBRARY!" Tick yelled, drawing looks. "THEY WANTED ME TO TELL YOU TO MEET THEM IN SPECIAL COLLECTIONS!"

"Er. Thanks!" Sky called back.

"I NEVER GO THERE!" Tick continued, yelling far louder than he needed to. "TOO DARK! AND I THINK THERE ARE SPIDERS! OR MAYBE DUST BUNNIES WITH LEGS! ARE THOSE DANGEROUS AT ALL, DO YOU THINK?"

"He's been following us since that last intersection," said Hannah, not bothering to keep her voice down. "He's always trying to carry my books and walk me to class! HE DOESN'T REALIZE HOW ANNOYING THAT IS!" she added loudly.

"I CAN'T *NOT* WALK YOU TO CLASS!" Tick yelled back. "WE HAVE THE SAME CLASS AND THIS IS THE ONLY HALLWAY TO IT!"

Sky felt distinctly uncomfortable. Everyone was watching Tick and Hannah and whispering behind their notebooks. Sky wanted to bury his head. When presented with a choice between facing monsters or Hannah's social life, he'd take monsters any day.

"Hmpf," Hannah harrumphed. "Likely story."

"Uh, I think this is where I take my leave," said Sky.

"Oh. All right, then," said Hannah, sounding surprised.

Sky fled up the hallway, speed walking.

"Let me know if you need a ride home later!" Hannah called after him.

"Lovely day, think I'll walk!" Sky yelled back, fearing her driving as much as her social life.

"But it's raining outside!" Hannah replied.

"Like the rain! Cleans the pores!" Sky retorted, quickening his pace.

"When it rains, *it* pours—it doesn't clean your pores!" Hannah corrected.

"Good to know! Keep that in mind when I get dirty pores!" Sky yelled, finally turning the corner.

He glanced out a window as he shuffled past. Rain fell in sheets thick as curtains . . . or maybe curtains thick as sheets. Either way, it was a lot of rain, and he'd just committed to helping Nikola move instruments later that afternoon.

"Perfect," he muttered.

CHAPTER 16
Dedications, Revelations & Lies

Sky found T-Bone and Hands huddled around a small table, looking at books beneath a sputtering incandescent bulb.

If possible, special collections looked even messier than last time he'd visited, and it was just as big, if not bigger—several times larger than the library itself—which was just messed up.

Hands glanced up at him, a broad grin on his face. "Nice Valentine's Day shirt. I didn't realize you could fit so many pink hearts on a shirt that small. Weren't you wearing an ugly hoodie this morning?"

"I'm not a shifter, if that's what you're asking," Sky retorted.

"I have no doubt you're the real Sky," said Hands. "Shifters have too much self-respect to wear a shirt like that. Or possibly not enough. . . ."

Sky sighed. He pulled off his backpack, set it on the table, and then flopped into a chair. "So have you figured out where we can find Alexander's blade, or have you simply been scanning fashion catalogs?"

"Sure, we know where to find it," T-Bone replied.

"You do?" Sky asked.

"No," Hands admitted. "But we've learned a bit more about it, and we know where it was supposed to be."

"Where?"

"Ah, that answer requires a story," Hands said, seemingly enjoying himself. "You see, centuries ago, Alexander and Solomon went to fight the Arkhon—just two forlorn heroes against an unstoppable enemy. Alone. With no one and nothing to accompany them save their own tragic destinies."

"Can you just skip to what happened?" Sky asked.

Before Hands could continue, T-Bone jumped in. "They fought the Arkhon, something went wrong—we don't know what—and only Alexander came back. He told everyone that Solomon had died at the Arkhon's hands. A short time after, Alexander was found dead in his study, stabbed through his neck with his own shimmering blade."

"You think Solomon did it?" Sky asked, sitting up straighter. "You think Solomon could have the blade?" His stomach sank as he considered the possibility. If Solomon had the blade, then there was no way to recover it short of opening the prison.

"We thought of that," said T-Bone. "But more digging showed us that Solomon was trapped at the time. He couldn't have done it, not personally."

"So who killed Alexander, then? And where is the blade?" Sky asked.

"We don't know who killed Alexander. It looks like the

hunters never figured it out," said Hands. "After his death Alexander and his rusted blade were buried in the Grove of the Fallen. Every record we can find points to the Grove."

"Well, they're not there now," said Sky, "and the only clue is that riddle on the coffin lid: 'With Hunter's Mark the buried dead shall shimmering blade hold in my stead.'"

"It makes it sound like someone with a Hunter's Mark could get the blade by burying themselves in the coffin," said Hands, looking pointedly at Sky.

"I know," Sky replied. "That's what I'm afraid of. But if the blade was buried with Alexander, then who left the riddle? And wouldn't the blade still be there? It has to mean something else."

"Are you sure you don't just *want* it to mean something else?" T-Bone asked.

Sky didn't reply. He'd seen enough dead bodies in the Sleeping Lands to last a lifetime; he had no desire to join them by burying himself alive.

"The weird part of it all is that several hunters claimed to have seen Alexander walking out of his study moments before they found the body," said Hands.

"I think I have an answer to that one." T-Bone slid a book across the table.

Sky glanced at the title. "*Botany Most Botanical*? Don't think I've read this." He opened the cover and found the dedication:

To my father, who took me in when no one else would, and to Solomon Rose, may he find in death the answers he lost in life.

"It's Alexander Drake's last book," said T-Bone. "Unfinished. It simply ends in the middle of a formula for making something called Slippery Wick Brew."

Sky nodded. "I've heard of it before. In *The Slippery Wick of Windenshum*, Alexander uses it to change his appearance in the Mountains of Moldy Foreboding"—Hands chuckled—"to stop a renegade hunter who's eating up all their cabbages."

"Cabbages? Seriously?" said Hands.

Sky shrugged. "The hunter liked his cabbage; what can I say? Anyway, Alexander befriends a Marrowick near the town, and the creature teaches him to create a beverage out of bits of Marrowick wax, chaotic Gloom, and other stuff that allows him to change his appearance: the Slippery Wick Brew."

"You mean the drink lets you shift like a Whisper?" T-Bone asked.

"Hardly," Sky replied, "it's not a true shift. Whisper *become* the creature they shift into over the three days of the full moon, any creature they taste minus the memories. And then, of course, they're stuck that way until the next full moon unless they want to risk turning into a mindless Gloom. Slippery Wick, on the other hand, only allowed Alexander to move his fat around."

"What good is that?" Hands asked.

"Well, he could change his surface appearance," Sky said. "He could make his nose bigger, his cheeks hollower, or even grow an inch by giving himself a fat head. That, plus a little hair dye, and he could look like just about anyone. It couldn't make you stronger or change your bones or give you tentacles, for example."

"Too bad," said Hands. "I've been thinking of growing me some tentacles." Hands paused and then shook his head, seemingly amazed. "But seriously, let me get this straight: We have shifters that can look like hunters; we have Bedlam who can possess hunters; and now we have hunters who can look like other hunters? Is that about right?"

"Don't forget Solomon Rose—a hunter who took over a monster's body and booted out the monster," T-Bone added. "The moral here is: Always ask for ID."

"No kidding," said Hands. "Since last year, I just sort of assume nobody is who they say they are and go from there."

"You guys are missing 'hunters and monsters that become the same person the moment they're Changed,'" Sky said quietly.

They both looked at him.

"Right," said Hands. "Well, that goes without saying. The point here is that whoever killed Drake could've taken the Slippery Wick Brew and made himself look like Alexander so he or she could escape unnoticed. That would explain how all those hunters saw Alexander leave his study moments after his death."

"Let's ignore all the impostors and everything else for the moment," said Sky. "Right now the only thing that matters is Alexander's blade. What else did you find out?"

T-Bone closed *Botany Most Botanical* and slid it to the side, grabbing another book from his stack. "This is *The Shimmering Blade of Aranoth*."

Sky perked up. He'd never heard of Aranoth before, and the book sounded promising.

"Aranoth was a hunter during the War of Legend—you're familiar with that, right?" T-Bone asked.

Sky nodded. "Somewhat. Most of the stories Phineas gave me were from the time of Solomon and Alexander, or thereabouts—the time of the Edgewalker Wars. The War of Legend was much earlier, a thousand years or more. I did some research a while back. To be honest, I couldn't find much."

"Neither could we," T-Bone admitted. "But we found enough. Legend was an unbelievable horror, a big monster. Scared everything. He nearly destroyed the world, like, the actual planet. The First Hunter formed the Hunters of Legend to stop him. Monster turned against monster, hunter against hunter, and Legend's five children—Bedlam, Vulpine, Erachnus, Mar, and the Arkhon—fought first for him, and then against him until eventually Legend was thrown down and his power broken. Does that about cover it?"

"More than I found," said Sky, who didn't know anything about Vulpine, Erachnus, or Mar, even though he'd heard their names on occasion. He'd also figured out that the statue of the woman standing over Solomon in the Grove of the Fallen was the First Hunter, his ancestor, according to Chase. He tried to imagine Phineas as the "consort" to such a woman, as Morton had claimed. If Phineas was married to the First Hunter, did that mean Sky was actually descended from Phineas? Had Mom and Dad simply told Sky that Phineas was his uncle to stop him from asking awkward questions? Whatever the case, if Phineas was married to the First Hunter, Sky really, really hoped her statue wasn't built to scale.

"So, at one point, Bedlam was a good guy?" Sky asked.

T-Bone shrugged. "He helped the hunters defeat his father, but who knows why he did it? For all we know, he could've wanted to replace him."

Sky nodded, but he wasn't convinced. Every story he'd ever

read about Bedlam made him look like a villain, but these stories were written by the same people who'd tried to kill him last night, the same people who thought Solomon Rose was a hero. If Sky could just talk with Bedlam . . . Of course, to do that he'd have to find him first.

"The shimmering blades were created during the War of Legend, one for each of the thirteen original hunters, including Phineas, Morton, and Winston, among others," said Hands. "*The Shimmering Blade of Aranoth* calls the blades 'sticky.'"

"What's that supposed to mean?" asked Sky.

"Do you remember what Phineas told you about black rutabagas?" asked T-Bone.

Sky nodded. "Take a rutabaga, tie a Barrow Hag's nose hair around it, and bury it under a harvest moon to get a black rutabaga. Eat it, and you can jump as high as a Barrow Hag for a time, with some uncomfortable side effects."

"Exactly," said T-Bone. "The thing is, if you stab a black rutabaga with a shimmering blade, the blade will eat it."

"Like, literally? 'Cause that's kind of gross," said Sky.

"Not literally," T-Bone snapped. "It absorbs the important bits and converts them into tiny shimmering gems—gems the hunter can use later. The more gems, the more powerful the blade."

"Beats carrying around a bunch of black rutabagas, I guess," said Sky. "Or barrow weed, or Slippery Wick, or DNA samples for shifters . . . Okay, I'm beginning to see its usefulness."

Hands nodded. "The shimmering blade is a storehouse for a hunter's most closely held secrets. Each blade is unique. That's why Morton can't use his own blade to free Bedlam."

"Or keep him trapped forever," Sky added. "Not to mention how many other secrets it must hold, tricks even Morton hasn't discovered. Alexander was probably the greatest botanist the world has ever seen."

"But first Morton would have to claim the blade," said T-Bone. "Meaning the current owner would have to give it to him, or Morton would have to kill him and take it."

"So if Bedlam wanted to free himself from the Chrysalis prison, he'd need four things," said Sky. "First, the blade. Second, ownership. Third, his body. And fourth, he'd need to know what made Alexander's blade unique—what's the secret ingredient within it that can free Bedlam?"

"Not to complicate matters, but it's also possible that there's nothing hidden within," Hands pointed out. "Those gems can be removed from the blade at any time. Alexander may have taken out the secret ingredient to make it harder for someone to free Bedlam."

Sky shook his head. "Let's find the blade first and worry about the rest later."

Sky closed *The Shimmering Blade of Aranoth* and slid it back to T-Bone.

"There's one more thing to consider, something that might lead us to the blade." Sky opened his backpack and withdrew the letter he'd taken from Ursula's office. "Someone raided Ursula's office today—she's safe, by the way, on vacation somewhere—but I found this in her desk." He set the note on the table. "I think I know what some of this means, but not all. Maybe we can fill in the blanks."

Sky looked over the letter:

U,

Still hunting C. P and E are Slippery and in place. Give love and picture to N. Look for the Marrowick delivery on the setter in the pit between the bedposts—sponsor is unclear . . . beware. C wants it, too; watch out for Harrow Wights.

-M

On his paper, Sky took his best guess and wrote:

Ursula,

Still hunTing Cassandra. Phineas and Errand are Slippery and in place. Give love and picTure To Nikola. Look for The Marrowick delivery on The seTTer in The piT beTween The bedposTs—sponsor is unclear (i.e., I don'T know who The Marrowick is working for or why They're giving us The delivery) . . . beware. Cassandra wanTs iT, Too; waTch ouT for Harrow WighTs (children of Bedlam ThaT look human, buT can bursT inTo flame, Throw molTen meTal, and develop hardened armor as They cool).

-Malvidia? MorTon?

"You think Phineas is alive?" Hands asked.

"Morton does, and I've got suspicions of my own as well, especially if Phineas drank Slippery Wick Brew," said Sky. "And Errand . . ."

He filled them in on his dream from the previous night.

"We don't know anything for sure," said Sky. "I'm not going to get my hopes up again. Maybe P is someone else—this is all guesswork; I'm just filling in puzzle pieces. But until we know more, P is Phineas. And I think N is Nikola, the janitor."

"The janitor?" Hands asked.

"Long story," Sky replied, not wanting to go into all the details, "but basically, I ran into him last night and he had half a picture—a woman who looked familiar. He dropped it before he ran off. Here, I've still got it."

Sky pulled out the picture of the dark-haired woman and showed them.

"Never seen her before," said T-Bone.

"Me neither," Hands added.

Sky stared at it . . . Where had he seen her? He put the picture away. "Well, apparently it was supposed to jog some memory in Nikola. He's a former hunter and he helped Phineas build the prison. It could be important."

"And M?" said T-Bone. "I don't see how M could be Malvidia or Morton. Malvidia doesn't know Ursula lives in Exile, and Morton wouldn't help anyone except, apparently, Solomon Rose."

Sky took a deep breath. One crisis at a time.

"Well, 'on the setter in the pit between the bedposts' is talking about the bowling alley," Hands observed.

"It is?" Sky asked.

"Yep. It's bowling slang: setter—i.e. pinsetters in the pit; between the bedposts, a seven-ten split," said Hands. "Whatever the Marrowick delivered, it's at the bowling alley—or was—and it's probably sitting on the pinsetter for lane eight or nine."

"The bowling alley again, huh? Well, I guess it's a start; we know the Marrowick was there, after all, and it didn't have anything with it when it left," T-Bone stated grudgingly, apparently wishing, as Sky did, that they had more to go on.

Sky couldn't imagine why the Marrowick would have the blade or why it would leave it at the bowling alley for Ursula, but clearly the Marrowick was wrapped up in all this somehow.

He tapped his finger against the table as he considered their options. "All right," he said finally, "it sounds like the bowling alley is our best lead to finding the blade. How about if we meet there in an hour?"

"An hour? Why not just go there now?" T-Bone asked.

Sky hesitated, not wanting to tell them about his promise to help Nikola out of fear they wouldn't understand. "I've got something to do—nothing important; just personal stuff. Besides, it'll take an hour to retrieve our gear and gather Crystal and Andrew; you two don't need me for that anyway."

T-Bone nodded slowly, his eyes full of suspicion. "Okay . . . we'll meet you in the sewer near the bowling alley in an hour, then."

"Good," said Sky. "The blade is the strongest piece on the board right now. Whoever controls it controls Exile's future, for better or worse. We have to find it before Morton and Bedlam."

CHAPTER 17
Tryouts of Doom

The sensation of falling is not unlike that of climbing, only in the opposite direction and with a much more disappointing end.

As Sky watched Felicity Anne Finley tumble toward the earth, he couldn't help but contemplate the strange complexities of girls and gravitational forces.

Last year Felicity had just been a girl trying to help him recover his pocket watch, using a kiss as a distraction. But now she was something else . . . something horrible . . .

"Nice dismount, Felicity! Keep those elbows tucked!" yelled Hannah as she and another cheerleader caught Felicity in their arms and set her on the ground.

Sky sighed. A cheerleader. Honestly.

"Trying out for the team?" asked a voice behind him as he lugged a saxophone up the bleachers.

Turning, he found Chase Shroud standing at the bottom of the steps, eating a large, soggy sausage.

"Do I look like I'm trying out?" Sky snapped. "Besides, try-outs were two months ago."

"Ah, but there's always room for talent," said Chase, taking a big bite of sausage. "Sorry, I'm being rude," Chase continued, mouth full. "Care for a bite?" Chase held out the sausage, offering it to Sky.

"No. Thanks," said Sky, watching streams of grease drip past the rain-soaked bun and onto the bleachers. "You realize your sausage is getting wet, right? From the rain?"

"If we waited for the rain to stop in England, we'd never eat sausage." Chase took another big bite and smiled through the resulting mustard-stache. "You're not still sore I trounced you this morning, are you?"

"No—should I be?" Sky headed back down the steps toward Nikola's instrument-filled shopping cart. They'd had to make a few trips, and it wasn't the smoothest ride, but it'd helped. He glanced around until he spotted Nikola carefully rearranging the instruments into geometric patterns, and completely messing up Mr. Dibble's seating arrangement. Sky sighed. He'd have to fix it. Again.

He'd tried to strike up a conversation with Nikola several times, to thank him for what he'd done, but Nikola hadn't said a word.

At least he wasn't on the field with Andrew and his step-whatevers, Jasmine and Ermine. Hannah had apparently let slip that Andrew was at the manor with Crystal, and Jasmine and Ermine had swooped in and snatched him up to do their dirty work, threatening to tell their mother that he was playing hooky if he didn't do everything they told him to. Andrew held their pom-poms while they formed a human pyramid with the other cheerleaders and bossed him around with fake Shakespeare lines—evidently their required reading for English class.

"Drop the pom and pom once more, dear friend, and to the breach with you and your dumb head!" yelled Jasmine as Andrew dropped a pom-pom.

"Up and up you go and with breaking chords, you fall with whole discord and bottom breaks!" Ermine chirped as several cheerleaders tackled Andrew and started hoisting him to the top of the pyramid against his will.

"That's horrible! It doesn't even make sense!" Andrew exclaimed, struggling to break free. "Wait, was that a flatulence joke?"

Sky just shook his head. He felt bad for Andrew, but he couldn't help him at the moment, not until he was finished. Then they could make good their escape and meet up with the others in the sewer near the bowling alley.

"Sure you wouldn't like a bite?" Chase offered again.

"No. Really. I'd better not," said Sky, watching in disgust as Chase took another huge bite.

"Suit yourself," said Chase, shrugging, his mouth full of food. "Nothing like a good banger."

"I'll take your word for it," said Sky. "Where did you get that anyway?"

"Made it," said Chase. "In London we slaughter our own sheep."

"Really?"

"Just taking the mick, mate," Chase replied.

"Oh. Right." Sky had no idea if that was good or bad. "Did you want something, Chase, or did you just come to lie to me some more?" he said, lugging up another instrument.

"Morton asked me to keep you company."

"You mean he wants you to watch me in case I find the blade," Sky retorted.

Chase grinned. "Sure you wouldn't care for a bite?"

Someone screamed on the field—a wild, feral sound.

Sky jerked his head around expecting some horror to come crawling out of the earth. Instead, he saw the football coach, Coach Blackburn, waving his clipboard and screaming at the top of his lungs as he followed Tick across the field. Tick looked exhausted and fed up with practice.

Squid and Lazy Eye, looking perplexed, followed a few steps behind the coach.

"Well," said Chase, "this looks interesting. You know, I've always secretly fancied American football."

Coach Blackburn stopped midfield and threw down his clipboard. Tick kept walking, removing his pads as he marched toward the cheerleading mats.

Sky smiled. It seemed like small pleasures were the only pleasures he got these days. He'd learned to take advantage of them whenever he could, and this particular pleasure, however small, was going to be very pleasurable indeed.

Hannah glanced up, noticing Tick for the first time, a look of absolute dismay crossing her face. Tick stopped in front of Hannah, and the cheerleading squad went silent.

Hannah held her breath.

"I'm here to try ou—"

"No!" Hannah shouted, cutting him off. "Tryouts ended two months ago!"

"Come on, let him try," said Felicity, coming to Tick's defense. "It's not like you didn't get your own special tryout last year."

"The siren's lips call truthful sounds ashore," said Jasmine, smirking.

"I—" Hannah started, but Tick turned away, jaw set, and walked toward Jasmine and Ermine, who tittered as he approached.

"I was just joking in the hall!" Hannah cried. "I'm sure quarterback's a very challenging position! Why don't you go back to it? *This isn't putting you in my good graces!*"

Tick grabbed Jasmine and raised her above his head. Jasmine balanced on his hands on one leg, holding the other leg out.

"Well, that's fine and all but—" Hannah began.

Tick launched Jasmine into the air. She flew upward, kicking out in splits before landing in Tick's outstretched arms. Jasmine put her arms around his neck and kissed him on the cheek, but Tick had eyes only for Hannah.

Sky might have been seeing things, but he could have sworn Hannah's cheeks turned a deeper shade of pink.

"That's impressive, but—"

Tick set Jasmine down, nearly dropping her. She stumbled to her feet, glaring, but Tick had already started backing away to the far side of the mat. He took a breath and then started running. He planted his hands, becoming a blur of spins and flips, twists and turns—a symphony of incomprehensible motion—coming to a perfect stop in front of Hannah, his chest heaving.

"I—"

Before Hannah could finish, Lazy Eye and Squid tackled Tick and dragged him back across the field, gathering his pads as they went. Tick kicked and screamed about wanting to be a cheerleader—clearly he had snapped—but Squid and Lazy Eye didn't let go.

Hannah watched silently as Coach Blackburn berated Tick and Tick yelled back, refusing to play tonight unless the coach called off practice and let them rest. Tick threatened to go back to the cheerleaders again. Coach Blackburn finally relented, and the players headed for the showers.

As the last player left the field, Hannah turned back to the cheerleaders, most of whom were smirking at her. "Practice is over!" she yelled.

Sky smiled. Small pleasures.

"That's quite a show," said Chase, finishing off his sausage. "I think your friend's given you the slip."

Sky glanced down and saw Andrew still on the field.

"Not him, the other guy," said Chase, pointing at the instruments.

Nikola was gone.

And he had taken Sky's tuba.

CHAPTER 18
Friends of Mystery

T-Bone lifted Sky up so he could see through the sewer grate. Rain runoff streamed through, splashing them both, but Sky had a clear view of the back of the bowling alley.

"They've got it taped off—crime scene," Sky said. "Looks like a new back door, too." Sky could hear music thumping. "Sounds like they're open. Okay. Set me back down."

T-Bone lowered Sky.

Sky brushed water from his clothes. It'd taken him a while to unload the rest of the instruments and get rid of Chase, and still more time to get here with Andrew. He'd never found Nikola, though at one point, he'd caught a glimpse of him heading north with his checkered blanket and Sky's stolen tuba. By the time Sky reached the spot, Nikola had disappeared, leaving absolutely no sign of his passing. He hoped Nikola wasn't doing anything unseemly with his tuba, such as using it to bake urinal cakes.

"Back door's not an option," said Sky. "Any other ideas?"

Nobody said anything.

"Well, we have to get in there," said Crystal. "If we can't use the back door, maybe we should go through the front."

"Andrew and I can go in; we're not suited up yet," said Sky.

"No good," said Hands. "Andrew comes here too often for disco night."

"I'm a jive machine," said Andrew, grinning.

"It's true," said Hands. "Andrew can groove like nobody's business and still hit the pins. He'd be recognized, as would I. If something happens in there, we don't want it traced back to us."

Crystal looked thoughtful. "All right, Sky will come with me. You three wait here. Andrew, get suited up. If anything happens, come in and get us. The note warned of Harrow Wights. I don't expect anything would attack us with people around, but you never know."

While Andrew suited up and Crystal suited down, Sky sifted through the duffel bag that held his gear. In the bottom, he found three poorly wrapped presents. He pulled the top one out and shook it. "What's this?"

T-Bone glanced over. "Presents. We're not singing."

"I'll sing," Hands offered.

"We're *not* singing," T-Bone stated again.

Sky shook the first one. "A scarf?" he guessed.

"Open it," said T-Bone. "It's from all of us—Beau, too. We couldn't have done it without his mad metallurgy skills."

Sky opened it. Inside, he found a large circular mint tin. "Is this a hint or something?"

T-Bone took the mint tin and slid his hand through a small

metal handle welded to the bottom. He squeezed the handle and the lid flipped open. A piece of material exploded out and unfolded in the blink of an eye, locking into a pearl-tinted transparent shield about four feet across.

"Ah . . . very nice," Sky lied. "A cloth shield. Very useful."

T-Bone smiled. "Andrew, the matches please."

"Of course, oh bossy one," said Andrew, pulling a match-book from his pocket and lighting a match. He held it next to the smoky, transparent material and put his hand on the material opposite the match.

"Impervious to fire." Hands threw a rock and T-Bone deflected it effortlessly. "Impervious to damage." T-Bone pivoted and threw the shield like a frisbee. It shot into the stone wall of the sewer, sinking to the tin. "And very, very sharp."

"That seems dangerous," said Sky, looking at the sharp edges and imagining himself with a missing head.

"It is," said T-Bone as he ripped the tin out of the sewer wall. "Push the handle here with your thumb and it'll fold the edges a bit—take off the sting."

T-Bone squeezed the grip and the shield collapsed back into the mint tin, the lid flapping shut behind it. "After that, lock it up. We call it the 'Tin.'" He twisted the handle and popped it off. Then he tossed both the Tin and the handle to Sky.

"We wouldn't want anyone chopping their fingers off," said T-Bone, grinning. "We've been working on this for months, but that letter you found warned of Harrow Wights nearby. Hands and I did some research—those things burst into flame. We figured it was best to get you the Tin now. There's also a new cloak waiting for you when you get back. We wove in some of the same materials we used on the Tins, so it's now resistant to fire and damage as well—not impervious, like the Tins, but much better than they were."

"Er . . . thanks," said Sky, impressed. "Much cooler than a cloth shield."

"Wait until you see mine," said Hands, tossing Sky the next present.

Sky caught it with as much trepidation as he'd caught the decapitating shield.

"This one's just from Hands," Crystal clarified. T-Bone and Andrew nodded vigorously.

When the present didn't explode, Sky opened it. Inside, he found two oven mitts embroidered with characters from Hands's favorite book series: *Embrace of the Vampire*. "Er . . . let me guess . . . These are loaded with sleeping darts that shoot through the fingertips?"

"No. But that's a good idea," said Hands. "Those are oven mitts. They're for taking hot things out of ovens. For baking cakes and stuff."

"Ah, okay . . . ," said Sky, "thanks."

"No prob," said Hands, smirking at some joke Sky couldn't begin to fathom.

"You've got some serious issues to work through, Hands, you know that?" said T-Bone, shaking his head.

Hands laughed.

Sky tossed the oven mitts in the bag and started to open the last present.

"This one's from me," said Crystal. "Sort of."

Sky ripped off the last bit of paper and found one of Uncle Phineas's old coats.

"T-Bone and Hands mentioned your Valentine's Day shirt," said Crystal, smirking. "Thought you could use a coat to hide those pretty pink hearts. Plus, it's kind of cold out and the coat has lots of pockets for your stuff. I found this one in an old bedroom at the manor. Good enough, you think?"

"I could kiss you right now . . . ," said Sky, staring at the coat.

"I'd rather you not," Crystal stated flatly.

Sky glanced up. "What? Oh . . . I was talking to the coat."

Crystal frowned.

"Not that I wouldn't!" Sky hurriedly added.

Crystal's frown deepened.

T-Bone and Hands laughed. Andrew looked at the ceiling.

"I mean . . . you know . . . or would," Sky stumbled. "But, that is to say, I'm very appreciative and—"

"Are you done yet?" Crystal cut in.

"Very," said Sky.

"Good. Let's go, then," Crystal snapped.

Sky put on the coat and shoved a few canisters of Fog and Jumper fuel into his pockets. Crystal had apparently spent part of the day, when she wasn't watching over her mom, refilling and repairing their equipment, because the canisters were full.

Crystal and Sky exited the sewers and made their way around to the front. Sky pushed on the door and found it locked.

They peeked through the windows. The lights were on, music was playing, and they could see people moving around inside.

"That's weird," said Crystal.

Sky tapped on the glass.

The door cracked open and a woman poked her head out.

She was old—wretchedly old—with saggy wrinkled skin that was caked in a thick, almost orange makeup. Long wisps of white hair, like cotton filaments, fluttered from her head, struggling to escape the horror that was her mole-speckled scalp. Despite her apparent age, her eyes were all fire.

"What do you want?" the woman asked.

"We just, ah . . . ," Sky started.

"If you're looking to bowl, you should know we're closed," the woman cut in.

"Oh," said Sky. "What are all those people doing, then?"

The woman glanced over her shoulder, looking at the crowded bowling alley.

"I don't see how that's any of your business," the woman replied tartly.

"What my brother means to say is that we were here a few nights ago and he left his shoes behind—wore the completely wrong shoes home," said Crystal, rustling through her backpack. She pulled out a very worn pair of bowling shoes. Sky tried to hide his astonishment at her preparation. "We'd like to return these and search your lost and found, if we could."

The woman wrinkled her brow. "I don't know . . ."

"There you two are!" a voice snapped behind them. Sky turned and saw a familiar-looking woman with charcoal hair marching toward them, but he couldn't place her. "What's taking you so long?"

"I . . . ," Sky began, but the woman reached them and put her arms protectively around him and Crystal.

"Were my instructions unclear, children?" The newcomer raised an eyebrow, clearly encouraging them to play along. "Perhaps my message got lost in translation. Let's find the shoes quickly and leave—I need to pay a visit to my friend Miss Terry to teach her how to keep better track of her things."

The woman sounded upset.

Sky opened his mouth. Closed it. Her friend, Miss Terry . . . For a moment Sky considered the possibility that this was Ursula herself, upset that he had taken the encoded note from her desk. As a Whisper, Ursula could shift into anything if she had a biological sample of the subject, but the full moon was still a few weeks off. Besides, the woman seemed upset with Ursula, not with him, and it wouldn't make any sense for her to be upset with herself.

Sky examined the woman more closely . . . her charcoal hair, so familiar . . . not Ursula, and yet she clearly knew about the note he'd found in Ursula's office, which meant she was probably the sender, "M" . . .

Everything suddenly fell into place, and Sky realized with a shock why she looked so familiar: She was the woman from Nikola's picture, a hunter he had seen at least twice before.

She was M—not Malvidia or Morton, but "Em," as in "Emaline." And like Nikola, she had been there the night Sky was Changed by the Shadow Man. She was Nikola's wife, who had carried him away and fought to give Phineas time to escape with Sky.

Sky knew who Nikola's son was, the son he had mentioned last night and long ago. Sky stared at Em, so stunned he could hardly think. . . . How was it even possible?

Crystal narrowed her eyes, obviously thinking hard, but she didn't have the information he had. She didn't know.

"You look like a fish when you do that with your mouth," Em observed.

Sky closed his mouth.

"Who are you?" the old woman at the door barked. "Why are you bothering me?"

"My name is Ju—"

"Em," Sky blurted before he could stop himself.

He saw Crystal stiffen when she heard the name; she'd figured it out.

The old woman narrowed her eyes suspiciously, watching them.

"Er . . . M, as in Mom, is what I meant," Sky corrected pathetically. "She's our mom."

The old woman's eyes narrowed even further, until they were just visible beneath her flabby orange wrinkles.

Em stepped in. "Yes, I'm their mother—an unfortunate position, as you can clearly see. . . ."

The old woman nodded in agreement, her wrinkles retracting a bit.

"But most people call me Juliet," Em continued, apparently not wanting to tell the woman her real name. "Now, if you'll just allow us to—"

"Incident last night," the old woman stated gruffly, interrupting her. "Closed till further notice."

"I'm sorry to hear that Miss . . ."

"Hazzleweed," said Hazzleweed. "No Miss, just Hazzleweed."

"Well, *Hazzleweed*," said Em, smiling politely, "as you can see, we're not here to bowl. We just need my son's shoes, and then we'll be on our way. You can't expect him to go without his shoes, can you?"

"What's wrong with the ones he's got on?" Hazzleweed asked.

Everyone looked at Sky's shoes.

"Those? You can't expect him to wear *those* shoes; he'll be a laughingstock!" Em declared.

Sky frowned, wondering what was wrong with his shoes. Sure, they were a little scuffed. Sure, there was a tear or four and they were covered in sewage, but for all that, they were very comfortable shoes.

"Oh no," Em continued, "these shoes would never do. We just pulled them out of the garbage so he'd have something to wear."

Hazzleweed nodded as if that was a perfectly acceptable answer.

"Please, Hazzleweed," Crystal chimed in. "Can't you find it in your heart to spare my brother the humiliation of wearing these shoes? I'm sure a woman of your caliber, with such a fine name, must have an equally fine disposition to match."

Crystal was laying it on a bit thick, in Sky's opinion, but it seemed to work.

"All right," Hazzleweed barked. "But you're in and you're out—find the shoes and leave. No lollygagging."

"We'd never dream of it," said Em.

Hazzleweed harrumphed and stepped to the side.

Then Sky, Crystal, and Andrew's dead mother—Emaline Livingstone—walked through the door.

CHAPTER 19
Hazzlebark and Hazzleweed

Crystal handed the bowling shoes to Hazzleweed, who grimaced and held the shoes at arm's length. Sky couldn't blame her; those bowling shoes looked even worse than the shoes he was wearing.

Hazzleweed locked the door behind them.

"This way," Hazzleweed barked, leading them toward the shoe counter.

Sky hung back with Crystal. Now that they were inside, Sky noticed that there were far more people in here than he'd first suspected. What's more, the place was a mess: pins everywhere, tables overturned, the pool table busted into pieces. The bowling alley patrons were putting on a good show now, acting like they were bowling, but it was obvious they had searched the place before he, Crystal, and Em had arrived.

"It's not possible . . . ," Crystal whispered, looking at Em, who walked a few feet ahead of them talking to Hazzleweed.

"She's dead! She's been dead for twelve years, since Andrew was one!"

"Hannah and I ran into her in the prison last year, a trapped hunter," Sky whispered back. "She nearly shot me in the face! I knew she looked familiar. Remember how Andrew told us her tomb was empty—that they'd never found her body? She was there the night I was Changed. She was with Phineas. Her husband, Nikola, was my protector—he's the janitor now. He's Andrew's dad!"

Crystal covered her mouth in shock. "Poor Andrew . . . I can't imagine how he'll react to this. Raised by that horrible uncle of his and those step-cousins . . . and all this time his parents were alive. Sky, what are we going to do? Where has she been for the last year?"

"Hunting your mom, by the sounds of it," Sky replied, thinking of the note. If Em was really the "M" from Ursula's note—and he felt certain that she was—then that's precisely what she'd been doing for the last year.

Crystal's expression changed dramatically, going from sympathetic to dangerous. "You think she shot my mom? You think she's Bedlam?"

"I don't know," said Sky. He glanced at Em, but he couldn't tell whether she was the one he'd seen running away in the Grove of the Fallen or not. "I didn't get a good look." He shook his head in frustration. "Let's just find whatever the Marrowick left here and get out. We'll sort out the rest later."

Crystal narrowed her eyes and nodded once. "Do you notice anything weird?" she asked.

"What? Aside from the fact that we're following an orange-skinned woman named Hazzleweed and our friend's dead mother?" said Sky.

"Like the fact that no one is *bowling*," Crystal hissed.

"I noticed," Sky replied.

"Hazzleweed!" barked a gravelly voice.

Turning, Sky found a tall man with a long pointy nose, pockmarked skin, and a sinister chin nearly as sharp as a beak.

"What is it, Hazzlebark?" Hazzleweed spat.

"Who're your friends here?" asked Hazzlebark, surveying them with sickly buzzard eyes.

"Looking for shoes," said Hazzleweed.

"Looks like they got shoes."

"Looking for other shoes," Hazzleweed stated.

Hazzlebark grunted and picked something from his teeth, which he inspected for several seconds before responding. "Well, get 'em out fast. We got *cleanin'* to do."

Hazzlebark walked to the wall a few feet away, still inspecting whatever he'd pulled from his teeth, and then he turned around and stood there. Doing nothing.

Sky and Crystal exchanged glances before following the woman, Hazzleweed.

"Stupid Hazzlebark thinks he's so smart," Hazzleweed mumbled to herself. "Got cleanin' to do—I'll show him cleanin' . . . clean him right across the head, I will . . ."

"So, Hazzlebark and Hazzleweed . . . ," said Crystal, clearly trying to break the tension, "unusual names. Are you two related?"

Hazzleweed stopped and turned her fiery eyes on them. "No."

"It's just . . . *Hazzle*," said Crystal, laughing uncomfortably, "seems like an uncommon name."

"I don't know any Hazzles—so's I suppose it is," said Hazzleweed. She pivoted her arm like a sprinkler and dropped the bowling shoes into a garbage can. Her finger shot out. "Lost and found's over there." She pointed. "Help yourself."

Her arm dropped and Hazzleweed wandered off muttering curses under her breath. "Get 'em out fast, right. I'll show him how fast I can get 'em out . . . get 'em out fast across his head, I will . . ."

Several people wearing heavy makeup glanced their way as they huddled around the lost and found box and began sifting through its contents, but Sky ignored them.

"*What are you two doing here?*" Em hissed.

"What are *you* doing here, *Juliet?*" Crystal retorted quietly. "Don't think we don't know who you are. Aren't you supposed to be dead? Because I thought you were dead—your son still thinks you're dead!"

"Shhh," Em hissed. "Unless you want to burn this place to the ground, I'd recommend you keep your voice down."

"What are you talking about?" Sky asked.

"You first," said Em.

"We found a note you sent to Ursula," said Sky, watching her closely.

Em's face gave nothing away.

"The note said that a Marrowick was supposed to deliver something here," Sky continued. "Last night we ran into a Marrowick as it was leaving, so we know it was here. Your turn. What's the delivery? Is it Alexander's blade?"

"No," Em stated without hesitation.

"How do you know?" Sky asked.

Em pulled the other half of Nikola's picture out of her pocket. The picture showed Nikola dressed in a white button-down shirt. On his eye Sky saw the white monocle, one of the keys to Solomon's prison. Nikola's arm was wrapped around

Em, while the other arm held a toddler: Andrew.

"I don't—" Sky started, but then he saw it. The rusted sword hung on a band around Nikola's shoulder. Nikola had fought the Shadow Man with that exact sword, Sky remembered. "Nikola has the blade."

"It's never shimmered for him," said Em. "It's never shimmered for anyone since Alexander."

"Are you saying Nikola killed Alexander Drake?" Sky asked, clarifying.

"No!" Em snapped. "Nik was in Austria at the time." Sky ignored the fact that Andrew's dad was more than four hundred years old, and he let Em continue. "He only showed up to help with the body. The story that Alexander was buried with the blade was fabricated to keep hunters from finding it. Nik's protected the blade since Alexander's death—or he did, I should say. He lost it in his madness. I sent him the picture hoping to jog some memory loose, but so far it hasn't."

"So if Nikola has the blade, what are you doing here?" Crystal asked. "Were you hoping to shoot some other innocent hunter?"

Em narrowed her eyes. "I've hunted your mother for the last year, Crystal. She is one of my closest and dearest friends. I promise you, I wouldn't do anything to endanger her life. I used a Harksplitter arrow. Harksplitter traps edgewalkers in their host—the arrows don't ever kill, even through the heart. Harksplitter is used for that very reason. If the host died, Bedlam would just jump to another."

Sky shook his head. "Cass told me that Bedlam had left her. He attacked me last night. Cass could've gotten away then and used the barrow weed to keep him from reentering her mind."

"Bedlam put her to sleep when he attacked you," said Em. "I know. It's the only reason I was able to catch up to him. Barrow weed only keeps Bedlam and other edgewalkers from entering your mind; it doesn't do any good once they're there. Bedlam has been pushing Cass's body hard, making her run faster, making her stronger, healing her over and over again; she's exhausted. I'm sure you must've noticed?"

Sky thought back. He remembered how Cass had leaped from Alexander's grave and how she had thrown the coffin over her shoulder as though it weighed nothing. Of course, that didn't prove anything. He'd seen hunters do those kinds of things as well.

"If Cass was Bedlam," said Sky, "then why didn't he try to take control of me in the Grove of the Fallen? Why give me barrow weed to keep him away?"

"If *I* was Bedlam, what would stop me from ripping that barrow weed from your nostrils and taking control of you right now?" Em countered.

Sky gulped. "Nothing, I suppose."

"Precisely," Em replied. "It's simple misdirection. Bedlam is the master of mayhem. You've shown that you can stop him. He's unlikely to try a direct assault again, even if he wasn't trapped in Cass. Maybe he thought you could be useful some- how. But the point is that no matter what she told you, Bedlam is still in there. He let her think she was in control to make her more cooperative, but now he's trapped. It'll take days for the Harksplitter to work itself out of Cass's system."

"And in the meantime, Bedlam's army will arrive and destroy Exile," Crystal observed.

"Bedlam is more powerful than his army," said Em. "I took out the greater threat and gave the hunters a chance. Bedlam still has creatures looking for the blade, and Morton is after it for his own reasons. Right now Bedlam is weak, but if someone freed his body, he could escape the Harksplitter. Fortunately, the odds of anyone finding the blade—let alone getting it to work—are almost zero."

"So if that's all true, then why are you here? Why look for the blade?" Crystal asked. "It seems like you could find a better use for your time, like maybe letting your son know you're alive."

"I was told that the Marrowick would deliver the means to stop Bedlam's army," Em replied, ignoring the jibe.

"And where did you get the information?" Sky asked.

"An anonymous letter," said Em. "I was casing the place when you two showed up. I was hoping Ursula would arrive."

"She's on vacation," Sky stated.

Em raised an eyebrow. "I seriously doubt that."

"And what about Andrew?" Crystal jumped in before Sky could reply. "What do you plan to do about him?"

Em was quiet for a moment. "I honestly don't know. I was only a mother for a year before I was trapped. . . . Nik is insane. We're hardly fit parents."

"So you're not going to say anything? You're just going to keep it a secret and pretend to be someone else?" Crystal snapped.

Em glanced at her. "Crystal, I'd have thought that you, of all people, might understand that some secrets are best left unshared—especially among friends."

Crystal blanched. "What are you talking about?"

"I've been to your house," said Em, sounding on the verge of tears. "I know what you're hiding."

"What's she talking about?" Sky asked, confused.

"It's nothing," said Crystal, refusing to meet his eyes. "We should get moving."

"Found your other shoes?" Hazzleweed gargled from immediately behind Sky, making him jump.

"What, this?" said Sky, holding up a pair of sunglasses he'd found in the box. "This is a pair of sunglasses."

"Hardly seems fit for walking 'round in," said Hazzleweed sagely. "Where do you put your toes? There ain't no toe pockets."

"That's sort of what I thought, too," said Sky, afraid to ask what toe pockets were. "It appears that my shoes aren't here. I think I might've put them in the ball return, or maybe in the pit. I think I bowled with them once while I was waiting for my ball."

"Oh, son," said Em, her voice carrying an is-that-seriously-the-best-you-can-come-up-with kind of vibe, "what am I going to do with you?"

Sky shrugged.

Em *tsk*ed. Without waiting, she stood and headed for the bowling lanes. Sky and Crystal hurried to follow.

"Well, Hazzleweed, if we can just take a peek at the pinsetter on lane nine . . . Was it eight or nine, dear? I can't remember," said Em.

"I—"

Em cut him off. "I suppose we'd best check both."

"You can't go there," Hazzlebark croaked, stepping away from his wall as they passed and falling into step behind them.

Hazzleweed took one look at Hazzlebark, another look at Sky, and then she scurried away.

"You've done it now, boyo," Hazzleweed muttered as she fled.

"Excuse me?" said Em sweetly, addressing Hazzlebark

without slowing. They reached the head of lane nine and started walking toward the pit.

Sky glanced around nervously. Everyone had stopped what they were doing and had slowly started gathering around the lanes. Someone turned off the music and the place grew eerily silent.

Sky thumbed a canister of Fog in his pocket, and he could see Crystal doing the same.

"I said you can't go there!" Hazzlebark growled.

Em stopped a few steps away from the pit and slowly turned to face Hazzlebark. She spoke soothingly, as if afraid to startle him. "I'm quite sorry, Mr. Hazzlebark—"

"Just Hazzlebark!" he shouted. His pockmarked skin seemed to be boiling, turning a deep copper, and smoke actually rose from the surface.

"Oh no . . . ," Sky muttered. He glanced around and noticed that everyone's skin seemed to be coppery and smoking. "This is not good. . . ."

"What?" Crystal whispered.

"Sorry . . . *Hazzlebark*," said Em gently. "We're just looking for shoes, nothing more."

"You will go!" Hazzlebark breathed heavily. "Now!"

Sky grabbed Crystal's arm and pulled her away from Hazzlebark, little by little.

"What's going on, Sky?" Crystal hissed.

Em moved closer to Hazzlebark, her voice soft and comforting. "Hazzlebark—that's a lovely name. Is it Dutch?"

Hazzlebark narrowed his eyes. "Leave . . . don't make me . . . you need to . . . you need to go." Air wheezed in and out of his lungs and he planted his hands on his thighs as if recovering from a long race.

"We will," said Em. "I'm walking to the door now, see?"

Hazzlebark seemed to calm down, the smoke lessening. His eyes focused on Em.

Sky was a few steps away from the pit. He saw movement through the far windows: T-Bone, Andrew, and Hands creeping up.

He took another step toward the pit. If something on the pinsetter could save Exile, it was worth the risk.

"Hazzlebark! The boy!" someone screamed.

Hazzlebark spun away from Em and his smoldering eyes locked on Sky.

"Not good . . . ," Sky chirped.

"I think you made him mad," Crystal whispered.

Hazzlebark's eyes were *literally* smoldering. "I . . . warned . . . you . . ."

Hazzlebark burst into flame.

CHAPTER 20
Harrow Wights

Time seemed to slow, and then everything happened at once. Hazzlebark threw a giant glob of fiery, fleshy copper just as Sky grabbed Crystal and jumped into the pit. The copper struck the thin facade over the pit, sailed through it, and crashed into the reinforced outer wall, splattering and setting it aflame.

Sky felt around on the pinsetter. His hand brushed across a package too small to be a sword. He snatched it from its hiding place just as the music flipped back on.

> Burn, baby, burn, disco inferno!
> Burn, baby, burn, burn that mama down!

T-Bone, Hands, and Andrew crashed through the door, crackling with electricity and holding Tin shields in front of them.

Everywhere, people screamed and burst into flames.

Hazzleweed, who was safely locked away in the DJ booth, cackled above the noise and sang along, adding her own lyrics.

"Got you mad now, Hazzlebark! Burn, baby!" she hooted, looking the same as before except healthier, happier, and far more insane.

Fiery balls of copper splattered everywhere. Em flipped out of the way of one fiery ball, dropped into a split to avoid another, rolled, and spun back to her feet, avoiding several more, almost like she was dancing. Glancing at Hazzleweed, Sky saw that she *was* dancing as she switched on a new song, something hard and thumping.

"I take it those are Harrow Wights?" Crystal shouted.

"Yep!"

Sky and Crystal jumped the gutter to the pit on lane eleven, searching for a path to the door.

"When they get mad," Sky continued, ducking down to take another peek, "their blood boils and melts pockets of copper scattered throughout their bodies! The hot metal ignites their skin as it seeps out and they burst into flames! When their fire goes out, the copper will cool, and then we'll be in real trouble!"

"I can only imagine how horrible that would be!" Crystal yelled sarcastically.

They dove into the pit on lane twelve just as fiery metal crashed into lane eleven. Sky and Crystal leaped onto the pinsetter.

A copper ball blasted into the pit, knocking out the pins and leaving the Harrow Wight with a seven-ten split—a difficult shot even under the best of circumstances.

Another flaming ball crashed down the lane, just missing the conversion, and the sweeper arm dragged the remaining tenpin into the pit.

Sky and Crystal watched the melted and smoking pins

bounce in the pit and get sucked up into the pinsetter while the burning copper balls rolled into the ball return and disappeared, leaving ruin in their wake.

"We've got to get out of here!" Crystal yelled.

Metal punched through the facade, sailed between them, and smashed into the outer wall. Through the hole, Sky saw Hazzlebark glaring back at him.

"Run!" Sky shouted.

Sky and Crystal scrambled from one pinsetter to the next.

The thin facade exploded all around them. Molten balls flew past again and again, splattering everywhere. Pinsetters malfunctioned, spitting out flaming pins.

Sky leaped to the side, dodging a burning pin. He jumped to the next setter, racing after Crystal.

Through a giant hole, Sky saw a fiery ball headed for Crystal.

"Crystal! Drop!" Sky screamed.

Without hesitating, Crystal twisted and fell off the pinsetter, crashing hard to the lane below. The fiery ball flashed through the facade, just missing her.

Looking down, he saw Crystal lying motionless, with Harrow Wights closing in.

Ripping the mint tin from his pocket—and silently thanking his friends for the timely birthday present—Sky leaped through the burning facade and activated the shield. Flaming rubble collapsed around him as the shield spun out.

He landed in front of Crystal and raised the Tin just as molten metal hit, driving him sliding backward. The fiery ball bounced off the shield and crashed back into the Harrow Wight, knocking her to the ground.

With the shield in one hand, Sky grabbed Crystal by the

arm and dragged her away from the facade as a huge chunk broke free and plowed into the lanes. They'd nearly reached the last lane and the outer wall, but they were trapped and Sky knew it.

The fire sprinklers kicked on and spit out a pathetic stream of rusty water. The drops popped and sizzled against the molten skin of seven advancing Harrow Wights, filling the alley with steam.

Just before the steam enveloped them, Sky saw copper seep into the Harrow Wights' palms, and they reared back, preparing to throw.

Sky dropped Crystal's arm and brought his Tin shield up as the balls hit. He pushed forward against the onslaught, striving to keep the Harrow Wights from Crystal.

Clearing the rusty water, the fire sprinklers sputtered and then spat out a massive stream that dissolved the steam and brought everything into focus.

Through a gap, Sky spotted T-Bone, Hands, and Andrew fighting their way to the exit with Em. Andrew yelled something at Sky, but it was lost within the thumping music.

Hands disappeared under a wave of Harrow Wights, and T-Bone and Em jumped forward, struggling frantically to free him. Andrew yelled again, pointing at the outer wall just behind Sky.

Before Sky could figure out what Andrew meant, a Harrow Wight stepped between them, blocking Sky's view. Its fire had burned out and its body was encased in a splotchy rusted copper, shiny and flexible as flesh in some places— greenish blue, formless, and unyielding in others. Its arm chopped down.

Sky ducked, expecting to see the shield's sharp edge cut

through the arm just as it had cut into the sewer wall. Instead, the monster's arm rebounded into the air, undamaged save for a small cut that quickly filled with more copper.

The monster took a step back. Its face was partially corroded and hard—bereft of features—while other parts were fleshy and bright.

Looking at that fleshy part, Sky realized he was fighting an insane Hazzlebark. Sky clicked the Tin handle, and the sharp edge rolled safely inward.

Hazzlebark swung again. Sky pivoted, knocked Hazzlebark's arm aside with the shield, and rammed him with his shoulder to no effect.

Sky yelped in surprise.

Hazzlebark roared. Sky pulled a Fog canister from his coat and clicked it on, but before he could throw, Hazzlebark grabbed his wrist and *squeezed*. Sky screamed and dropped the Fog.

Hazzlebark kicked the canister into the burning rubble of the facade and it exploded weakly. And in that moment Sky knew what Andrew wanted him to do.

With a click, Sky sharpened the edges of the Tin shield and swung at Hazzlebark with his free hand. Hazzlebark let go of Sky's wrist and stepped back.

Sky let the momentum carry him, grabbing another canister from his coat as he spun. Before Sky could throw it, Hazzlebark snatched his wrist again. Sky dropped the canister and it crashed uselessly against the outer wall.

Sky brought his Tin shield around, but Hazzlebark snatched his other wrist so that he now held both. Another squeeze and the Tin fell from Sky's limp hand and landed upright in the gutter, the sharp edge lodging into the wood.

Hazzlebark rotated Sky's arms and lifted him. He head-butted Sky. Once. Twice.

Sky tumbled to the ground. Blood streamed from his face. Through the blood, he saw Em and T-Bone collapse under the weight of more than a dozen Harrow Wights. Andrew raised his Cross-Shocker, but a Harrow Wight tackled him, and he too disappeared in a mountain of smoldering bodies.

Sky closed his eyes against the pain. He was all that was left.

Hazzlebark kicked him to his back and his Hunter's Mark warmed as Hazzlebark spoke, his voice like grating iron. "Give me what you found."

The other Harrow Wights closed in, their fires spent, their faces and bodies like Hazzlebark's, but each uniquely grotesque.

Sky pulled out the package. "What? This?" he slurred, his lips feeling too big for his mouth and his mouth feeling too big for his head.

Every Harrow Wight in the alley stopped what they were doing and turned to face him. Hazzleweed shut off the music.

As Harrow Wights moved closer, Sky could see the others pinned to the ground. Hands wasn't moving. T-Bone, Em, and Andrew looked beat-up, but conscious. Sky could see Andrew's hand slowly drifting toward his Core.

Sky turned his attention back to Hazzlebark. "The package is mine," Sky spluttered, his mouth feeling like it was full of molasses. "Special delivery."

"You cannot stop us," Hazzlebark croaked. "You betrayed us long ago. Tonight Exile will burn."

Sky slipped a Jumper canister from his pocket.

Hazzlebark reached down and lifted Sky up by his coat.

Flames shot from Hazzlebark's hands. Phineas's old coat resisted, but Sky could feel his ugly pink shirt burning where Hazzlebark's hands touched.

"You want the package?" Sky spat. "Then catch."

Sky flipped the package into the air.

The Harrow Wights watched, mesmerized.

From the corner of his eye, Sky saw Andrew kick out at the Harrow Wight pinning him down. The Harrow Wight let go and Andrew hit his protective Shimmer. A crackling blue nimbus popped up around him, pushing the Harrow Wight away.

Andrew rolled and snatched up his Cross-Shocker.

In that instant, Hazzlebark released Sky and reached for the package. Sky locked his arms behind him and clicked on the Jumper canister. The force propelled him up toward the package.

As he snatched it from the air, Andrew pulled the trigger on his Cross-Shocker. Two electrified prongs shot through the alley, between a Harrow Wight's legs, then bounced off the Tin shield Sky had strategically lodged in the gutter, went behind the crowd of Harrow Wights, and smashed into the Jumper canister Sky had dropped against the outer wall earlier.

The canister exploded.

The concussion punched a massive hole through the brick and sent Harrow Wights flying.

Shock waves caught Sky as he grabbed the package, and flung him tumbling through the air. As the ground spun toward him, he pointed the Jumper canister and squeezed to slow himself. Even with the boost, he crashed hard and rolled to a stop.

The place was a charred and soggy ruin. Harrow Wights were scattered everywhere, groaning. Sky spotted T-Bone racing for the hole in the outer brick wall, with Hands slung over his shoulder. Andrew ripped Sky's Tin from the lane while Em carried Crystal gently in her arms.

"Come on!" Andrew cried.

Sky shook himself and ran for the hole as Harrow Wights stirred around him. Many were out cold, and he could see the copper seeping back into their skin. In a few hours they'd grow new flesh, but until then they'd be ugly, ugly, ugly.

Sky reached Andrew and the others.

"Are you all right?" Em asked, looking worried.

Sky wiped blood from his nose. "Yeah, I'm okay." He felt like death.

Outside, he saw T-Bone opening the sewer grate.

As they started to leave, Hazzleweed called out to Sky, "Bedlam can save her, you know!"

Sky stopped and turned to face Hazzleweed, who stood a short distance away on the upper level by the DJ booth.

"Save who?" Sky asked.

"Your sister—the one you came with," Hazzleweed said. "But he won't do it for free!"

Sky got a sick feeling in his stomach. He scrambled frantically through the rubble until he caught up with Em and Andrew. Very slowly, Sky rolled Crystal forward in Em's arms until he could see her back.

"I'm sorry, Sky," Em said quietly.

Crystal had dropped, just like Sky had told her to.

But she hadn't dropped fast enough.

CHAPTER 21
Orphan Among Us

They laid Crystal on her stomach on a table next to her mother. Em had slipped away to warn the hunters about the arrival of the Harrow Wights, without telling Andrew who she really was. Sky had wondered at that: Hadn't Andrew ever seen a picture of his mom? But then, Sky supposed, any family rotten enough to lie about Nikola, to tell Andrew his father was dead rather than crazy, probably wasn't into family moments. Em, who had assumed the name of Juliet once again, had promised to return later to explain everything. Still not quite trusting her, Sky had kept the package.

"What in the world were you doing, Sky?" Mom demanded. She rushed around the kitchen, grabbing bits of this and that: Jack seeds, knives, a small blowtorch.

Sky held a bag of ice against his face. Mom had thrown several weird pastes and gels at him and told him to smear it on his cuts, bruises, and burns. T-Bone, Andrew, and Hands were doing the same, smearing on the pastes and gels and icing themselves. They watched quietly as Mom gathered her supplies.

T-Bone was mostly burned and banged up like Sky, but Hands had taken a nasty knock to the head and still looked dazed. Andrew sat on a barstool a short distance away from the others. He stared at nothing, his brow creased in thought.

Sky wasn't sure what to do for Andrew, who had to suspect something about the mysterious woman who had fought beside them in the bowling alley and then run off with hardly a word. Em had chickened out, as far as Sky could tell. Was it Sky's place to tell Andrew about his mother? He honestly had no idea.

Footsteps echoed in the hall. "Helen?" Beau called out. "Helen? Are you home?"

"In the kitchen!" Mom yelled as she sterilized the knives.

"Herman should be along soon," Beau continued as he walked down the hall. "We're about as ready as we can be for Bedlam's army. I would've stayed, but there was a fire, and with Sky's track record . . ."

Beau walked into the kitchen and spotted the beleaguered monster hunters, scorched, battered, and bleeding, and then he saw Crystal. "Oh . . . oh no . . ."

Beau strode to the table. "What happened?"

"That's what I'd like to know!" Mom shouted. "Everyone get out of my way!"

Mom stepped to the table and began examining Crystal. She blanched as she probed the wound, and her face went whiter and whiter as the exam continued.

"We ran into Harrow Wights at the bowling alley," said Sky, his voice hollow.

Beau nodded as if he had expected as much. "Bedlam's army is nearly here."

"Where's Edward?" Mom cut in. "Crystal could use her father, and I'm sure Cass could use her husband. Did you find anything at her house?"

Mom gently turned Crystal onto her side. T-Bone and Hands stepped forward to hold her in place while Mom started pouring a thick substance down Crystal's throat.

"I'm afraid Crystal's father won't be coming," Beau said hesitantly.

Mom scowled. "And why not?"

Beau was quiet for a moment. "Because Edward died over two years ago."

Everyone stopped what they were doing. Silence filled the room.

"But then . . . who's been taking care of Crystal?" Mom asked.

"No one," Beau replied.

"That's not possible," said Andrew, emerging from his stupor. "You're telling us that Crystal's been living on her own for over two years and *nobody has noticed*?"

Beau nodded. "Has anyone actually seen Edward in the past two years?"

Nobody spoke.

"Wait," said T-Bone. "What about the phone number at her house? She said she'd called his hotel today and left a message."

Beau shook his head. "I'm sorry. There is no phone number— I looked. It's not there. Edward Bittlesworth died over two years ago on an overseas assignment from his paper. Crystal had a letter of condolence tucked under her mattress, and little else of value in the empty house."

Sky glared at him; it couldn't be true. "You're lying."

"I'm sorry, Sky," said Beau.

Sky didn't say anything. He just stared at the thick layer of coppery metal stretching from Crystal's mid back to the base of her neck, where the skin was charred and pockmarked like the moon. Sky remembered Em's cryptic words at the bowling alley about keeping secrets and Crystal's evasions when they had offered to retrieve the phone number at her house. He thought of her baggy secondhand clothes and all the times he had seen her leave the lair early in the morning, never realizing that she had probably slept there.

She was the glue that held them together, and yet she was the most broken of all.

"Can you fix this?" Sky asked Mom, tears streaming from his eyes.

"I'll do what I can," Mom promised, her tone carrying a hopeless weight. "I can make her comfortable."

"How long does she have?" Sky croaked.

"It's hard to say," Mom replied. She carefully applied a thick gel to the metal on Crystal's back, which started to steam. "A few hours, perhaps."

"A few hours . . . ," Sky muttered in shock.

Mom flipped on the small blowtorch and started moving the flame back and forth across the gel.

Sky looked at Crystal, and then his eyes drifted to Cass. If she was really Bedlam and if what Hazzleweed had said was true . . .

He wiped the tears from his eyes. "Mom, do you know why someone would shoot Cass with Harksplitter?"

Mom dipped several sheets of what looked like orange paper into a blue liquid and placed them on Crystal. Even though Crystal was unconscious, Sky saw her body relax, and the worry lines on her forehead slipped away.

"We have our suspicions," Mom hedged, glancing at Beau.

Sky waited, refusing to speak. He already knew the answer, but he needed confirmation.

Mom sighed and brushed her tears away. "Harksplitter was used against Edgewalkers during the wars. It was one of the few things we found that worked against them. Whoever shot Cass must have known the secrets of Harksplitter and believed that Cass was Bedlam."

"You say it like you were there, but the Edgewalker Wars happened centuries ago," Sky pointed out, catching the familiarity in her tone. "How old are you?"

Mom smiled. "It's impolite to ask a lady's age," she quipped evasively. "What is this about, Sky?"

Sky watched her as if he had never seen her before, and it occurred to him that he might not be the only one keeping secrets. "Is there anything that counteracts Harksplitter?"

Mom frowned. "Counteracts? I don't think that would be a good idea." Mom handed the blowtorch to Beau and showed him where to use it, and then she wiped off her hands and crossed to the refrigerator. Sky joined her as she sorted through various bottles and containers filled with strange botanical substances.

"Humor me," said Sky. "If Bedlam was really in there, and someone—say an Edgewalker—wanted to talk to him without allowing him to escape, and without getting trapped by the Harksplitter themselves, how could they do it?"

Mom stopped sorting and examined him as if he was one of her patients. "That's quite a question. If it was any other Edgewalker, I would say good luck, but with Bedlam . . . He's not just an Edgewalker, he's Master of the Edge. It was rumored during the wars that even though Bedlam was trapped in his

Chrysalis, his children could still occasionally reach him in the Edge, in what they called Edge Memories."

Sky inhaled sharply.

"Bedlam couldn't escape to another body—he couldn't actually walk the Edge himself," Mom continued. "But his children could call him to these Edge Memories and talk to him. It was quite a bother. I take it this isn't an academic question?"

"Not exactly," Sky replied. "Do you trust me?"

"Not in the slightest," said Mom. "But I love you. That will have to be good enough."

Sky grinned. He started to walk away, but Mom grabbed him and hugged him tightly.

"Don't do anything stupid, Sky." Mom pleaded.

"Of course I won't," said Sky, "I only do smart things."

Mom released him with a final squeeze, and then she went back to her bottles, seemingly determined to avoid watching whatever he was about to do.

Sky walked back to Cass and sat next to her—close, but not too close. He pulled the barrow weed out of his nose, sniffing. Just last night Errand had shown him a nearby Edge Memory, one of the manor itself and Solomon's prison. It struck Sky as almost too convenient that Errand had shown him such a place just when he would need it. It made him wonder how much Errand knew about Bedlam and what Errand's role was in all this. Clearly Errand wanted something, and clearly he knew more than he had told Sky. But what was he after?

Sky forced the thoughts from his mind and focused, recalling how Errand had pulled him from his personal memory of Skull Valley into the Edge Memory of Exile. Sky studied the

details of the event in his mind, remembering how he had felt
and what Errand had done; he studied it until he thought he
understood how it was done.

"Sky, what are you—" T-Bone started.

But at that moment Sky reached out with his senses. He
got a quick impression of Bedlam lurking within Cass, and
then Sky grabbed ahold and yanked Bedlam into the Edge
Memory with him, doing it the same way Errand had.

Sky tumbled down and crashed in the woods where he had
landed with Errand. He rolled to his feet and took in his
surroundings, which hadn't changed in the slightest since last
night. He saw the wall to Solomon's prison a short distance
away, and the manor beyond.

"Sky Weathers," Bedlam hissed, his voice coming from
everywhere at once. "How nice of you to visit."

Sky felt his Eye of Legend grow cold. Bedlam was trig-
gering it somehow, releasing Legend's power and will just as
Morton had.

"I want to make a deal!" Sky managed through clenched
teeth. Pain swelled within him. Black veins started to spread
through his hand. Sky fought against it, struggling to push it
back. He calmed himself—too much was on the line for him to
fail. Crystal had nothing. He had to give her at least this after
he had cost her so much.

As he calmed, the Hunter's Mark seemed to warm, and
slowly the veins began to recede.

"A deal? You hunters are like a murder of crows plucking
one another's eyes until none can see. Why would I make a
deal with a murder?"

"Not with the hunters," said Sky. "Just with me!"

Everything went silent, and then Bedlam fell from the night like a comet and crashed directly in front of Sky. The ground exploded, throwing Sky backward. Before he could regain his feet, Bedlam grabbed his head and lifted him from the ground while Sky clung to Bedlam's arm. Sky could feel Bedlam trying to force his way into his mind, but the effort was weak. Sky pushed him out easily.

Bedlam chuckled. "Why keep me out, Sky? The two of us could make a wonderful team. Aren't you curious about all the lovely things I could teach you?"

"I don't have to keep you out," Sky spat. "You're stuck in Cass. You couldn't get in even if I let you, not until the Harksplitter wears off, or your body is freed. This is as far as you come unless you make a deal with me."

Bedlam growled and dropped Sky. "You are a pawn in this game, Sky, but you could be a king."

"The king's the worst piece on the board," Sky retorted. "He just sits around until someone traps him. At least the pawn has the chance to reclaim a better piece."

"Only if he survives long enough to reach the far edge," said Bedlam. "And odds are not in your favor."

"Why do you hate us so much?" Sky asked.

"BECAUSE YOU BETRAYED ME!" Bedlam shouted. "I, who helped you overthrow my father. I, the first to join your cause against Legend. I, who taught you my secrets only to have you hunt down my Edgewalkers, my children, and send them to oblivion simply to keep me bound! Your murder of crows is corrupt—betrayers!"

"I don't understand," said Sky. "The stories I read claimed that you were seeking your father's power—that Solomon and Alexander trapped you until your heart was pure and filled with love."

Bedlam growled at him.

Sky held up his hands defensively. "I'm not saying I believed it!"

"Hunters lie, and Solomon and Alexander lied worst of all," said Bedlam. "They convinced the other hunters that I was in league with my brother to reclaim my father's power, to reforge the darkness in the Eyes. When all along, it was they who were plotting to take it. Solomon and Alexander believed that the Hunter's Mark would allow them to control it. And they call me mad! The First Hunter herself—the greatest of your kind—held my father's power in her hands, and she gave it up. She broke the power into parts and gave half to her chosen thirteen and half to Legend's five remaining children, and she bound the power in the Eyes. She understood. To reforge Legend's power is to reforge Legend! But I saw Solomon and Alexander's plan; I would not give up the Eye willingly and they would not kill me. If they tried to take the Eye by force, dire consequences would follow. So for hundreds of years I slept, until Vulpine, my sister, sent Cassandra to awaken me."

"So when Solomon and Alexander realized they couldn't get the Eye from you, they—" Sky stopped himself, but it was too late.

"They stole my brother's body and his Eye?" Bedlam offered.

"How did you—"

"I know because I taught them how to do such a thing, fool that I am! My Edgewalkers visited me for a time and kept me informed before Solomon exterminated them.

I knew of Solomon and Alexander's plans for my brother, though many of the details I have learned since awakening."

"So Solomon and Alexander succeeded—they got your brother's body—but something must've happened because Alexander returned alone, claiming that the Arkhon had killed Solomon."

"Perhaps Alexander finally betrayed Solomon in the hopes of breaking free."

"Breaking free?" Sky queried, feeling confused. "Free from what?"

"Free from being a Changeling with Solomon, of course," said Bedlam, grinning.

Sky's heart stopped. "Solomon and Alexander were Changelings?"

"Yes," Bedlam replied. "Just as you are Changelings with Solomon's apprentice."

"Errand isn't Solomon's apprentice anymore," Sky retorted, wondering how Bedlam knew about Errand.

"We shall see." Bedlam chuckled.

"Why haven't I ever heard about this?" Sky asked. "None of the stories mention that they were Changelings, though that would explain how they both had a Hunter's Mark at the same time."

"They were very good at hiding it. Solomon used Slippery Wick Brew to disguise himself. And Changelings are so very, very rare. The knowledge of how to create one was lost for centuries before Alexander rediscovered it. I only uncovered their secret during training, and I kept it until the end. But tonight Morton will free Solomon if I do not stop him first."

"Your army is coming to stop Morton?" Sky asked hopefully.

"My army is coming to wipe you hunters from the face of the earth. I will burn Exile to the ground and make it my new home, near my sleeping brother, Erachnus, and my future prisoner, Solomon Rose."

"Can you help my friend? Can you help Crystal?" Sky demanded.

Bedlam stared at him for a second, and Sky could feel Bedlam rifling through his mind for images of Crystal. Sky didn't resist.

"I can help," Bedlam finally said. "But not from here."

"But if I let you out, could you?"

Bedlam considered him. "With my body, perhaps."

"You'd have to help her first, no matter what," said Sky. "And you'd have to stop your army from destroying Exile and go back to Skull Valley."

Bedlam scoffed at the proposal. "And what do I get in return?"

"Your freedom," said Sky.

"A bigger prison, you mean."

"The Caribbean has got to be nicer than a Chrysalis," Sky replied. "Or being trapped in someone's mind."

"And should Solomon escape?"

"Then take him—trap him somewhere if you can; do whatever you want with him," said Sky. "But heal Crystal first."

Bedlam examined Sky. A broken smile slipped across his face. "Perhaps the First Hunter has an heir after all. Very well, Sky Weathers. Deliver me and I will deliver your friend."

Bedlam touched Sky on the forehead and Sky felt something slip into his mind. He stumbled back. "What was that?"

"A message for the Darkhorn telling her to help you should you need it."

Sky rubbed his forehead. "So, the Darkhorn . . . is she really your . . . er . . . wife?"

Bedlam raised a rusty eyebrow.

"Uh . . . never mind," Sky muttered, backpedaling. "On second thought, I don't really want to know."

Bedlam laughed maniacally, darkness swirled around him, the forest fell apart, and Sky tumbled back into his own head and fell to the kitchen floor.

"—ing," T-Bone said, apparently finishing the sentence he had started before Sky slipped into the Edge Memory. Sky knew from experience that time didn't move the same way in the Edge.

"Sky! Are you all right?" Mom asked, rushing over from the fridge to help him up.

"I'm fine," said Sky. He grabbed the package they had retrieved from the bowling alley and started to leave the kitchen.

"Where are you going?" Mom asked.

"To fix this," Sky replied.

But before he could leave, he spotted a small piece of paper sticking out of the coffin in the cemetery replica he'd built from utensils the night before. He snatched the paper. The lid closed, the coffin slipped into the grave, and tissue fell on top, covering the coffin like dirt.

Sky opened the note:

Dear Apprentice,

Sorry I missed you earlier. Bedlam's army

appears larger than we anticipated. After careful consideration, we have determined that Exile is a loss and that a hasty retreat is in order to allow us to gather our strength in a more defensible location. As such, we will be leaving for the Academy of Legend tonight after a few remaining matters of business. Please make sure you pack plenty of clean underwear, a sharp knife, and a toothbrush. I can't wait to introduce you to the other Hunters. Once you are packed, attend me at the Grove of the Fallen—I believe you know the place. Please hurry. We have much to do, and I require your assistance with a matter of grave importance. Hope to see you soon. Come alone if you value your friends and family, and make sure to say your good-byes.

—Morton

Sky crumpled the note. Morton was running and taking his hunters with him, just as Errand had predicted.

"What is it?" T-Bone asked.

Sky inspected the kitchen and realized that Alexander Drake's coffin was missing. "Mom, did you move the coffin?"

Mom looked up from what she was doing, her brow furrowed as she glanced around. "No. Your father must've moved it."

"Ah. That would be it, then," said Sky, grinding his teeth. Morton had taken the coffin—their one clue to the blade's whereabouts, aside from an insane hunter. Bedlam's army was too close and Morton was out of time. Sky suspected that this was Morton's last-ditch effort to find the blade before freeing Solomon and abandoning Exile entirely.

And if the coffin really led to the blade somehow, then this was Sky's last chance to find it, no matter the risks.

"Sky, what's going on?" T-Bone asked.

"It's nothing," said Sky, shoving the crumpled note in his pocket. "You guys wait here."

Hands scoffed. "Yeah. Right."

Sky filled his pockets with canisters from his backpack and the duffel bag. "I'm serious," Sky insisted, shoving the package into a pocket inside the coat to open on the way. "They need help here. I'm just going out for a bit. Nothing dangerous."

"The fact that you feel the need to assure us that nothing's dangerous means that something is dangerous," Andrew observed.

Mom glanced up at Sky, narrowing her eyes.

"It's fine! Really. I'll be back in an hour, two hours tops, well before dark."

Beau shook his head. "I don't know what's going on here, but someone had better explain it to me."

Cassandra moaned.

Beau glanced over at her, and Sky slipped out while everyone was distracted.

"Sky!" Mom called after him.

"Be back soon!"

The front door opened just as Sky reached it and Dad walked through. "Sky! Just the son I've been looking for! You look horrible. Did you burn down the bowling alley?"

"I didn't burn down the bowling alley!" Sky exclaimed, slipping past Dad and out the door.

"Oh. That's good," said Dad. "Where are you going?"

Sky ran down the porch steps. "Out! Mom's waiting for you in the kitchen!"

"She is?" Dad asked, looking confused.

"Oh, and Dad—Morton's hunters are about to abandon Exile to Bedlam's army," Sky said, pausing.

"What?" Dad exclaimed. "How do you know that?"

"Call it a hunch," Sky replied. "Also, in an hour or two Morton's going to try to break into our house to free the Arkhon, who's really Solomon Rose, his former apprentice."

"I know who Solomon Rose is," Dad said, sounding far less surprised than Sky would have expected. "We'll be ready for him."

"I—" Sky started, choking up, not sure what he intended to say, but feeling the need to say something. "I'll be back in a little while. Good-bye."

"Good-bye? Sky! Sky! Where are you going?" Dad yelled after him.

But Sky kept running.

CHAPTER 22
Erfskin Biscuits

Sky slowed as he approached Crenshaw's family crypt on the edge of the Sleeping Lands. ARGRAVE IS YOUR GRAVE the plaque read. But he hadn't slowed because of the plaque. Unlike last night when he had passed this place, the giant stone door was now open.

He was in a hurry—he needed to get to the Grove of the Fallen—but he also knew that Nackles and Rauschtlot were hiding in the Sleeping Lands and that they preferred dry places to wet places, and this area was about as dry as it got in the Sleeping Lands. He didn't know exactly what Morton had planned, but he felt fairly sure that this "matter of grave importance" involved burying him. "With Hunter's Mark the buried dead shall shimmering blade hold in my stead." Sky was the only one besides Errand, wherever he was, who had a Hunter's Mark, and thus the only one besides Errand who could truly solve the riddle. The question was: Once Morton buried him, would he dig him up again?

Morton's message was vague. He'd told Sky to pack, which implied that he intended to take Sky to the Academy of Legend and subject him to further humiliation. But Morton had also told him to say good-bye to his family and friends. That could imply that Morton meant to kill him. Either way, Sky could use an ally, and a Gnomon who could burrow through the earth seemed like the perfect choice.

Sky crept into the Argraves' family tomb. Inside, he found a room that might once have looked stately and impressive but now was old and moth-ridden. Stained paintings hung askew on the walls, and the fixtures were tarnished, the stones cracked and moldy.

In the center of the room he saw a giant stone coffin—a sarcophagus—the top of which had been carved into the shape of a grumpy man who appeared very much put out by his death.

"Well, I can see where Crenshaw got his looks," Sky muttered.

He crouched down, put his hand on the stone floor, and tuned his Hunter's Mark to Earthspeak. Rauschtlot's voice came through as a faint whisper, too quiet to make out, but nearby. Beyond that, Sky felt the earth rumbling strangely to the southeast near Arkhon Academy, like thousands of feet stomping on bleachers to "We Will Rock You."

With a pang of guilt, Sky realized that the homecoming game had begun. Of course, even if he could have kept his promise to Mr. Dibble and attended, he didn't have an instrument to play; Nikola had stolen his tuba.

Sky started to pull his hand away, but then he noticed one more vibration coming from deep, deep below. At that moment, he realized how Bedlam's army was coming to Exile without anyone noticing: They were coming from under the earth.

Sky shivered. The tremor felt as if it was still far away, but there were so many vibrations . . . thousands of them. He was running out of time.

Sky took a deep breath and surveyed the stone floor of the Argraves' tomb, noticing that the mold was slightly discolored and worn, as if someone had walked upon it recently. He followed the discolored path and found himself standing in front of a tarnished torch holder on the far wall.

"You've got to be joking." He reached up and turned the torch holder sideways. The top of the sarcophagus opened, revealing a ladder within.

Sky laughed. "Real clever. No one ever would've figured that one out," he said sarcastically. "Rest assured, dead Argraves, your trap-building expertise has been passed on."

Sky crossed to the open tomb, listening for voices, but his ears couldn't detect anything.

He climbed down the ladder into the darkened catacombs below. He found water at the bottom that came up to his knees and a tunnel leading into the dark. Sky's eyes adjusted and he saw that the passage was broken and branching, with bits caved in and other parts sloping downward into pools of water and, beyond, the burial rooms of the pickled dead.

Placing his Hunter's Mark on the wall, Sky felt his way toward the nearby vibrations, which he could make out as voices now. The sound traveled through the earth to his Hunter's Mark, and he heard it as if he was standing next to the speakers, listening with his ears.

"I think our break is about over. We should relieve Nackles and the others," said a familiar voice. Sky hesitated for a moment: The man was speaking Gnomon. With a British accent. Almost no one spoke Gnomon, or any monster language, for that matter.

"Yesss, *Winston*," Rauschtlot replied. She made a hissing, popping sound and Sky realized she was laughing.

"Oh, don't laugh!" snapped Winston Snavely, the hunter who had appeared so dramatically during training that morning. "Winston's a fine chap. A fine chap with a fine first name and Snavely's not a whit behind it, so don't call me anything else unless you intend to get me into trouble. These biscuits are delicious, by the way! Wherever did you get them?"

"I maaade themmm," Rauschtlot hissed.

Something fishy was going on, and Sky suspected that whatever it was had little to do with the creepy one-eyed fish circling him. He veered into a sloping passage that led upward and out of the water, which now reached his waist. A faint light flickered up ahead.

"Really? I had no idea you baked! And you just mixed the erfskin right in?" asked Winston.

"Yesss," said Rauschtlot. "Nacklesss gatherrred the erfssskin before the collapssse."

Sky remembered what Andrew had said, about how Nackles had only come to the east cemetery last night to gather some sort of baking fungus—erfskin, by the sounds of it, whatever that was.

"Ah, yes . . . last night," said Winston quietly, a note of sadness in his voice. "I really wish I could have arrived in time, but I was unfortunately detained below. Sky performed exceptionally well, wouldn't you agree? Beyond what I could have imagined. And, as they say, all's well that ends with biscuits." Sky heard crunching sounds, and then Winston started up again. "These biscuits really are remarkable, and I can hardly taste the erfskin at all! It should really come in handy next time a tunnel decides to collapse on me. Thank you for the gift, Rauschtlot."

"My pleasssure, Winssston," said Rauschtlot, sounding pleased at the compliment.

Sky reached the end of the passage and peeked into a small burial room. He gawked at what he saw. Rauschtlot and Winston sat on two large rocks, one on each side of a sunken sarcophagus. A woman was carved into the top of the stone coffin, hands resting on her chest, and within those hands, Rauschtlot and Winston had placed a pot of tea. They each drank from dainty ceramic cups while snacking on cookies, or biscuits, as Winston had called them.

Winston gobbled up the last of his cookies and drained his tea. His clothes were a mess; it looked like a tunnel really had collapsed on him.

"Well, Ubiquitous," said Winston, patting the stone woman's stomach as he stood, "you were a horrible hunter, but you make an exceptional table."

Rauschtlot picked up the pot of tea, the cups, and the plate with the remaining cookies, and swallowed it all in one big gulp, storing it, Sky knew, in one of her stomachs for later use.

Winston glanced over and Sky ducked back into the shadows, but it was too late. "I see Morton has already taught you to be sneaky—a useful skill, all in all. It must be nice to have such a fine master."

Sky exhaled and stepped into the room. "I wasn't being sneaky—I was being cautious."

"An interesting way of putting it," said Winston.

"You and Morton don't seem to get along," said Sky, slowly walking into the room, his eyes drifting from Winston to Rauschtlot and back again.

"You could say that," said Winston calmly. "Things have been a bit peckish between us since he murdered my son."

Sky stopped where he stood. "Morton Thresher killed your son?"

"Not in a way anyone could prove," Winston replied. "What exactly is it that you want here, Sky? It seems to me that there are safer places you could be at the moment. Of course, if you were looking for safety, you could have heeded Chase's warning to flee Exile last night and saved us all a spot of bother."

"How did you know Chase warned me?" Sky asked.

"Because he told me," Winston replied. "And now you've put yourself in Morton's hands and given him the keys to the Arkhon's prison."

"I didn't have a choice," said Sky defensively.

"That's the way traps work," said Winston. "If it gave you a choice, it wouldn't be a trap. Now, what is it you wanted?"

"I saw the door open," Sky replied. "I thought I might find Rauschtlot and Nackles here."

"Of course," said Winston. "How rude of me. Rauschtlot, are there any biscuits left?"

Rauschtlot opened her mouth and pulled out the plate of cookies. Sky looked at the cookies, curling his lip in distaste. "No thanks. I'm good."

"Here, take some for later, then," said Winston, giving

Sky several large handfuls. "They might come in handy if you find yourself in a tight spot—a not altogether unusual circumstance for you, from what I hear. Erfskin is quite a rarity. It can make you as strong and resilient as a Gnomon, if you take my meaning."

"I think I do—take your meaning, that is," said Sky, shoving the cookies into a coat pocket. "Thanks."

"That's a smashing coat," said Winston admiringly. "I used to own one just like it. Bit scratchy."

"Yeah," said Sky. "It's less itchy if you wash it."

"Ah . . . that's the secret then," said Winston, smiling.

"Would you mind if I talked to Rauschtlot in private?" Sky asked.

"Not at all," Winston replied. "I'll just wait over here."

Winston strolled off down the tunnel, whistling to himself.

Sky rushed over to Rauschtlot. "Rauschtlot, are you all right? Is Nackles okay?"

"Yesss," she hissed in Gnomon. "Winsssston and I are old friendsss."

"What are you doing here?" Sky asked.

"Collapsssing tunnelsss," Rauschtlot hissed. "Bedlam's army comesss. We lead them to Erachnusss to face huntersss. Keep Exile sssafe."

Sky nodded. It made sense. The area where the hunters trained was familiar, out of the way, and full of traps. It was the only place where they might have an advantage against whatever monsters were coming through the earth.

"Smart," said Sky appreciatively. He was glad someone else was thinking about saving Exile, because right now all he really cared about was Crystal. Fortunately, finding the blade and freeing Bedlam saved Crystal and Exile—but

Crystal first. "So you've been here the whole time?"

"Deeeeper," Rauschtlot replied. "Tunnelsss of earrrth eeeater."

"The earth eater? You mean Paragoth?"

Rauschtlot nodded fearfully, her eyes darting around as if saying Paragoth's name would make her magically appear. No hunter, as far as Sky knew, had ever seen Paragoth and lived. All they'd ever found was evidence of her passing and the gargantuan otherwordly tunnels she had left in her wake far, far below.

"She is clossse," Rauschtlot hissed. "She makesss the tunnels for Bedlam's arrrmy."

"Is she working with Bedlam?"

"Yesss," Rauschtlot replied. "But they fearrr her. They ssstay far away or die."

Sky frowned. Paragoth, according to the stories, lived deep down where it was warm and dark, and where she could eat the molten earth to fuel her fires and heat her belly. She left behind tunnels that were hundreds of feet across and teeming with strange life. It was even rumored that Paragoth was the mother of the Gnomon, though Sky wasn't about to ask Rauschtlot if that was true; she looked frightened enough as it was.

The news complicated matters because it meant Rauschtlot had more important things to do than help him.

Sky glanced back at Winston to make sure he wasn't listening. Winston was whistling happily, a tune Sky recognized from the song "There Once Was a Flowering Botanist." He'd heard it many times while growing up. Winston did a little jig to his whistling, ending it with a twirl.

From the minute Winston had appeared that morning,

Sky had been suspicious of him. Like Hands and T-Bone, Sky just assumed that anyone he met was a fraud or a shifter of some sort, until proven otherwise. Winston's strange conversation with Rauschtlot had heightened Sky's suspicions, but that song—sung to him so often when he was young—confirmed it: Winston wasn't who he appeared to be. And now Sky knew exactly who he was. Part of him was thrilled beyond belief, but another part of him—the more vocal part—was swelling with anger at the deception and the pain it had caused. For now, at least, Sky was content to let Winston keep up his charade since Winston didn't seem to care enough to end it. But Sky wasn't going to make it easy for him.

"I need your help," Sky continued, ignoring his anger and pain as he turned back to Rauschtlot. "Crystal's hurt and—"

The whistling stopped. Sky glanced over and saw Winston standing right next to him. "How did you—"

"What happened?" Winston cut in, his voice stern, demanding an answer.

"Harrow Wights," Sky replied. "They threw this fiery molten ball and—"

"It's bad?" Winston asked, cutting him off again.

Sky nodded and wiped away a tear he didn't remember crying. "Very. She only has a few hours."

Winston appeared grief-stricken. "That poor girl. Rauschtlot, can you continue without me?"

Rauschtlot hesitated. "Perhapsss."

"Do your best," Winston stated. "Send word to the manor if you locate Morton's allies and Bedlam's body."

"Yesss," Rauschtlot hissed. Then, turning, she dove into the wall as if it were water rather than hardened stone and earth. She filled the hole in behind her—dirt and gravel shooting out of mouths that suddenly appeared on her legs and feet. Idly, Sky wondered what the process would look like in reverse. He shivered and decided he really didn't want to know.

Winston stared after Rauschtlot, looking forlorn. "She was my ride . . ."

Winston spun and strode down the tunnel.

Sky scrambled to catch up. "Who are Morton's allies?"

"The Whisper and the Wargarou: Ambrosia and Gourmand," Winston replied. "They've been working with Morton since their failed attempt to open the prison last year. They haven't given up, though Morton has kept them ignorant as to who they'll find should they succeed."

"And yet somehow you know exactly who they'll find. How is that?" Sky asked, raising an eyebrow.

Winston glanced at him. "The Arkhon has been telling hunters that he was Solomon Rose for years; it's not my fault if no one else believed him."

Sky harrumphed. That was a bad answer, but he wasn't going to press. "So Ambrosia and Gourmand have Bedlam's body? I thought Bedlam's army had it."

"They did," said Winston, wading down into the water and the one-eyed fishes. "But Ambrosia and Gourmand stole it from them earlier today. Now they're hiding somewhere in Paragoth's domain while Bedlam's army rushes to the surface to destroy us. I suppose Morton figured that if he couldn't find Alexander's blade, Bedlam's body would do. Either way, Morton gains a bargaining chip he can use with Bedlam, and Exile is destroyed."

"So he's given up his search for the blade?" Sky asked, his stomach sinking. If Morton wasn't looking for the blade anymore, then that meant he truly intended to bury him.

"I suspect Morton still wants Alexander's blade, not only as another bargaining chip, but for more sentimental reasons," Winston replied, his voice bitter.

"You mean because he used it to kill your son?" said Sky, guessing.

Winston glanced at him, but didn't say anything.

"It's true, isn't it?" said Sky, his mind racing as he connected the pieces together. "You said Morton killed your son and that you hate him for it. Alexander was killed with his own blade, but they never found the killer—you think it's Morton, and you think he wants the blade not just to stop Bedlam, but as a memento, or maybe as a symbol that he's beaten you—a sentimental reason. Alexander Drake was your son, wasn't he?"

A single tear fell down Winston's face, and Sky knew: It was time to end the game, whether Winston wanted him to know who he truly was or not. Sky couldn't take it anymore.

"Uncle Phineas . . . why didn't you ever tell me?"

Winston looked at him sharply . . . and then he smiled, and Sky knew it was true.

"Phineas, it *is* you!" Sky threw his arms around Phineas, who hugged him back. Sky was still mad and he still wanted answers, but for now he was content to wait. Phineas was alive!

"You've always been far too clever for your own good," said Phineas, grinning.

"You weren't exactly subtle," Sky accused. "'There Once Was a Flowering Botanist'? Really? You couldn't have picked a more obvious song to whistle."

"Ah, yes," said Phineas. "I sang that to you when you were small, until you figured out what the lyrics meant."

"It was horrible—worst song I ever heard," said Sky, smiling. "Limericks were never meant for music."

"Your mother was of the same opinion, as I recall, and explained her reasoning quite vigorously," said Phineas.

Sky laughed.

"Aren't you curious to know why I look like this, how it's possible?" Phineas asked.

"You're using Alexander's Slippery Wick Brew," said Sky. "I mean, it makes sense. . . . He really was your son, wasn't he?"

"Hunters like myself can't have children of our own, an unfortunate side effect of a prolonged life," Phineas said. "But Alexander was adopted, and yes, he was my son in every way that matters."

"And you believe Morton killed him?"

"Yes," Phineas replied. "I do."

"But . . . that would make Morton the owner of the blade," said Sky, his stomach dropping. "If Morton is the owner of the blade, then we can't use it to free Bedlam unless Morton gives it to us willingly or . . ."

"He dies," said Phineas, finishing Sky's thought. "I am aware of the situation."

"But you can't kill him. Bedlam said that if someone with the Eye of Legend dies, dire consequences will follow," Sky pointed out. "Of course, that didn't stop Morton from hunting me, so maybe the consequences aren't so bad."

"They are bad," Phineas confirmed. "Potentially catastrophic. It's hard to predict, but it's always horrible, and fixing things is even worse; that is why we prefer to trap creatures with the Eye who turn evil. In your case, Morton convinced a majority of the Hunters that you were a big enough liability to be worth the risk."

"I feel so honored," Sky said blandly. "You have an Eye, don't you? Like Morton. Like me. You've lied to me all these years."

Phineas raised an eyebrow. "It's possible," he evaded. "Have you talked to Bedlam, by chance?"

Sky nodded. "He's trapped in Cass, though somehow I suspect you already know that."

Phineas smiled, but didn't expand.

"We have a deal," Sky continued. "Bedlam will save Crystal and take his army back to Skull Valley if we free him."

Phineas sighed in relief. "Excellent."

"Can we trust him?" Sky asked.

"Yes," said Phineas. "Bedlam is one of the most honorable creatures I have ever met. If he promised you that he would heal Crystal and leave, then that is precisely what he will do."

"Good," said Sky. "The only problem is that we don't have the blade or Bedlam's body, and even if we had both those things, we don't know how to use the blade to free Bedlam, not to mention that Morton owns the blade, so we couldn't use it even if we had it."

"That is one of the most confusing sentences I have ever heard," Phineas said appreciatively. "Congratulations, Sky— we might make a hunter of you yet."

Sky grinned.

They reached the ladder leading out of the catacombs. Sky's grin faded. Their time was short. Once he climbed that ladder, he would have to leave Phineas again. It was time to ask the question that had bothered him more than any other.

"Why did you let me think you were dead?"

Phineas smiled sadly. "Many reasons, and none of them good, I'm afraid. Mostly it was to protect you and Exile. I've been undercover at the Academy of Legend for the past year trying to steer the events Bedlam has now set in motion. It's very dangerous. But I suspect it was also for the same reason you never told your parents about Errand: The longer you keep a secret, the harder it is to share."

"You've been with Errand for the last year, haven't you? He was there with you, at the Academy, wasn't he?" The words came out sounding more bitter than he had intended. He knew it was stupid to feel jealous, but Sky couldn't help picturing the two of them traveling the world together, laughing about how they had really pulled one over on that fool Sky.

"Not for the full year, no, but enough," Phineas replied, his voice level and cautious. "It took me some time to find him, and even more to convince him to come with me. Errand was instrumental in getting the hunters to come to Exile—a backup plan should our efforts to free Bedlam fail, though I'm afraid they won't be enough."

"Especially since they're leaving," said Sky. "Morton has called a retreat."

"I'm aware," Phineas replied. "I've talked to Hagos. I suspect the retreat may not go as well as Morton has planned."

"And Errand's here? In Exile?" Sky asked.

"That's not for me to say," Phineas replied. "Errand's secrets are his own to share, as yours are yours. Secrets are a hunter's currency, after all."

"Ah. I see," said Sky. "I think I can guess who he is."

"I'm sure you can," said Phineas. "In fact, it would surprise me if you couldn't."

Sky thought for a moment. "So there really is a Winston Snavely?"

"One of the few friends I have left among the Hunters of Legend. He's currently taking a much needed vacation in

the Caribbean with hopes of meeting a flowering botanist."
Phineas smirked and Sky laughed.

Phineas grew serious again. "Sky, I know the last year has
been hard. I'm sorry I arrived here too late to stop the hunt
last night. I spent eleven years training you for these sorts of
things; from the time you could crawl, I've watched over you.
Don't begrudge Errand his time with me. He has a far harder
road ahead than either of us, and he will need you before the
end. He will need both of us."

"What end? You make it sound like something horrible is
coming," said Sky.

Phineas smiled sadly. "Have I ever complimented you on
your coat? It's quite fetching."

"You're evading," Sky pointed out.

"Did you know I once met a woman named Eva Ding?
Lovely lady," said Phineas. "Though she had the strangest fas-
cination with pudding tarts . . ."

Sky rolled his eyes and climbed up and out of the sarcophagus.

As he reached the top, a thought occurred to him. "Phineas,
if Morton killed Alexander, then why did he leave the blade
behind? Why didn't he take it with him?"

Phineas frowned. "An astute question, one I've asked
myself for years, but I've never given myself a satisfactory
answer. It wasn't until recently that Morton learned the blade
could be used to free Bedlam, so he didn't fully appreciate
its value. But even so, shimmering blades are incredibly rare,
and Alexander's holds more secrets than almost any other.
Morton could have taken it and hidden it away, or come up
with some story to explain how he got it. He's a powerful
Hunter—few would have had the courage to doubt him. To
be honest, I have no idea why he left it."

Sky thought about it and couldn't come up with a good answer, either, but the question troubled him. Why wouldn't Morton take the blade?

They exited the tomb and Fred the Piebald swooped down and landed on the awning above them.

"Fred! Where have you been? Are the other Piebalds okay?" Sky asked.

"CAW!"

"Well, tell them to stay hidden," said Sky.

Phineas looked up and spotted Fred. "Fred, is it? I've never trusted Piebalds; their brains are smaller than peas, you know."

"CAW!" Fred croaked.

"I've never heard such rude language in all my years," Phineas sputtered. "Do you kiss your mother with that mouth?"

"CAW!"

"You've never kissed my mother in your life," Phineas retorted. "And I'm still of the opinion that butter pecan is the better flavor."

Sky guffawed, remembering Morton's story about Phineas arguing with a bird over ice cream flavors. "You know this bird?"

"CAW!"

"Fine, Piebald, whatever," Sky corrected.

"We've met," Phineas replied guardedly. "Though I haven't seen him for some time. I wonder what you could possibly be up to, Fred? . . ."

"CAW! CAW!"

"I've been busy—I haven't checked yet," said Sky.

"What package is he talking about?" Phineas asked.

Sky pulled out the package from the bowling alley. "It's the reason we went to the bowling alley. Someone sent a letter saying a Marrowick would deliver a package that would stop Bedlam's army."

"I suspect Bedlam is the only one who can stop his army should the hunters fail," said Phineas.

Sky opened the package. Inside, he found a small, bloodred seed no larger than an acorn. A note in the package read:

When Hope, Patience, and Vengeance fail,

and the broken world around you breaks,

plant this seed within your heart, and avail

to free a soul and mend mistakes.

"Sounds cryptic," Phineas observed.

Sky checked the packaging, but there was nothing else inside. On the outside, all he found were a few splotches of Marrowick wax.

"Did you send this?" Sky asked.

"No," said Phineas.

"But you could be lying to hide something from me. It wouldn't be the first time."

"I could be, but I'm not," Phineas replied, looking troubled.

"So who sent it?"

Phineas took the seed and examined it. "No idea, really.

I've never seen a seed like this before." Phineas held it up to the light, and the bloodred shell turned clear so that Sky could see a golden glob in the middle.

"What is it?" Sky asked.

"It appears to be some kind of golden glob," Phineas replied.

Sky rolled his eyes. "I can see that."

"Then why did you ask?" Phineas retorted.

Fred cawed, swooped down, and snatched the packaging from Sky's hand.

"Hey!" Sky shouted. But Fred simply flew away with the envelope.

"Someday soon that bird and I are going to have a very long talk," Sky promised.

"I expect you shall, and longer than you might suppose. You have many of those in store, from what I understand," said Phineas, handing the seed back to Sky. "You'd best keep that and the letter until we ascertain their purpose."

Sky put the seed in his pocket. He watched Phineas, tempted to tell him about Morton and the Grove of the Fallen and how Morton planned to bury him. But if he told Phineas what Morton was up to, Phineas would come with him, which meant that he wouldn't go help Crystal, and Crystal needed all the help Sky could send her.

"I've got a few things to do," Sky said. "I'll catch up with you at the manor later."

"Hurry, then." Seemingly preoccupied, Phineas strode off.

Sky didn't have any allies to help him with Morton, but he still had the erfskin cookies Phineas had given him. If the cookies really gave him the strength and resilience of a Gnomon, he might just survive his burial. Or maybe he would die from gross-cookie poisoning. Either way, it was his best bet, and the blade was his only real hope of saving Crystal. He had to try.

With the erfskin cookies in his pocket, Sky turned and raced north for the Grove of the Fallen.

CHAPTER 23
Buried by Porp-a-lorps

*H*ello, Sky," said Morton. "You've forgotten your underwear."

"And my toothbrush," Sky replied as he approached Alexander's gravesite. "I didn't have time to pack, and since I'm not going anywhere, I didn't see the point."

Alexander's coffin sat beside his open grave and Sky eyed it anxiously, knowing the sort of "grave business" Morton needed him for. "With Hunter's Mark the buried dead shall shimmering blade hold in my stead."

They meant to bury him.

The only problem was that the blade was never in the coffin, according to Em. Nikola had carried it the entire time, until he'd gone insane. So unless Nikola, in his madness, had left the riddle and somehow hidden the blade below, this whole experience would come to a terribly disappointing end.

Morton stood on one of the piles of dirt, staring down into Alexander's grave. Chase was there as well, along with Solange Avaray, but there was no sign of Hagos Adera.

Three Hunters of Legend to bury one thirteen-year-old boy.

Chase winked, but Sky ignored him. He wasn't sure how to handle Chase just yet.

Solange, on the other hand, glowered and seemed very unhappy to be there. Sky wondered what'd happened to Hagos.

"Hagos had a . . . change of heart, so to speak. Rather than inviting him, I've asked him to prepare our hunters for the retreat back to the Academy of Legend," said Morton, seemingly reading his thoughts. "Winston has thankfully disappeared, so, alas, it's just the four of us here to mark this splendid occasion: The recovery of a shimmering blade is not a small matter. Nearly all have been lost or taken by outcasts like Malvidia and Phineas."

"So you're really leaving? You're just going to abandon the Exile hunters to face Bedlam's army alone?" Sky asked.

"Yes," Morton replied.

Sky waited, but Morton didn't expand.

"We've searched the hole," Morton continued, "and it appears there is nothing down there."

"Does that mean you're not going to bury me?" Sky asked.

"Oh, no—we have every intention of burying you," Morton replied, smiling.

Sky grimaced. "Let's get on with it, then."

Sky walked over to the coffin, trying not to shake.

"There are a few conditions before we do this," said Morton, before Sky could open the coffin.

"Conditions?" said Sky incredulously. "You're about to bury me alive and you're giving me conditions?"

Morton grinned. "Of course. Should this work, you will give the blade directly to me. As a *gift*. Freely and wholeheartedly."

"Why would I need to give it to you? Don't you already own it?" Sky asked, watching Morton closely.

Morton scowled. "No."

As far as Sky could tell, Morton wasn't lying. But what did that mean, exactly? Was it possible that Morton hadn't killed Alexander? But if he hadn't, who had?

"And what do I get if I give you the blade?" Sky asked.

"You are my apprentice. You will come with us to the Academy of Legend during our retreat. In other words, you get to live," said Morton.

Sky shook his head. "Not good enough. I'll give you the blade, but *I* get to set the conditions."

"And what, precisely, are your conditions?" Morton asked, looking amused.

"Your hunters stay here to defend Exile," said Sky. "And you use the blade to free Bedlam."

"And why on earth would I do that?" Morton asked.

"Well, you've already got his body," Sky replied. "And the main reason you want the blade is so you can have another bargaining chip to use with Bedlam should you need it. That tells me that you're already considering freeing him to save your own hunters. Just make the deal now—save your hunters and Exile as well. Honestly, with Phineas dead or gone, there's no reason not to. Besides, Bedlam was your ally once. He could be again."

"Interesting," said Morton, still smiling. "Though I suspect my objectives are no longer compatible with Bedlam's, and I can see many reasons not to save Exile. Out of curiosity, what's to stop me from simply killing you and taking the blade once you have it?"

"You can bury me, but you can't make me take the blade

if it somehow appears," said Sky. "I want a promise—on your sword—that you'll do what I've asked, or I won't touch the blade. And if I don't touch it, I don't own it, which means if you kill me, you still won't own it."

Sky knew he was taking a huge risk, but this was the best he could ask for. In the stories, hunters who swore on their blades always kept their word. He could only hope Morton would do the same.

Morton considered. "You are a confusing little boy. Very well. I swear on my sword that should you recover the blade, and should it shimmer, and should you give it to me freely and wholeheartedly, I will order my hunters to defend Exile and I will free Bedlam. Is that satisfactory?"

Sky examined Morton's words, looking for a trap. "And you will stay yourself," he added.

Morton's grin fell a little. "As you say—I will stay as well. Good enough?"

Sky nodded.

"Excellent!" Morton exclaimed. "Chase, if you'd do the honors?"

Chase opened the coffin lid. He stared inside, looking perplexed.

Sky stepped forward and saw a checkered picnic blanket and his tuba, minus the case, sitting in the coffin.

"It's a tuba," Chase muttered.

"Excuse me?" Morton moved closer, followed by Solange.

"It iz ze tuba," Solange confirmed.

Morton picked up the tuba while Solange grabbed the picnic blanket, sniffing it.

"Zis blanket smellz of nacho cheese." Solange stared at the blanket in disgust.

Morton inspected the tuba and then played a few notes. "It is indeed a tuba."

Chase raised his eyebrows questioningly at Sky. Sky shook his head—he had no idea why these things were here. Obviously Nikola had put them here since the picnic blanket belonged to him and he had stolen Sky's tuba earlier. But why, and where was the tuba case? Was some part of Nikola's jumbled brain trying to tell him something?

"Let us get on wiz zis—ze Moonriders are waiting," said Solange. "And zis town is for ze birds."

"Yes . . . well," said Morton, tossing the tuba to the side.

Sky cringed. He hated the tuba, but that was *his* tuba.

Solange threw the blanket on a pile of dirt.

The coffin was now empty.

"In you go!" said Morton cheerfully.

Sky took a deep breath and . . . and . . . He couldn't do it. He stared into that cramped space; he imagined the earth surrounding him. "I . . . I can't."

"Oh, come now!" said Morton. "It'll only be for a few minutes, then we'll have you right back up. The Porp-a-lorps are highly accomplished diggers."

Sky looked at Chase, who gave a slight nod of his head, promising Sky that he would be all right. Sky took a deep breath and climbed into the coffin.

The coffin bumped against the walls as they lowered him into the earth. He closed his eyes. *Breathe. Breathe.*

He heard dirt raining down on the lid and the sounds of the hundreds of fireflylike Porp-a-lorps zooming past, pushing the dirt onto the coffin.

A few minutes.

A few minutes more.

Porp-a-lorps thumped into the coffin, shaking it.

Morton opened the lid. "See? That wasn't so bad?"

Sky sat up, gasping for air. Morton stood next to the coffin, but they were still in the hole—they hadn't pulled him out yet. And that made Sky nervous.

The smile on Morton's mouth fell away. "Where is the blade?"

"Nothing happened," said Sky.

"Are you certain?"

"Positive," Sky replied. Over Morton's shoulder, he could see Chase staring down into the pit, looking worried. There was no sign of Solange.

"A pity," said Morton. "Perhaps if we gave it more time?"

"I'm not going back in there!" Sky declared. He started to rise, but Morton put his cane across Sky's chest, stopping him.

"Hmm . . . that does create a dilemma," said Morton. "I can't have you running off, and you don't seem inclined to help me. You wouldn't consider telling me how to open the prison, would you? I've used the keys before, but I can't for the life of me figure out how to make them work on the prison."

Sky shook his head. "I don't know. I've only closed it, never opened it."

Morton sighed. "I suppose I'll have to figure it out on my own, then. You realize, of course, that our deal is off. Without the blade, I can't exactly free Bedlam and save Exile, now can I? It's too bad. I'd hoped to make a present of Alexander's blade to Solomon to replace the one he lost when they trapped Bedlam, but seeing as how we can't find it, Solomon will have to make due without for the time being. Really, I should've taken it with me when I had the chance."

Sky stared at Morton. "You killed Alexander."

"Most certainly," Morton replied. "I stabbed him through

the neck with his own blade. But the blade never shimmered for me, I'm afraid, or I never would've left it behind. I thought it was worthless. For the life of me, I've never understood why it didn't work. I was its rightful owner. I even set aside my own blade for it so I could make the new connection, and still it rejected me. It was very frustrating."

"But why did you kill Alexander? You told me you and Phineas were friends once, and yet you murdered his son!" Sky said accusingly.

"Oh, many reasons," said Morton. "A grudge against his father. Personality differences. But mostly it was revenge for killing Solomon."

"But Alexander didn't kill Solomon," Sky pointed out. "Solomon became the Arkhon."

"Yes, I realize that now. It's an unfortunate situation. When Alexander returned alone after their hunt of the Arkhon, I confronted him. He told me that Solomon had died a hero, but his story was full of holes and he refused to give me details. But I knew Alexander and, at the time, I believed his cowardice had cost Solomon his life. My greatest apprentice, my son, dead because of a cowardly boy who was like a brother to him! I found Alexander in his study, and I stabbed him with his own blade."

"And you're calling *him* a coward?" Sky prodded. "I still don't get why you used his Slippery Wick Brew to imitate him."

Morton stared at Sky as if he were crazy. "I did no such thing."

"But there were reports that Alexander was seen leaving his office a short time before his body was found," said Sky, feeling like he was missing something.

Morton waved his hand dismissively. "Rubbish."

He lifted his cane from Sky's chest and Sky sighed in relief. He had honestly thought that Morton intended to bury him again.

"Well, we'd best be off," Morton chirped.

Sky started to climb out, but Morton's cane swung back into place, stopping him. "Not you."

With a quick thrust, Morton pushed Sky back down into the coffin and closed the lid.

Sky pounded on it as dirt rained down once again and Porp-a-lorps zoomed past.

"Chase! CHASE!" Sky screamed. "You can't let him do this! CHASE!"

Sky heard Morton's voice growing softer and softer with each clump of falling dirt. "This is for your own good, Sky—a punishment to remind you that I am your master now. We'll return for you right after we release Solomon; I'm sure he'll be terribly happy to see you. It's better this way, really. You'll see. Until then, try to stay alive."

Sky fought to get out of the coffin, but it was no use.

He felt a vibration coming through the wood—Earthspeak. His Hunter's Mark surged with light, and he heard Chase say, "I'll be back for you, Sky. I promise."

But the words that started in Chase's voice ended in Errand's. And then Sky knew for certain. Chase and Errand were one and the same.

"Don't leave me, Errand!" Sky shouted back through the earth. "Don't leave me!"

"I promise I'll return," Errand said one last time. "As soon as I can."

Sky screamed, pounding against the lid.

"Get me out of here! Get me out! Errand! ERRAND!"

CHAPTER 24

A Gift Freely Given

Sky closed his eyes and tried to breathe slowly. It would have been much easier to calm down if that person would stop screaming. Sky realized *he* was the one screaming, so he closed his mouth.

"All right . . . all right, just stay calm," said Sky to the confining darkness.

He took a deep breath.

"Just . . . be . . . calm." Sky took another deep breath.

Then he lashed out, pounding at the coffin with his legs and fists.

"Get me out of here! Get me out! Get me out—"

The coffin dropped a foot and Sky stopped freaking out. He could hear something slithering through the dirt above and below, and then to the sides, wrapping around the coffin.

"Hello?" Sky whispered.

The coffin fell again, and this time it didn't stop. It plummeted down and down. Sky started screaming in earnest.

Something thumped into the coffin's sides, wrapping around, enfolding him in a very dangerous hammock. Sky heard crackling and popping, and then he jerked to a stop. Whatever was outside began to constrict.

The coffin cracked and a trickle of dirt fell into Sky's mouth. He spit it out. "Give me a minute here!"

The crackling of the pine box grew louder.

Sky pulled out one of the erfskin cookies Phineas had given him. He stared at it, feeling almost as frightened of the cookie as he was of whatever was outside the coffin. Phineas had said the cookie would give him the strength and resilience of a Gnomon. It was also made with baking fungus and had been regurgitated by a Gnomon. Only imminent threat of death could make him eat this cookie. He closed his eyes and took a tiny nibble. . . .

His eyelids flipped back open: It was better than he had expected.

As he swallowed that tiny bit, he could breathe more easily. He felt his pores open to an alarming degree, and air rushed in, making him light-headed. His skin seemed to harden and his muscles tightened.

"Whoa . . . nice."

He shoved the rest of the cookie back into his pocket with the others, fearing to eat too much, unsure of the side effects. They wouldn't be too dangerous, or Phineas wouldn't have given him the cookies. But Phineas had a weird sense of humor; he might find it funny to see Sky with a terrible rash for a week or an extra ear growing out of his forehead. Character building, Phineas would call it.

Sky didn't know how long the erfskin cookie's effects would

last, but he could always take another nibble if he needed it. Then, experimenting, he pushed at the sides of the coffin with his newfound strength, and they cracked.

A tree root immediately rushed through the crack, slithered across his chest, and slipped out the other side. Then it constricted and started crushing him. Hundreds of maggots—some the size of his fist—crept through the opening and crawled over his body, and Sky remembered the warning outside the Grove about maggots. He gagged as the creatures coated him in slime.

"Bad . . . idea . . . ," Sky wheezed, struggling to breathe through the root's crushing pressure.

He put his Hunter's Mark against the root to see if he could talk to the tree above. Any tree smart enough to know he was trespassing had to be smart enough to stop crushing him.

"Please . . . stop. . . ." He felt his Hunter's Mark warm, and light spilled out. The root began to let up.

He took a deep breath.

And then, on the lid, in the light of his Hunter's Mark, the words changed. Instead of "With Hunter's Mark the buried dead shall shimmering blade hold in my stead," he read, "Place Hunter's Mark here to live."

Sky shoved his glowing mark to the spot, and the root on his chest began to tighten again.

More words appeared:

I GIVE YOU THE GIFT,

OF THE SHIMMERING BLADE,

THOUGH NOT IN MY HANDS,

AND TAKEN AWAY.
I GIVE IT FREELY,
COMPLETELY,
AND WITH MY WHOLE HEART.
THE BLADE IS NOW YOURS,
YOUR GIFT TO IMPART.
SINCERELY,

ALEXANDER DRAKE

P.S. IF YOU'RE DESPERATE ENOUGH TO BURY YOURSELF FOR THE BLADE, YOU DESERVE IT.

P.P.S. IF YOU'RE SOLOMON ROSE, I TAKE IT ALL BACK.

Sky felt a warm sensation flow through him, the light got brighter, and then the words disappeared completely. Sky waited for the blade to drop through the earth or something, but there was nothing more. What in the world? . . .

The root on his chest constricted, growing tighter and tighter, and this time it wouldn't let go when he asked it to. Maggots crawled all over him, and he could feel them gnawing at his hardened skin.

Sky punched the pine box again and again, shattering it

to pieces. Dirt cascaded in around him. He gulped in air and forced the root from his chest. He clawed at the earth, pushing his way up. Maggots clung to him. Roots lashed at him.

Sky held his breath, struggling, until he inhaled and dirt filled his lungs. He stopped breathing. His skin leeched air from the dirt, and he kept driving upward. A root caught his ankle and dragged him back down. Sky jerked his leg, snapping the root.

His fingers broke through the surface. Grabbing hold, he yanked himself up, clawing and scraping. His head popped out. His chest. His hips. Finally he tumbled out of the earth, flopped to his back, and knocked the maggots from his body.

Sky rolled to his knees, spitting out dirt. He barfed and coughed until there was nothing left, until his lungs and stomach were empty. He inhaled deeply, savoring the sweet air.

He sat that way for a time, breathing, until his trembling subsided and the terror left him. He felt his skin return to normal, and the Gnomon-like strength disappeared as the nibble of erfskin cookie wore off.

Noticing his tuba nearby, he crawled over and set it on his lap. It was badly dented and several of the valves had broken off. He put it to his mouth and blew out a sad-sounding note.

Based on the strange message, Sky now felt certain that he owned Alexander's blade. He could use it to free Bedlam, if he ever found it. But the only person who could have given him the blade was Alexander's killer and—based on the message—Alexander's killer was none other than Alexander himself, which didn't make any sense at all.

Whatever the case, it didn't matter anymore; he now owned the blade, which took him one step closer to saving Crystal, and he didn't have time to ponder four-hundred-year-old riddles. Right now only one thing mattered: finding the blade.

Glancing up, he saw T-Bone, Hands, and Andrew running toward him.

"Sky! Are you okay? What happened?" T-Bone exclaimed as they ran up.

"Crystal . . . is she alive?" Sky asked, climbing to his feet, fearing he was already too late.

"When we left, she was," Hands replied. "Winston—or I should say, *Phineas*—and your mom are keeping her alive, but it's a close thing."

"How did you find me?" Sky asked. He started walking through the monuments toward the Grove, staring up at the sky, watching.

"Phineas told us where you were," said Andrew.

"Phineas? How did he know?" Sky asked.

"Errand appeared in his head, or something," Hands replied. "Told him Morton was finally on his way to free Solomon and that they'd buried you. Phineas is setting up defenses around the manor, but Malvidia dragged Beau and your dad down to the Finger of Erachnus. She's grabbing every hunter and former hunter she can find to fight off Bedlam's army. It's not looking hopeful."

"That about sums it up," said Sky.

"Sky, what's going on?" T-Bone asked, sounding frustrated. "Because I'm utterly confused. How is Errand back? Where has he been?"

"Errand's posing as Chase Shroud," Sky replied. "From what I understand, he and Phineas have been spying on the Hunters of Legend and Bedlam for the last year, trying to 'steer events,' as Phineas put it. I don't know the full story, but it appears that they're the ones who manipulated the hunters into coming here in the hopes of stopping Bedlam's army—a backup plan that's likely to fail, by the sounds of it, but might buy us some time."

"So Phineas and Errand are behind the hunt on you?" Hands asked.

"I'm not sure about that," Sky said hesitantly, hoping it wasn't true; he couldn't see Phineas doing that, but Errand . . . "Morton hates Exile. He would love to see it burn to the ground. Once Bedlam's army started marching, I think Errand must've leaked information about Solomon and the blade as a way to lure Morton here. As Solomon's former apprentice, Errand is the only one besides Solomon who could've known about the link between Alexander's blade and Bedlam's Chrysalis—a link that's not mentioned in any of the stories."

"It seems like bringing Morton and all these hunters here is kind of risky," T-Bone observed. "What if Morton manages to free Solomon?"

"I don't think they ever intended to give Morton the monocle—they did that to save me. I'm still not sure how they got it. But Phineas and Errand had to convince Morton to come here somehow," said Sky. "At least, they believed they did."

"Why's that?" Andrew asked.

"Because Phineas thinks Morton used Alexander's blade to murder Alexander, Phineas's son," said Sky. "But Phineas could never prove it to the other Hunters."

Hands whistled. "No wonder they hate each other."

"That would make Morton the owner of the blade," said Andrew, "the only one who could use it to free Bedlam."

Sky nodded. "Phineas was right about one thing: Morton murdered Alexander with the blade; Morton told me himself," said Sky. "But Phineas was also wrong: Morton was never the owner."

"What's that mean?" asked T-Bone. "Are you saying Alexander didn't own the blade when Morton used it on him, so ownership never transferred?"

"Or that Morton only thought he killed Alexander," said Sky. "Alexander left a message in his coffin that only someone with a Hunter's Mark could see. So either Alexander somehow knew he was going to die and left the message beforehand, or someone else with a Hunter's Mark left the message in Alexander's name. Or, another possibility—"

"Alexander isn't really dead," Andrew finished.

Sky frowned at the thought. "It seems like a lot of hunters are returning from the dead these days."

"Really?" said Andrew. "Who else?"

Sky bit his tongue. Andrew still didn't know about his parents, Em and Nikola. "I was just referring to Phineas and Errand," Sky lied. "The point is, I now own the blade, even if I don't have it, so we'll never know who the previous owner was."

"Between killing Phineas's son and the blade stuff, I'm surprised Morton's alive," said T-Bone.

"Phineas can't kill him—or he won't, anyway," said Sky. "Apparently, bad stuff happens when you kill someone with the Eye, bad enough that hunters trap creatures like Bedlam and Morton rather than kill them, assuming they even *could* kill them."

"But you have the Eye and hunters tried to kill you," Andrew pointed out.

"I think having both the Hunter's Mark and the Eye of Legend makes the hunters doubly worried. Enough so that killing me seems worth the risk," said Sky.

"So if Phineas and Errand aren't trying to kill Morton, what are they trying to do?" T-Bone asked.

"Trap him," said Sky. "Phineas was never able to prove that Morton killed Alexander. If he could prove that, then the Hunters of Legend would turn against Morton and imprison him. If Phineas didn't have their support, they'd simply undo any trap he built."

"But the blade won't prove anything, and I doubt they'll take your word over Morton's," said Hands. "The trap failed."

"That part of it," said Sky. "But Phineas never lays just one trap."

"Solomon Rose is the second," said Andrew, nodding appreciatively.

"It's a double-bogey trap," said Sky. "Very risky. Hunters don't believe Solomon is the Arkhon. Nobody trusts the Arkhon. So if they learned Morton had tried to free him, Phineas could make a case for imprisonment."

"And if Solomon escapes?" Hands asked.

"That's the risky part," Sky replied. "With Solomon free, and Morton backing him, he might be able to sway the hunters to his side. If he manages to convince them of who he is, things will go against Phineas."

"So why take the risk?" T-Bone asked. "Seems stupid to me."

"I didn't give them an option," Sky admitted. "I was supposed to leave Exile. By staying, I forced Errand and Phineas to give up the monocle to save me. If Solomon escapes, it's my fault."

"So the first trap's a flop, and the second trap might blow up in our faces." T-Bone shook his head in dismay. "This is giving me a headache. Remind me not to play pinochle with any of you."

"Pinochle?" said Hands, raising an eyebrow.

"What? I like pinochle," said T-Bone defensively.

"So what's next?" asked Andrew. "Do we go to the manor to help Phineas?"

Sky shook his head. "Phineas will have to hold off Morton, and Malvidia and the hunters will have to deal with Bedlam's army. We need the blade and Bedlam's body. Ambrosia and Gourmand—Morton's allies—are hiding Bedlam's body deep beneath the earth in Paragoth the earth eater's tunnels. And we need to figure out how to free Bedlam, something I'm hoping will be apparent once we have the other two things."

"So what first? Blade or body?" asked Hands.

"Blade," said Sky. "We're going to the homecoming game."

"Why?" asked Andrew.

Sky looked at Andrew and came to a decision; for better or worse, Andrew deserved to know. "Because that's where we'll find your dad."

CHAPTER 25
Ride of the
Darkhorn

Andrew took it better than Sky had expected. Sky explained everything—about Nikola, about Em, about what had happened. Andrew listened silently. Sky finished with the story about Em at the bowling alley.

Andrew stared at him. Sky couldn't tell whether Andrew was on the verge of tears or maniacal laughter.

"I thought she looked familiar," Andrew muttered.

Andrew was in shock, then, it appeared.

"You don't have to come with us, Andrew," said Hands. "We understand if you don't want to see your dad right now."

"I've seen my dad almost every day since I started going to Arkhon Academy," said Andrew bitterly. "I just never knew it, and my stupid uncle and his stupid family never saw fit to tell me. I don't see what's so different now."

Sky glanced at T-Bone and Hands, not sure what to do. This wasn't quite the reaction he had expected.

"You're okay?" Sky asked.

"Can we just not talk about this right now?" Andrew snapped. "I'd rather forget it until this is over."

"Sure, Andrew," said T-Bone. "If that's what you want—"

"IT IS!" Andrew shouted.

T-Bone held up his hands defensively. "Okay. Sorry I asked."

Andrew stormed ahead, setting a brisk pace.

Sky wandered after him, lost in his own thoughts, wondering if he'd done the right thing by telling him.

As they passed by the First Hunter's broken stone sword, a dark shadow flashed overhead, blotting out the moon. Hands, T-Bone, and Andrew went for their weapons, but Sky held up his hand. "Hold it! I called her here!"

"Called who?" T-Bone asked warily.

A gigantic jet-black horse, with a mangled horn on her forehead and a ball of light dangling from the horn, landed on the gaudy tomb of Esteban, the one-named hunter.

"I've called the Darkhorn," said Sky. Since he had crawled out of Alexander's grave, he'd been opening his mind and reaching out with his senses, broadcasting his location to anything capable of sensing it, searching for the Darkhorn. "If you have any more barrow weed, shove it up your nose now, and whatever you do, don't look at her horn."

The Darkhorn neighed and stomped a hoof, shaking the ground. She sniffed at the air like a bloodhound taking in a scent, and suddenly Sky was looking at the most beautiful woman he'd ever seen before, an angel, wreathed in flowing light.

The Darkhorn reached out and touched Sky's forehead, and Bedlam suddenly appeared, standing next to him. Sky jumped, but then he saw Bedlam's eyes—distant and unfocused, and his voice came through like a recording. And Sky realized that Bedlam had somehow implanted a memory of himself in Sky's head. Sky glanced at T-Bone, Hands, and Andrew; they didn't seem to notice Bedlam at all. They just stared dumbly at the Darkhorn. "Assist them, my love. Let their thoughts guide you. Soon we will be together again," Bedlam whispered.

The Darkhorn—the beautiful woman—smiled and then emitted a horrible neighing sound that Sky took for happiness.

Bedlam turned to Sky, his eyes unfocused. "Betray me, Changeling, and I will skin you and wear you to dinner parties."

"That's really disturbing," Sky replied. "I hate dinner parties."

The Darkhorn reared, and then Bedlam was gone, as was the image of the beautiful woman.

Sky walked up and slowly put his hand on the Darkhorn's leg. She lowered her head close enough for him to pat her on the nose.

"Looks like it's time to fly," Sky said. "Bedlam said to guide her with our thoughts."

T-Bone tossed a duffel bag in front of Sky. "You'd best suit up."

Sky put on his gear. He ached all over, and it hurt to pull it on. The music of the nearby Grove did little to soothe or rejuvenate him, as it had before. It wasn't discordant, as when Cass had been shot, but it wasn't quite peaceful, either.

"All right," Sky said as he pulled on his battered cloak with a quiet, painful groan. "Let's go."

Since the Darkhorn's back was easily three times his height, Sky hit his Jumpers and sailed up and on, followed by Andrew.

"I'm not getting on that thing," T-Bone declared.

"You fly all the time with your Jumpers," said Hands. "What's the problem?"

"I don't fly on things with big spears sticking out of their foreheads!" T-Bone exclaimed.

Hands shook his head, hit his Jumpers, and landed on the Darkhorn behind Sky. "Just get on, you big baby."

"Fine," said T-Bone. "But I get to drive."

T-Bone hit his Jumpers and landed in front of Sky. There was plenty of room.

The Darkhorn's hair was longer than Sky had expected. It wrapped around his legs and hips and tightened snugly. Sky yelped.

The Darkhorn leaped into the air, rocketing out of the Grove and the surrounding cliffs.

"How do you steer this thing?" T-Bone yelled as the ground flashed by below them.

"With your mind!" Sky yelled back.

The Darkhorn darted and veered, swooping toward the trees, only to level out again and climb higher and higher. She whinnied in complaint.

"Who's doing that?" T-Bone screamed.

"Sorry, that was me," yelled Hands.

"What were you thinking?" Andrew yelled.

"I was thinking how that bog really does look like soup, and how those clouds look like salt shakers!" yelled Hands.

"You know . . . I think you're right!" Andrew yelled.

The Darkhorn veered down again, and then up.

"Would you stop that!" T-Bone shrieked.

Hands and Andrew laughed, but as quickly as Andrew's smile appeared, it disappeared even faster.

Looking down, Sky saw Morton and his hunters cutting through the swamp.

"How much time do you think we have before they reach the manor?" Hands asked.

Sky looked at the manor in the distance. "I don't

know—maybe a half hour, and then it's up to Phineas. Plus, Morton still has to figure out how the keys open the prison, and I suspect Phineas didn't make it easy!"

They veered east toward Arkhon Academy.

T-Bone pointed at the ground as they swooped over the Argraves' crypt. "What is that thing?"

A giant spiderlike creature climbed out of the earth and shook itself, sending dirt everywhere.

Sky groaned. "It's a Gossymer! They shouldn't be here! The Gnomon were supposed to lead them to the Finger of Erachnus!"

"Maybe this one got lost!" Andrew yelled.

"I hope so. . . ."

Ahead, they saw the lights of the football stadium and heard the roar of fans. The stadium was packed with spectators.

Sky spotted two more Gossymers as they swooped toward the stadium, but the Gossymers burrowed back into the earth at the sight of the Darkhorn. Sky steered the Darkhorn around the stadium, feeling sick as he took in the crowds of people.

"I think we're in trouble, guys," said Sky.

"We're only down by seven points," Hands yelled, apparently watching the scoreboard. "Touchdown and a field goal and we pull ahead—that's not so bad!"

"I was talking about the monsters and those crowds!" Sky yelled.

"Oh. Yeah. That's pretty bad," said Hands.

They circled the stadium once, flying higher and hoping the lights would blind the spectators. Sky scanned the bleachers, looking for Nikola. Nikola had left a message for him at Alexander's grave. Sky felt certain of it; he just didn't know what that message meant. He had to jog Nikola's memory to help him recall where he had put Alexander's shimmering blade.

The crowd went wild. Looking down, Sky saw Tick complete a spectacular pass.

"I can't see Nikola from up here! We're going to have to land!" Sky yelled. He steered the Darkhorn to the forest on the west end of the field, a forest that spread up the hill to Pimiscule Grounds.

They landed and used their Jumpers to dismount. The Darkhorn let out a loud neigh and then seemed to slip back into the shadows, disappearing completely from view.

"So how are we going to do this?" Andrew asked. "We can't just walk out there dressed like this." He gestured at his cloak.

"Got it covered," said T-Bone. He pulled the duffel bag from his shoulder and set it on the ground. Opening it, he withdrew two nasty football jerseys and threw one to Sky and one to Andrew.

Sky caught a whiff of it and nearly gagged. "What is this?"

"Practice jersey," said T-Bone, pulling off his cloak and putting on his own, less disgusting jersey over the top of his gear. Hands did the same.

Sky and Andrew stared at their jerseys in distaste.

"It's huge," Sky complained, holding up T-Bone's practice jersey. "It's like a pup tent."

"And they smell like football rolled in hockey," Andrew added, curling his lip.

"At least you didn't get T-Bone's," Sky moaned. "Seriously, I could prop this up and sleep under it. Rainstorm? No problem. Perfectly dry. Fall from the sky? Not an issue—I've got a parachute big enough for us all."

"Just put them on and stop whining," T-Bone snapped. "They're not that bad."

"Says the guy with a properly sized jersey," said Sky. He slipped out of his cloak and pulled on the jersey while T-Bone and Hands wrapped their arms in KT Tape to hide the more obvious bits of gear.

"You guys need some of this?" Hands asked, offering Sky and Andrew the athletic tape.

Sky looked down at himself. The bottom of the jersey went to just past his knees, while the sleeves reached nearly to his wrists. Andrew looked a bit better. He was only a few inches shorter than Hands, so the bottom of his jersey wasn't too far off from where it should be. Unfortunately, Hands had much broader shoulders, so the shirt hit Andrew mid forearm.

"Thanks, but I think we're more than covered," said Sky sarcastically.

Hands grinned. "I think you look pretty."

T-Bone snickered.

"Might I have the next dance?" Hands asked, giving Sky a formal bow.

T-Bone burst out laughing.

"You guys are both jerks, you know that?" said Sky.

Glancing over, Sky saw that even Andrew was grinning.

"Let's just get this over with," Sky declared, storming off toward the field.

"As you wish," said Hands breathily. "Milady."

"Jerks, all of you," Sky muttered, leaving them laughing hysterically behind him. Despite his pique, he was glad to hear Andrew laughing. He knew Hands and T-Bone were trying to cheer up Andrew. The laughing wouldn't change things in the long run, but it might make Andrew forget about his parents for a while, and that was worth being the brunt of a few jokes.

Sky tried to tuck in the jersey as he walked, but he ended

up with awkward bulges. Finally he tied the bottom of the shirt in a knot and let it dangle to the side.

He was nearly to the bleachers when he felt the ground rumble slightly. Andrew, T-Bone, and Hands quickly caught up to him.

"That can't be good," said Hands.

Sky placed his hand on the ground and heard all sorts of random vibrations through the Hunter's Mark. To the northeast—around the finger of Erachnus, he guessed—there were terrible rumblings. And closer—far too close—he detected a smaller number. He focused on the more immediate threat. Something was burrowing up beneath the field. Lots of somethings.

"I think we're too late," Sky muttered and sprinted for the stadium.

Bedlam's army had finally arrived. Just in time for homecoming.

CHAPTER 26

Homecoming Queen

The stadium was packed with thousands of fans. Sky stood in the shadow of the bleachers, his stomach sinking. There were so many people. The homecoming game against Arkhon Academy's bitter rival, Quindlemore, was the biggest game of the year. It looked like all of Exile had shown up to watch.

"Sky!"

Turning, Sky saw Cordelia running up.

"Cordelia? What are you doing here? I thought you'd be at the Finger of Erachnus with all the other hunters."

"Malvidia sent some of us here to guard the perimeter in case any stragglers from Bedlam's army come this way," said Cordelia. "What are *you* doing here?"

"We need to find Nikola—the janitor," Sky replied, making an effort not to glance at Andrew. "Have you seen him?"

Cordelia furrowed her brow. "He left a short time ago, headed north. I tried to convince him to come back because it's not exactly safe up there, but he ignored me. Weird guy.

He kept muttering 'a kindness for a kindness,' and 'a bled for a but.' When he spouted off a limerick about urinal cakes, I sort of tuned out."

Sky's ears perked up. "Wait . . . say that again."

"What? The limerick?" Cordelia asked, laughing. "'O' round puck that water seeps, not a cake that peoples eats, but sitting in the briny, nowhere near foul heinie, you make every scent so sweets!'"

Hands and T-Bone laughed, but Andrew only scowled.

"Not the limerick—the other part," said Sky, worried that Andrew might think he was making fun of his dad. "The kindness for a kindness thing."

"'A kindness for a kindness, a bled for a but.'"

"Abled for abut . . . blade for tuba—it's an anagram," said Sky. "I helped him move the instruments . . . a kindness. I think he wants to give me the blade for the tuba."

Sky cast his eyes around the field. On the far side, he spotted Mr. Dibble and the marching band. Hannah and the other cheerleaders had formed a pyramid and were partially blocking his view. But as they dropped down, he saw his tuba case, sitting in the honorary first-chair position.

"We need that tuba case."

The ground trembled.

"What was that?" Cordelia asked fearfully.

"What we need is to get these people out of here!" said T-Bone. "Why haven't the hunters cleared the stadium?"

"Why would we? The battle's happening up north at the Finger," said Crenshaw as he approached from behind, along with Ren, Marcus, Alexis, and a few of Morton's hunters who Sky didn't know.

The others were dressed in dark clothes, ready to hunt, but

Marcus was totally unprepared, as was apparent by his large furry hat and hangdog expression. Marcus was in the band with Sky, and it looked like Crenshaw had dragged him away against his will. Marcus played one of the few instruments that Sky considered worse than the tuba: *the castanets.*

"I didn't expect to see you here, Sky," Crenshaw continued. "I'd heard Morton had a special surprise for you."

The ground shook again. The football fans screamed and stomped their feet on the bleachers, oblivious to the shaking.

"We don't have time for you to be an idiot, Crenshaw," said Sky. "You need to clear the stadium. Now."

"Wish we could, but Morton needs us at that manor of yours. He's ordered the hunters to retreat," said Crenshaw. "Hagos is trying to convince them to stay, but most—the smart ones, at least—are flying back to the Academy of Legend on the Moonriders. Exile will have to fend for itself."

"You're insane," said Sky. "You can't just leave Exile to Bedlam's army! What about your family?"

"My father's leaving, too," Crenshaw replied. "And my mother is dead. Even her body is gone now. It dropped through the east cemetery with all the others, thanks to you. There's nothing in Exile I care about." Crenshaw looked at Cordelia, his expression somewhere between anger and desperation. "Are you coming?"

"You've got to be kidding," Cordelia scoffed.

Crenshaw's expression darkened. "Fine. Maybe I'll just drag Sky to Morton. Bet you'll come then."

The Cross-Shocker slipped into Andrew's palm, and T-Bone and Hands tapped their crackling metal Shocker gloves together, leaving a trail of sparks. "Try it," T-Bone said, grinning as if he'd like nothing more.

"You're outnumbered," Crenshaw pointed out.

"And you're outsmarted," Hands retorted. "And outclassed. And your ears are too small for your face. Don't they look small, Andrew?"

"They are disproportionately small," Andrew replied, nodding in agreement.

Crenshaw looked over their electrified weapons and suddenly scowled, as if he'd just realized exactly how big T-Bone was. "I don't have time for this. Come on."

Crenshaw turned and walked away. Morton's hunters fell in behind him, but Ren, Marcus, and Alexis stayed behind with Cordelia.

Crenshaw noticed they weren't following. He turned on them, and his expression grew even darker.

"Our families aren't leaving like yours," Marcus squeaked. "We can't run away to save ourselves while they die."

Crenshaw examined Ren, who shrugged. "Marcus is right. I won't leave my family, even if I don't like some of them very much."

T-Bone nodded approvingly, but Ren wouldn't look at him.

"Fine," Crenshaw barked. "Stay and die. See if I care. I don't need any of you!"

With that, Crenshaw spun and walked away, taking more than half a dozen of Morton's hunters with him.

"What do you want us to do, Sky?" Ren asked.

Sky turned back to the bleachers, searching for a way to get these people out. A girl's voice came on over the sound system, narrating the play-by-play.

Before Sky could say anything, Hands took off, running up the bleachers. "Announcer's box—I'm on it!"

"We'll mess up the game!" T-Bone offered. T-Bone and Andrew rushed onto the field.

Sky inspected Cordelia. "I hate to ask this since I know you're not Shadow Wargs anymore, but can you still jump through shadows?"

"You mean shadow slip?" Cordelia asked. She glanced at Ren, Marcus, and Alexis, who nodded back at her. "We can, but we're not supposed to. Malvidia said it could draw the attention of a Wargarou who might try to enslave us again."

"The nearest Wargarou is far underground," said Sky. "I think you'll be okay. I need you guys to stand back and watch. If it looks like anyone's about to get hurt, I want you to slip in and get them out. Can you do that?"

"Sure. But hurt by what, Sky?" Cordelia asked. "We've watched the perimeter—nothing's even close to here."

The crowd roared and Sky saw Tick running with the ball. A Quindlemore linebacker dove. Tick leaped over him and kept running for the distant end zone. The crowd was in a frenzy.

Sky put his hand on the ground and felt the rumblings. Time was up.

"The stragglers from Bedlam's army aren't coming from out there," Sky said, pointing toward the woods. "They're coming from *beneath*."

The ground rumbled, shaking the bleachers. This time the crowd noticed, and an eerie silence began to settle.

As Tick reached the end zone, a giant hand burst out of the ground, stopping him a few yards short. Tick ripped off his helmet and started backing away.

From the corner of his eye, Sky saw Hannah racing across the field toward Tick, her long blond hair blowing in the wind.

"Hannah . . . ," Sky whispered fearfully.

Another hand appeared next to the first, and then an enormous Harrow Knight crawled out of the earth. Its skin was a mishmash of dirty flesh, copper, and rust, and it rose thirty feet into the air, towering over the goalpost. The Harrow Knight stood silently for a moment, looking over the stadium.

"Please ignore the giant monster in the end zone and kindly proceed to the exits in an orderly fashion," Sky heard Hands say over the loudspeakers, *way* too little, too late.

Someone screamed, and then the entire stadium erupted in chaos.

The Harrow Knight roared and burst into flames. Reaching down, it ripped the goalpost from the ground and swung it in a massive arc, sending football players flying everywhere. Tick flipped over the post and then dodged again as it swung back at him.

The Harrow Knight raised the goalpost over its head like a trident, with the tip pointed directly at Tick.

Sky found himself bolting across the field, screaming.

The trident dropped.

Hannah bowled into Tick, knocking him out of the way. The edge of the goalpost caught Tick on the side of the head as he fell, and sent him sprawling to the ground beside Hannah.

With a desperate cry, Hannah grabbed Tick and tried to drag him away. Tick wasn't moving.

The Harrow Knight drew back for another strike.

Hannah dropped Tick's arm and stepped in front of him, putting herself between Tick and the Harrow Knight. She stood bravely before that fiery terror, her hair blowing in the wind, her small fists clenched, her beautiful face raging. Sky had never seen her look so radiant and so terrible, and his heart broke at the sight as he screamed and screamed. She faced down that Harrow Knight alone—small and fragile. Waiting to die.

There was a flurry of shadows and then the goalpost smashed into the ground and snapped at the tip. Sky dropped to his knees in anguish.

The Harrow Knight roared and flung the goalpost into the nearby bleachers. Sky saw another flurry of shadows and people started disappearing. Sky then realized that Cordelia, Ren, Marcus, and Alexis had done exactly what he'd asked them to.

He turned around just as Cordelia appeared with a wide-eyed Hannah and an unconscious Tick.

"Hannah!" Sky cried, wrapping her in his arms.

Hannah huffed, but hugged him back. "Now maybe you know how I feel when you go traipsing off after monsters."

"Please use only designated exits when leaving, as there is a giant flammable monster on the field," Hands said over the loudspeaker.

Tick groaned and Hannah dropped down next to him. "What happened?" Tick muttered.

"A monster hit you in the head with a goalpost," Hannah replied.

Sky glanced at Cordelia; she looked exhausted.

"It's not as easy as it looks," Cordelia said, breathing hard.

"Can you get me to my tuba case?" Sky asked, pointing past the storming Harrow Knight to the bleachers near the opposite end zone, where dozens of kids in fuzzy hats ran for their lives.

Cordelia shook her head. "Ten yards is easy. Twenty is possible. But that's over a hundred yards—it's too far."

The ground rumbled. The Harrow Knight's fire died and wisps of smoke rose from his mottled coppery skin as it hardened. The Knight pounded the nearby bleachers, which were now empty thanks to Ren, Marcus, and Alexis.

"What's so important about the case, Sky?" Cordelia asked.

T-Bone and Andrew came running up with most of the Arkhon Academy football team, including Squid and Lazy Eye. Several of the players had singed and blackened uniforms.

Sky surveyed the team, frowning, a bad and desperate idea forming in his head. "I think Alexander's shimmering blade is in my tuba case. If we get it, we can free Bedlam. This Harrow Knight is just the first of many. There are *thousands* of other monsters on their way—the hunters won't be enough to stop them, especially if most of Morton's hunters abandon us. But if we free Bedlam, *he* can stop this. This is his army. He's the only one who can."

Cordelia nodded. "Get me close."

"I have no idea what you guys are talking about," said Squid, "but if it helps, I think we can get you past the Harrow Knight and to that tuba case."

The other members of the football team nodded, their expressions grim. Sky hated to ask—it was going to be dangerous—and he knew from the vibrations coming through the earth that this one Harrow Knight was the least of their worries, but they needed that blade. It was the only way to save Crystal and Exile.

As if in answer to his thoughts, the ground rumbled again. And then, in the middle of the field, a single Gossymer appeared.

"That doesn't look so bad," Lazy Eye commented.

"Looks like a Quindlemore cheerleader to me," Squid quipped. "All legs and hair and hairy legs."

"Please ignore the giant spider in the center of the field," Hands announced over the loudspeaker. "Your panic will only cause it to burst into flames."

The screaming began anew and the Gossymer promptly burst into flames.

"He's got a bright future in announcing," Tick said groggily, staring up at the announcer's box. Several of the players nodded in agreement.

"Hands! Get down here, you idiot!" T-Bone yelled, sounding annoyed.

At that moment the Harrow Knight clawed up a chunk of earth and launched it at the announcer's booth. Hands jumped through the door as it hit, and the announcer's booth toppled off the bleachers. Hands brushed himself off, then hit his Jumpers and sailed over the rapidly thinning crowd. He crashed next to Sky in a wave of shimmering light and rolled to his feet. "Did I miss anything?"

A dozen more Gossymers crawled out of the ground with smaller, human-size Harrow Wights on their backs. The Gossymers sat silently near the center of the field as the Harrow Wight riders took in their surroundings.

Sky pulled out his Tin shield and flipped it open. Hands, T-Bone, and Andrew did the same. T-Bone threw them their cloaks and coats, and they put them on, tossing their nasty jerseys to the side. There was no point hiding anymore. Their new cloaks were resistant to fire and damage, like the Tins, and would serve them far better.

"You—give me your pads," said Hannah, pointing at one of the smaller football players.

"Me?" the player asked, looking confused.

"Hand them over," Hannah demanded. The player

glanced around, shrugged, and then pulled off his helmet and shoulder pads.

Tick struggled to sit up. "What are you doing?"

"I'm tired of watching from the sidelines," said Hannah, putting the shoulder pads over her shirt. "And you're in no condition to lead this team."

"What makes you think you can?" Tick asked.

"Oh, please," said Hannah, rolling her eyes. "For the last year all you've talked about is football. You three"—Hannah pointed at the player without pads and two others—"carry Tick and try to keep him from doing something stupid. You and you—tell Jasmine and Ermine to organize the cheer-leaders and get these people into the school. The rest of you, line up! Double-wing, hard V formation on my mark. Spread offense at case. Option run to line. Hot route out. Got it?"

The players all grunted.

"I have no idea what you just said," Sky muttered.

"Just stay between me and Hands," said Hannah, pulling on her helmet. "You too, Cordelia."

Sky and Cordelia nodded dumbly.

"Break!" Hannah yelled.

The line formed up in a sort of V-shape, with wings. T-Bone took his place at the tip of the V. Lazy Eye and Squid took positions next to Hannah, and the others fell in line. Sky found himself next to Cordelia, protected in the center of the wedge—the quarterback position—with Hannah to his left, Hands to his right, and Andrew directly behind him.

Hannah surveyed the field; more and more Gossymers burst from the earth with each passing minute and several were already rushing toward them.

"Red forty-two!" Hannah shouted.

The line shifted to the right.

"Hike!"

The line surged forward.

T-Bone barreled into the first fiery Gossymer with his shield while Squid and Lazy Eye tackled the legs. The Gossymer toppled to the side and the line rushed past. A coppery silk web shot from the downed Gossymer's spinnerets, enveloping one of the players, who fell to the field as it constricted around him.

Hands threw his Tin. It spun through the air and severed the thread before the Gossymer could reel in. Sky snatched up the Tin, folded the sides, and threw it back to Hands as Cordelia shadow slipped the player to safety, reappearing at Sky's side a moment later.

"What are those things?" Hannah called as they pushed forward.

"Gossymers!" Sky yelled back.

"As in Gossymer threads? As in the threads that wiped Derek's memory and took his beautiful eyebrows away from me?" Hannah cried as they ran.

Sky nodded.

"Yellow ninety-six! Black thirteen!" Hannah yelled.

Sky waited for the line to adjust position, but nothing happened.

"What did you tell them?" Sky asked.

"I told them not to eat the Gossymer threads because they're the thing that took Derek's luscious golden eyebrows away from me!" Hannah replied.

"They had a code for that?" Sky asked in surprise.

"Not really," Hannah replied. "It means something more

like 'Don't eat the food of your enemies'—they had an incident last year."

Sky snorted.

"Red forty-seven!" Hannah yelled.

The line veered left and closed around them.

Ahead, Sky saw nearly a dozen Gossymers headed their way with Harrow Wights on their backs. Beyond the end zone, he could see Ren, Marcus, and Alexis leading the giant Harrow Knight away from the crowds. And still in the bleachers, sitting patiently, he could see his broken tuba's bright white case.

They passed the fifty-yard line and rammed into the Gossymers, entering a terrifying gauntlet of fire, hairy legs, webs, and exploding earth.

T-Bone knocked the legs out from under one. The Harrow Wight swung a flaming sword at him and he batted it to the side. T-Bone threw his shoulder into the Gossymer and knocked the beast and rider to the ground.

Sky fired his Pounder over and over, drenching the Gossymers and Harrow Wights in ICE and snuffing out their flames while the football team blocked and tackled, getting scorched. Andrew shot a Gossymer with his Cross-Shocker. The prongs sank into the Gossymer's body and it darted away, dragging Andrew behind it as he frantically tried to hit the release. Sky sprang onto Andrew's back as he passed by and slammed the release, then they were on their feet and running.

They pushed through to the forty, the thirty-five. Players fell everywhere Sky looked and Cordelia flashed around, struggling to get them back within the safety of the V formation. A Gossymer and its rider shot out of the ground directly beneath Sky, sending him tumbling.

The Gossymer stepped over him, and giant pincers

dropped, clacking and snapping. Sky brought his Tin up and smacked the pincers away, but the Gossymer twisted, caught the Tin, and flipped it from Sky's grasp. Hands leaped onto the Gossymer and knocked the Harrow Wight off. Then he dug his heels in and they shot forward, over the top of Sky, and rammed another Gossymer that had pinned Squid.

From his back, Sky shot the Gossymer Hands was riding with his Pounder before it could burst into flames and fry Hands. Other players got the same idea and began commandeering Gossymers.

Hannah and Cordelia grabbed Sky and dragged him to his feet. Sky scooped up his Tin and they raced up the bleachers. There was a groaning sound. Metal buckled, and then a Harrow Knight erupted through the seats in front of them.

Cordelia grabbed Sky and Hannah and shadow slipped from seat to seat, dodging through a shower of padded cushions and mangled metal as the bleachers collapsed. Sky's stomach lurched with each jump, and his mind spun. It felt so much like edgewalking that he kept checking to make sure he hadn't left his body behind. They made a final jump, landing near the tuba case.

The Harrow Knight turned around to face them. It raised its hand and a molten copper ball the size of a car began to form.

Sky snatched up the case and they slipped away again as the fiery ball burned through the bleachers where they'd been standing.

Another jump and they were back on the field.

Cordelia collapsed.

"What's wrong with her?" Hannah asked, dropping down to make sure she wasn't hurt.

"She's exhausted—that last jump was too far!"

Hannah scooped up Cordelia in a fireman's carry, but before they could get away, a Gossymer stepped in front of them, blocking their path. Hands peeked around the Gossymer's giant head. "Need a ride?"

Sky looked over and saw the football team nearby, struggling toward the end zone and the school beyond. Squid and Lazy Eye, also on Gossymers, like Hands, covered their retreat along with T-Bone, Andrew, and a few players who weren't injured or carrying the injured.

"Yes!" Hannah declared. "We need a ride!"

Hands helped her put Cordelia on the back of the Gossymer, where it was wider, and then she climbed up behind Hands and grabbed ahold of his waist, a detail that seemed to please Hands immensely.

Sky jumped up next to Cordelia and held on to her and the case as the Gossymer darted forward. As they raced to rejoin the football team, dodging through the legs of Harrow Knights and leaping over other Gossymers, Sky reached out with his senses, searching. He called out to the Darkhorn. They had the shimmering blade; it was time to find Bedlam's body. And to do that, he needed the Gnomon, who were, he hoped, at the Finger of Erachnus, where they had led most of Bedlam's army.

Sky and the others caught up to the football team, and the Darkhorn flashed past overhead. Quindlemore's football team emerged from the school ahead, along with all the cheerleaders, and rushed toward them, reinforcing their line and helping with the wounded. Among the cheerleaders, Sky spotted Felicity—the girl he'd kissed last year—and his stomach did a little flip.

"T-Bone, Andrew! Come on!" Sky yelled. He turned to Hannah. "I—"

"Have to go," Hannah cut in. "I know. I'll hold them off as long as I can, and I'll take care of Cordelia."

Sky nodded, and a quiet understanding passed between them. Hannah smiled sadly, a tear running down her cheek. "I understand why you have to do this, Sky. I really do. I'm beginning to suspect that you might not be the only one caught up in Phineas's legacy. I just wish I could keep you safe."

Sky smiled back at her, his smile every bit as sad. "No one can keep me safe—there are no safe places left for me. I'm not sure there ever have been. But Phineas taught me how to think and how to survive. And you and Mom and Dad have loved me, even if you don't know what I am. That's got to count for something. Besides, safety is for prey—I'm a hunter. It's others who need safety from me."

Several more Harrow Knights burst from the ground behind them, joining the growing army of Harrow Wights and Gossymers driving them toward Arkhon Academy. The army dropped back slightly, waiting for the Harrow Knights to take the lead, as the Darkhorn circled above.

Sky hugged Hannah and then slid down from the Gossymer.

"Hey, I'm not safe, either," Hands complained.

Hannah laughed. "Hasn't Sky warned you about me, Hands?" Hannah cocked an eyebrow and Hands gulped. Then she leaned forward as if she was going to kiss him. With a quick shove, she launched him from the Gossymer. She smiled down at him. "I've got enough boy problems already. Come back when you get bigger eyebrows." She dug her heels into the Gossymer, driving it forward again. "And keep my brother alive!"

The Darkhorn landed directly in front of Sky as T-Bone and Andrew arrived.

The players passed by, staring in wonder at the glorious light and the beautiful woman who had suddenly appeared. The line started to break. The woman licked her lips.

"Stop that!" Sky ordered. The woman scowled at him, and the illusion disappeared.

The Harrow Knights bellowed and the Darkhorn reared back, issuing a challenge. Bedlam's army started to charge. Sky hit his Jumpers and leaped onto the Darkhorn's back, followed by T-Bone, Hands, and Andrew. They left the ground just as the army's front line reached them. The Darkhorn smashed into a Harrow Knight, plowing it over, and then they were soaring over the decimated field and out of reach.

The stadium was a disaster. The bleachers had collapsed, the announcer's box lay in ruins, and hordes of monsters rushed across the field, charging the school.

"I'm going to count that last run as a score—a tie, then," said Hands as the scoreboard fell over.

"Shut up, Hands," said T-Bone. "And if anyone says we're about to go into overtime, I'm going to punch you."

Below, Sky saw Hannah leading the football team into Arkhon Academy. To the west, he saw lightning strike the manor dome and the beginnings of plasma clouds forming into great funnels.

"I don't think it's overtime," said Sky fearfully as they rose higher and higher and the terrifying battle around the Finger of Erachnus came into view. A giant hole sat open near the northern edge of the field, and wave after wave of Bedlam's massive army spilled out, engulfing the hunters' pitiful resistance. Along the southern edge, where they fought to block the army from the school, Sky saw dozens of shadowy silver creatures—Moonriders, he supposed—flying away, carrying the majority of Morton's hunters to safety as they abandoned Exile.

"I think we've started an entirely new game," Sky whispered.

A swelling ball of crackling energy spread out, growing larger and larger, with the manor at its epicenter.

The Darkhorn veered. The energy crashed around them in a raging storm. And then they were falling and falling, down and down, without veering, without swooping, and without a sound.

CHAPTER 27
Army of Bedlam

Sky, T-Bone, Andrew, and Hands hit their protective Shimmers as the massive Darkhorn crashed through the forest, smashed through some wooden bleachers, and plowed into a column of advancing Gossymer riders near the Finger, leaving a deep furrow of earth and wood and devastation behind.

The Darkhorn's hair released them and Sky tumbled off, clinging to the tuba case. He scrambled away as the Darkhorn rolled to her feet. She let out a mournful wail and slipped into the shadows.

Hundreds of monsters lurched through the woods, and a small group of hunters—maybe fifteen in all—dropped from the trees, landing among the monsters. Sky spotted Dad leading the charge and swinging a massive shimmering ax, his normally smiling face contorted in a madness and rage that Sky had never seen before, an expression he would never forget, an expression that terrified him and chilled him to his bones. Beau stormed next to him, screaming and swinging a pair of shimmering knives faster than Sky could track. Em chased after them, filling the monsters with arrows, followed by T-Bone's mother and Hagos Adera. They plunged into the hordes, leading the other hunters, oblivious that their children were standing nearby, watching.

"Did that just happen?" T-Bone asked in awe, rubbing his neck.

Andrew scowled and spun away, marching toward the Finger of Erachnus. Sky, T-Bone, and Hands followed. The woods all around were filled with the sounds of fighting—monsters shrieking, hunters yelling, creatures dying.

They picked up their pace, racing across the open space around the Finger. They found Malvidia there, barking commands.

She frowned as they approached. "Why do I have the feeling you're bringing me bad news?"

"They need help at the school," Sky replied, breathing hard, still trying to process what he had just seen. "Some of Bedlam's army popped up on the field."

"I have hunters there," Malvidia replied.

"Most of whom left to join Morton at the manor," Sky retorted, feeling annoyed.

Malvidia stared at them with cold eyes. She turned back to the hunter she had been talking to before they'd arrived and spoke quietly. The woman nodded and ran off. "I'll send what I can, but I don't have much to spare. I'm beginning to fear that Morton had the right idea."

Malvidia began circling the Finger, shouting orders at the hunters as she passed. Many were in sorry shape, bleeding and bandaged and laid out on stretchers and makeshift cots.

"Morton is releasing the Arkhon," Sky stated, watching a hunter treat a woman with a missing arm.

"I've noticed," said Malvidia, glancing at the strange storm clouds swirling in the distance.

"I've found Alexander Drake's shimmering blade, but we need Bedlam's body," said Sky. "Are the Gnomon here?"

Malvidia stopped walking. She narrowed her eyes. "You've found Alexander's blade?"

Sky nodded.

"Show me," said Malvidia.

Sky opened the case and pulled out a long, rusted blade. The moment he touched it, the blade shimmered to life, and he could feel it and the secrets it held, almost as if it were a part of him.

Malvidia inhaled sharply. "You exceed all expectations, Sky."

Sky grinned.

"Don't feel too proud," Malvidia cautioned. "I have very low expectations."

Just then Rauschtlot and Nackles popped out of the ground a short distance away, along with a half dozen other Gnomon, many of whom looked injured.

Malvidia quickened her pace. "Osmer, I need you! I can't understand a word these Gnomon say!"

Rauschtlot and Nackles had been talking to the other Gnomon, but they turned to face Malvidia and noticed Sky for the first time. Nackles smiled with nearly all her mouths.

"Sssky!" she exclaimed in Gnomon, giving him a big hug that made his bones creak.

"Okay! Okay! That's enough!" Sky squeaked. Nackles released him with a shy smile.

"Greetingsss, Sssky," Rauschtlot hissed. She had a nasty cut on her arm and patchy discoloration on her skin in places.

At the mention of Sky's name, the other Gnomon all turned to watch him, their skin going icy blue as they stilled, listening and looking far too attentive for Sky's liking.

"Are you two all right?" Sky asked in Gnomon.

"Never mind, Osmer," Malvidia said as a somewhat dashing old man came strolling up. "I'd forgotten about Sky and his lifetimes of study to learn all monster languages."

"Balderdash, Malvidia!" said Osmer. "Go easy on the boy."

"Grandpa?" Hands said incredulously. "What are you doing here? You were supposed to go back to the nursing home!"

Osmer waved his hand dismissively. "Pah! I just stay there for the ladies. I'm not *that* old."

"Sky, I need you to ask the Gnomon what they found," said Malvidia.

"Okay. Rauschtlot, what did you find?" asked Sky.

Malvidia sighed. "In *Gnomon*, please."

"Right," said Sky. Switching to Gnomon, he asked the question again.

"The Whisssper guards the body with the Waaargarou," Rauschtlot hissed. "They willll not come up."

Sky translated, adding, "Winston said Ambrosia and Gourmand are working with Morton to free the Arkhon."

"I am aware." Malvidia surveyed the battle, looking pained.

Sky turned to Rauschtlot and, in Gnomon, asked, "Rauschtlot, do you know where Bedlam's body is?"

"Yesss," Rauschtlot hissed. "But Paragoth is clossse. She is unpleasssant."

"So I've heard," said Sky. He turned back to Malvidia. "Rauschtlot can take us down."

"Excuse me?" said Malvidia.

Sky realized he was still talking in Gnomon. He switched.

"You don't have to send your hunters—we'll go. You just need to hold off the monsters up here until we free Bedlam."

Malvidia examined him. Then she surveyed the battle. "Hunters will die. Morton will free the Arkhon long before then. If we leave now, we could save some of Exile's populace and regroup with the hunters. Bedlam won't stop, and there's a wide world to consider beyond Exile."

"Start evacuating, but give us until the second wave of energy is released from the manor before you retreat with the hunters," said Sky. "The first wave just means Morton has opened the front gate. But the Arkhon won't wake up until the pendulum stops and the second wave hits."

"We may all be dead by then. . . ." Malvidia stared off into the woods to the north. "Very well, Sky."

Malvidia drew a long shimmering blade from a sheath and stabbed it into the ground. She adjusted a few straps on her black mourning dress. "I will give you until the second wave to return, if I can. Don't disappoint me, or Exile's destruction will be on your shoulders." She took up the sword and marched into the northern woods.

Osmer whistled. "I don't know how you got on her good side, Sky, but someday we'll have to talk."

Sky stared at Osmer. Good side? Seriously?

Sky strapped the shimmering blade on so that it hung from his shoulder, and then he handed T-Bone, Andrew, and Hands each one of Rauschtlot's cookies.

"Eat up—they're good," said Sky. "Rauschtlot baked them."

Everyone glanced at Rauschtlot, who smiled back at them. Then they popped the cookies into their respective mouths.

"Wow. That really is good," said T-Bone appreciatively, licking his fingers. Rauschtlot's smile grew even bigger.

Andrew and Hands nodded in enthusiastic agreement.

"The Gnomon made those? I've never heard of Gnomon sharing secrets before. Any idea what's in them?" Osmer asked suspiciously.

"Something called erfskin, I think," said Sky.

"Most interesting," said Osmer.

Sky felt stronger, his skin thick, his pores open. Even his eyeballs felt hard, which was a very strange sensation, almost as strange as the wind blowing through his skin.

"All right, Rauschtlot, we're ready," said Sky. "Lead on."

Rauschtlot grabbed Sky and slung him onto her back. Rauschtlot's skin parted just under her arms and a mouth opened up on each side, swallowing Sky's hands and closing to hold him in place.

"Whoa! That wasn't part of the deal!" Sky exclaimed.

The largest Gnomon, who was several feet taller than Rauschtlot, grabbed T-Bone and flung him into place as if he weighed nothing. Two other Gnomon grabbed Andrew and Hands.

Nackles held her hand palm out—the Gnomon sign for good-bye.

"Good thing we reinforced our cloaks, I suppose," said Andrew, staring at the ground apprehensively. "Since it appears we're going for a swim."

"Hhhold on," Rauschtlot hissed.

And with that, she dove into the ground.

CHAPTER 28

Paragoth, the Earth-Eater

Sky inhaled. Dirt rushed into his mouth and lungs, and then out again through his pores. He could feel it spilling from his skin, through his clothes. A rock bashed into his forehead and bounced harmlessly into his wake.

He cranked his head around and saw the rock tumble into a small air pocket directly behind them, and then the rock was lost amidst the dirt streaming through his and Rauschtlot's bodies. He realized he still had his eyes open. He shut them, but that felt worse.

They dropped into a tunnel and sailed through the air.

He caught a brief glimpse of the other Gnomon falling to his sides, and then Rauschtlot plunged into the tunnel floor without slowing. She spun and twirled, charging through the finer sediment and punching through rock, until Sky lost all sense of direction.

It was horrifying.

Another tunnel, another glimpse of the others, and then through again.

Earth crashed all around him and they moved fast, like an avalanche.

Time passed; how long, Sky couldn't say. Just when he felt like he couldn't stand it anymore, they popped into a tunnel and Rauschtlot came to a sudden halt. She released his hands and Sky slid off, collapsing to the ground. He coughed out dirt and rocks and bits of things he couldn't even identify.

The Gnomon carrying T-Bone, Andrew, and Hands dropped into the tunnel nearly a minute later. Sky stood and brushed himself off, emptying dirt from several unmentionable places.

"Are you guys all right?" Sky croaked.

T-Bone, Andrew, and Hands nodded, still hacking up dirt like cats with stubborn hairballs.

The tunnel sloped down, the heat growing more and more intense as they ran. A green glowing fungus illuminated the walls, and Sky heard running water ahead. After a few minutes they reached a gargantuan tunnel. In several places water fell from the ceiling hundreds of feet up. It crashed into giant pools and raced along an underground river.

Near the river Sky saw Bedlam's body, entombed in the hardened and waxy Chrysalis.

Over three dozen Gossymer riders guarded the Chrysalis, along with two people Sky recognized all too well: Ambrosia the Whisper and Gourmand the Wargarou.

"Rauschtlot, how close can you get to the Chrysalis before the Gossymers know you're there?" Sky asked.

"Clossse," Rauschtlot hissed.

Sky glanced around the tunnel, thinking.

"Could you get Paragoth to come here without getting caught?" Sky asked.

Rauschtlot examined him. "It isss unwissse."

"Probably," said Sky.

Rauschtlot hissed. Then she turned to the other Gnomon and spoke rapidly, telling them to get the Chrysalis while she found Paragoth. The Gnomon looked frightened. They grabbed T-Bone, Andrew, and Hands, and slung them onto their backs.

Rauschtlot began to grab Sky, but he stopped her. "No, not me. Get me on the way back. Paragoth first. I have a feeling we'll need the distraction."

"Sky, what are you doing?" T-Bone asked.

"Paragoth is our double bogey if things don't work out," said Sky. "She might give us a chance to escape if things go bad."

"The double bogey . . . that's the super-high-risk secondary plan, right?" Hands asked.

"Look, get the Chrysalis and leave. Rauschtlot will pick me up on the way out," said Sky. "If anything happens to separate us, I'll meet you up top by the Finger of Erachnus."

"Idiot," said Hands. "You're going to get yourself kill—"

The Gnomon dove into the ground, and Hands's mouth was promptly filled with dirt.

"Be sssafe, Sssky," Rauschtlot hissed. And then she too was gone, leaving Sky alone.

He took a deep breath, waited a minute for them to get into position, and stepped from cover.

"Ambrosia! Gourmand!" Sky yelled as he slid down the side of the tunnel and strode toward the river. "Morton didn't tell me I'd find you two down here!"

The Gossymers leaped forward, quickly surrounding him.

The ground shook, and something horrible trumpeted far down the tunnel, causing Sky's bones to tremble and making him seriously reconsider the advisability of his plan.

While everyone's attention was diverted, Sky saw Bedlam's Chrysalis disappear into the ground.

Ambrosia narrowed her eyes as Sky approached. "Sky Weathers. Most unexpected."

Gourmand growled at him.

"It appears you've upset Gourmand," said Ambrosia. "If he loses control, it'll take me a week to coax him back into that form, so please don't do anything stupid."

Gourmand's eyes flashed red.

"No, I won't. I will only do smart things from now on," said Sky.

"Patience, Gourmand. What is it, precisely, that you want, Sky?" Ambrosia asked.

"Morton sent me down to collect Bedlam's body—I'm his apprentice now," said Sky. "Honestly, you'd think he would've mentioned that you two were in charge, but I suppose he didn't realize that we knew each other."

"I hope you didn't spend too long coming up with that *terrible* story," said Ambrosia.

"Not too long," said Sky. "Would you believe I got lost? Because I did. If you two could just point me in the right direction . . . Oh, wait—I think I see it way over there. Well . . ." Sky yawned and stretched. "I should probably be off, then."

Sky started walking away, but Gourmand was suddenly in front of him, growling, the Wargarou's mouth full of pointy teeth.

Sky backed away.

"Now, Sky," Ambrosia chastised, "was that a smart thing?"

The ground trembled and then split apart. The Gnomon burst out, like water from a geyser, and collapsed to the ground, bleeding and battered. Two dozen Gossymer riders poured through next, carrying Bedlam's Chrysalis, as well as T-Bone, Hands, and Andrew, whom they threw to the ground.

"You didn't really think I'd be so unprepared, did you?" said Ambrosia.

The ground continued to shake.

"Not really," said Sky. He studied Ambrosia. "Why are you trying to free the Arkhon?"

"Because he's my father," Ambrosia replied tartly. "If I locked up your father unjustly, wouldn't you try to free him?"

"But what if he *isn't* your father?" Sky asked.

"You mean because he's Solomon Rose?" Ambrosia retorted, raising an eyebrow.

"You know?"

Ambrosia waved her hand dismissively. "My father has been telling the hunters that lie for years, and it's finally paid off. We've finally found one stupid enough to believe him."

"Morton's not stupid," said Sky. "Solomon stole your father's body. If you open the prison, you will free the hunter who might have killed him."

Ambrosia frowned. "Nice try. But you're not going to win me over that easily."

"I don't need to win you over," said Sky. "I've got a double bogey."

The rumbling grew louder and louder. Ambrosia glanced up the tunnel. "What have you done, Sky?"

"Something stupid, I think."

The Gnomon climbed to their feet, looking nervous.

Far down the tunnel, where it curved, the glowing fungus began to wink out, the light disappearing.

Just then Rauschtlot shot out of the ground next to the Chrysalis. Sky leaped onto her back, dodging past Gourmand. Rauschtlot snatched the Chrysalis, holding it under one arm.

The strange fungal lights went out.

The injured Gnomon grabbed T-Bone, Andrew, and Hands, and ran for the river.

There was a scream of rage, and then Gourmand shifted into a giant wolflike creature of tusks, swirling fire, and darkness. The ground rumbled. Paragoth shrieked from somewhere up the cavernous tunnel, and the Wargarou answered with a terrible roar.

With a backward glance, Sky saw Ambrosia jump onto a Gossymer, throwing a Harrow Wight from its back.

Sky darted for the river with Rauschtlot.

Harrow Wights and Gossymers burst into flame.

Sky and Rauschtlot shoved Bedlam's Chrysalis into the river and grabbed hold. The other Gnomon dove in after them, latching on as well. The enormous tunnel curved behind them, hiding Paragoth, but Sky saw wisps of darkness and a horrifying shadow as large as the gargantuan tunnel itself, and then they turned a bend and the river whisked them away.

Gossymer riders rushed along the riverbanks with Ambrosia in the lead.

Sky heard a new type of rumbling.

"Waterfall!" Andrew screamed.

"Dive! Now!" Sky yelled.

The waterfall came into view, and the Gnomon abandoned the Chrysalis and dove just before reaching it.

They found the river bottom and kept diving, burrowing

into the earth. Water rushed in behind them. Down they went, and down again, down, down, a hundred yards or more, all the way to the bottom, and when they reached it, they shot under the falls and back into the river.

The earth under the waterfall, weakened by burrowing, slipped away and millions of tons of rock cascaded down into the river, creating a tidal wave.

Far away, Sky heard the Wargarou roaring and the shrieks of Paragoth as they fought, but as the wave crashed down, he fixed his eyes on Bedlam's Chrysalis ahead and clung to Rauschtlot.

The tidal wave smashed down on him, yanking him from Rauschtlot's back. He tumbled in the surf, struggling to breathe as water leaked through his earth-breathing pores and filled his mouth.

And then he felt Rauschtlot's four-fingered hand grab his waist. They slammed into the riverbed, through it, and then popped out on the riverbank. Sky coughed and hacked up lungfuls of dirty brown water.

Rauschtlot dove back in, reappearing a moment later with Bedlam's Chrysalis.

There was no sign of T-Bone, Andrew, Hands, or any of the other Gnomon.

"W-w-where are they?" Sky gasped. He heard scuttling behind him. The ground trembled. He looked over, hoping to find his friends.

"We mussst go, Changeling," Rauschtlot hissed.

"But . . ."

Without waiting, Rauschtlot grabbed him and threw him on her back. Sky heard a sucking sound as little mouths on Rauschtlot's four-toed feet glommed onto Bedlam's Chrysalis.

Then they plunged into the earth, dragging the Chrysalis behind them just as dozens of Gossymers exploded from the ground.

They rushed through the earth. Rauschtlot spun and twisted. Gossymers darted past, raking at Rauschtlot and Sky with sharp legs.

Sky sensed the waterfall nearby and they raced upward. But the Chrysalis slowed them, and Rauschtlot only had her arms to dig with. More and more Gossymers circled.

A terrible wailing shook the earth below and Gossymers charged in, slamming down on Sky from above.

Sky caught a brief glimpse of Ambrosia smiling from the back of a Gossymer, and then Rauschtlot dropped and they were falling, falling, falling through the roof of the gigantic tunnel. Water streamed down from the ceiling around them, and into the river far, far below.

A whip of fire and darkness flashed past. Sky glanced right and his mind seized, for there was Paragoth, the earth eater, monstrous, dark, vaguely Gnomon-shaped, bits of rock crackling from her skin, lava flowing like hair, mouths everywhere, gray skin seeping fire.

They fell past, tendrils of darkness and mouths within mouths shooting out like tongues, crashing through earth, deep, deep, leaving holes where they devoured. Tongue-mouths licking and fretting, slipping past above, below, everywhere Sky looked, just missing as they fell, writhing shapes and flaming gouts shooting by.

Fiery whips from the Wargarou tangled with Paragoth's tendrils, lashing and ripping. The two fought, smashing and tearing at each other.

Sky's brain shut down, and he clung to Rauschtlot, gibbering and crying.

Gossymers fell all around them, silk streamers trailing behind like parachutes, and Paragoth smashed and swatted them like flies.

With arms spread out, Rauschtlot angled for an open tunnel going straight down.

They fell through. Sky rotated just so and slammed his chest against Rauschtlot's back, activating the protective Shimmer just before they crashed into the shaft. They rolled, flopping and flailing, to a stop. Even with the Shimmer, it felt to Sky as if every bone in his body had snapped, but his erfskin, and the Gnomon resilience that came from it, were still working.

Rauschtlot grabbed the Chrysalis under one arm and started running.

Paragoth's mouths plunged through earth, shooting past them, just missing time and time again.

Rauschtlot dove into a wall, grabbed the Chrysalis with her feet, and they were swimming through the loam.

Ten minutes later they emerged from the earth, battered and torn, and in entirely the wrong place.

CHAPTER 29
Slippery Wick Brew

We're under the manor," Sky croaked after coughing the dirt from his lungs. "I recognize this place—the tunnel that collapsed the night I became a Changeling."

Sky jumped up and drew the shimmering blade. He stepped toward Bedlam's Chrysalis. He found a thin opening on top, large enough for the blade. He slid the blade in, but nothing happened.

He still had no idea how to open the Chrysalis.

"The Fffinger is overunnn," Rauschtlot hissed, her body bleeding and torn. "I . . . mussst . . . rrr . . ."

Rauschtlot slumped to the ground, her skin turning bright white.

Sky dropped his shimmering blade and fell next to her. "Rauschtlot? Rauschtlot!"

She didn't move. She didn't breathe.

She just lay there, still as the earth.

Sky collapsed back against the wall, the horror of all that

had happened finally catching up to him. He cried, his body rattling with heavy sobs.

He'd failed everyone. Crystal was going to die. Exile was going to burn.

Above, the manor rumbled.

"I can't do this anymore," Sky whimpered. "I just can't."

Then he heard something at the far end of the tunnel, where the ceiling had collapsed. He leaped to his feet, wiping his tears away.

He tried to activate his Pounder, but nothing happened. Glancing over his shoulder, he saw that the Pounder, along with most of his new cloak and gear, had been shredded to bits. Only Phineas's old coat remained.

Dirt poured out of a small hole in the wall. Rocks shifted. Sky backed down the tunnel.

The hole got bigger and bigger, and Sky could hear voices coming through.

A moment later Winston Snavely tumbled out of the hole.

"Phineas?" Sky exclaimed, hardly believing his eyes.

"It's Sky!" Phineas yelled back into the hole. He turned back to Sky, holding out his hand. "Come along now. Quickly."

Sky heard a noise directly above him, and before he could move, a Gossymer crashed through the ceiling, landing on top of him.

"Sky!" Phineas cried.

"I bury you in one place and dig you up in another," said Morton Thresher as he grabbed Sky roughly and threw him in front of Ambrosia on the Gossymer before climbing back on. "Up we go!"

Sky caught a fleeting glimpse of his shimmering blade, lying useless on the ground, and Phineas rushing toward them, and then they were up and gone, appearing amidst the chaos in the yard outside the manor. Storm clouds swirled above and lightning crashed down, but the monsters that had been trapped in the prison slept on. Sky, Morton, and Ambrosia had arrived far back from the manor, just inside the glowing stained glass wall that marked the boundary of Solomon's prison.

Ambrosia shoved Sky off the Gossymer and he tumbled hard to the ground, then rolled to his back.

"Give you a hand there, mate?"

Sky looked up and saw Chase smiling hesitantly down at him, offering his hand.

Sky ignored it and stood. "Thanks. I can get up on my own."

"I can see that," Chase replied.

"Keep an eye on him," said Morton. The Gossymer carrying Morton and Ambrosia shot back into the ground.

"Will do," said Chase.

Sky noticed Crenshaw and a small group of Morton's hunters hovering a short distance away. Crenshaw gave Sky a sour look before turning his attention back to the distant manor.

"What's going on?" Sky asked, loud enough to be heard over the roaring storm, but not loud enough for Morton's hunters to hear.

"Pendulum's not degrading," Chase replied. "Should've stopped some time ago, but Winston's keeping it going somehow. They've blocked off the house—giant Shimmer, I think. No one can get near it. It only just dropped when you arrived."

"So Morton and Ambrosia are burrowing into the manor," said Sky.

Chase tapped his nose. "Spot on, mate."

"Sometime you and I need to have a little talk about not burying your mates, *mate*," said Sky.

"Couldn't be helped. Here, take this." Chase handed Sky a small vial.

"What is it?"

"Something to help you survive," Chase replied.

Sky frowned. The last time someone he knew had drunk an unknown liquid, he'd lost his memory. On the plus side, Derek had forgotten having kissed Hannah, so maybe it wasn't all bad.

"Trust me," said Chase.

"Trust you? You're a liar, Errand," Sky hissed. "You've been right in front of me this whole time and you didn't say a word."

"And you're not a liar? Pots and kettles, Sky, pots and kettles," Errand replied. "Now drink up."

Sky glowered, but Errand, or Chase, or whoever he was, was right. He'd been no more honest than Errand, and no more trusting. Besides, whatever was in the vial wasn't likely to put him in a worse situation. Probably.

"Fine," Sky muttered. When no one was watching, Sky drank it down. Surprisingly, it tasted sweet, like honey.

"Tell me when your skin starts drooping," said Errand.

"Wait—what?" Sky grabbed his skin and pulled, stretching it much further than should've been possible. "You gave me Slippery Wick Brew?"

Errand glanced over. "Hmm . . . might've put too much dung in it. Good enough, I suppose." He raised his voice. "Crenshaw, I need your help here!"

Sky saw that Crenshaw and the other hunters had moved closer to the manor to watch Morton's approach.

Crenshaw came over, but he didn't look happy about it. "What?"

"I found this on our boy," said Errand, holding up another

vial. "You're a smart one—any idea what we've got?"

Crenshaw took the vial from Errand. Their hands touched. "Ow. What was—"

Errand caught Crenshaw under the arms before he could fall and, on Errand's finger, Sky saw a small ring holding a Dovetail thorn.

"Concentrated Dovetail," said Errand, shuffling Crenshaw behind a tree, where he dropped him. "Learned that trick from the Shadow Man."

"You call him that, too, huh? The man who Changed us?" asked Sky.

"What else is there to call him? We've no idea who he is," said Errand. "I've searched everywhere, Sky. Not even Bedlam knows who the Shadow Man is. Only Solomon knows."

"You don't still believe that, do you?" asked Sky.

"He wasn't lying, Sky—not about that," said Errand. "He *knows*."

"Are you really working with Phineas and laying a double bogey?" Sky asked. "Or have you decided to team up with Morton to free Solomon, even after all the trouble we went through to lock him up?"

"*You're* the one who became Morton's apprentice, as I recall," Errand countered.

"Whose side are you on, Errand? Be straight with me for once."

"I'm on *our* side," said Errand.

"I wasn't aware we had a side," Sky retorted. He glanced at his hand. "Why am I all saggy?"

"The brew might need some adjustments—I was in a hurry." Errand stretched his own hand and Sky saw the skin peel back, revealing Errand's marks underneath.

"You have to fold the skin just right to hide it," Errand continued. "Phineas taught me that trick."

"I'll bet he did," said Sky bitterly.

Errand grabbed Sky's face. "Try not to cry—I need to make a few adjustments to your fat."

Sky felt his skin slide this way and that. It hurt. "So do I look like you now?"

"You look like him," said Errand, pointing at Crenshaw. "And *he* looks like you. Now, put on his clothes while I fix him up."

Sky stripped down to his boxers and put on Crenshaw's clothes, tossing his shredded cloak to Errand. He paused at Phineas's old coat.

"Come on, the coat, too," said Errand, holding out his hand. "You can wear Crenshaw's, just empty the pockets."

"It's not the same," said Sky, moving his Tin and a few canisters to the new coat. He paused as he pulled out the seed and note they'd retrieved from the bowling alley.

"What's that?" Errand asked.

"I'm not sure . . . ," Sky replied, thinking. He added the seed and note to his new coat and put it on. "How do I look?"

"Like a little girl trying on her daddy's clothes," said Errand, putting Sky's old coat on Crenshaw. "Roll up the cuffs and sleeves. Hopefully they won't notice what a scrawny git you are."

"Thanks," said Sky drily. "And you can drop the accent around me."

"Believable, right?" said Errand in his normal voice, which is to say he sounded exactly like Sky, even though he still looked like Chase. "I spent a few weeks in South London practicing."

"I don't know . . . ," said Sky. "You sound more Australian to me."

"Shows what you know. The European hunters find my accent very believable. They haven't said a word."

"That's probably because they think you're Australian," Sky observed.

"Just shut up and grab his legs," Errand replied tartly.

Sky grabbed Crenshaw's legs, and together they carried him out from behind the tree.

"What are you two doing?" a girl demanded before they had taken two steps. She glanced at Crenshaw, who, Sky noted, really did look like him now. If Crenshaw wasn't several inches taller than him, and several muscles larger, they could've passed as twins.

"Our boy was causing trouble—had to give him what for," Errand supplied, switching back into his faux British-Australian accent and dropping Crenshaw's arms so that his head banged against the ground.

Before the girl could respond, thunder cracked and a swirling ball of crackling energy rolled out of the manor, knocking them all to the ground.

Morton's hunters jumped to their feet, cheering as the monsters around them—the ones that couldn't burrow, jump, fly, or climb, and therefore couldn't escape the prison last year—began to twitch and wake up.

Sky and Errand glanced around uneasily as they crawled back to their feet.

"Great. Excellent," said Errand drily. "Most glorious."

Sky didn't say anything. Accents and imitation weren't really his thing, not to mention that he had nothing to say. In a few minutes Solomon Rose would escape, Malvidia and her hunters would retreat, Crystal would die, and Bedlam's army would burn Exile to the ground.

"Well, ah, we should be heading out, I suppose," said Errand as he and Sky backed away.

The girl turned to look at them again.

"You blokes watch him till we get back," Errand commanded, pointing at Crenshaw. "We've got important things to do. Understand?"

The girl frowned. "What important things?"

"Morton wanted us to come and find him," said Errand.

The earth rumbled, and the Gossymer carrying Morton and Ambrosia shot out of the ground.

"And there he is," said Errand.

Morton shook the dirt from his clothes and hair. "What happened to my apprentice?" he asked, staring down at Crenshaw.

"These two gave him what for," said the girl, pointing at Sky and Errand.

Morton stopped dusting himself off and looked at them.

"We sure did," said Errand. "The rotter tried to escape."

Morton nodded, apparently accepting the story. "Put him up here—and you lot follow us."

Sky and Errand slung Crenshaw in front of Ambrosia on the Gossymer and it darted forward, racing into the heart of the awakening monsters.

Sky and Errand had no other choice but to follow.

CHAPTER 30
A Tangled Web Unwoven

Solomon Rose stood alone and unmoving in a forest of fallen trees. He looked like Sky remembered from earlier that morning—like an Echo—with leathery black wings spread out and branchy arms raised. White gobbets of ruined eye clung to Solomon's lacerated trunk, and his mouth was open wide so that Sky could see the Eye of Legend staring out at him through the darkness.

As they approached, Sky saw lightning strike Solomon's upheld branches.

Solomon shivered. Then his branches swept down and he let out a terrible roar that shook Sky to his bones.

The roar turned into a bellow and Solomon thrashed around, clawing at his eyes. One of his branches swept over Morton's small group, and he stopped. "Who is there?" Solomon rumbled. "What year is this?"

The question surprised Sky, but then he remembered that only Errand had been able to edgewalk outside the prison, and then only because of his unique link with Sky. Without Errand, Solomon would have been completely cut off from the world.

"The year of your freedom, and the year of our reconciliation, *Solomon Rose*," said Morton, sliding off the Gossymer and approaching Solomon.

Sky glanced at Ambrosia and saw her stiffen. Did she believe him now? She had come expecting to free her father, the Arkhon, and instead she'd found his usurper, just as Sky had told her.

Solomon growled, low and deep. "That is a dangerous name, even from you, Morton Thresher."

"So it's true? When this boy," Morton gestured at Chase, "fed me this fanciful tale about the legendary Solomon Rose, my former apprentice, dwelling in the Arkhon's body, I had to admit to a bit of skepticism. But it's really you in there, isn't it?"

Solomon laughed, and it shook Sky like thunder. "Now you believe? Have you come to kill me then, *master*?"

"Of course not!" Morton snarled. "All these years, Solomon, I could've helped you! When Alexander brought your body to the Academy, everyone thought you dead by the Arkhon's hands. And I thought you dead by Alexander's cowardice. I stabbed him through the neck with his own blade."

"Did you *really*?" Solomon chuckled, sounding quite amused.

"Yes . . . ," said Morton slowly. "We've brought you something."

Morton signaled, and Ambrosia slid off the Gossymer with Crenshaw in her arms. As she did, Crenshaw's arm popped out, dangling to the side. Ambrosia glanced down and stopped. Her eyes lifted to meet Sky's: Crenshaw didn't have any marks on his palm.

She knew.

Sky's heart beat pitter-pat. If she gave him up, he and Errand would be toast.

Then Ambrosia did something entirely unexpected: She grabbed Crenshaw's arm and tucked it against her so the hand was hidden. Ambrosia nodded once at Sky, and then walked off to join Morton.

"Excellent!" Morton exclaimed, turning back to Solomon. "I believe you are familiar with Sky Weathers?"

Solomon hissed, his branchy arms reaching greedily for Crenshaw. Ambrosia pivoted her body, stopping him.

"For four hundred years I've struggled to keep you free and help you, like a good daughter. I've honored you despite your mistakes and cruelty. You told me you lied to the hunters, that you told them you were Solomon to taunt them. But you lied to me. I am not *your* daughter," Ambrosia spat. "Does my father live?"

Solomon lowered his useless eyes as if to stare into Ambrosia's. Sky knew Solomon couldn't see, not with his eyes, at any rate, but his branchy arms were every bit as sensitive, if not more so.

"You have known me longer than you knew him, Ambrosia," Solomon rumbled. "We have passed through darkness and glory and ruin together, you and I. Have I not been like a father to you?"

"DOES HE LIVE?" Ambrosia screamed.

Solomon growled. "No. I do not believe he does."

Ambrosia's head dropped, and when she looked up again, Sky saw tears in her eyes. "Thank you, Solomon. That is all I needed to know."

She offered Crenshaw to Solomon again.

Solomon paused, as if considering, and then his branchy arms wrapped around Crenshaw.

Sky glanced at Errand, wondering what to do. Crenshaw was a despicable jerk, but they couldn't just allow Solomon to kill him. "We've got to stop him," Sky whispered.

"Relax," Errand whispered back. "Solomon needs one of us. He won't hurt Crenshaw . . . much."

Solomon roared. Sky jerked his head around and saw Crenshaw lying on the ground and Ambrosia hanging from one of Solomon's arms by her teeth. Solomon flipped his arm and sent Ambrosia flying. She crashed to the ground among the fallen trees, lying motionless.

"Ungrateful spawn!" Solomon rumbled.

"Not spawn you have to worry about, fortunately," said Morton. "You have the boy, and soon you can reclaim what is rightfully yours. You are a hero! The Hunters of Legend will rejoice at your return!"

Morton's hunters cheered at his words.

"Yes . . . a hero . . . ," Solomon rumbled.

Sky nearly gave himself away, he was so mad. Solomon was no hero. He was a power-hungry vulture of the worst kind.

"It's time to depart," said Morton.

Solomon rumbled in agreement and reached for Crenshaw again, but as his arms slithered around him, he hesitated. "Morton, what is this?"

Crenshaw's arm had flopped out at a weird angle, clearly showing the absence of the marks.

"Oh, crap," Sky whispered.

Morton knelt down. The skin on his palm peeled back, and Sky saw the Eye of Legend. Black veins spread through Morton's skin, turning his entire hand midnight blue. He tapped several spots on Crenshaw's face. The spots turned black and Crenshaw's skin drooped, cascading down in huge wrinkly waves.

"Double crap," said Errand.

"That's not going to happen to us, is it?" Sky hissed quietly, staring at Crenshaw's flabby waves of flesh.

"Not if we die first," Errand whispered back.

Morton turned suspicious eyes on them and squeezed the pommel of his cane. The black casing folded up to become the crosspiece, revealing the shimmering blade beneath.

"You gave him what for, eh?" said Morton walking slowly toward them as they backed away.

"That we did," said Errand. "Just look at the fellow."

"Knocked the marks right off of him, I see," said Morton, holding the shimmering blade casually at his side. "And what about you, Crenshaw, did you give him what for?"

"Jolly right, I did," said Sky, doing a horrible imitation of Crenshaw's voice and adding the British accent for no apparent reason.

The Gossymer scuttled behind Sky and Errand, blocking their retreat, and Morton came to a stop right in front of them. He tapped both of their faces, not with his hand, but with his shimmering blade, filling it with darkness. Their skin sagged horribly, and then slapped back into place with a smacking sound.

Their disguises were gone, and they were now identical.

"Changelings," Morton sneered.

Solomon laughed. "Surprise."

At that moment Phineas exploded out of the ground, knocking Sky and Errand one way and Morton the other.

Phineas—still posing as Winston Snavely—landed and pointed his blade at Morton.

The grove went silent.

Phineas started to cough, choking on the dust. "One minute," Phineas wheezed, holding up his index finger—the universal sign for "give me a minute."

Morton used the break to scurry away. The Gossymer and Morton's hunters joined him as he hid beneath Solomon Rose's protective branches.

Solomon laughed, a deep belly chuckle that shook the dead grove. "Don't worry, Morton, *I* will protect you."

"You could've had him," Errand hissed, dusting himself off as he and Sky stood. Sky pulled on his skin, and when it snapped back into place quite normally, he sighed in relief.

"I'm sorry—was my entrance not dramatic enough for you?" Phineas coughed. "I can go back and try it again, if you like."

"Winston, your timing is most unfortunate," said Morton, unaware of Phineas's disguise.

Phineas held up his index finger again, hacked, lowered the finger, hacked again, raised it, raised it, almost hacked, and then stood and composed himself, lowering the finger entirely.

"Morton," Phineas coughed. "Sorry I'm late for the party. I had a detour that couldn't be helped."

"You shouldn't have come, Winston. We have no quarrel."

"Bully that," Phineas spat. "You killed my son."

Morton's eyes went wide, and for the first time Sky saw true fear on his face.

"Phineas . . . ," said Morton, sounding terrified.

Phineas's face drooped and then slapped back into place. And where Winston Snavely had stood, Sky saw Phineas T. Pimiscule.

"You've hidden behind the Hunters of Legend for four hundred years, Morton, but you've stuck your neck out too far this time," Phineas snarled.

"In all fairness," said Morton, regaining his composure, "Alexander was your *adopted* son. His untimely death was hardly worth ruining a friendship over."

"Untimely? You stabbed a sword through his neck!" Phineas exclaimed.

"Not in a way that could be proved," said Morton.

Solomon started laughing. "Ah, Alexander, my brother, you've trapped us all!" Solomon laughed and laughed.

"It appears that it's time for us to depart," said Morton, stepping closer to Solomon.

"I'm not leaving without what I came for," Solomon rumbled, his useless eyes turning on Sky and Errand. "The Hunter's Mark is mine."

"By all means, Solomon," said Phineas. "Don't let me stand in your way."

"Patience, Solomon," said Morton, eyeing Phineas warily. "They will come to us in time."

Solomon grumbled.

Sky spotted a clublike branch with a good knot on the end and picked it up. He had Crenshaw's sword, but he feared he might poke someone with it harder than he intended. He wanted to incapacitate these hunters, not kill them. He'd treat them the same way he treated monsters, even if Morton and his hunters didn't deserve it.

"Who was it, Solomon? Who made us Changelings?" Errand cried out. "Tell us! If you ever cared for me, tell us!"

Solomon growled. "Come with us and I will tell you everything you want to know, Errand. Even now, you have not gone far from me. Only I can give you what you need, the power you crave, the family you desire. I can give you a life worthy of song and story, a name no one will ever forget. Come with me, Errand. By the law of the Hunters of Legend, you are still my apprentice. You belong to me."

Sky saw Errand hesitate, his body shaking as if he was actually considering Solomon's offer. Sky began to open his mouth, but Phineas shook his head ever so slightly.

Errand's mouth opened and closed a few times before he finally spoke. "Just tell me, Solomon. *Please* . . . ," he begged.

"Soon, Errand. Soon," Solomon rumbled.

Sky heard a distant roar above the booming thunder of the ongoing plasma storm and the shaking earth. Then through the stained glass wall a short distance to the east, he saw Bedlam's army rushing through the trees. Dozens of towering Harrow Knights with coppery, smoldering skin charged the wall, followed by hundreds of fiery Harrow Wights and Gossymers.

"I wish we'd had time to talk, old friend, but I see that your other guests have finally arrived," said Morton. Solomon's branchy arms dipped down and Morton climbed aboard, along with Morton's hunters.

Errand drew his silver sword.

"Always a pleasure, Phineas," said Morton, tipping his bowler hat to them.

Sky pulled out his Tin shield and flipped it open, curling

the edge. He held the Tin in one hand and the knotted branch in the other.

With a blood-pounding scream, Sky, Errand, and Phineas charged, but before they could reach Morton, an Echo rose out of the darkness and slammed into Solomon.

Ambrosia, daughter of the Arkhon, had finally managed her monumental shift after biting Solomon—a shift that would, in the absence of the full moon, rapidly change her into a mindless Gloom. She had all but given her life for the attack, and it appeared she had every intention of making the most of it.

CHAPTER 31

Solomon Rises

Chaos erupted.

Echo limbs flailed madly, smashing into people and sending them flying through the air.

Sky, Phineas, and Errand rushed toward Morton and his hunters.

Morton raised his midnight-blue hand and smoky darkness erupted out of the Eye. Sky felt it slam into him, repelling him, and then he was flying backward with Errand.

As Sky flew through the air, he saw Phineas raise his shimmering blade and cut through the darkness. Phineas swung down, and a physical, smoky light erupted out of the blade, catching Morton in the chest and pitching him tumbling toward Solomon.

Sky and Errand climbed to their feet as Morton's hunters closed on Phineas. Sky saw Phineas slide his palm along the blade, and an Eye of Legend appeared on his hand, revealed somehow by the blade.

Sky and Errand charged once again, but the smoky light swirling around Phineas pushed them back.

Sky watched helplessly as Morton's hunters attacked. Phineas became a whirl of motion, smacking hunter after hunter with the flat of his blade to knock them out, his movements so precise, so perfect.

Morton Thresher dove into the ground like a Gnomon.

"Phineas! He's gone underground!" Sky warned, still trying to get in close enough to help.

Phineas must have heard him because he thunked a hunter on the head, knocked him down, and then dove blade first into the ground.

With Phineas gone, Sky and Errand rushed in. Only six of Morton's hunters remained, leaving three each for Sky and Errand.

Sky swung with his branch and had it blocked by a kid with a sword. The kid smiled. The other two hunters attacked. Sky caught the first sword with his Tin shield. As the girl swung down, Sky uncurled the Tin, making it sharp. The sword slammed into it and split cleanly in two, leaving the girl stunned. Sky used the opening to ram her with his Tin, avoiding a slash from the second hunter at the same time.

The first hunter came at him and Sky blocked with his branch. The sword sheered into the wood and hit the knot, getting stuck. Before the hunter could react, Sky twisted the branch, yanking the sword from the kid's hands, and then he flicked his wrist and smacked the kid on the head with the sword handle, driving him back.

The second hunter attacked again, and Sky blocked with his L-shaped sword-club—the sword still stuck in the knot. Sky spun the club and smacked the hunter on the head.

She stabbed, and Sky stepped to the side so that her sword went through the handle of the sword wedged into his club. Spinning, Sky yanked the sword from her hand so that now he was holding one end of a U.

They both stared at his strangely shaped weapon. But before either of them could do anything, Errand stepped up behind the girl and clocked her on the side of the head with the hilt of his sword, knocking her out.

"I was handling it," said Sky.

Errand looked at Sky's weapon, turning his head from side to side. "Nice weapon. What do you do with it? Spell 'U stink'?"

Sky threw down the club. "Where's Phineas?"

The earth rumbled, low and deep, sending Sky and Errand stumbling, and then Phineas and Morton shot out, swords locked together, darkness streaming from their marks.

The darkness hit Sky and Errand, sending them flying in opposite directions.

Branchy limbs struck all around as Sky landed next to the flailing Echo and scrambled to his feet. The Echo began to roll. Sky leaped onto a limb, racing along its length to avoid being squashed. Another limb flashed by, and he jumped, landing hard. The limb curved upward and he ran and ran, leaping and scrambling from one limb to the next, the Echo rolling over and over.

He reached the edge of a limb, clinging to it as it carried him up and up. He'd nearly reached the wall. Through it, he saw a giant Harrow Knight draw its fist back.

"Oh no . . . ," Sky muttered, knowing what was coming. He'd seen these kinds of walls blow up before, and it was never pretty.

A shadow passed by overhead. "Sky! Jump!" Andrew yelled.

Without thinking, Sky pulled a Jumper canister from his coat, pointed down with a stiff arm, and activated it.

The Harrow Knight's burning fist hit the nearly unbreakable wall and passed right through it, igniting the plasma within.

The explosion was deafening.

Sky sailed up, and then T-Bone, Andrew, and Hands were yanking him onto the Darkhorn's back.

The Darkhorn darted forward, racing the flames from the exploding wall. They pitched and teetered, but stayed in the air as the shock waves washed over them.

Sky looked down into utter devastation. Plasma had ignited along the entire length of the wall, leveling it and everything within fifty yards.

Through the haze, Sky saw flashes of light and ribbons of darkness as Phineas and Morton fought on.

The plasma storm went mad. Bright lights swirled above, washing the landscape in eerie colors. Lightning crashed down again and again, and funnels touched the cornfields and gardens, gobbling them up. The Darkhorn rocketed through it all, weaving and rolling as they hung on for dear life.

Rain poured from the plasma clouds in torrents, dousing the sputtering fires and washing away the haze. They swooped over Phineas and Morton, and Sky saw Errand fighting alongside Phineas.

Phineas swung at Morton. Their blades crashed together. Errand shadow slipped behind Morton, stabbing with his sword. Morton shadow slipped out of the way, reappearing behind Errand, then wrapping his arm around Errand's neck.

Phineas raised his hand and darkness flooded out, sending

both Errand and Morton flying. Even from where he was, Sky could feel that terrible darkness.

Before Errand flew too far, Phineas raised his blade. Vines shot out, wrapped around Errand, and kept him on his feet.

As Morton flew, he, too, pointed his blade at Errand and snatched him with vines. Errand cut both sets with his sword and then dove into the ground, followed by Phineas and Morton.

And then, above the ever-rolling thunder, Sky heard Solomon Rose laughing.

Near the shattered wall, Sky saw what remained of Bedlam's army streaming over the ruins and, closer, he spotted the two burning Echo. Solomon stood tall, and the rain doused out his fires. Sky watched in horror as Solomon's eyes—the eyes Errand had destroyed the year before with a candleholder—regrew and became white and pupil-less once again. The wall was finally broken. Solomon could shift. The world was doomed.

Solomon laughed maniacally, raising his great Echo mouth to the sky in triumph.

Ambrosia lay at Solomon's feet, her body shrinking and growing and writhing chaotically as it burned. The Gloom had taken her, if she wasn't already dead.

From high up, Sky saw hordes of monsters streaming toward the manor from the Finger of Erachnus. A small band of hunters stood on the Finger's tip, fighting against overwhelming numbers.

And farther south, he saw the surviving hunters fleeing for Arkhon Academy. Monsters closed from all sides, overrunning the school and heading for Exile.

"We've lost," Sky muttered in shock.

Sky! The blade!" Andrew shouted, shoving Alexander's shimmering blade into his hands. "Phineas gave it to us after you left it behind. He didn't want Morton and Solomon to know you had it. We can still stop this—where's Bedlam?"

"It doesn't matter. I tried to open the Chrysalis, but I don't know how."

"Think, Sky; there has to be an answer!" Hands yelled.

Sky frowned. He pulled out the seed and the note they'd recovered from the bowling alley. "It occurred to me earlier that this might be related, but I don't know how. Whoever sent it claimed it could stop Bedlam's army, but the only way I know how to stop Bedlam's army is to free Bedlam. Maybe you guys can figure it out." He read:

When Hope, Patience, and Vengeance fail,

and the broken world around you breaks,

plant this seed within your heart, and avail

to free a soul and mend mistakes.

"What does it mean?" T-Bone asked.

"I don't know," Sky replied. "But I think it's related. According to Morton, the First Hunter named the two monocles Hope and Vengeance, and the watch Patience."

"And them failing could refer to the prison opening," said Andrew.

Below, Sky saw Solomon marching toward Phineas and Errand as they fought Morton.

"Well, the seed is obviously that seed you're holding," said T-Bone. "But how are you supposed to plant it in your heart?"

"And the soul could be Bedlam—the mistake Alexander's," Sky added. "Bedlam never should have been locked up."

"It's love!" Hands cried.

"What?" said Sky.

"The answer to the riddle is love! When Hope, Patience, and Vengeance fail, you plant this seed—love—in your heart to make things better. That's the thing that will stop Bedlam's army! We need to love them!"

Everyone was silent.

"That's the worst interpretation I've ever heard," Andrew muttered.

T-Bone nodded, but Sky started laughing.

"The answer is love!" Sky exclaimed. "*The Edge of Oblivion* claims that Bedlam can only break free when he has a pure heart filled with love! The seed is the answer! But how?"

"Hands, take over flying the Darkhorn. And try not to kill us. We'll do the thinking," T-Bone said.

"It was a good solution—I was right," Hands replied, sounding offended as they plummeted in a way that made Sky's stomach shoot into his mouth.

"Hands!"

"Sorry, got it now!"

"It's a good solution, but all it tells us is that the seed is part of this," said Sky. "I still have no idea what to do with it!"

Below, Solomon roared. Sky glanced down and saw Solomon staring back up at him. Solomon's wings beat down once, twice, and then he was off, his body shifting and rippling until he looked like an even larger version of the Darkhorn.

"Think faster!" Andrew yelled.

Sky ignored him, his heart beating madly in his chest as he examined the seed.

The Darkhorn swooped.

They plunged toward the earth, twirling. Solomon darted over their heads. The Darkhorn pulled out, racing away from the manor. They soared over the Finger of Erachnus.

Malvidia stood on the tip, fighting alongside Em, T-Bone's mom, Hagos, and a few others as monsters swarmed them.

The Darkhorn curved south, Solomon bellowing and raging behind them.

They flew over the school. Below, Sky saw Osmer, Beau, Dad, and Hannah leading the hunters and students in a final, desperate charge.

They banked west, soaring over the broken stadium. The Darkhorn closed her wings and sailed through the remaining goalpost. Solomon followed, but his overlarge body slammed into the sides, ripping the post from the ground. Solomon spread his wings again with a roar, and the goalpost split in two and tumbled to the ground.

The move had gained them a few precious seconds.

"Ha!" Hands exclaimed.

The Darkhorn faltered left, then right.

"If you're going to drive, then drive!" T-Bone bellowed.

Hands turned his attention back to the Darkhorn.

The ground around the manor trembled.

Solomon closed on them.

"The blade . . . it eats things! The gems can be removed! This is it! The seed is the gem!" Sky cried. "I've got it."

He held the seed and stabbed it with the sword. The golden ichor inside the seed—Bedlam's lifeblood—flowed out and into the blade.

Sky felt a jerk, and then the blade shot out of his hands and spun in the air. Faster and faster it went, shimmering like a star.

Light burst out, followed by a shock wave that sent the Darkhorn reeling, and then the sword plunged into the earth.

A moment.

A breath.

One.

Two.

The earth exploded, sending ripples across the yard and ripping the front porch from the manor.

Bedlam shot out.

Darkness rolled around him in waves, and his face was terrible to behold, half rusted green copper, half gray flesh, and all mad.

Bedlam looked up, and Sky saw the Eye of Legend staring

at him, not as a puffy mark of swirling dark, but as an actual *eye*, alive and menacing.

The land beneath Bedlam's feet began to crack and die.

Solomon dove at Bedlam. But before he could get even halfway to him, writhing darkness rocketed out of Bedlam's Eye, swatting Solomon from the air. Solomon plummeted, plowing a deep furrow through the cornfields.

As Bedlam's army surged across the yard, Bedlam stomped his foot, the ground rippled, and the entire army fell, flames dying, copper disappearing.

Sky watched the wave crash down the hill, all the way to the Finger of Erachnus. He saw Malvidia and the others struggling for their lives on top of the Finger. As the wave washed over it, Bedlam's army toppled.

Bedlam chuckled. "Now this is more like it!"

The Darkhorn lurched and Hands cried out.

"What happened?" T-Bone yelled.

"He's taken it! Bedlam wants his horse back," said Hands, rubbing his temples.

"I think it's his wife," Andrew corrected.

Sky saw Solomon climb to his feet and assess the situation . . . and then fly off.

"He's running!" T-Bone yelled. "The great Solomon Rose is running!"

Several shadowy creatures—Moonriders—rose from the trees south of the Finger, and Sky saw Hagos Adera and a small group of hunters chasing after Solomon.

The Darkhorn landed next to Bedlam.

"Off!" Bedlam ordered.

"You can't!" Sky said, refusing to move. "You promised! Crystal and her mom first! You have to heal them!"

Bedlam growled. "You would allow Solomon Rose to escape?"

"If it saves Crystal and her mom, I'd let Legend himself escape," Sky declared.

"You wouldn't say that if you'd met him." Bedlam glowered at them and stepped forward, preparing to throw them bodily from the Darkhorn.

"You promised," Sky pleaded. "You *promised*."

Far away, they saw Hagos and Solomon growing smaller and smaller until they disappeared completely over the horizon, but Sky kept his eyes on Bedlam. Bedlam ground his teeth. "Let's see to your friend."

CHAPTER 33
Called from the Edge

Bedlam was too big to fit in the manor, but before they even reached the door, Mom came out carrying Crystal. Behind them, Sky saw a pale-looking Rauschtlot carrying Cassandra.

"Rauschtlot! You're alive!" Sky wrapped Rauschtlot in a bear hug after she set down Cassandra.

"For nnnow," Rauschtlot hissed, her voice hollow and sickly as it reverberated out of her various mouths.

Mom came over and hugged Sky.

Bedlam knelt next to Cassandra and placed his giant hand on her head. After a moment he muttered, "The Harksplitter has run its course; she will wake soon."

Bedlam turned to Crystal and placed his hand on her back. Sky held his breath. The copper on Crystal's flesh bubbled and then disappeared into Bedlam's palm. Bedlam rolled her onto her back and brushed the hair from her face almost tenderly. "She has wandered far . . . but I have wandered further. She has heard my call—I believe she will come back, in time."

Sky cried. They were the most beautiful words he'd ever heard.

CHAPTER 34
Twin Blades

Sky found Phineas and Errand near the cornfield a short time later, walking toward him looking tired and dirty. Phineas took off running immediately when Sky told him the news about Crystal.

Sky and Errand walked silently for a time.

"What happened to Morton?" Sky asked, breaking the silence.

"Escaped," said Errand. "Hopped on Solomon's leg before he took off. The cowards. We got the three keys back, though—he had them hidden in his bowler hat." Errand held up the bowler hat, showing Sky.

Sky nodded, unsurprised; at least the bowler hat was good for something, because it made a very ugly hat. "Maybe Hagos will catch up to them."

"He'd better hope not," said Errand. "Hagos and the hunters he had with him are pretty good, but they're no match for Morton and Solomon."

"So what now?" Sky asked.

Errand shrugged. Then his face drooped and stretched and he looked like Chase Shroud again.

"Back to the Academy of Legend for me, mate," said Errand.

"That's the worst place you could go!" Sky exclaimed. "What if Morton goes back there? Or Solomon?"

"I hope they do," said Errand darkly. "We might still be able to convince the hunters to side against them."

"You don't have to go," said Sky. "You could stay here with us."

Errand shook his head. "Solomon was right about me. I'm not like you, Sky. I'm not a good person."

"Don't say that! Everyone in Exile would be dead if it wasn't for you!"

"That's just it, Sky. I don't care about everyone in Exile. No matter how much I try to deny it, in the end I nearly gave in—even after all Solomon had done, even after the way he'd treated Ambrosia, even with all of Exile and the world on the line."

"But you didn't!" said Sky.

"I didn't because of *you*," Errand stated. "You and Phineas. If you two hadn't been standing right beside me, I would've done it. The fact is, I want those things Solomon promised. I want to learn the secrets. I want creatures everywhere to remember me. Someday, if I have any say about it, the world will forget Solomon Rose, and the only name they will remember is *Chase Shroud*."

Sky felt a chill go down his spine.

"So what about you, Sky? What now?" Errand asked.

"I don't know," said Sky. "Bedlam's already left with his

army, and we got word from the school that most everyone's all right, though dozens of hunters died—mostly Morton's—and Hands's grandfather appears to have sustained some injuries after making a pass at the lunch lady. T-Bone and Hands went to the school to see if they could help, and then Em showed up on a Moonrider a few minutes later and dragged Andrew away to search for his dad, who still hasn't shown up. Andrew barely said two words to her, but at least he went—it's a start, I guess."

"What about Solange?" asked Errand.

"Come and gone," said Sky. "She was furious at Hagos for not following through with the retreat—blames him for the deaths. She collected Morton's remaining hunters and took off on her Moonrider."

"You could always come back to the Academy of Legend with me," Errand offered. "Just think of it, Sky, the two of us, running around, having adventures . . ."

"I'm sort of tired of adventures, to be honest," said Sky.

"Well, there's a library there bigger than the manor—bigger than all of Arkhon Academy, even! You could come with me and learn everything you ever wanted to know about the hunters," said Errand. "Just sit there all day if you want. You wouldn't be the only one. Several Exile hunters are planning to come."

"Really?" asked Sky. "Wait . . . let me guess: Crenshaw and Ren."

"*And* Cordelia and about a dozen others," said Errand. "They all agreed to come."

"Cordelia, huh? . . ." Sky considered the possibility and then shook his head. "I can't, Errand. I'm afraid of what they'd turn me into. Besides, they need me here. With Phineas back, and half the town in rubble . . . I just can't."

"I suppose I expected that," said Errand. "Did you ever figure out who left that message in Alexander's coffin?"

"I don't know," said Sky. "I honestly don't. I don't know who sent that seed via Marrowick, either—could be the same person. Or not. But whoever it was, they're long gone by now."

They reached the hole that Bedlam had shot out of, and at the bottom Sky saw *two* shimmering blades. He and Errand scrambled down, but Errand got there first and snatched up both blades.

One of the blades lit up at Errand's touch. The other stayed rusted.

Sky watched Errand as he looked the blades over, turning them in his hands, his expression hungry. "*Two* shimmering blades, Sky! Do you have any idea how rare these are?"

"Some," said Sky slowly. "Where did the second blade come from?"

"It was Solomon's," Errand replied. "Alexander accidentally locked it away in Bedlam's Chrysalis when they trapped him. Solomon wouldn't shut up about it when he was training me. He found a new blade centuries ago, before he became the Arkhon—killed a hunter for it—but a hunter can't own two blades at the same time. Once he took the new one, he lost the old one. This blade's been free for the taking ever since. So many of Solomon's secrets, locked within . . ."

Sky frowned. Something about Errand's look disturbed him more than he could say.

Errand ran his Eye of Legend over each of the blades. Solomon's blade became dark and terrible, but Alexander's didn't respond at all to his touch; Sky had already claimed it.

Errand glanced up and must've noticed Sky's frown because

his expression quickly changed from wolfish to friendly. He offered Alexander's blade to Sky. "One for each of us."

As Sky took his blade, light spilled out of it, and the blade twinkled brightly. It felt strange in his hand, alive and foreign, and yet almost like a part of him.

Errand stared back and forth between the blades—one dark, one light—his eyes full of wonder, and hunger. "Twin blades, Sky. Just like us."

"Come on, Errand," said Sky. "Let's go find Mom. We've got a lot of explaining to do."

Sky started to climb out of the hole, but he stopped when he saw that Errand wasn't following him.

"I'll come," said Errand, "but you can't tell her about me, Sky. You have to promise."

"What? Why not?" Sky asked in exasperation. "I thought that's what you wanted!"

Errand shook his head. "That's what I *used* to want, but the Errand you knew is dead, gone, say bye-bye. I'm Chase Shroud now—that's what you'll call me, or I'll leave right now. Promise me, Sky."

Sky looked over this person he used to know, the boy who'd spent eleven years watching the world through Sky's eyes, experiencing the same things he'd experienced, but never in control, always trapped . . . a boy who now called himself Chase Shroud.

"I'll call you Chase in public," said Sky, "and I won't tell Mom and Dad our secret just yet. But in private, you're Errand, and I won't call you anything else. Take it or leave it."

Errand watched him and then nodded. "Done."

"Done, then," said Sky.

Errand took a running leap, bounced off one side of the

hole and then the other, back and forth he went, up, up, until he reached the top.

Sky watched in annoyance and then started climbing after him. He was really going to have to learn some of those tricks.

But for now, he had friends who were going to need him.

EPILOGUE

Fred the Piebald

Fred the Piebald soared over the thick jungle, following a small white dot far below. The dot—a rather troublesome Marrowick—flew casually along a pockmarked dirt road. Fearing he would lose its trail, Fred dropped closer until he could see the light of the full moon reflecting off the Marrowick's waxy skin. The Marrowick wound through a luscious green valley that twinkled with strange, unnatural lights, before climbing a steep and treacherous mountain. When the Marrowick reached the top, it landed on a rocky outcropping beside a young man who looked no older than twenty, but was in fact far, far older.

Fred swooped down, landing on a nearby tree.

The man turned to the Marrowick. "Everything worked out okay, I presume?"

The Marrowick bubbled strangely and emitted a few chirping noises.

"Ah. Ah. That's most unfortunate," said the man. "I'd hoped

Sky would free Bedlam before that occurred. If Solomon is now free, we'll have to change our plans considerably."

"Why do you say that?" asked a woman as she rose out of the ground, her giant body made of earth, rocks, and leaves, with vines and plants sprouting everywhere. Streams of water ran down her back and a giant Eye of Legend rested on her stomach.

The Marrowick burbled happily.

"You have done well," said the woman. "My brother is finally free."

The Marrowick bowed to her.

"We can't continue like this, Vulpine," said the man. "Soon they will know that I live. Solomon already suspects as much—maybe even my father. Too many creatures now know that Solomon and I were Changelings. It's not long before they realize that the Arkhon was recovering in Solomon's body when Morton mistook him for me and stabbed him with my blade. The Hunters of Legend are weak. Solomon will win them to his cause as he did once before."

"You committed to this path long ago, Alexander—do not doubt yourself or turn from it now," said Vulpine. "Just because your trap did not capture all the creatures you'd intended does not mean that it failed."

Alexander was quiet, thoughtful.

"I must return to the Academy of Legend," Alexander declared.

"Are you certain that is wise?"

"It is *necessary*," Alexander replied. "I can't allow Solomon to get a foothold there. If the Academy of Legend topples, the others will follow, until Exile is all that remains."

"And there is another reason . . . ," Vulpine hinted.

"Yes," said Alexander, "Errand will be there, though I understand he goes by a new name now: *Chase Shroud*."

"A dark name," said Vulpine. "Do the Exile hunters know that he was behind the hunt on Sky? Do they know he was the one who suggested it to Morton?"

Vulpine and Alexander looked at the Marrowick.

The Marrowick bubbled.

"No, then," said Alexander. "Though, it would surprise me if Phineas and Sky didn't at least suspect it. It's possible Errand was just looking for another way to lure Morton to Exile, that he didn't realize the danger he was putting Sky in."

"And do you believe that?"

"No," said Alexander. "I don't believe Errand does anything accidentally."

"You think he meant him harm?"

"Hard to say," Alexander replied thoughtfully. "Sky seems to be one of the few things in the world Errand honestly cares about. And he didn't leave Sky completely unprotected—he himself imitated Sky and led many of the hunters into Sky's traps the night of the hunt, though Sky never realized it."

"Hopefully Sky is enough," said Vulpine.

"We took a serious gamble with them," said Alexander. "If one or the other falls, I fear our entire cause will be lost. We will need both of them to stop what is to come."

"Are you having second thoughts about what we did?" asked Vulpine.

"Always," Alexander replied.

Fred had heard enough. He swooped down behind Alexander. As he did, he shifted, his skin rippling and stretching, until a young woman—no older than twenty-five—stood in Fred's place. She had long, flowing blond hair that cascaded down her back like glittering stardust, and eyes as deep and blue as ocean ice. She wore blue jeans, a T-shirt, and a long black trench coat.

Before Alexander could react, the woman put a knife to his throat.

"Ursula!" Alexander cried, sounding frightened.

Vulpine started to move.

"STAY BACK, VULPINE!" Ursula drew blood from Alexander's neck.

Vulpine paused and then withdrew.

"How did you know—how did you find me?" Alexander asked.

With her free hand, Ursula drew out the empty package she'd stolen from Sky—the one he'd recovered from the bowling alley. She dropped it in front of Alexander.

"You licked the envelope," Ursula hissed. "A biological sample is all I need."

She shifted and suddenly she looked just like Alexander. She shifted back.

Alexander groaned.

"Which one, Alexander?" Ursula hissed.

Alexander shook his head, regretting it as the knife cut into him. "I can't tell you, Ursula; right now that knowledge is the only thing keeping me alive."

"TELL ME! You stole him! You! You stole him from me! Now, TELL ME!" Ursula took a deep breath. "Which one is my son?"

HUNTER'S JOURNAL ADDENDUM, SKY WEATHERS

For reference, I've compiled some notes on a few of the monsters I've come across, read about, or heard about so far.

While I've included a few survival tips, your first and best course of action is always to RUN. I mean it. Flee. Vamoose. Hotfoot it out. Shake a rug. Just get out of there. If that doesn't work, try a friendly "hello"; it won't help at all, but at least you won't die impolite.

SHADOW WARGS:

Shadow Wargs are hunters who have made a pact
with a Wargarou: The hunter agrees To become The
Wargarou's minion and, in exchange, The hunter gains
The ability To shift into a Shadow Warg. Shadow Wargs
are Clydesdale-size, wolflike, and very annoying. They
are made of darkness, can slip between shadows without
being seen, and are practically invulnerable.

HOW TO SURVIVE AN ENCOUNTER:

The Shadow Wargs of Whimple menTions Three
weaknesses: silver, fire, and wolfsbane.

WARGAROUS:

Wargarous are vicious, vaguely wolflike, and impossible
To kill. They can change shape over The Three days of
a full moon by eating The body of The victim They wish
To change into, and They keep ThaT shape until They eat
anoTher, or reverT To Their *True* form—a Terrible monsTer
of darkness and fire.

Wargarous can fliT Through shadows, disappearing and
reappearing like knives in a sheaTh. They can creaTe
Shadow Wargs and, if They find Shadow Wargs ThaT
oTher Wargarous have creaTed, They can bind Them.
Once bound, The Shadow Warg is bound for life unless
The Wargarou frees iT, has iTs pack Taken from iT
(usually afTer losing a fighT To anoTher Wargarou), or dies.

Wargarous seem To have a love for fine Things and eaTing small children. Usually, They keep a low profile, lying in waiT, buT when They change inTo Their fiery form—look ouT.

HOW TO SURVIVE AN ENCOUNTER:

According To *Wicked, Wicked Wargarou*, waTer and cold can someTimes quench a Wargarou's fire, buT iT won'T sTop iT. Driving off a Wargarou's pack will weaken iT. And, supposedly, a "hunTer's blade" can kill iT—whaTever ThaT is.

Also, being able To change inTo a Wargarou yourself doesn'T hurT.

GNOMON:

> "*Four To The fooT,*
> *larger Than man,*
> *long of The arm,*
> *and noT very Tan,*
> *They look like gnomes,*
> *wiTh less-poinTy haTs,*
> *and if you find one,*
> *you beTTer skee-daTs . . . Tle.*"

—Taken from *The Tourmaline of ForesighT*

*NoTe: Gnomon are *noThing* like gnomes! They are monsTrously Tall wiTh large, black eyes, noseless, wrinkled faces, and pale, whiTe-gray TranslucenT skin ThaT pulses with red and blue and black veins (*Blue as it stills, Black as it flies, Red as it kills*—a description of their color-changing skin from *Much Ado About Gnomon*). They wear caps over their heads to hide dozens of tiny mouths, all of which are lipless and full of razor-sharp teeth, which they use for tunneling. Few things can match a Gnomon's strength. Some stories claim that Gnomon may even be descended from Paragoth of the Deep, the earth eater.

HOW TO SURVIVE AN ENCOUNTER:
Gnomon don't have opposable thumbs.

WHISPER:
These sneaky creatures are masters of infiltration. In my experience, they prefer human form, and even their true form seems human. But don't let that fool you: Whisper can change into almost anything (even Shadow Wargs and Wargarous, as I found out the hard way). Their body densities increase with age so they can shift into larger forms, so watch for sudden weight changes in those around you. Unlike their father, the Arkhon, Whisper can only shift over the three days of the full moon—not all the time. And Whisper need a fresh biological sample of the creature they want to change into (though older Whisper have some limited control of their features without a sample). Whisper feel a consuming urge to shift all the time, but if they shift outside of a full moon, their bodies become increasingly chaotic until they lose control completely and become Glooms—fallen Whisper.

HOW TO SURVIVE AN ENCOUNTER:
NEVER hunt a Whisper under a full moon (you might as well be hunting The Arkhon; seriously, They're just as bad).

ECHO:

The Evil Echo of Solomon Rose describes Echo as vaguely Treelike, with large, black, leathery wings that fold out of Their Trunkish bodies. Their branchy arms can be inflexible as iron one moment, and slithery as Tentacles The next, and when The wings spread out, The branches sweep downward into a rickety protective shell. Or, if They choose, outward like writhing spears To flay and Terrify Those below—a Tree one instant, a nightmare with wings The next.

Great pupil-less white eyes run half The length of The Trunk—or at least, They did until Solomon Rose gouged Them out, one by one, when The Echo refused To follow him against a monster he claimed would destroy The world. Robbed of Their sight, Echo began To "see" Through highly sensitive organs in Their branches and mouths—Tasting The scents, sights, and emotions around Them.

Echo keep To Themselves, hiding in The old, dark forests of The world. Tangled roots spread deep, deep beneath Them, clinging To The roots of other Echo like children holding hands, and They spend days and nights lost in a haunting sort of collective dream.

According To The Echo narrator of *The Evil Echo of Solomon Rose*, breaking an Echo from its roots ends The dream, effectively exiling The Echo, and is one of The cruelest Things That can happen; it is also one of The best, because a rooted Echo can't fly, and flying, as The narrator claims, is a dream worth waking up for.

HOW TO SURVIVE AN ENCOUNTER:
Echo have highly sensitive sensory organs all along Their limbs. So long as The limbs are flexible (i.e., not in protective mode), They can be attacked. At best, This will temporarily "blind" The Echo, giving you Time To run.

PIEBALDS:
Mottled black-and-white crows. If you shine a black light on Them, Their skeletons will glow. Piebalds Thrive on high levels of phosphorus and The scales from Their feet can drive away some Types of poison (like DoveTail).

HOW TO SURVIVE AN ENCOUNTER:
Don't give a Piebald crackers (especially phosphorus-laced crackers) and it will leave you alone.

THE JACK:
The Jack is a sprawling, living, fire-breathing pumpkin patch. According To *The Journal of Alexander Drake*, each of The Jack's gourds (some of which are The size of houses) has its own brain. A gourd can work independently, attack what it wants, but if The big brain

gives a command, the thousands of little brains have to follow. Distract the big brain and you distract the rest.

The Jack sleeps most of the time, but it's a light sleeper. Fortunately, the only eyes are on the main head. Unfortunately, it has an incredibly strong sense of smell through glands on each of the gourds. And if it smells you and thinks you're a threat, it wakes up, and when it wakes up, it's nearly as bad as Hannah in the morning.

Jack seeds, from the gourds, can accelerate healing. They are also poisonous to DoveTail.

HOW TO SURVIVE AN ENCOUNTER:
Two known weaknesses: attract the big brain and distract it with the biggest threat, and then, second, hit it with DoveTail, which might slow it down or just make it angrier. *The Journal of Alexander Drake* says that hunters who faced the Jack didn't survive long enough to discover any other weaknesses. Based on my own experiences, I can attest to this.

DOVETAIL:
A giant, boron-eating hedge maze. White leaves like feathers cover thick black branches. Red and black budding flowers on the DoveTail are strangely inviting (just watch out for the poisonous thorns!).

The earth around DoveTail is usually red and barren, due to the fact that the DoveTail has eaten most everything else.

HOW TO SURVIVE AN ENCOUNTER:
DoveTail moves slowly, unless it views you as a real threat. Don't threaten it, and you should be fine. If it does decide to attack you, make sure you have Jack seeds and crow's feet on hand. Whatever you do, DON'T FALL ASLEEP!

THE ARKHON:
Terror of the Night, Bringer of the Dark, One of Three, The Immortal, The Blood Thief, The Wasting Hunger, The Shifting Horror, The Moon Goblin, The Night. The Arkhon is the ultimate shifter, the father of most other shifters. He can change into anything so long as he has tasted it before.

The Arkhon is ancient and not all he seems . . . AVOID AT ALL COSTS!

HOW TO SURVIVE AN ENCOUNTER:
While he's in a form, he acquires the form's weaknesses, but the second you try to corner him, he shifts. The only way to stop him is to stop his shifting.

GLOOMS:

According To *The FanTafsTik Book of Myfical MofnsTers*, Glooms are "Fallen Whisper"—Whisper who couldn't resist The urge To shifT outside of a full moon and losT conTrol. Like Whisper, Glooms Take on forms by ingesTing biological samples, buT unlike Whisper, Glooms can'T susTain Those forms and will frequenTly spin Them off, leaving behind a fleshy mess. They are like "rolling chaos," "unpredicTable," and "insane"—"forever losT in madness."

HOW TO SURVIVE AN ENCOUNTER:

Glooms hibernaTe in winTer. Cold and cemenT slow Them.

CHANGELINGS:

Changelings are noT born; They are made. You sTarT with Two of any number of creaTures, buT aT leasT one of Them musT be a shifTer with "old blood" (blood of The Arkhon, I'm guessing). Blood is Traded with blood under a birTh moon. From Then on, no maTTer whaT They were before, boTh are Changelings ThereafTer, becoming alike in every way and permanenTly linked. The Change is compleTe and ToTal in a way ThaT no oTher shifTer or creaTure, no maTTer how powerful, can ever achieve. To Change again, and link with anoTher, a Changeling musT kill iTs counTerparT. Blood musT reTurn To blood, and The murder musT be by iTs own hand.

HOW TO SURVIVE AN ENCOUNTER:
Depends on what form it takes. But usually, They're easy to kill (far *too* easy, if you ask me).

EDGEWALKERS:
Before They became extinct, Edgewalkers could travel through people's minds, leaving Their own hideous bodies behind. They were dream-stealers, gorging on a person's hopes and fears until There was nothing left—feeding a wasting hunger They could never satisfy.

In *The Edge of Oblivion*, Solomon Rose led a group of hunters against The Edgewalkers. They found The Edgewalker's wasted bodies, one by one, and killed Them while They slept—leading to The monsters' complete and total extinction, if The story is to be believed.

Before Their extinction, when Edgewalkers entered a mind or a dream, all They had with Them was what They took from The waking world: Their self-images and The things on Their own sleeping bodies. Once inside a mind, They could use what They found There to get out again (if They wanted to). Edgewalkers (and Those trained in edgewalking) could slip from one mind to another undetected, but once detected, They became stuck in The host's mind until: 1. The host let Them out. 2. They drove The host insane and took control. 3. They died.

HOW TO SURVIVE AN ENCOUNTER:
Edgewalkers are, by all accounts, extinct. But if you happen across one (and I really hope you don't), don't let it drink your blood; this is how they strengthen their bond with you and gain power in your mind. If you find yourself stalked by a persistent and pernicious Edgewalker, your best bet is to find its body and destroy it; if you try to take it on head-to-head, in your mind, you are very likely to lose.

DARKHORN:
A hairy black horse the size of a Wargarou, with a lance of darkness protruding from its forehead, and a glowing esca dangling from the lance. The lance and esca apparently perform some kind of "mesmerizing stirring" on those who see it, putting them to sleep.

Sheriff Beau once told me that the Arkhon approached an old hunter stronghold—Bedlam Falls—disguised as a Darkhorn. Before they could stop him, the Arkhon shifted into a Harrow Knight and destroyed half the town.

HOW TO SURVIVE AN ENCOUNTER:
Can be captured with a dog-hair net.

HARROW KNIGHTS:
Giants with some limited shifting abilities (enough to blend in with their surroundings, look like rocks, etc.). The oldest ones are rumored to be the size of small hills, and

spend Their Time sleeping, buT mosT are smaller—a mere
fifTeen To TwenTy feeT Tall.

When They geT aggravaTed, Their blood boils and Their
skin caTches on fire. A burning, copperlike subsTance
oozes Through Their skin, covering Them from head To
Toe in a flexible, Though impeneTrable, coppery armor.
As They cool down, usually afTer everyThing around Them
is dead, The coppery subsTance hardens and breaks off,
revealing a fresh layer of skin beneaTh.

HOW TO SURVIVE AN ENCOUNTER:
Foxglove will speed up Their hearT raTe and cause The
copper To oxidize (rusT). This exposes Their skin and
makes Them more vulnerable.

HARROW WIGHTS:
Like Harrow KnighTs, buT human-size and human-looking.
Harrow WighTs spend a loT more Time around humans
Than Harrow KnighTs and, as a consequence, are nearly
all insane (if your skin was always caTching on fire and
going all coppery, you would be Too!). Like The Whisper,
They are masTer infilTraTors.

HOW TO SURVIVE AN ENCOUNTER:
Foxglove and kind words.

GILEADS:
BoTanical monsTers. The main parT of a Gilead's body is

made up of snaking roots that rest underground. It can have any number of appendages aboveground, and these appendages shift into a variety of plants and trees to fit in; but according to *The Journal of Alexander Drake*, Gilead appendages usually appear as Dragon Trees.

Gilead roots provide a burst of adrenaline and can accelerate healing.

HOW TO SURVIVE AN ENCOUNTER:
No idea.

BARROW HAGS:

Barrow Hags have big, froglike eyes and scaly skin and can jump enormous distances.

Apparently, if you wrap the nose hair of a Barrow Hag around a rutabaga and bury it under a full moon, you will get a black rutabaga. If you eat the black rutabaga, you can jump like a Barrow Hag (just watch out for the side effects!).

HOW TO SURVIVE AN ENCOUNTER:
Can be frozen with the right gear.

HUMANATEES:
Half man, half manatee. Need I say more?

HOW TO SURVIVE AN ENCOUNTER:
Humanatees are notoriously docile; don't get it angry and you should be fine.

UMBERLINGS:
Umberlings mimic The shadows of creaTures around Them. They are hard To spoT, and even harder To sTop.

HOW TO SURVIVE AN ENCOUNTER:
No idea.

SEEPING CREEPERS:
Formless. Seeping Creepers appear as lumps of dirT, meTal, waTer, or sludge. They are incredibly poisonous and hard To predicT.

HOW TO SURVIVE AN ENCOUNTER:
No idea. Maybe you can freeze iT, or use cemenT mix?

SATYRNS:
SaTyrns have nighT-black, leaThery skin ThaT can sTreTch and shifT. MosT of The Time, They appear as half one creaTure and half anoTher. Animals, monsTers, people—noThing is off limiTs. The only Thing ThaT never shifTs is Their Thick skin, which (by all accounts) moves disturbingly as Their innards reorganize Themselves.

HOW TO SURVIVE AN ENCOUNTER:
No idea. LeT me know if you find ouT.

ERABIN:

Erabin are massive, Wargarou-size creatures that are somewhere between scarabs and spiders. They can spin webs like spiders and dig underground like scarabs and their bite is poisonous.

HOW TO SURVIVE AN ENCOUNTER:
No idea.

MARROWICKS:

Towering, with waxlike skin that melts in the sun. Waxy wings rise from its back and the Marrowick uses these wings like extra legs. The Marrowick will frequently try to mimic the appearance of hunters it encounters.

The Journal of Alexander Drake claims that hunters used to make equipment out of Marrowick wax—though I have no idea how or why.

HOW TO SURVIVE AN ENCOUNTER:
No idea.

MOROSPAWN:

Ocean-dwelling giants. Morospawn wander the unfathomable crevices of the ocean in search of light.

HOW TO SURVIVE AN ENCOUNTER:
No idea. I've never encountered one and I hope I never will.

PARAGOTH OF THE DEEP:

The earth eater. Paragoth lives deep underground, in the hard-to-reach places of the earth. I've never read a firsthand account of an encounter with Paragoth, but rumors say that Paragoth is like a rolling ball covered with thousands of silent mouths snapping and chewing.

HOW TO SURVIVE AN ENCOUNTER:
Feed it and beg for mercy.

NITHOK:

Hideous, with fiery wings and gruesome features that will drive a person mad just by looking at it.

HOW TO SURVIVE AN ENCOUNTER:
Don't look at it.

LEGEND:

An ancient evil, long since dead, who nearly ripped the world apart. Literally. His power was broken by the First Hunter and trapped in the Eyes of Legend. Thirteen Eyes were given to the Hunters of Legend and five were given to Legend's children, who fought against their father. To use the dark power in the Eyes, you have to control Legend's will, and the more power a particular Eye possesses, the harder that will is to control.

HOW TO SURVIVE AN ENCOUNTER:
He's dead. You should be okay.

ERACHNUS:

Legend's oldest son. He's huge. Enormous. His body is buried under Exile and his finger juts out like a tower in the old hunter training grounds.

HOW TO SURVIVE AN ENCOUNTER:

As far as I know, he's dead. At least, I hope he is; otherwise being buried like that for more than a thousand years would be very uncomfortable.

BEDLAM:

Legend's oldest surviving son. He's the father of the Edgewalkers, the Harrow Wights, the Harrow Knights, and the Gossymers. He likes fire and driving people insane. He's master of the Edge and he's got a "thing" going with the Darkhorn. Weird, I know.

HOW TO SURVIVE AN ENCOUNTER:

Barrow weed can keep him out of your mind, though once he's there, it's not all that helpful. You're better off trying to make a deal for your life. If you face him head on, you're very likely going to die or go mad.

VULPINE:

Legend's oldest surviving daughter. Honestly, I don't know much about her, but I think she's some kind of plant.

HOW TO SURVIVE AN ENCOUNTER:
Hopefully, I never have to find out.

THE ARKHON: (Updated Entry)
From what I can determine, the Arkhon is Legend's fourth child. I don't know what happened to him, but the impostor, Solomon Rose is still traipsing around in the Arkhon's body, which he apparently took to gain control of the Arkhon's Eye of Legend and the dark power it holds. Solomon is dangerous and not to be trusted.

HOW TO SURVIVE AN ENCOUNTER:
Keep him trapped. If he escapes, I fear we're all out of luck.

MAR:
Legend's youngest daughter. She has something to do with water, but I couldn't find a record of her anywhere. It's quite possible she's dead.

HOW TO SURVIVE AN ENCOUNTER:
No idea.

GOSSYMERS:
Gossymers are giant spiders that burrow through the earth and catch on fire. They are the favored mount of the Harrow Wights when they go to war.

HOW TO SURVIVE AN ENCOUNTER:
Run like crazy and apply generous amounts of aloe vera.
Also, if you can get on one's back, you might be able to
take control if you don't mind the flames.

PORP-A-LORPS:
Tiny firefly-like creatures that like to bury things. Like
people.

HOW TO SURVIVE AN ENCOUNTER:
They mostly leave you alone unless you upset them.
Shoving barrow weed up your nose can also keep them
away. The downside is that you have barrow weed shoved
up your nose.

BOLGERS:
Ugly green-skinned creatures that tend to shrink to the
size of pine needles and hibernate when hungry, but grow
to the size of pine trees when fed Yule logs (either kind,
but they prefer the dessert).

HOW TO SURVIVE AN ENCOUNTER:
Cover yourself in mud. If you have any areas of exposed
flesh, they will sense you and sting you, and their sting
is poisonous and very unpleasant. If you are stung, you'll
need to obtain the anti-venom as quickly as possible or
you'll wind up hibernating until spring. As their brains grow
larger, you can occasionally reason with them, but don't
count on it.

ACKNOWLEDGMENTS

First, I'd like to thank the usual suspects: my tremendous agent, Steven Malk; and everyone at Simon & Schuster who played a role in bringing this series to life and helping it find its way into the hands of readers, especially my publisher, Justin Chanda, for supporting this series; my designer, Laurent Linn, for the amazing art direction; my publicist, Anna McKean, for the PR; Julia McGuire, for making stuff happen; and my editor, Courtney Bongiolatti, for standing by me through a rather difficult year. Courtney, you've decided to join the FBI; I hope that wasn't because of me.

A special thanks to John Rocco for his stunning artwork. I couldn't stop smiling when I saw the cover to *The Legend Thief*. I've never seen anything like it before. Simply incredible!

Many others have contributed to the success of this series in a variety of ways, so prepare for a plethora of random acknowledgments (yes, I used the word "plethora").

Brandon Mull and James Dashner, you read *Return to Exile* and said nice things about it. My writing group: Dave Butler, Platte Clark, Erik Holmes, and Mike Dalzen. My assistant, Diana Ault, who organized my chaos. Sam Bernards, who went above and beyond the call of friendship. My parents, in-laws, and other family, for everything.

An ultra-big-mega-special thanks to my readers and fans for your encouragement and for spreading the word! Recommending this series to others is the biggest compliment you can give me, so thank you!

Finally, and most importantly, I'd like to thank my wife, Katie, and my kids: Jordan, Lucas, and Connor. I love you. What more can I say?

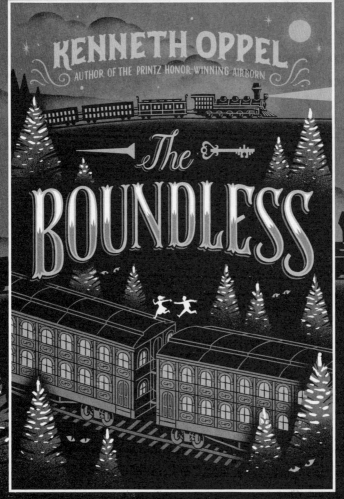

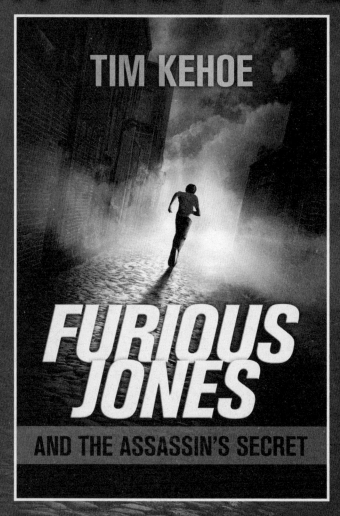